I0590061

SPIRIT OF THE BAYONET

BETRAYAL

TED RUSS

Portions of this book were previously published in the book: *Spirit of The Bayonet* (2019)

Published by Chinook Publishing LLC.

First Edition: 2025

ISBN: 979-8-9986894-0-6

Cover design & interior formatting:

Mark Thomas / Coverness.com

For Bart.

OFFICER ASSESSMENT AND TRAINING COURSE

Chapter One

27 June 2061
Fort Benning, Georgia

Paul walked down the barracks hallway, a large duffel bag on his back, another in each hand. Sweat darkened his gray T-shirt and ran down his head in tickling, itching rivulets that made him want to rub his face.

The problem was his hands were full.

The barracks on Fort Benning seemed ancient, constructed of cinder block almost a hundred years ago—just before the Vietnam War. Beads of water oozing out of the humid summer air of Georgia clung to the painted walls. The air in the hallway was a damp mixture of disinfectant and mildew.

Each barracks room doorway was full of a couple of brand-new lieutenants hanging out, half paying attention to each other's listen-to-what-I-did-on-leave stories. They all kept one eye on the newcomers, stumbling out of the stairwell and walking down the hall, looking for their assigned barracks room.

The more alpha among them sized up each passerby like wolves examining a new pack member. *Can I take him? Where will they rank in the hierarchy? Will she be one of the lieutenants who makes it through? Will I?*

Paul's muscular, six-foot two frame drew many sidelong, assessing glances from his fellow lieutenants as he moved down the hall. He ignored them and walked into his room. Dropping his bags just inside the doorway, he worked his fingers to regain circulation. Then he grabbed the biting shoulder straps that held the last overstuffed duffel on his back and slid them off.

The bag made a loud thud, and he exhaled, trying to uncoil the tension in his back.

"Who the hell are you?" said a female voice.

Startled, Paul's head jerked to his right.

A female lieutenant, wearing only a towel, stared at him.

"Uh…" Paul stammered. "What room am I in?"

"Mine," she answered.

"So, not 312?"

"310."

"Ah," Paul said. "Shit."

The female lieutenant shook her head and put her hands on her hips. Paul noted her triceps muscle. She had the toned physique of a professional tennis player. Her black hair was like his, shorn down to an even, skull-covering stubble. High cheekbones. Hazel eyes.

She looks like someone who will make it through; Will I?

"Room 312 is next door to the left," she said, pointing past Paul into the hallway. "You will recognize it because it has the number '312' on the door."

"Thanks for the tip," Paul said. He gave an embarrassed grin, hoping to tap into a little empathy before he left.

He got nothing.

She crossed her arms and glared.

Fuck you, he thought as he bent over to pick up his bags again.

Paul left without saying goodbye.

She slammed the door behind him.

The hallway seemed livelier to Paul now, even though only a few minutes had passed. Lieutenants walked back and forth from the latrines. Some in towels. Some partly in uniform.

Dress blues. As ordered.

I'm running late, Paul thought, stepping into his room and closing the door. *Gonna be a quick shower for me.*

Seventeen minutes later, just before 1800 hours, Paul entered the auditorium in his dress blues along with more than a thousand of the military's newest second lieutenants. Paul stepped into a row of seats, not realizing until it was too late that he was standing next to the inhospitable female lieutenant from earlier.

She noticed him and frowned.

"Give me a fucking break," she said under her breath, but loud enough for Paul to hear.

Paul tried to reverse course, but the file of lieutenants close behind him prevented it.

He faced the front of the auditorium again as Colonel Filson, the Commandant of the Officer Assessment and Training Course, walked onto the stage in the old auditorium.

Filson wore the Combat Corps dress uniform, a dark green jacket over khaki pants with brown shoes, dating back over a hundred years ago to the Army. His chest was covered in ribbons and insignia and the buckled belt over his jacket held a bayonet on his left hip.

Paul's eyes fell on the bayonet. Worn only by members of the Combat Corps, the bayonet was a rare but powerful sight in the modern military.

"Look at that scar," the female lieutenant whispered to Paul. "Did you know he was one of the first Centaurs?"

Paul leaned away from her. He didn't know why she was talking to him, and he did not want to get caught talking in formation. Particularly not to her.

And, of course, he knew Filson was a Centaur. They all did.

Filson was part of the army's first generation of Centaurs, augmented combat soldiers implanted with electronics that enabled them to command and control drone weapon systems via brain-to-machine interface. They had read about his exploits at the Academy. His actions at the Second Battle of Santiago were the subject of an entire semester of modern strategy and tactics classes. And if someone didn't know the colonel's record, the large scar that circled his head just above his ears was a giveaway.

Colonel Filson was also a legendary hard-ass.

He wore his hair skintight on the sides. Above his augmentation scar, gray hairs gave his flattop a weathered look, and deep crow's feet ran from the sides of his eyes into his temples.

But as tired as his face appeared, his six-foot body radiated energy and seemed to want to break into a sprint as he walked across the stage. There was something lupine about the old colonel. He stepped up to the podium and surveyed the room from what seemed like more of a fighting stance than a speaker's posture.

"Take your seats," Filson commanded.

Over a thousand second lieutenants sank into their seats. A few of them muttered to each other as they did so.

"It doesn't take any fucking talking!" the colonel yelled. "I said sit. Not speak." A jarring squelch of feedback spilled out of the speakers as Filson's rage overwhelmed it.

The class was startled into silence by his ferocity. He was living up to his reputation already.

"Welcome to the Officer Assessment and Training Course," the colonel said without warmth. "I am Colonel Filson, commandant of this school. It is my duty to prepare each of you for service as officers in the United States Military. I want to congratulate each of you for successfully earning your commissions as second lieutenants. And I want you to know that your commissions don't mean shit to me."

Filson swiveled his head from left to right in silence, taking in the auditorium full of brand-new officers.

"I am talking to all of you. All the valedictorians, all the sports stars, all the class presidents, all the fraternity rush chairmen and sorority big sisters, and especially all the goddamn debate captains. You have done nothing. None of you. Your road to becoming an officer starts here!"

He jabbed his finger on the podium.

"Tonight!"

Another swift jab.

"And does not end for the next one hundred and eighty days unless you quit, or fail out."

A final solid jab of his finger landed on the podium like a bayonet driving into a block of wood.

"And, please, those of you who know you are going to quit, do so now and save my cadre the hassle." He paused, letting the thought sink in. "Come on. I know you're out there. It will be over in a moment. Sergeant Major McGowan is here and can process you out before the mess hall closes."

A tall, muscular black soldier wearing Combat Corps greens stepped out of the shadows at the front corner of the auditorium beneath the stage. He also bore the augmentation scars of a Centaur, as well as a bayonet on his hip. His left hand was an advanced prosthetic, hinting that the rest of that arm was as well. He walked to the center of the stage beneath the podium and smiled as he held up a stack of paper in one hand and pens in the other.

The colonel and his sergeant major looked around the auditorium. And waited.

And looked.

And waited.

Paul thought they were belaboring their point until he heard a shuffling noise to his right.

Every head in the auditorium swiveled to see a lieutenant stand up. He made his way to the aisle and then kept his eyes on the floor as he walked down to the sergeant major.

Several other students stood up and worked their way to the front as the first, sad lieutenant took a piece of paper and pen from the sergeant major.

"No fucking way," someone near Paul whispered.

The colonel waited as four officers signed their resignation papers in front of the entire class.

A staff sergeant walked out and corralled the four shamed junior officers and led them away.

"Any more takers?" Colonel Filson said to the room. "The dropout rate for O.A.T is twenty-five percent," the colonel finally continued. "That's right. One-quarter of you will quit before the course is over. Might as well get it over with."

The colonel looked around until he was satisfied that no one else was going to make the walk of shame. He nodded to the sergeant major, who turned and walked back to the side of the auditorium.

"At least another twenty-five percent of you are going to fail," he continued. "Look around this room. Less than half of you will graduate in six months."

The colonel paused again to let the number sink in. As he did so, Paul thought he heard a noise behind him, past the closed auditorium doors. He looked around at the lieutenants next to him. No one seemed to notice anything.

"A less-than-fifty percent graduation rate!" he yelled. "It's a ridiculous number. The Pentagon gives me shit about it every cycle. 'How in the world can you fail fifty percent of the officers that we have just commissioned?' they ask me.

"I'll tell you the same thing I tell them. Because they are commissioning weak, spineless, and cowardly men and women."

The colonel glared at the auditorium for a long moment.

"Helluva motivational speaker, huh?" the female lieutenant whispered in Paul's direction.

Paul shrugged her off, not inclined to be her friend and terrified of drawing attention.

"The purpose of this course is threefold," Filson said.

Again, Paul thought he heard something. A noise from the lobby. A few others must have also, as their heads swiveled around, looking to the rear.

"First!" The colonel held a finger in the air. "I regard it as my solemn duty to root out as many of you as I can, to not allow you to get out into my military and weaken it. I have seen what happens when just one weakling slips through the cracks. Soldiers die. I will never allow that to happen on my watch."

Colonel Filson's chin jutted forward in determination.

"Second," he continued, holding up two fingers. "This course is designed to give every commissioned officer a common foundation that grounds them in what the military is for. And that is, fighting wars."

Now Paul was sure. A crowd was building just outside of the auditorium. It sounded boisterous. Several lieutenants around Paul heard it too. They shared what-the-hell faces before swiveling back toward the colonel, who seemed oblivious to the growing noise.

"Those of you who graduate, no matter which candy-ass corner of the military you go on to serve in, you will goddamn know, for fucking certain, what being a real officer is all about. No matter what cushy REMF assignment you serve in, you will know, deep down in your bones, what the real war-fighting soldiers are doing. And you will be able to draw a straight fucking line from what you are doing at that moment, no matter how clean and shiny, to what the real war fighters need. And you will fucking do it for them. On time. Every time."

"Third!" Filson held up three fingers. "This course thoroughly tests and assesses newly commissioned officers to find those candidates best suited for the Combat Corps." The colonel paused again and looked at the crowd. He crossed his arms as his eyes swept slowly over the class from left to right. He was in no hurry.

Paul's back stiffened as Filson's eyes passed over him.

The female lieutenant next to him sat straighter as well.

"I always achieve goals one and two." Filson uncrossed his arms.

The noise from the lobby was getting louder. *How many people are out there?* Paul wondered. *How is that not pissing off Colonel Filson? And what is about to happen?*

"The third goal?" the colonel said, almost to himself. "Well, with you lot, I don't hold out much hope for the third goal. We'll address that later if we need to."

Now there was shouting outside of the auditorium. Hundreds of closely shaven lieutenant heads looked around nervously.

Colonel Filson was notorious for beginning each Officer Assessment and Training Course differently. Junior officers were a chatty, secret-sharing bunch, and he was determined that everyone would face a terrible surprise on their first night. After a week, the course settled into its grinding, predictable rhythm, and that was fine. At that point, it didn't matter. It was going to suck, and there was no way around it. It was designed to test wills and to teach skills.

But the first night, and the following couple of days, were meant to terrorize. To frighten. To test one's ability to deal with uncertainty and the unknown, as well as the uncomfortable and hostile.

"I wish you all good luck." The colonel stepped back from the podium. "Sergeant Major! Take command of the class."

The sergeant major walked back out to the center front of the auditorium, under the podium. He saluted the colonel and then turned to face the class.

There was banging on the auditorium doors now. Frightened lieutenants looked over their shoulders back toward the noise.

"On your feet!" the sergeant major yelled.

The class jumped out of their chairs to the position of attention.

Here we go, Paul thought.

"On the command of fall out," the sergeant major began, "you will exit this auditorium and take direction from your training cadre."

The sergeant major paused to let the roar outside of the auditorium take full effect. The sound outside the doors sounded like a pirate ship disembarking. It sounded angry. It sounded violent. It sounded hungry.

"Fall out!"

The class surged for the exits. Paul and the female lieutenant ran side by side through the doors with their classmates.

Blows to the head knocked them to the ground as they stepped through.

Paul saw stars. His first thought was, *Shit, I just lost my hat.* But then he blinked and looked up at the scene.

Cadre in black riot gear were beating the shit out of the candidates.

The cadre wore padded gloves and boots, but the blows still hurt. Noses were breaking. Eyes were blackening. And guts were bruising.

Paul gaped at the surreal brawl. The candidates in their dress blues looked ridiculous next to the black-clad cadre. Their formal uniforms were not designed for fighting. Seams were ripping. Buttons were flying. Dress jackets were splitting.

The cadre, veterans of close-quarters combat, overwhelmed the candidates despite being outnumbered at least ten to one.

The candidates were not all handling it well.

The instant transition from civilized lecture to physical threat was too sudden. Candidates who could not make the mental turn either froze or wept. They would be processed out of the class that night. The first washouts.

"It's road march time, candidates!" a cadre member yelled through a megaphone. "Your rucksacks are waiting for you just outside the building. You will grab a rucksack and follow the route! Those of you who are first out of the building can pick a light one! Those of you who are later can have the heavy ones!"

A new urgency surged through the class. Candidates redoubled their efforts to get through the cadre. But not with any more success. The blows came hard and fast. More candidates fell to the ground.

Bodies were piling up just past the auditorium doors. Paul was stuck under a couple of flailing candidates.

"Come on!" the female lieutenant yelled as she grabbed Paul's wrist. "Get the fuck up!"

She yanked him up, and they both charged forward.

"Together!" Paul yelled.

"Roger that!" she answered.

"Him!" Paul pointed at one of the black riot suits absorbed in pummeling an unfortunate candidate.

They hit him at once. Paul took another punch to the head, but they overwhelmed him for an instant.

It was enough.

Paul fell forward.

The cadre member kicked the female lieutenant in the back in retribution as she slid by. She fell hard.

The cadre turned back to face the surge of other candidates trying to get out.

Paul leapt to his feet. They were now less than twenty feet from the exit. He could see the pile of rucksacks just outside. He pulled the female lieutenant off the ground.

"You good?" Paul asked, shoving her forward.

Wincing, she pointed at the door without answering him.

Paul pushed her forward, and they sprinted out.

"Candidates, halt!" yelled a voice as they got outside.

Paul and the female lieutenant skidded to a stop and came to the position of attention, both panting.

"Names?" asked the cadre member, looking at his clipboard rather than them. They were both relieved to see that he was wearing the olive-drab overalls of a battle-suit driver, not black riot gear. The sounds of the melee roared behind them.

"Kata Vukovic," she said.

"Paul Owens," he said.

The cadre member scanned his list. He nodded to himself as he put a check mark next to each of their names.

"Grab a ruck and get moving," he said, gesturing over his shoulder at the pile.

"Halt!" the cadre member yelled at another cluster of candidates stumbling out of the auditorium. He turned from Paul and Kata and hurried away.

"Names?" they heard him ask the newcomers.

Paul and Kata jogged over to the pile.

There were hundreds of rucksacks in a mound that loomed over their heads. They scanned the various sizes of rucks. Most seemed moderately full. But there were many that were overstuffed and several that were obviously empty.

Paul leaned over to test one of the overstuffed ones.

"Shit!" Paul said. "Has to weigh a hundred pounds."

Kata grabbed a medium, and he did the same. It didn't feel right to grab one of the empties.

Kata adjusted the shoulder straps and then set her rucksack on the ground. She took off her battered dress blue jacket and threw it aside.

"It's hot as balls out here," Kata said. "And it's trashed, anyway."

Paul yanked his jacket off. He shook his head at the sight of it. One sleeve was nearly pulled off, and none of the buttons remained. One of the side seams had burst open.

"Fuck it," Kata said, yanking off her starched white dress shirt. Her undershirt was already drenched with sweat.

"Good idea," Paul said, taking off his dress shirt.

They slung their rucks onto their backs and then acknowledged each other with a shake of their heads. Their sweaty white T-shirts, accented by the olive-green rucksack shoulder straps, looked ridiculous over their dress blue pants.

Paul chuckled.

"What?" Kata asked.

"Your dress pants have holes in both knees."

"Yeah? I tore them saving your ass. So, you owe me."

A cadre's voice interrupted them. "Candidates, halt!"

They crouched as they scanned the area, fearing the return of the black-suited aggressors. But the voice had come from back toward the building. More candidates were emerging, and cadre members with clipboards were all over them.

"Let's keep moving," Kata said.

A green chem stick glowed in the middle of the parking lot to their front, fifty meters from the pile of rucksacks. Another burned in the distance in the middle of the road that stretched away and up a steep rise. At the top of the rise, over half a mile away, lay another dim green light, just before the road dipped down the other side of the hill and into the darkness.

"I guess that's the route," Paul said. "Let's go."

They walked as fast as they could. Not knowing how far they had to go, they were reluctant to jog. Who knew how much energy they would need tonight? They crested the small rise and went over the other side, the noise of the chaos behind them fading.

Soon, they were in marching mode. Their strides in sync, their breathing measured, they tried not to wonder how far they had to go.

Kata broke the silence.

"So, did I hear right?" she asked in a transactional tone. "It's Paul?"

"Yeah," he said.

They walked a few more minutes in silence before Paul asked, "What kind of name is Vukovic, anyway?"

"Croatian. Grandparents on my dad's side came over back in the nineteen-nineties during the war."

They walked along, both wondering about the other. Kata finally came out and asked, "So, are you going for Combat Corps?"

"Yes. I want to be a soldier. Not a REMF."

Kata nodded at the answer.

"You?" he asked.

"Same."

They walked in silence for a long time, both wondering how many Combat Corps slots their class would have and knowing that it was just one.

Paul stopped dwelling on it first. His dress shoes, which he had purchased a week ago and were not yet broken in, had been biting into his heel and the top of his toes for miles.

He kicked them off.

"What are you doing?" Kata asked him.

"I don't know how long this road march is going to last. But my guess is that it is going to be much longer than I want to walk in those damn things. I figure, this way, I am fucked the least."

Kata kicked her dress shoes off as well.

They walked farther into the darkness, their socked feet a final blow to their dignity.

"I think it's going to be a long night," Kata said.

It was.

Chapter Two

Paul was wet, filthy, and exhausted.

It was the last night of phase one. The class was on a seven-day field exercise that pulled together everything they had been taught to that point: land navigation, survival, marksmanship, close-quarters combat, first aid, etc. Six days ago, the cadre had put each trainee alone in the mountains of West Virginia with a map, a compass, two canteens of water, and a week's ration of food. No GPS. No radios. No drones. No nothing. So not only had the class been dropped into the empty, mountainous armpit of America, they had been dropped over a hundred years back in time.

"This is some real bullshit," Kata said to no one, holding up her magnetic compass as they walked to the drone copters.

Paul and several other heavily laden candidates in the file nodded in exhausted agreement.

"It's like we're training to be doughboys," Kata added, shaking her head.

"Huh?" a candidate next to her said.

"Doughboys," Kata repeated.

The candidate looked back at her.

"You know," she said, looking around at the group like an impatient schoolteacher. "World War I soldiers."

Paul avoided eye contact with her. *So arrogant,* he thought.

"Idiots," Kata said to herself with disbelief as they filed into the idling aircraft.

It was nighttime, with only a sliver of the moon providing illumination.

The drone flew with its doors open. Paul was sure that Filson had arranged it to do so. The blustery combination of rotor wash and night air tugged and pulled through the cabin, wrapping everyone in a chill despite it being August.

Paul looked around. There were two dozen candidates on board, including him and Kata. Most looked miserable. But a handful wore the same intense face Paul did. Class standings were well known at that point, and Paul was in the running for the one Combat Corps slot. So was Kata. And so were about twenty other candidates. So, the phase-one results were important.

After twenty minutes of flight, the drone's nose rose slightly, and it began to shed airspeed and descend.

Sixty seconds later, the aircraft's four large turbofan thrusters swiveled and howled as it came to a hover. The small red light over the door changed to green, and the lone cadre on board kicked the coiled fast rope out the door. He turned and pointed at the first candidate, yelling, "Move!"

The candidate stood up and headed for the door. He wobbled for a few steps under the weight of his pack. The shifting floor of the aircraft did not help. It was windy.

He gave the cadre a thumbs-up, grabbed the fast rope, swung out into the darkness, and slid out of sight.

The cadre leaned out to observe. Satisfied the candidate had not killed himself, the cadre hauled in the fast rope. He coiled it neatly on the aircraft floor in smooth, efficient motions borne of repetition.

Then the cadre took his seat next to the door. The engines whined louder, and the drone's nose dipped slightly as it accelerated and climbed away.

Paul noted the augmentation scar visible just below the cadre's black knit skullcap. He was a Centaur, and there was no need for him to speak to command the drone. Verbal communication was only required with the soft meat of the candidates.

After ten more insertions, there were only a few candidates left on board.

At the next insertion point, the cadre pointed at Kata and said, "Move!"

She popped up and walked to the door.

The aircraft swayed in its final deceleration, but Kata was unperturbed. She didn't even reach up for one of the hand grabs.

The light changed to green.

The cadre gave a thumbs-up.

Kata vanished down the rope.

The test was simple; the trainees had to locate themselves on the map and make their way to the extraction point, eighty mountainous miles away, in seven days. Along the way, there were testing stations, which they had to navigate to and arrive at within one minute of an assigned "time on target."

If a trainee missed a TOT, they were done. A drone copter arrived within five minutes to yank them off the mountain. When they arrived back at Fort Benning, they were given the option of resigning their commission or recycling back to the first day of phase one.

Most resigned rather than start over.

At one station, they had to field strip and reassemble a weapon within two minutes and then progress through a firing range. At another, they had to correctly assess and render first aid to several types of injuries. There were about five stations a day, and trainees had one chance at each. If they failed a station, they were done. The drone copter was on the way.

So, each day and most of each night consisted of hours of trekking up and down mountains, punctuated by high-stakes military skills tests.

It was raining on the last night, and Paul was sheltering under a small rock overhang. After studying the map, he calculated he had about two hours before he needed to start humping again. He had just taken off his waterlogged boots and was trying to dry out his socks in front of a tiny fire he had built when Colonel Filson appeared.

The colonel seemed to materialize at the edge of the dim firelight. Paul was startled. He hadn't heard an aircraft or Filson approach and could not conceive of how the colonel had found him. But Filson could do that. He did it to Paul more than once during O.A.T. He would step out of the darkness during the dirtiest, wettest, most lost and isolated moments of the training.

Paul fumbled around on the ground, trying to get to a position of attention, but before he could stand up, Filson said, "As you were, Owens. Don't get up."

"Yes, sir."

The colonel sat down across the fire from Paul and leaned in to warm his hands. Paul noticed Filson was soaking wet.

"Good fire, son," Filson said. He looked around. "Good hide-site selection also. Your fire is concealed, and you have good cover. Nice."

"Thank you, sir."

"Most of your class is worthless. But you and a couple others have potential. Particularly Vukovic."

Paul just nodded and stared at the fire. *Damn it. I knew she was doing well.*

"What do you think of O.A.T so far?" Filson asked, pulling a plastic bag out of the breast pocket of his field jacket.

"It's pretty tough, sir," he said as he shifted his weight and thought, *Terrific, there goes my plan to get some sleep.*

"It was a lot different before I got here, you know," the colonel said as he pulled a cigar out of the plastic bag. He returned the bag to his pocket and bit off one end of the cigar, spitting it into the fire. "It was a joke. Two weeks of bullshit they called 'fieldcraft,' which wasn't much more than roasting marshmallows and playing grab ass in the woods."

Filson leaned forward until one end of the cigar touched the small fire. The red glow of the flames lit his face from below, highlighting his augmentation scar. The sharp horizontal shadow across his forehead looked like a seam that suggested you could lift open the cap of his skull. Which, of course, they had, over fifteen years ago.

"You know, when they first asked me to be the commandant of O.A.T, I told 'em no. When they asked again, I said, 'Fuck no.' I was stationed out West at the time. I had just gotten back to my unit after healing up. I was ready to get back into the fight. They asked a third time, and I just ignored it. So I was surprised when the Supreme Commander, General Tom Havron, showed up. In fucking person."

Filson made a wide-eyed, mock-surprised face to emphasize the point. It was the most human thing Paul had seen him do yet, and it almost made him laugh out loud.

"It was late afternoon," Filson continued. "I had just gotten in from working out with a combined-arms drone team on the maneuver range. The general was waiting for me at the armory. 'Get the fuck out of that exo and meet me in my office, Filson!' he yelled.

"Tom didn't have an office there, of course. It was my office. I could tell he was pissed, so I jumped out of the exoskeleton and double-timed to meet him. One of my platoon sergeants walked my equipment back to the armory.

"'What's your goddamn problem, Don?' he asked from behind my desk as soon as I shut the door.

"'I don't understand, sir?' I responded.

"'Why are you fighting me on this assignment?' he asked me.

"'What do you mean fighting you, sir? I've just been back and forth with personnel. I didn't know...' I started to say.

"'I'm the Supreme Commander of the US Military, you moron!' he yelled at me. 'You fight with personnel, you are fighting with me!'

"Now, you have to understand," Filson said to Paul with resignation. "I would have then, and still would now, do anything the old man asked me to. Anything. But... I really didn't want this assignment."

Filson stared at Paul until he was certain Paul understood. Then he continued.

"'So, it was your stupid idea to put me out to pasture as the commandant at Fort Benning, sir?' I said to the general, getting mad. 'I thought I was just dealing with the faceless bureaucratic stupidity of the institution! But now that I know it is your specific brand of stupid, you better believe I'm gonna fight it!'

"That made General Havron chuckle. He smiled and nodded. 'Don,' he said to me. 'What have you been bitching about for years now?'"

The colonel took a long drag from his cigar and then leaned into the fire and looked at Paul.

"You have to understand, Owens," Filson said. "I was one of his company commanders when we fielded the first real ground drone and Centaur units, and he was just a maverick lieutenant colonel. We co-developed a lot of the first organizational and tactical principles for employing the increasingly complex units the US Army was fielding. We saw a lot of shit together. He had asked for me and my battalion, by name, when he was scraping together a force to go south and kick the Chinese out of Santiago. And along the way, we had grown more and more dismayed together."

Filson paused, staring into the small fire.

Paul grew uncomfortable as the silence extended. He tried to stare into the fire also.

"You see, son," Filson finally continued. "For as long as there have been soldiers, they have lived on one side or the other of an ancient schism."

Filson outstretched both arms to emphasize his point.

"And I'm not talking about the divide between the soldier and society. I'm talking about the schism between the soldier and the REMF. For as long as there have been armies, the warriors have despised the logisticians and administrators, the 'Rear Echelon Motherfuckers,' sitting far back from the fighting, safe with their clean sheets, warm showers, and hot meals.

"And the REMFs," Filson continued, "have despised the warriors right back, looking down on the knuckle-dragging brutes with their colorful medals, bullshit stories, and hulking egos. The REMFs were fine letting the warriors get all the glory because they thought they were smarter than us. You heard that bullshit that 'amateurs study tactics, while professionals study logistics'?"

Paul nodded.

The colonel spat into the fire.

"Nonetheless, for millennia, a grudging truce and understanding persisted. The system worked. But over the past twenty years, the ancient system has slowly been turned upside down by all the goddamn technology we've been fielding. Most of which, by the way, has benefitted only the defense industry. It's been almost a hundred years since Eisenhower warned us about the military-industrial complex, and I'm telling you, Owens, it's never been stronger. Those bloodsucking profiteers have accelerated the widening of the schism, dazzling the REMFs with shiny objects, overly complex systems with no soul and often no fighting ability."

The colonel rubbed his eyes.

"Some days," he said, "I think we really are just cannon fodder, and the military-industrial complex is eternal. It is the one part of this story that will never, ever change."

Colonel Filson shook his head in disgust at his own statement.

"Over the course of our careers," he continued, "General Havron and I watched as the number of fighting robots increased every year, while the number of fighting men and women decreased. I remember taking command of my first company and being shocked to learn I had more robots assigned to me than human soldiers. Then, when I was a battalion commander, I actually commanded fewer men and women than when I commanded a company!

"And don't think the military has gotten any smaller as this has gone on," the colonel said, shaking his head. "Quite the fucking opposite. When I was commissioned in 2037, the active-duty military was about one-point-two million strong, and less than three hundred thousand of those were real combat forces. The military you were just commissioned into is one-point-three million strong, and less than twenty thousand of us are combat soldiers."

Filson's eyes got big and he arched his eyebrows for emphasis.

The colonel stared at Paul for a moment, and then said softly, "Think about that, son. Less than one percent of the population serves in the military. And little more than one percent of the military actually fights."

The colonel shook his head.

"Ever since the French Revolution and Napoleon's Grande Armée almost two hundred and fifty years ago, the percentage of a society's population that serves in the military has been steadily decreasing. And in the past few decades, the percentage of the military that actually fights has fallen off an even steeper cliff.

"General Havron and I bitched to each other often about the direction of things as we slogged through some of the world's garden spots. The ancient schism was out of whack. Permanently. It was never going to be right. The REMFs run things now. Always will. The problem for over a decade was, they had no idea how to run it. That's how Santiago happened.

"But when the general sat behind my desk that day in my office and asked me what we'd been bitching about for twenty years, I just looked back at him like an idiot. Not sure what he was saying.

"'Don, I want you to go to Benning and fix the officer course,' he said to me.

"'Sir, you won't like what I do with the place,' I told him.

"'Yes, I will,' he said, without blinking.

"'It won't work unless I have total, unfettered authority to do what needs to be done,' I demanded, looking for him to waver.

"'You will,' he told me.

"I thought about it for a minute and then said, 'If you're serious, sir, I'll do it. But I'm going to quit the first time I encounter bullshit.'

"'It's a deal, Don,' General Havron said, smiling with excitement. 'I've got your back.'

"And, son of a bitch, he sure did. I wrecked the place," Colonel Filson said with satisfaction. "Got rid of all the instructors and replaced them with real warriors I had served with. I established the course structure you're going through. Sixty days of intense individual instruction, followed by sixty days of small-unit leadership, followed by sixty days of combined-arms training and assessments.

"Then, after the first iteration, when I failed over half of the class, the chief of military personnel, a four-star REMF general at the Pentagon, called me. Left a long voice mail about what an arrogant idiot I was and told me to pack my bags because he was sending a new commandant the next day."

The colonel took another tug from his cigar.

"I forwarded the voice mail to General Havron with a message from me that said, 'Your pick. Me or the REMF. No hard feelings either way, sir.' The next day, I got up early, packed my bags, and waited for the aircraft with my replacement to arrive. Around lunchtime, though, I saw the announcement of the military's chief of personnel's sudden retirement on the *Military Times* website."

The colonel chuckled at the memory.

Paul smiled at Filson from across the fire, trying to picture the surprised four-star general when he was relieved by the Supreme Commander for crossing a lowly colonel.

Filson caught Paul smiling and nodded back at him.

"After graduation, ninety-nine percent of your class will never have mud on their boots again," Filson said. "But I goddamn guarantee you they will understand what it means to be a soldier. And those REMFs will support you better because of it."

Filson stood up and stretched his back. He took one last tug on his cigar and then threw the butt of it into Paul's small fire.

"You understand, son?"

"Yes, sir," Paul lied.

"Good. Don't miss your TOT tomorrow, or I'll fail your ass."

"Yes, sir." But the colonel had already disappeared into the shadows.

Chapter Three

Paul trudged up the Colorado mountainside just a few steps behind the Geek, another O.A.T candidate. It was almost 0100 hours, and their platoon had been moving up the steep incline, in full unaugmented combat gear, for more than three hours.

Kata, who had been marching behind Paul, took a few quick, long strides to catch up to him.

"He's not going to make it," she whispered, gesturing with her weapon at the Geek, whose wobbly and uncertain legs threatened to collapse at each step.

"Shut up," Paul hissed. "He's going to make it."

Paul sped up to separate himself from Kata and bumped into the Geek from behind.

The Geek, unable to take a hit at this point, lost his balance.

"Shit," Paul said, grabbing the stumbling candidate by his rucksack shoulder strap to steady him.

"Sorry, Geek," Paul said. "My bad."

The Geek nodded, not able to spare the breath to speak.

"Just think of that photo," Paul whispered to him. "And keep going."

After a few seconds rest with Paul's steadying grip on his rucksack, the Geek turned back uphill.

Paul gave him a moment to get some separation between them. Kata stepped up and next to Paul, glared at him, and threw one hand up in the air.

"Fuck you," Paul muttered before turning uphill.

Paul and the Geek, Wallace Hartwell, had become friends over the past months of Filson's crucible. There was no pair of candidates more dissimilar.

Paul seemed born for a life of military service. Hartwell seemed destined to be cast out of it.

Wallace stood only about five and a half feet tall. He wasn't fat, exactly. But he was chunky and a weakling. He was also the smartest candidate in the class. Wallace had graduated from Georgia Tech with a double major in nuclear engineering and robotics.

Wallace was also self-aware. He knew he was not well suited to Filson's gauntlet. He also knew that none of his fellow trainees thought he would make it through O.A.T. But Wallace was resolved to try.

Wallace did not hide his geekiness. It would have been impossible to do so. And within a day of the start of O.A.T, everyone referred to him as "that fucking geek."

Wallace took no offense. He embraced it and kept his head down. By the time he shocked everyone, especially Colonel Filson, by making it through phase one, the jeer had been transformed into a nickname.

Paul respected the Geek's intellect, but he was intrigued by the Geek's spirit. He never quit. Ever. Paul had recognized that fire within Kata the moment he'd met her. That's why he regarded her as competition for the Combat Corps slot. But it took him a while to see it in the Geek.

He sought to understand it weeks earlier, one night in the high desert west of Kirtland Military Base near Albuquerque. They sat on the cold ground and leaned against each other's backs, unable to sleep as they tried to stay warm.

"Why do you want this so badly?" Paul asked the Geek.

"I am a fourth-generation officer," the Geek answered. "A fourth-generation Georgia Tech to military commission, as a matter of fact. There are photos of my father, my grandfather, and my great-grandfather on the wall of my ROTC battalion's headquarters in Atlanta."

Paul waited as the Geek paused for a moment. He pulled his Mylar thermal blanket tighter.

"I should have said I *want* to be a fourth-generation officer. I want to continue the tradition," the Geek continued. He looked at Paul with a weary smile. "I am not one yet. And it's clear that Filson doesn't want me to be one."

Paul nodded to himself. It was true. Filson despised the Geek.

The class was well into phase two now. Most of Filson's technology prohibitions still applied as they roved from base to base across the country. They trained in mountain, swamp, desert, and urban conditions as each candidate rotated through positions of leadership from squad to platoon leader. In a system modeled after the army's old Ranger School program, each candidate's turn in a leadership role was graded by both instructors and peers. They got very little sleep, lived on one meal a day, and never came out of the field or showered.

Filson was ahead of his normal pace for O.A.T and had already run out over a third of the class. Now, in the thick of phase two, he was failing candidates at a rate of almost one a day. He was determined to get the Geek and made no secret of it. But, somehow, the Geek kept soldiering on.

"How do you keep going?" Paul asked him.

"You mean, despite my unsuitability?"

"Um… no. That is not what I meant. I just…"

"It's OK, Paul. Sincerely. I'm playing with you."

The Geek chuckled as Paul shifted in his thermal blanket.

"It's true, after all. I am poorly suited to all this." The Geek looked around at their austere surroundings. A dozen other exhausted candidates, huddled in pairs and wrapped in thermal blankets, were dispersed around them. All trying to force themselves to sleep. They would be on the move again before daybreak.

"But you know the REMFs that Filson scorns? The ones he rails against? Well, I can do that job. The military needs REMFs, after all. Especially in the Space Corps. And, if I make it through this, I think I'll be a really good one."

"There is no doubt in my mind about that, Wallace."

The Geek smiled at the comment from his friend.

"Why do you want this so badly, Paul?" the Geek asked.

"Dunno. Guess I've never thought about the why."

The pair was silent for a few minutes.

"My father served," Paul said, long after the Geek thought the topic had passed. "It's really all I've ever wanted to do."

The Geek smiled again. "That makes me happy."

"What?"

"That, as different as we may be in capability, we are similar in motivation."

"I guess we are," Paul said.

"I know you want to make it into the Combat Corps, Paul," the Geek said. "And I hope you do. Me? I just want to serve in uniform like my family has for generations. That's what keeps me going. You know those three photographs I told you about? In my most lonely, droning, and zombie-like moments, I picture my photo on the wall next to them, and I just keep walking toward it. And I won't stop until my heart quits beating, or Filson tells me to go home."

Paul nodded, his intrigue with the Geek becoming awe. Paul and Kata were doing well at O.A.T. They were in the running for the one Combat Corps slot. Their wills were fierce, their bodies strong, and Filson curious to see who would win. The Geek, though? His body was weak. Filson wanted him out. All he had was his spirit.

Could I make it if I were him? Paul wondered.

As they slogged up the mountainside, Paul thought about that conversation in the desert. Then he thought about the colonel.

Earlier that day, as Filson was assigning the Geek platoon-leader duties for that night's mission—an assault on a mountaintop position that would require them to hike all night—Paul and Kata made eye contact. They both thought that Filson was stacking the deck against the Geek.

The Geek collapsed, falling face-first on the rocky slope.

Paul jumped to the Geek's side and started pulling his rucksack off. Kata walked up quickly and leaned over the Geek.

"What the hell do you want?" Paul asked her.

"Give me his pack," she said.

Paul regarded her for a moment. "No," he said. "We'll split it."

They emptied the Geek's rucksack and divided the load. A couple of other platoon mates followed. One took the Geek's weapon, and another grabbed his ammo.

"What are you guys doing?" protested a nearby candidate, who stood watching. "He's not going to make it. He's failing."

Paul lunged at him.

"Yeah. He is failing," Paul said, grabbing the candidate by the collar. "But he's not quitting."

"Easy, Paul!" Kata shouted, stepping between them and breaking Paul's grip. "We've got a lot more to do tonight. We all need our energy."

Paul shook his head in disgust and turned back to the Geek.

The candidate nodded in agreement with Kata, as if she had taken his side.

She shoved him hard. He stumbled back a few meters.

"What the hell?" he said, taking two aggressive steps forward before stopping at the sight of Kata in a ready position.

"What is wrong with you two?" he said.

"The Geek is doing his best," Kata said. "If he weren't trying so hard, I'd say, fuck him also. But he fell on his face, moving forward up the hill. He never sat down. Never complained. Never quit." Kata paused to make sure the candidate understood her when she said, "So, he is coming with us. Every step of the way. You got it?"

The candidate sneered and looked around for support. But the other platoon members stared back, hands on their hips, and nodded.

"Yeah," he said. "I got it."

Kata returned to the Geek's side.

"I thought we were saving our energy?" Paul said.

"Fuck you," Kata answered.

They had to clean blood off of the Geek's face. He had busted his lip and nose open in the fall. Then they propped him up and shoved him up the rest of the mountain.

The assault was successful.

Paul and Kata had made sure that everyone in the platoon marked the Geek's performance as a success when it was time to turn in peer ratings.

Most were happy to do so. No one thought the Geek was actually going to make it through and graduate from O.A.T. But it felt good to foil Colonel Filson in some small, temporary way.

The respite was short-lived.

Swamp training was the most hated part of phase two. They trained for three weeks in a nasty part of northern Florida and were in at least ankle-high water the entire time. The heat and humidity were oppressive. It felt like breathing through a dirty, wet sock. Every candidate got rashes and skin infections, and by the third week, their skin would slough off at any rough contact. It had lost all its strength. Their knees, elbows, and backs were raw.

By the end of swamp training, Paul's platoon was down to twenty-four candidates, and it was the Geek's turn to lead the mission again. And, again, the colonel circled like a hungry buzzard. The whole platoon knew that if they failed at the night's assault, the Geek was done.

They groaned when they got the mission. It was a direct assault on a machine-gun nest dug into a small rise in front of which lay a putrid stretch of chest-deep water thick with mangroves and leeches. It had been raining for over a week, and the water was high. So high, in fact, that the cadre gave them four rubber rafts to assault in. Colonel Filson was sufficiently worried that, in their exhausted state, some of the weaker candidates would drown.

"Well," the Geek said in an insincere voice, "the man does have a heart."

Paul shook his head.

"What?" the Geek asked.

"We're fucked," Kata said. "Notice how they did not give us any paddles? We're going to have to drive those pieces of shit with our rifle butts. We won't be able to steer, and we're going to be moving slow."

"And we have only one very obvious avenue of approach to the objective," the Geek said.

"And they know it," Kata said.

"And we're going to be noisy," Paul said, standing up.

The platoon watched as he walked over and climbed into one of the black inflatable boats. Squeaky rubber barking noises marked his slightest movements. He sat in the boat in silence for a few seconds before climbing back out. The symphony of chirps and squeaks began again.

"Each boat holds six," Paul said, walking back. "So, we're going to make so much noise the enemy will hear us coming long before we can get to the beach and begin the assault."

The dejected platoon huddled and tried to come up with a plan. They were exhausted, so they sat cross-legged in the shallow, fetid water that came up to their navels. They were miserable.

"I think this is it for me," the Geek said. "Just want you to know it has been my honor to work with all of you." He spoke to the platoon, but his eyes rested on Paul and Kata.

"Bullshit!" Kata said. "We can do this!"

The Geek shook his head. "I appreciate your enthusiasm, Kata. But I don't see a way to successfully pull it off in these boats." He gestured at the cluster of boats tied to a mangrove behind him. They made loud squeaking noises as they jostled together.

Paul remembered how Filson had smiled when the cadre had given them the boats.

"What if we don't use them?" Paul mumbled to the group.

Kata looked at Paul and smiled, getting his meaning instantly.

The Geek looked at Paul. "The colonel said we had to use them. For safety."

"Oh, we'll use them," Paul said.

Kata belly-laughed.

The Geek looked at Kata. Then back at Paul. Then smiled as he looked back at Kata. By the time he looked back to Paul, the Geek was also laughing.

"I don't have the slightest idea what you have in mind," the Geek said to Paul, breathless from laughter and fatigue. "But it must be better than what I was thinking."

Half the platoon rolled in the water, laughing. Kata was slapping platoon mates on the back and punching them in the shoulder. They winced as they felt their skin slough off and went right back to laughing.

The rising morale spread through the platoon like a tonic. By the time Paul had finished briefing them on his idea, they all felt like they had just taken a shower. They felt refreshed and alert in a way they had not in months, excited to try to pull one over on the colonel.

Paul knew that the cadre would be expecting them to assault in the boats as they had been told to. So he divided the platoon into two teams of ten and one team of four. Paul and Kata each took a ten-man team and stripped down to their basic uniforms. They put their packs and gear into the boats but kept their weapons on them.

Then the team of four—the Geek and three others—each got into one of the boats. The four of them started paddling up the lone route to the objective.

Paul took his team wide to the left of the main assault. Kata took hers to the right. Unburdened from the seventy-five pounds of equipment they carried everywhere, they were able to swim and bound quickly in the water without making a sound.

The boats were so slow that Paul and Kata had their teams in perfect position on the flanks of the enemy position by the time the Geek was able to begin his assault.

The rubber boats had been so loud, the cadre had not suspected any other threat.

Paul and Kata waited for the cadre to engage the Geek's force, then attacked on the flanks.

It was a total surprise and a perfect envelopment. They captured the enemy position in just a few minutes and took no casualties.

Colonel Filson seethed. Paul could tell later, during the debrief, that the colonel wanted to explode. But he allowed the victory to stand. The Geek recorded a successful assault.

The colonel exacted a price out of them, though. The whole platoon was punished for "employing unsafe tactics." They were given extra duty for the next week.

But their morale was so high, they didn't care. They felt not only like they had gotten one over on the colonel, but that they had also saved a buddy.

Chapter Four

9 December 2061
New York City

"Are you absolutely sure about this, Fiona?" Martin Pruden asked.

Fiona Malloy looked up from her computer. Pruden, bleary-eyed from lack of sleep, stood across from her on the other side of her desk. The sleeves of his customary blue button-up shirt were rolled up to his elbows, and his khakis showed the stained wear and tear of a string of late nights. She glanced down at herself. Her jeans and grey sweatshirt weren't in any better condition.

Fiona stood up and stretched.

She scanned the room as she reset her long, brown hair into a tighter ponytail. The room was a mess. Pizza boxes, dirty dishes, beer cans, and empty water bottles were scattered about the large office she was renting in Midtown Manhattan. The leather sofa, where Fiona had been sleeping for weeks, was also serving as her clothing storage area and was obscured by dirty clothes and a single uncovered pillow. Thick white notebooks were strewn about the hardwood floor like wayward steppingstones. Two printers and a couple of reams of paper sat in one corner against the floor-to-ceiling window, next to large plastic trash bags of shredded paper.

Fiona smiled at the mess. It made her feel good. Evidence of homework done, preparedness.

Their two analysts had left about an hour ago. Faithful Pruden had stayed, of course. It was crunch time. Fiona had until nine a.m. to accept the last and final counter offer from Spitting Metal, a promising but deeply indebted AI weapon systems designer and manufacturer she had made a bid to acquire.

"Yeah," Fiona said, turning her gaze to Pruden. "I am sure about it. We've been over the numbers a hundred times. I think they work."

He nodded, unconvinced, as she walked by him toward the windows.

She rubbed her neck and looked out at the city. It was well after midnight. Cleaning drones worked the streets and sidewalks, taking advantage of the reduced traffic which would surge again in a few hours as the human work day approached. Above, the ever present cloud of delivery and taxi drones scintillated. Every few seconds one of the tens of thousands would swoop down from the coursing multitude in a descending arc that looked suicidal, before flaring aggressively to decelerate and land on a towering rooftop.

"Martin," Fiona said, turning from the window. "How long have we been at this?"

Pruden looked at his watch, but Fiona shook her head.

"Not tonight," she said. "I mean on our strategy. Our plan."

"Oh." Pruden scratched his head. "Two years, I guess?"

"More like almost five," Fiona said.

He shook his head in weary disbelief.

Fiona Malloy met Martin Pruden the day she started at Harvard Business School over four years ago.

He was standing over an expansive table of nametags looking lost when she stepped up to scan for her own.

"Whatcha looking for?" she asked, sensing his lack of progress.

"Martin Pruden." A sheepish grin spread across his face as he extended his hand. "You'd think they would do these things alphabetically or something."

"Maybe it's our first test?" she said, shaking his hand. "Fiona Malloy."

"Malloy? There's a Roberta Malloy right here." He grabbed the nearby nametag. "Relation?"

"No." Fiona scowled and took the nametag from him. He watched as she fished a pen out of her backpack, lined through Roberta, and replaced it with Fiona. "No one calls me that."

Pruden smiled and nodded. "Understood, Fiona."

She winked in thanks before turning her gaze back to the table. "Alright, Martin Pruden. Let's find you."

The two were a mismatch: a guy from a tight-knit working-class New Jersey family who had slaved for four years as an analyst at a bottom-tier investment bank before somehow making it into HBS, and a girl from a dysfunctional, ultra-wealthy bloodline, straight out of undergrad with no work experience, who gained easy access to Harvard because of her family name.

In addition to being four years older, Pruden, at six feet, was also four inches taller than Fiona. Somehow, though, he came across as slighter than she. His short blond hair, pleasing smile, unimposing posture and slight paunch cloaked him in a blandness that obscured his high intelligence.

While Pruden's appearance made no impression at all, Fiona looked like she could step back onto her college lacrosse team and still deal out serious punishment. She'd discovered CrossFit early in college and had still not slowed down at it. She wore her hair in a tight athlete's ponytail all the time and was often seen wrapping up her day just before midnight with a jog through campus.

They didn't seek each other out. Their work ethics and class loads synchronized them. They were assigned to the same core curriculum classes in their first semester. Soon, they started pairing up regularly when small teamwork projects were assigned. Within a few months, whether it was in the business-school study rooms, the library, or just venting at the pub, they were spending the majority of their time together. They chose all the same electives their final year.

The rumors that they were sleeping together began immediately. They were not, but Fiona and Pruden exerted no effort to dispel them. They were uninterested in the social scene and focused on their studies.

Fiona managed her time at Yale and then Harvard Business School like an architect, building the structure of skills she would need later. It was surprising to most how hard this attractive trust-fund baby applied herself.

Entering their last semester, they were close. Their classmates were surprised whenever they were seen apart. But they were not friends, more like soldiers who had shared the same foxhole for a long time. They were intimately familiar with the other's habits and thought processes. But that was it. When the war was over, they would part ways forever.

As they neared graduation from business school, though, Pruden was offered a job at Goldman Sachs. He was excited as he told Fiona about it over beers in a booth at their favorite pub in Harvard Square.

"No," Fiona responded, surprising herself as well as Pruden.

"What do you mean, no?" Pruden asked. "I wasn't asking you a question. I'm telling you about a great opportunity."

Pruden's parents worked at the local high school, back home in New Jersey. His dad taught math and coached the basketball team. His mom was a career counselor. Goldman was offering Pruden a starting salary that was more than his parents made, put together, in five years.

"You're not going to waste your time with that crap, Marty. You're going to come work with me, and, I promise you, you are going to be happy you did. What did they offer you?"

Pruden was quiet.

"I'll double it. Whatever it is. And give you an equity stake in everything we do."

Pruden hesitated as he grappled with the interaction. He had always known they were from different worlds. But this was the first time since meeting Fiona that he'd felt the yawning socioeconomic chasm that separated them.

It didn't feel good.

"Are you serious?" was all Pruden could get out of his mouth.

"A hundred percent," Fiona said, feeling her commitment well within her as she spoke. She wanted Pruden to come with her.

It was a great offer. But what exactly were they going to be doing? Pruden wondered. And if it failed, how would it translate to another potential employer?

"Marty," Fiona said, seeing the raging risk assessment play out on his face.

"Do you want to be part of a big, safe, slow-moving machine, or do you want to take a shot at building something?"

Pruden leaned back in his chair, put off by her reaction to his good news.

"Hey," Fiona said. "No hard feelings either way. All I will say is that the big, safe jobs will always be there. There will always be room for another sheep at the trough."

"Learned that from your billionaire's vantage point, did you?" Pruden said.

"Touché," Fiona answered, smiling at the barb.

Pruden didn't throw many brushback pitches, but when he did, they had heat on them. Fiona liked that. Fiona liked a lot about Pruden. She wanted him on board. She was going to need his help.

"Let me start over." Fiona leaned forward toward Pruden. "Goldman is a great outfit. You should be proud. Shit, I'm proud of you. You've busted your ass to get to this point. I know we've got different backgrounds. Nonetheless, the last two years proved we work well together, and I respect your judgment, intelligence, and work ethic. I need your help. And I'm willing to pay for it."

"Why?" Pruden said. "Working on what? I don't even know what you are trying to do. This is the first time in two years you've talked about what happens for you after graduation. To be honest, I assumed you'd go back to your family office to help manage activities and investments. Like, part time."

Fiona leaned back in the booth.

Pruden waited for her to speak.

"I would rather die than do that," Fiona said.

Something in her face told Martin she meant it.

Fiona and Pruden set up shop in New York City after business school. It was irritating for Fiona to be close to her family. But it was where her network was strongest and where her name would be taken the most seriously. People would not realize she was going rogue.

They spent six months flying in the top thought leaders in the world: economists, technologists, anthropologists, historians, philosophers, anyone who struck them as a potential source of information and insight. They did not claim their activities were related to the Malloy Family Investments, but they did not say they weren't.

At the end of these sessions, they made their decision.

"Artificial intelligence," Fiona said to Pruden across a pizza box after midnight, surrounded by their laptops and notebooks. "That is where we focus."

"Military applications," Pruden added with a nod. "They still haven't figured out a good answer to the kill chain problem that both works well and complies with the Tokyo Accords," he said.

"They are going to be the biggest customer for AI solutions for decades," Fiona said. "And after the big Department of Defense reorganization a few years ago, their buying behavior is even more concentrated."

"That's right," Pruden agreed.

After the Santiago debacle, Congress restructured the armed forces. The images of the US military running into the ocean begging for sealift embarrassed and enraged the country. Americans don't like to lose.

A handful of military veterans in Congress led the crusade for reform, spurred on by an irate electorate and a vocal veteran community. Skeptical of the Pentagon's ability to transform itself, they forced change by dismantling the Joint Chiefs and making the majority of the bloated general officer corps retire.

Then they tapped a young, visionary field commander to lead the transformation. They named General Tom Havron, the man who had led the liberation of Santiago, the supreme commander of US military forces.

He walked into the Pentagon and tore the place apart.

Havron demolished as much of the old bureaucracy as he could. In Havron's eyes, you either fought, or you supported those who fought. The old concepts of the Army, Navy, Air Force, and Marines were no longer valid to him or anyone else who understood the changes technology had wrought upon warfare. He'd got rid of the separate military branches and anything else he viewed as bureaucratic artifice. When Havron was done, the military chain of command was flatter, more streamlined, and more focused.

In Fiona's and Pruden's eyes, a more concentrated and rational customer had been created, and buying power had been focused and streamlined.

Fiona's decision to invest in military AI had launched another deep dive that lasted a year. They learned the market, the players, the technologists, and mastered the entire landscape.

Fiona enjoyed scheduling meetings with artificial-intelligence companies under the guise of due diligence for Malloy Family Investments. The meetings always started out awkwardly as the visiting company leadership tried to take measure of the young pair. *Is this a serious meeting?* They would wonder.

Until the questions came.

Fiona lashed them with a laser of strategic curiosity and Pruden, obviously a few years older than her, honed in on all the flaws in their financial statements.

The cash-starved start-ups or debt-ridden mature players would tell her everything as Fiona would pretend to get excited about their robotics, algorithms, or whatever their secret sauce was. She and Pruden would suck their brains dry and then break their hearts. They never invested.

By the summer of 2061, they had narrowed their focus to three target companies. The first was a group headquartered in Silicon Valley called Spitting Metal. They were scary, driven only by hard-core killing efficiency at scale. They wanted their robots to be the deadliest ever, and to be global. Their vision was big: battleships, nuclear submarines, aircraft squadrons, and orbital platforms.

They frightened Pruden. He called their vision "apocalyptic."

Fiona loved them, especially their "driver in a box" architecture. But they were a long way from profitability, and their grand vision had a price tag. Hundreds of millions of dollars and a few lucky breaks. Pruden worried it would be a black hole, sucking Fiona's money into oblivion.

And Pruden valued Fiona's money.

The second was a DARPA spin-off. A group of MIT robotics experts that was more focused on solving extreme mobility challenges like, "How can we get our robot to climb a wall of wet ice in a hailstorm?" or "How do you intercept a hypersonic aircraft while pulling as few Gs as possible?" They didn't directly address the kill chain problem, but their mobility solutions were the best in the world. Fiona loved them for that reason, and because their management team was easy to manipulate. Best of all, they had numerous patents and didn't cost much to operate. Fiona called them the DARPA Boys.

Then there was a man named Dr. Musashi.

Musashi ran a small company of roboticists. A tight team with history and deep connections in the space industry which they left with Musashi to pursue more terrestrial goals. They didn't focus on mobility questions, like the DARPA Boys. And their goal was not maximizing destruction, like Spitting Metal. They were trying to create reliable soldiers that could be led by and counted on by human small-unit leaders who would command the robots and provide kill chain compliance. They were on the verge of what they believed would be a breakthrough, but needed a quick infusion of capital to make it happen.

After initial enthusiasm, Fiona decided she didn't like them very much. "They don't think big enough," she'd told Pruden.

"But the Combat Corps loves them," Pruden countered. "Of all the companies we have evaluated, they have the most current revenue and surest path to profitability."

Fiona nodded. Pruden knew that, in Fiona's world, revenue and profits won every argument.

Fiona acquired a controlling interest in Dr. Musashi's company and the DARPA Boys and put both in a holding company she named Determined End States. She avoided associating her name with the holding company and the two subsidiaries. Fiona never wanted her grandfather to discover her connection to them.

Now, almost five years after meeting, and two and a half years since starting their business endeavor together, Fiona and Pruden were poised to do the same with Spitting Metal. The problem was that it required Fiona to borrow a large amount of money.

"It's two hundred and fifty million dollars that you have to personally guarantee, Fiona," Pruden said as Fiona walked away from the desk toward the windows. "You will owe the two hundred and fifty million dollars whether Spiting Metal comes through or not. It would bankrupt you."

"If they come through, we'll make billions," Fiona said.

Fiona stared out of the window at the lights of Manhattan, the sparkling swarm of drones above.

Pruden decided he would make one final run at it. "It's a ton of money, Fiona. A lot more than you have. And it's too risky. Even the best scenarios we've modeled show these guys are going to need hundreds of millions of dollars to get to the finish line. You are only 26 years old and if this goes south, you will spend the rest of your life digging out from under it. I'm worried you will regret this one day."

"Always the downside with you," Fiona said.

"You hired me to help you. That is what I am trying to do."

"I know. But you're not looking at it the right way. Spitting Metal rounds out our portfolio."

Pruden sighed and leaned back in his chair.

"Think it through with me," Fiona said. "What do you like about Musashi?"

Pruden looked at his watch. He was tired.

"Please," Fiona asked him.

"Fine. But then I'm going to bed."

"Deal."

"I think Musashi's vision is ambitious and unique," Pruden said. "He has spent decades trying to develop dependable, even noble, AI soldierbots. Then he bonds those soldierbots to a human leader who is on the battlefield with them. Then, through data links and enhanced situational awareness, he enables that human to authorize or deny kill permissions.

"Musashi's architecture does put a huge burden on the humans who are forward with the soldierbots," Pruden continued. "Mentally, conceptually, and emotionally. But he believes that is where the burden is best shouldered… forward, where the reality is. And I agree."

Fiona nodded and then said, "And the Spitting Metal architecture harks back to the early drone-control days during the turn of the century. Human controllers monitoring and controlling their units from high-tech command-and-control nodes back in the US. Any kill is authorized and enabled by the officers 'back in the box.' I'm no Clausewitz, but why put a human in harm's way if you don't have to?"

Fiona paused, but Pruden did not rise to the argument. He just shrugged.

"Truthfully," Fiona said, "I don't care which solution wins, as long as it is one of ours. And that is the beauty of what we're going to do. We'll have two different solutions to the kill chain problem. One ancient in inspiration. The other an updated, battle-proven architecture. The DARPA Boys will provide both with robotics and mobility solutions. That's a winning and diversified portfolio. Without Spitting Metal, we're half a loaf."

Pruden chuckled.

"What?" Fiona asked, deflated at the reaction.

"Only you would try to spin taking on two hundred and fifty million dollars of debt to acquire a risky start-up venture as a risk-mitigation action."

Pruden and Fiona stared at each other for a moment, both exhausted.

"Fiona, I think it's a mistake. I'm worried about you. I'm worried that…"

He hesitated.

"What?"

"I'm sorry… But I'm worried some of that Malloy family voodoo, and your desire to escape it, is clouding your judgement."

Fiona smiled and nodded. "It's a reasonable concern. But that's not what is going on here. This is a good play."

Her voice conveyed absolutely certainty. Pruden knew it was time to get on board.

"It's none of my business and I don't want it to be. I just want you to be successful."

"We will be," she said, smiling even wider. "With the two if us working together, partner. What can go wrong?"

Chapter Five

5 January 2062
Fort Benning, Georgia

Colonel Filson changed the suck for phase three. For those candidates who graduated, phase three would be their last and only exposure to "real military missions." So, the colonel's goal was to expose them to as many mission profiles as possible. The curriculum called for ten missions over the sixty days of phase three. Mission cycles lasted about six days. They kicked off with a mission briefing in the auditorium, where high-level tasks and unit assignments were given. Then two days for planning, three for execution, and one for recovery.

The good thing was the mission cycle meant the candidates got to sleep in their bunks in the barracks at least two nights a week. But it was an exhausting grind.

Like the rest of the candidates, Paul and Kata noticed that the cadre's tone changed. It was as if Filson, after running out over half of the candidates, was satisfied he had whittled the group down to its core. There was less yelling, more instruction. The cadence of candidates dropping from the course and being flown out on the morning drone was down to one every couple of days. And those were for injuries, not failures or resignations.

There was also a rising atmosphere of competition among those who believed they were in the running for a Combat Corps slot. Most candidates, like the Geek, were happy to have survived this far and were starting to allow themselves to believe that they were going to graduate. They were counting the minutes.

Filson was silent on the matter, giving no clue as to class standings or how many slots were actually available.

But the class knew. For the past few weeks, a group of seven real contenders had emerged. Paul and Kata were among them.

Now, with one week left before graduation, the class entered the final mission cycle. After the initial mission briefing, the class left the auditorium buzzing. Filson had orchestrated a complex and exciting combined-arms extravaganza for their capstone mission.

This one had everything: long-range drone insertions, armored blitzkrieg raids, combat engineering tasks, and even several unaided nighttime river crossings. The final objective was a wooded mountaintop fortress that would be assaulted by four infantry platoons in exoskeletons after midnight. It was the kind of military experience the REMFs would talk about for the rest of their lives.

But it was also obvious that Filson had set up the capstone mission as a winner-take-all competition. Leadership of the four infantry platoons was not yet designated. During the mission brief, the colonel said simply, "Leadership of the four assaulting infantry platoons will be assigned based on the tactical situation and unit strengths."

"Bullshit," Kata said to Paul later.

Paul nodded. "It will be assigned based on who is still in the running for the Combat Corps. Anyone that is not a platoon leader on this one is out of it."

"Yep," she said. "And whoever does best on the assault will get the slot."

Paul and Kata shrugged and followed the rest of the class to the mess hall for breakfast before joining their assigned units and diving into the mission planning.

Five days later, they both led a platoon of candidates in exoskeletons up the hill toward the objective, along with two other rival platoon leaders.

The exoskeletons were nothing special. They were underpowered and saddled with multiple governor settings to prevent candidates from hurting themselves. While they did succeed in giving REMF-bound candidates an augmented infantry experience, they were terrible assaulting platforms.

"Move!" Paul yelled at his platoon over the radio. He was frustrated by their progress.

Pyrotechnics exploded all around them as they slogged forward. Drone gunships, which were supporting their assault, shrieked by at treetop altitude.

Paul's platoon was tired. Fifty-six hours into the operation, all they wanted was to be done, to get a shower, and to graduate.

But Paul was still gunning for the Combat Corps slot.

"Come on, damn it!"

Paul checked his map display. One kilometer to go. He wondered if any of the other platoons were ahead of him.

Filson had warned them during that night's mission brief that "enemy jamming will prevent the transmission of friendly unit positions." The colonel had smiled as he'd continued. "So, unfortunately, the four assaulting platoons will not be able to coordinate their attack."

Paul was getting anxious.

"Come on, Second Platoon!" he yelled. "We can do this!"

Gunfire erupted all around them.

"Get down!" Paul yelled.

They had walked into an ambush.

Buzzers began sounding off around Paul. "Shit!" he said to himself.

When the simulation tracking team determined that a candidate had been killed or wounded, they rendered that candidate's exoskeleton inert. The suit emitted a loud buzzer sound for three seconds before immobilizing so that the wearer could get into as comfortable a position as possible. Sometimes it was hours before they were repowered. A second loud buzz accompanied the loss of power.

"We've got to get out of this kill box!" Paul transmitted to his platoon. "Everyone who is still able to fight, follow me!"

Paul jumped up and sprinted up hill.

Alone.

He covered about fifty meters before something charged out of the shadows and knocked him over.

He tumbled across the ground.

An enemy exoskeleton towered over him.

Paul tried to stand up, but his exo's right leg had been damaged. He was able to get to a kneeling position just before the enemy ran into him again.

Paul splayed onto the ground. Hydraulic fluid leaked from multiple joints. Red indicator lights flashed in his helmet.

His suit was faltering.

Paul rose again and reached for his pistol.

But the enemy was on him again, pinning him down. Paul fought. But it was over. His suit had lost all mobility and power.

The enemy exo ripped Paul's helmet off as a half dozen soldiers in black riot suits surrounded Paul.

They tore him out of the rest of his exo and put a black hood on his head. Paul cursed as they bound his hands.

It was over.

Someone grabbed him roughly by his bound hands and dragged him uphill. After five minutes, Paul was winded and stumbling. He had not slept in four days, and his captor was charging up the hill on fresh exo-aided legs.

Fuck you, Paul thought.

Suddenly the ground was level. It felt to Paul like they were on a dirt road. He heard the rumble of a diesel engine and the slam of what sounded like a large tailgate being dropped open.

The hands that had dragged him raised his bound arms until his palms touched metal.

"Get in the truck," the voice said.

Paul fumbled his way into what felt like an old cargo truck. Once he hoisted himself into the back, he felt for the bench seats and sat down.

A feeling of utter defeat washed over him.

Chapter Six

Paul heard the truck slip into gear. It lurched a few times before surging forward and cruising down the mountain. Someone grabbed his hands and cut away his binding.

"Take your hoods off," Colonel Filson said, putting away his large combat knife.

Paul pulled the black hood off.

The colonel sat across from him, swaying with the jolts and leans of the old truck.

Kata sat next to Paul.

Their eyes met, and they saw defeated reflections of themselves. Kata shook her head slightly as if to say, *This sucks.*

The roar of several assault drones passed overhead, shaking the canvas covering the back of the truck.

"Final wave of the assault," the colonel said, pointing an unlit cigar at the overhead sound. "Two platoons are still in the fight. They are doing well."

Paul wanted to punch him.

"Hey," the colonel said, feeling the disappointment radiating off of the two exhausted candidates. "You guys did your best. You have nothing to be ashamed of. You should both hold your heads very high."

Paul and Kata were too heartbroken to talk.

The colonel shrugged and lit his cigar. The flares from his igniting breaths cast a glow throughout the back of the vehicle. After a dozen puffs, Filson leaned back and inhaled deeply.

"When were you born, Owens?" he asked.

"2039, sir."

"Christ on a cracker," Filson muttered. "You?" he asked Kata.

"Same, sir."

The colonel cocked his head to one side in disbelief and then let out a long, exhausted sigh. "That's two years after I was commissioned."

Paul and Kata were silent, not in the mood for Filson's story time. But they were trapped.

"The whole military was going through a transformation back then. I didn't realize it at the time, because I was downrange for about ten years straight. First few years on the tail end of that fucked-up Global War on Terror and then whipsawing around the world when we finally woke up and started reacting to the Chinese," the colonel said, shaking his head.

"More automation. More AI," the colonel continued. "More and more technical shit. I remember when I was a new Special Forces captain commanding an A-team in Pakistan, they gave us a suitcase full of small, helicopter-like drones. They could fit in the palm of your hand. I thought it was the coolest shit I had ever seen."

Filson chuckled.

"What I didn't realize, and I don't think anyone did, was that human combat skills and stamina were being de-emphasized. I mean, me and the rest of the tough guys in Special Operations Command were still out there doing our thing. And getting all of the press coverage, by the way. So, it seemed like the military was still doing its job. But, high level, the dial was turning toward technicians, administrators, and analysts… away from the warriors. Not intentionally, maybe. But it happened.

"I wasn't following any of this shit at the time," Filson said. "I was a dumbass new major, staring down at least a decade of staff weenie assignments before getting a crack at battalion command. It looked to me like the new soldier-augmentation program was where the action was. So, I wanted in.

"The augmentation protocol sucked, of course," he continued. "But it was exciting, cutting-edge stuff. So many things were changing so fast in the army then. I remember when they discontinued Ranger School. A bunch of us wondered what the hell was going on. Ranger School was the soul of the army! How could they cancel it? Something about budgets and relevance and roles and missions."

Filson shrugged.

"It was going to be a brave new world," he said.

Filson put his cigar in his mouth and pulled his combat knife back out from his utility belt. He crossed his right leg over his left, leaned forward, and grabbed his boot. The cigar illuminated the colonel's face as he carved a large piece of dried mud out of his boot's tread with the blade. It fell to the floor of the rambling truck.

Filson smiled and leaned back. He sheathed the blade and took the cigar from his mouth.

"Couple years later," the colonel continued in a low voice. "In 2047. Santiago."

The colonel stared at the chunk of mud he had dislodged. It slid toward the rear of the truck in spurts as the truck bounced and vibrated along.

Paul and Kata did the same, waiting for him to continue and wondering when they would finally be alone so they could process their failure.

"You guys study Santiago in school?" the colonel finally asked, not taking his eyes off the chunk of mud.

"Yes, sir," they both said.

The colonel looked up at Paul. "Tell me what you know about it."

"Um..." Paul stammered. He knew Filson had been there. "I guess the consensus is they caught us napping."

"Ha!" the colonel burst out, startling Paul. "We were worse than napping, Owens. We were weak. They kicked our ass almost all the way out of Chile and into the sea. If they had succeeded, the red flag of China would be flying over that whole continent, as it does in Caracas tonight."

The colonel glared out of the back of the truck. Paul was uneasy.

"That First Battle of Santiago was our generation's Task Force Smith," the colonel said in a more reasonable tone. "The Chinese, of course, had some grotesque shit. Their equivalent of our augmentation program was over the top. Still is. I'll never forget some of the Centaur horror I saw down there.

"But our problem was we had evolved into a soft, overly technical force," the colonel continued, settling into one of his long stories. "Great tech, but no spine. And not just the Army, by the way. Air Force, Navy, and Marines—all weak. By then, we were more of a logistics and administrative outfit. No one knew how to fight without a joystick anymore.

"When Santiago fell, the Joint Chiefs shit their pants. They had no idea what to do. Luckily, one of them was familiar with a little-known two-star general named Havron.

"Commissioned infantry, Havron was a Green Beret during the tail end of the Global War on Terror. Saw some real shit. Tough bastard. A smart one too. When he got his first star, he was put in charge of the soldier-augmentation program. He spent two years trying to push the military forward, writing think pieces on hybrid man-and-machine units, Centaur theory, and tactics. Shit that no one else had the balls or foresight to write about. Hell, he was the first one to even use the term 'Centaur.'

"He had been so insistent about his ideas, they told him to put together a test unit to demonstrate the potential of hybrid man-and-machine units a couple years before Santiago.

"When Santiago fell, they asked him if his new unit was ready.

"Havron said they were not. But he pulled together all the combat veterans he could find across the Army. It was not enough. So, he sent word to every Ranger School graduate, every Special Forces vet, every SEAL graduate, every Marine infantry or special warfare graduate, asking for volunteers. And they came. Everyone. You should have seen some of those scrappy old fuckers," Filson said, laughing. "But, holy hell, could they fight..."

The colonel's eyes drifted back toward the rear of the truck.

"It was a crazy idea. Not only a man-and-machine hybrid unit. But also a cross-branch hybrid. Army, Navy, Air Force, and Marines all fighting side by side under a streamlined, unified command."

Filson looked at Kata.

"It took the old man more than a year to get it all pulled together. Then, you know what he did?" the colonel asked her.

She did not know what to say, thinking maybe it was a rhetorical question. It was.

"He led us back down there and kicked ass. By the end of the Second Battle of Santiago, we were pulling the enemy out of foxholes and bayonetting them," the colonel said with pride. "It got pretty old-school."

Paul and Kata nodded. They were familiar with what the colonel was talking about. As legend, though. As mythology.

"When we got back, all hell broke loose. Congress, the president, and the American people were pissed. That's when the Joint Chiefs realized they'd fucked up. They had created a monster. Havron was a hero."

Filson took a long tug on his cigar.

"Congress fired the Joint Chiefs and restructured the whole shop. They gave Havron the keys to the Pentagon, and the old man formed the Combat Corps," Filson said in a reverent voice. "The mission of which is to select, augment, and train human soldiers to fight our nation's enemies in direct combat. The Corps absorbed the Special Operations Command as well as the last remaining and scattered combat commands across the military, including the army combat divisions and Marine expeditionary units. The Corps also absorbed a few high-speed supporting units as well. If you fought, you were in the Combat Corps."

They all leaned forward as the truck decelerated. The vehicle hesitated and coughed as it changed gears before making a turn.

"By 2051, about ten years ago, it was all over. General Havron had reorganized the whole fucking show. For good. That was the year he asked me to take over O.A.T."

The colonel looked at his cigar and took a long last pull. He released the fragrant smoke slowly. It wafted through the back of the truck before being sucked out of the gaps in the canvas.

Paul watched the tendrils of smoke disappear like his dreams of joining the Combat Corps. He felt the truck decelerate and turn. It straightened out but did not speed up. It seemed like they were close to their destination.

"The Combat Corps does more than just complete the kill chain," the colonel said, snuffing his cigar out on the bottom of his boot. "We are the small group of real soldiers in a big military. We are its diamond-hard center."

Paul had heard enough. "We're familiar with the history, sir." He nodded toward Kata. "It's one of the reasons we both had hoped to make it."

"Well, Lieutenant. Like I said, you both did your best."

The truck finally came to a stop. Paul and Kata wanted off. Now.

Filson sensed their urgency.

"Give me a minute, candidates," he said, pulling the canvas to one side and hopping out.

They sat alone in the truck. After a minute, Paul turned and looked at Kata. She looked at him and shrugged. There was nothing to say.

"Owens and Vukovic!" the colonel hollered. "Dismount!"

Kata looked at Paul with a face that said, *I am so fucking over this.*

Paul just nodded. He pulled aside the canvas, and they climbed out of the truck.

Colonel Filson stood a few feet from the truck, smiling.

A walkway extended behind him for 150 feet, leading to a wide three-story building. The middle of the structure was dominated by a large cupola sitting on top of six tall columns. Two building wings extended left and right.

But it was the cupola structure that demanded their attention. A spotlight shone from its ceiling onto a large statue that stood over twenty feet tall. An infantryman, from a lost time almost a hundred years ago, charged forward, calling to his soldiers to follow him.

Paul realized they were back on Fort Benning, in front of the Infantry Museum.

Dim lights embedded in the walkway lit the path from where they stood between the two center columns to the base of the statue, where a lone person stood. As their eyes adjusted, Paul and Kata started to make out the outline of a crowd on either side of the walkway, which was lit by the soft glow of the pathway lights.

It was their O.A.T class, standing at ease, hands behind their backs, looking at them. Paul spotted the Geek. He was smiling in excitement.

"Sir?" Kata said, unable to put it all together.

"What is going on?" Paul echoed her confusion.

"Let's go," the colonel said. "The old man is waiting."

He turned and took a few steps. Noticing that the two exhausted junior officers had still not figured it out, he resorted to commands.

"Owens! Vukovic!" he said forcefully. "On me!"

That worked.

They walked quickly to catch up to him. Then the three of them walked, side by side, down the path.

Members of their class, fresh off the mountain and still in their filthy combat uniforms, nodded at them respectfully as they passed.

Soon they were walking by the cadre, who also looked at them with approval.

Halfway down the path, though, strangers stood in formation on each side. They were Centaurs. Some wore obvious prosthetics. Some faces were old. Older than the colonel's.

"Who are these people, sir?" Kata whispered.

"Every Combat Corps personnel who could make it," the colonel answered in a normal voice. "There aren't many of us, and this doesn't happen very often. You'd be surprised how far they travel for this when we put the word out."

"Word out about what?" Paul asked.

"For Chrissake," the colonel said, stopping. "I know you guys are tired, but you're going to have to be quicker than this going forward."

"But, sir, we failed the last mission," Kata said, hope building within her.

"Do you really think, after six months, decisions like this are made based on one mission?" Filson asked.

Paul and Kata gaped at the colonel mutely.

The colonel let a smile spread across his face and said, "And what makes you think that last mission even counted?"

Kata and Paul looked at each other, then the colonel, then around, and then at the lone figure at the base of the statue. The officer wore dress greens, but with the old "Ike Jacket," rather than the more formal belted jacket. Four stars gleamed on each shoulder. A bayonet hung on his hip.

"Is that—" Paul began.

"General Havron," Filson said. "Supreme Commander of the US military. Liberator of Santiago. Founder of the Combat Corps. Not a man to keep waiting."

The colonel turned and continued down the path. Paul and Kata followed, passing between the columns. The statue of Iron Mike loomed above them. His shouting face and upheld right hand called unseen comrades forward. His left hand held his rifle, bayonet fixed on the end of its barrel.

Colonel Filson and his two exhausted charges came to a stop in front of General Havron under the statue.

Filson saluted and said, "Sir, this is Lieutenant Paul Owens and Lieutenant Kata Vukovic."

General Havron returned the salute and Filson took several steps back.

Paul and Kata stood at attention.

"At ease," the general said.

Paul and Kata adjusted their feet to a shoulder-width stance, hands clasped behind their backs, as Havron looked them over.

Paul and Kata could not help looking him over as well.

Despite his broad shoulders, the general had a wiry air about him, the hint of a hidden quickness. His gray hair was closely cropped and contrasted with the dark pupils in his tired face.

The general smiled and said, "I've heard good things about you two."

"Thank you, sir," they said in unison.

"How was O.A.T?" he asked with a smile.

"Sucked, sir," Kata said.

Havron smiled broadly at the comment and nodded. "Good," he said. "Good." He shot Colonel Filson an approving look. "Do you know what they're all here for?" The general gestured over their shoulders toward the gathered crowd that had turned to face them.

Paul and Kata turned to look. The darkness lent the crowd an endless quality, faces extending out of the glow from the cupula and off into the eternal distance.

"There are less than five hundred ground combat officers in the US military," the general continued. "Four hundred and eighty-nine, to be exact. Our full authorization is five hundred and twelve. But I can't seem to keep us at that level. After tonight, there will be four hundred and ninety-one."

The general let the comment hang for a moment.

"I usually only let Colonel Filson pick one per class," he continued. "But he was insistent about you two. Said you were a team. Said it would be a damn shame." The general's voice feigned irritation and got louder as he went on, to be sure Filson could hear him. "Said I would be an idiot not to take you both. Said a bunch of other disrespectful shit about me."

There were a few chuckles from the crowd.

The general leaned in toward Paul and Kata. "He is a stubborn old bastard," he said in a voice only they could hear. "But he was right," Havron said, straightening back up.

The general gestured to an aide standing a few paces to his left. The lieutenant colonel stepped forward and held out the large wooden box in his white-gloved hands.

"Do you know the spirit of the bayonet?"

"To kill, sir," they both said as the general opened the box. Two large bayonets lay at rest on the felt box liner.

"Yeah," the general said, turning back to them. "That's what we train you to say. That's what it meant for a long time. For centuries, when things have boiled down to fixing bayonets, it was the last round of the fight. The situation was shit, and it was time to do or die. Chamberlain at Little Round Top. Cole at Carentan. Millet on Hill 180." General Havron looked at Colonel Filson. "That old bastard in Santiago," he said.

"But that's not all of it. Not anymore. The question is no longer: Can you stick this thing in the enemy's heart?"

The general patted the bayonet on his hip.

"I think most would at least try to do that in the right circumstances.

"In this dark age. The curse and blessing is that our bayonets are too powerful. They reach across the globe, into space, under the sea. They walk around, fly, swim, and talk. They are colossal. And they are microscopic. It's never been easier to kill. And it has never been harder to fight.

"The spirit of the bayonet is now about leadership. It's the sacred duty the military honors and burdens you with when you join the Combat Leadership Corps. You train, care for, and lead those who carry the bayonet. You decide how your nation applies the bayonet. Who we kill. Who we spare. You are the human being, the American human being, in our nation's killing machine. You are asked to be both the tactical mind and the value system. Sparta and Athens. And we ask you to be this philosopher-warrior downrange. Alone. In the worst possible circumstances."

Havron stepped closer.

"You are the spirit of the bayonet now."

The general paused. Paul realized that a loudspeaker had been pushing Havron's words to the assembled crowd.

"The insignia of the Combat Leadership Corps is crossed bayonets," Havron said as he turned and took one of the bayonets from the box, "symbolizing the leadership, toughness, and courage it takes to lead our forces in combat."

The general unsheathed the bayonet and held it up so that Paul and Kata could see it. The number "2476" was engraved in a large font on the blade.

"Contrary to what many believe, it is not a symbol of guts-in-your-teeth bloodlust and thirst for battle. Rather, it is an acknowledgment of the solitude we in the Combat Corps face. The load we carry." He returned the bayonet to its scabbard and snapped it onto the left side of Kata's utility belt. "No one else in the entire US military is authorized to carry a bayonet."

Kata felt the heft of the blade on her left hip and could not stop herself from smiling.

The general put his hand on her shoulder and nodded. Then he turned and grabbed the second bayonet from the box.

"These bayonets are symbols of your belonging to the small and elite core of the US Army," Havron said as he unsheathed the second bayonet and held it up. It bore the number "2477."

"And they are a reminder that it will, someday, for all of us, boil down to a singular killing thrust."

Havron fastened the bayonet onto the left side of Paul's utility belt and then stepped back. He looked around past the small group under Iron Mike and out at the crowd assembled in the night.

"Which officer vouches for these two?" he asked loudly, directing his question to the assembled crowd.

"I do, sir," Colonel Filson said, straightening up to attention.

Havron nodded.

"Which enlisted soldier vouches for these two?"

"I do, sir," Sergeant Major McGowan said, snapping to attention.

The general nodded.

"Which peer will vouch for these two?"

The Geek came to attention as he said, "I do, sir!" Paul and Kata had not seen him join the small group under Iron Mike. The Geek smiled and fidgeted with excitement. Colonel Filson looked down at his feet. Tradition dictated that the peer witness was elected by the class. The Geek, who no one thought would make it when they all started, was unanimously elected.

General Havron turned back to Paul and Kata.

"Lieutenant Vukovic, do you accept this nomination into the Combat Leadership Corps and the burdens that accompany it?"

"I do, sir."

"Lieutenant Owens, do you accept this nomination into the Combat Leadership Corps and the burdens that accompany it?"

"I do, sir."

"Very well," General Havron said.

He pulled a three-by-five card out of his flight suit's left breast pocket. He always read the orders, even though he had them memorized. It was too important, too sacred of a thing to fuck up.

"Attention to orders!" Havron commanded. Hundreds of heels scuffed and knocked as soldiers, officers, and civilians snapped to attention. "The president of the United States, acting upon the request of the secretary of the military, who, having heard the affirmation of the superior officers, enlisted soldiers, and peers that these two officers serve with, has placed special trust and confidence in the patriotism, integrity, and abilities of Second Lieutenant Kata Vukovic and Second Lieutenant Paul Owens. In view of these special qualities, their demonstrated potential, and desire to serve, Second Lieutenant Vukovic and Second Lieutenant Owens are accepted into the Combat Corps. Effective this twelfth day of January, 2062, by order of the secretary of defense, they are the two thousand four hundred and seventy-sixth and two thousand four hundred and seventy-seventh officers of the line."

Chapter Seven

"I can't believe how fast these guys go through money," Fiona said, standing up. She dropped the Spitting Metal financial statements on her desk and rubbed her neck. It was late. They had been at it for hours.

"Really?" Pruden asked, sitting at his own desk. "Their cash burn is exactly what we forecasted during due diligence."

Fiona's face hardened. She forced herself to smile at the comment.

Pruden looked away from her thin-lipped grimace.

Fiona sighed heavily and walked toward the windows of her office. The snow from the day before was gone from the streets and sidewalks, whisked away or melted by the city's robot maintenance and cleaning force. Inches of the stuff still clung to every horizontal surface above the streets, though. Window sills, gutters, and rooflines seemed softened and less reflective than usual as the bellies of dark, low clouds reflected the multi colored light of the tireless, coursing swarm of drones above the city.

"What about the Talisman option?" Fiona said, turning away from the window.

It was Pruden who sighed this time. He looked at the large white binder on the corner of his desk.

"What?" Fiona walked over to Pruden and grabbed the binder. "We never really walked away."

Pruden stood up and stretched. "No. But we haven't spoken with them in over a month."

Talisman Partners LLC was a hedge fund. Pruden had been trying to arrange a line of credit with them to help fund Spitting Metal's ravenous need for cash. The conversation with Talisman was the result of an extensive due diligence process involving Fiona, Pruden, a team of researchers, and Fiona's favorite private detective. The diligence objective was to optimize on a single attribute - the absence of connection to the Malloy family.

Fiona wanted a lender that had no association with her grandfather. She could not risk him finding out about her activities. He was a notorious and vindictive meddler. She was going to be operating too close to catastrophe for too long to risk Robert Malloy II gaining line of sight.

"Can you get us a meeting with them tomorrow?" Fiona asked.

"I don't see why not."

"Good," Fiona said. "Do it."

Pruden looked at Fiona with concern.

"We won't need them very long," she said. "But we really need them at the moment."

"What are you going to do?"

"Sweeten the deal," she said.

Pruden looked at Fiona.

She smiled. Without the thin lips this time.

"I won't do anything crazy."

"I know," Pruden said. "Because I am going with you."

* * *

The next morning around ten a.m., Fiona stood at the front of a conference room facing the six partners of Talisman. They had taken places on each side of a long conference table. The senior partner, Buck Dorrity, sat with his arms crossed at the head of the table.

The table had room for twelve, which left a couple of empty chairs between Fiona and them. Pruden sat to the side of Fiona as she concluded her pitch. She had been presenting their case for over an hour.

Pruden smiled as Fiona wrapped up. He loved to watch her pitch a deal. She was a natural.

"I appreciate the opportunity to present Spitting Metal's strategy, financial forecast, and capital requirements to you this morning. We are very proud and excited about where we are."

Fiona looked around the room, making eye contact with each partner. Then she glanced at Pruden, who nodded.

"I'd like to end with a bit of historical context, if you don't mind."

The high-definition display behind Fiona, which for over an hour had been showing graphs and spreadsheets, went black.

"As I am sure you all remember, in October of 2039, Russia moved to end their Ukrainian dispute once and for all," Fiona said. "They sent two divisions of autonomous robots into the country and conducted a raid into the capital, Kiev."

Behind Fiona, pictures of the carnage in Ukraine flashed onto the large display. Now-infamous photos of destroyed buildings, mangled bodies, and lethal robots clicked by in rapid succession.

"These AI-enabled war machines were given a mission to accomplish on their own, without human intervention. They invaded Ukraine in the middle of the night, and by the time the robots marched back across the border into Russia, they had killed over fifty thousand people, including civilians and children. It was murder. The world recoiled from the vision of autonomous robots killing humans. It struck a core nerve. A fear of the future was finally realized."

Fiona paused for effect.

"Then, months later, in April of 2040, world leaders met in Tokyo," she continued. "And on the fourteenth of April, the International Agreement Regarding the Prohibition of Machine-Based Killing Decisions was signed by every country with a functioning government."

A picture of the massive signing ceremony appeared behind Fiona. Formally dressed dignitaries assembled on a large outdoor staircase lined by blooming cherry trees.

"The agreement mandated that a human be involved in and approve every decision to kill another human. Known as the Tokyo Accords, it codified the requirement for a human-anchored kill chain and ushered a new level of complexity into warfare."

The display behind Fiona faded to black.

"Complexity due not only to the moral and legal risks of kill chain compliance, but also because of the effectiveness of machines in combat. Because, the fact is, strategists who were able to look at Ukraine dispassionately realized the Russians were on to something. The machines fought well and accomplished their mission. Repulsive or not, the strategy had worked."

Dorrity nodded. Fiona took a step forward, closer to the table.

"The politicians of the world want to be able to fight with machines. Their constituents are much happier when robots are sacrificed for their country instead of humans. Generals would rather fight with machines also. Machines don't get bored, scared, or forgetful."

Fiona looked directly at Dorrity.

"But no one wants to be charged as a war criminal."

Dorrity chuckled.

"The Russian general that conceived of and commanded the operation in Ukraine can't leave Moscow for the rest of his life. If he does, he's going to find himself sitting behind bars in the Hague being prosecuted."

Fiona paused, acknowledging the nodding heads around the table.

"We want machines to do the fighting for us," Fiona continued. "And the brave men and women of our military deserve the best AI-augmented fighting robots in the world. We have seen what happens when we don't equip our military properly and give them the means to win."

A picture of Santiago appeared behind Fiona. Smoke rose from the besieged city. Fiona paused as the image changed to the well-known photos of panicked US military personnel scrambling into the Pacific Ocean and climbing into boats fleeing the Chinese army.

"They also deserve a kill-chain-compliant architecture that doesn't leave them wondering if they are going to be prosecuted for war crimes. Because, ultimately, the essential character of this shitty world's conflicts has not changed. Humans will, at some point, have to be killed if we are going to win our nation's wars."

The photos behind Fiona dissolved, and the image of a waving American flag took their place.

"That is Spitting Metal's value proposition, gentlemen. Victory," Fiona said. "Efficient, kill-chain-compliant victory. Whether it be air, land, or sea."

The flag behind Fiona faded away and was replaced by the Spitting Metal logo, a coiled robotic cobra with bullets and missiles spraying from its fangs.

"Thank you for your time," Fiona concluded.

Dorrity uncrossed his arms and looked around at his partners.

"Are there any questions for Miss Malloy?" he asked the table.

No one spoke up. Their poker faces were strapped on tightly.

"OK, then," Dorrity said, standing up. "Miss Malloy, if you'd give us just a few minutes to confer in private, I would appreciate it."

"Of course," Fiona said, grabbing her bag.

Pruden stood up, and they all shook hands.

Pruden and Fiona each took a seat in the luxurious, cushioned velour chairs in Talisman Partners LLC's lobby.

"Well, what do you think?" Fiona asked Pruden as they watched the doors to the meeting room close.

"They'll sign it."

Fiona nodded in agreement as she looked at her phone.

"I mean, why wouldn't they?" Pruden continued. "You are offering them double the going rate on a line of credit as well as five percent in the company. And don't get me started about the debt-to-equity conversion clauses." Pruden shook his head. "It's a rich deal, and they know it."

Fiona looked up from her phone. "What's bothering you? You think it's too rich?"

"Way too rich."

"I told you not to worry. We're going to rotate out of this piece-of-shit LOC in twelve months. Don't worry about it." She looked back at her phone.

"It's not the richness of the deal that bothers me," he said. "It's the punitive measures if we fall behind on payments. They could end up controlling the company if we can't—"

"This is my brother," Fiona interrupted, getting up from her chair and pointing at her phone. "Grab me when they are ready."

Fiona turned toward the far corner of the lobby and walked away as she answered the call.

"Hey, Eugene. Where did you decide on? The Dolomites? How is the snow?"

Chapter Eight

Fiona's mother sobbed next to her in the front row. Her younger brother, Eugene, cried quietly on her other side. Fiona reached out and took her brother's hand without taking her eyes off her father's casket.

Members of their extended family filed by, offering condolences, some placing flowers on the casket.

Fiona took inventory of her family. She was only fifteen but had learned well the signs of alcoholism, drug addiction, and depression. She kept a running total of each affliction as Malloys stopped to lean over and console her, her mom, and Eugene.

Not a lot of happy Malloys, she thought.

She looked across her father's casket at the reason.

Her grandfather.

Robert Malloy II looked bored, sitting aloof, legs crossed, in a black suit and tie. Had Fiona not known it was his son's funeral, she would have thought he was enduring a tedious business meeting.

But it was his son's funeral. And her father's.

Fiona thought about the moment, three days ago, when she'd heard her mother moan in despair. Fiona was upstairs in her room. Her mother was in the living room on the first floor.

Fiona's uncle, her father's brother, had shown up for a surprise visit a few minutes earlier.

"Roberta," he said, calling Fiona by her first name. "I have something to discuss with your mother."

"Go on upstairs, darling," her mother said with a weary smile. Fiona went upstairs without protest or delay. She was used to the request. In the Malloy family, there was always some drama, grievance, or disappointment to discuss.

A few minutes later, her mother was sobbing.

Fiona ran to her brother's room.

He looked at her with wide eyes when she threw open his door and rushed to him.

"What is it?" he asked, tears beginning to run down his face. "What is wrong with Mother?"

"I don't know," she said, hugging Eugene. "I don't know."

Fiona fought off her own tears. Anxiety welled in her gut.

Minutes later, her uncle appeared in the doorway. They could still hear their mother crying downstairs.

Fiona looked at her uncle's face, and she knew.

Her father was dead.

"Died suddenly on his trip," was all her uncle would tell them.

No one told her the truth, but over the next three days, Fiona had listened closely to the adults around her and pieced together what had happened. Her father, supposedly on a duck-hunting trip with friends, had gone alone to one of their family's lodges and killed himself with a shotgun blast to the head. His body had been discovered by one of the staff.

No one, not even Fiona, was surprised. Her father had been depressed for her whole life. He was a sad, sensitive man. Fiona loved her father. She loved his softness and sensitivity. She basked in it when they were together. But she knew it made him fragile.

She knew she had to be careful with her father, and she knew why.

The day before the funeral, she'd overheard her mother telling Fiona's aunt, "He went his whole life without ever hearing the words 'I love you' or 'I'm proud of you' from the one person he needed to hear it from the most."

Now, Fiona stared across the casket at her grandfather. She hated him.

After her father's casket had been lowered, Fiona helped her mother get up, and they walked toward their car.

"Candice," her grandfather called to her mother.

Her mother squeezed Fiona's hand tighter as she stopped and turned to face Robert Malloy II.

"I'm sorry, Candice," he said, stepping closer. "He was a disappointment. But I know that you loved him. I am sorry." Her grandfather noticed Fiona crying. He looked down at her and said, "Roberta, stop crying. Everything is going to be fine, child."

But they were tears of anger. That was the day she decided she would never again answer to the name Roberta.

* * *

Fiona sat in the back of a chauffeured town car three years later on her eighteenth birthday as it worked its way through the clogged streets of New York City.

Fiona's phone vibrated. She reached into her coat pocket to retrieve it.

I love you, Fi, read the text from Eugene. *Don't let the bastard get you down.*

Thx. I won't, she responded. *How is Italy?*

Bella.

Good. Call you after.

Fiona put the phone back in her coat pocket as they pulled up to the tall building in midtown Manhattan. A doorman opened her door the instant the car pulled to a stop.

The elevator opened on the seventy-ninth floor, which was entirely dedicated to the Malloy Family Foundation and Malloy Family Investments.

It was an austere reception area with a single desk.

The lone receptionist recognized Roberta Fiona Malloy immediately and gave her a quick nod, which relaxed the security guard. The large, suited man stepped back from the elevator and spoke discreetly into his earpiece.

"Good morning," the receptionist said, approaching Fiona with an appropriate mixture of respect and indifference. "Right this way, if you will."

The receptionist led Fiona down a short hallway into a small meeting room.

"Mr. Malloy will join you in just a few minutes," the receptionist said before returning to her desk.

The meeting room was small. An oval, dark wood table surrounded by eight chairs sat in the middle of the room. One of the chairs at one end of the table, was much larger than the others and had arms and brass nail heads. One wall was entirely floor-to-ceiling windows looking south. The Statue of Bragg was a small dark shape on the silvery upper New York Bay.

Fiona walked to the window. From where she stood, almost a thousand feet above the avenues and cross streets, the view conveyed a sense of order. Fiona tried to plug into the fact that none of the thousands of humans her eyes could see cared about her family.

"Hello, Roberta," her grandfather said as he entered the room. "Thank you for making the trip."

He was the only one that still called her that. She tried to ignore it.

He was spry for seventy-eight. Slightly taller than Fiona, at just under six feet, with a back that was unbent. He had a rangy build, like a mountain climber and eyes that were quick and clear.

"Of course, grandfather. I appreciate your time."

"You are looking good!" her grandfather said as they shook hands. He squeezed Fiona's shoulders. "Indeed! I've seen videos of you on the lacrosse field. You're a bruiser! It has made you strong."

Her grandfather returned his arms to his sides and smiled.

"And congratulations on Yale," he added, his smile widening.

Fiona smiled back, hating that he could kindle feelings of pride within her. She stepped on the feelings and dissolved her smile.

"And how is your mother?" he asked.

"She's fine," Fiona said. But really, she didn't know for sure. She had only received superficial check-ins from her mother for a while now. Last year, after remarrying, she put Fiona and Eugene into boarding school and moved out West with her new husband. Fiona understood not wanting to be reminded. She understood the desire to escape. But it still hurt.

Her grandfather let the moment linger too long before saying, "Let's have a seat and talk."

He sat in the large chair at the head of the table.

Fiona sat next to him.

"So, I am sure your cousins have told you what this meeting is all about?" her grandfather asked.

"Sort of."

Her grandfather nodded.

When Malloys turned eighteen, they were summoned to meet with their grandfather. Momentous and terrifying events for the grandchildren, the meetings were the stuff of whispers and anxiety across the family.

"My father started Malloy Markets in 1970," her grandfather began. "He worked himself to the bone. Died of a stroke at age sixty-one in 2007. I was at his side when it happened. I had been working by his side at that point for more than ten years. I was the eldest of three children. My father split the business equally between us, but left control solely to me. Because he knew I was the only one worth a damn.

"We buried father the day after he died. The next day, I went back to work while my brother and sister contested the will. They did not want me in control of the business because they wanted to sell it. They wanted to cash out and walk away from my father's legacy.

"I was in the middle of executing my strategy to take Malloy Markets online, you see," he continued, looking out the window. Fiona had the sense he was recalling the story for himself, not for her. "It was something father believed in wholly. And something that my brother and sister regarded as foolhardy and expensive. They had no understanding of the endeavor and no stomach for the effort involved. So, they fought me.

"They failed, of course," he said, swinging his head back to Fiona. "And afterward attempted to mend fences and pitch in. An effort they stayed committed to for about a week. They soon lost interest when it became clear that the company was going to thrive under my leadership. They reverted back to being worthless."

Her grandfather spoke slowly, daring Fiona to react or object to anything he said.

Fiona knew better. Besides, she had heard this version of the family history before. She sat still and met her grandfather's gaze as the monologue filled the room.

"By the time I was sixty-one like my father, the business was fifty times bigger than when I'd taken the helm. My siblings and their offspring, and mine, were all very wealthy. Because of me."

Her grandfather pointed at himself with his thumb and then placed his fist on the table.

"Me. Alone. I ran the business while my brother and sister fucked off. I ran the business while our families grew and the subsequent generation proceeded to fuck off. Your father, his brother and sister, and all of their cousins, the third generation of wealthy Malloys, have done nothing but fuck off their whole lives. The greatest measure of exertion demanded of them is a walk to the mailbox to get their check."

The mention of her father, in such dismissive and uncaring terms, was like a peeling a scab off of her heart. It burned. Her sweet, soft father. She still missed him. Fiona shifted in her chair and tried to relax her jaw as the pain, a penetrating mix of anger and absence, smoldered inside her.

"Now comes your generation. Fifteen of you. Each of which I expect to do fuck all. To earn fuck all. To accomplish fuck all."

A side door opened, and the receptionist stepped into the room, a leather folio in her hand. The old man kept talking as the receptionist reached across the table and placed the folio in front of Fiona.

"As I'm sure you know by now, when a Malloy turns eighteen, they are given access to a twenty-five-million-dollar trust fund. It's their money, no strings attached, to do with as they wish. I do this for every Malloy. Even the ones who choose to go by their middle name, rather than carry forward the name of my father."

Her grandfather paused.

He stared at Fiona.

Fiona looked back at him, wondering if they were going to have that argument again.

But, the slight recorded, her grandfather continued after a few heartbeats.

"And I will also do it for little gay boys who prefer Italy to our own country."

Again, he paused, making sure his grievance was noted.

Fiona looked back at him. She pictured herself caving in the old man's head with her lacrosse stick and smiled.

Her grandfather reached across the table and opened the leather folio between them.

"I've been sued by members of my own family six times. I won each time. But it cost me time. Time is the most precious thing in the world to me. This document gives you total, unilateral, unfettered control of your trust. But it also writes you out of any more of the Malloy family fortune. Irrevocably."

Her grandfather leaned back in his chair.

"In exchange for a sizable fortune, which is more money than your great-grandfather and I had to our names when we were your age"—the old man gestured at the document in the folio—"you are forfeiting your right to scheme, connive, lie, and steal any more. Because that is what the people in this family invariably try to do."

Fiona looked down at the document. She estimated it to be about ten densely printed pages.

"You can leave the money with the Malloy Investment Fund to be managed by us, or you can do something else with it. Do with it what you will. I don't care."

Fiona placed her hand on the document and ran her finger along the edge, letting the top-right corner of each page hang on her fingertip before falling to the table.

"You don't have to sign, of course," her grandfather said. "You can choose not to. Then you can wait until I die to confirm that I have written you out of my will already."

Fiona was tempted. She hesitated. *Oh… to be free of this monstrous family.*

She chuckled at herself.

Who are you kidding, Fiona? she thought. *You're going to turn down twenty-five million dollars to spite the old man and your family? No. You're not an idiot. You're going to do something much better than that.*

"What in the world is going through that head of yours, child?" her grandfather said.

Fiona looked up.

He stared at her.

"You are a curious one, Roberta," he said with a different smile than she had ever seen. "Curious indeed."

Fiona picked up the pen in the center of the folio and signed the document. She was ready to be out of there.

"Thank you, young lady," her grandfather said, standing up.

Fiona stood up as well. The receptionist opened the door and stepped into the room.

"We're done here, Ms. Frank," Fiona's grandfather said.

"Very good, sir," she answered.

Her grandfather extended his hand to Fiona and said, "Happy birthday."

Fiona shook her grandfather's hand. "Thank you."

But her grandfather held on when Fiona tried to release her grip.

"Twenty-five million dollars," the old man said, pulling her slightly closer. "No strings attached. And no fucking safety net. That's it. You understand me?"

"Yes, sir."

Her grandfather released her hand, smiled, and left the room.

Chapter Nine

19 January 2062
Fort Benning, Georgia

Paul's Officer Assessment and Training Course started with 1,134 students. Six months later, on January 19, 2062, 398 graduated. The rest failed, quit, or were recycled.

The graduation ceremony was held on the parade field in the shadow of the Infantry Museum, where Paul and Kata had been accepted into the Combat Corps. It was well attended by military and civilian officials and also by family members. Paul's and Kata's parents beamed and swelled with pride all day.

Later that evening, most of the class spent a few hours at the officers' club after the graduation ceremony, saying their goodbyes. Their class was dispersing the next day, headed for assignments all over the world.

Paul and Kata sat at the bar and watched the revelry. Their minds had already turned toward their next challenge. They shipped off for duty with an exoskeleton battalion in the morning and would likely be in combat in a few months.

"There they are!" they heard the Geek say over their shoulders. "Paul. Kata. I've been looking for you!"

The Geek stepped through the crowded O club floor. A girl's hand in his, and an older man just behind him.

The older man's resemblance to the Geek was clear, but Paul and Kata were more surprised by the girl. Shorter by an inch or two than the Geek, she was a pretty blond.

Kata's eyebrow arched as she and Paul shared glances.

"Paul, Kata, I'd like you to meet my father."

The Geek's father smiled and offered his hand. "Congratulations to you two!" he said with enthusiasm. "Combat Corps! Just incredible! And Wallace has told me all about you both. Thank you for being such a good friend to my son. He told me he never would have made it without your help."

"That's bullshit," Paul said.

The Geek's father was startled by the force of Paul's voice.

"Yeah," Kata said, just as loudly. "Without this guy, I don't think I would have made it through."

The Geek's father straightened, trying to assess Paul and Kata.

"Toughest son of a bitch in the class, right here, sir," Paul said, pointing at the Geek. "We were lucky he was in our class."

"You going to introduce us, Wallace?" Kata said, glancing at the Geek and then the blond girl.

"Oh. Yes. This is Susan," the Geek said.

"Nice to meet you," Kata said, extending her hand. "Kata Vukovic."

"Thank you," Susan said. "The pleasure is mine."

Paul leaned forward from his stool so that his arm would reach. "Susan, I'm Paul."

Susan nodded as she shook Paul's hand.

"Yes," she said. "I have heard of you both. So nice to meet you."

"One hell of a man you've got there," Paul said, making eye contact with the Geek. "I'm going to miss him."

The Geek looked down at his shoes.

"He got the prime assignment of our whole class, you know," Kata said.

Susan looked at the Geek. "He told me what he would be doing. I didn't realize it was…"

"Those high lunar orbit jobs with Space Command are the toughest to get. Period," Paul said.

"Probably the most important, too," Kata added. "The way the Chinese are militarizing space so quickly, we need officers with balls up there."

Kata gestured at the ceiling to make it clear she meant the moon and Mars and beyond, unaware her reference to male anatomy made Susan blush and the Geek's father smile.

"And they asked for Wallace by name," Paul added, to move the conversation along.

The Geek's father and Susan both looked at him, pride and adoration in their eyes.

"That's enough," the Geek said, making a waving motion with his hands. "I really just wanted to be sure you all met."

"Yes," his father said, turning back to Paul and Kata. "Congratulations again."

"I've got to get them back to the hotel," the Geek said. "We leave early in the morning for Houston."

"Roger that," Kata said.

The Geek gave Paul and Kata each a quick hug and then led Susan and his father out of the O club.

"The Geek has it made, you know," Kata said, with no animosity in her voice.

"Yep," Paul said. "And good for him."

Paul and Kata knew that, despite Filson's railing and curses, the REMFs would inherit the earth. The truth was that REMF roles were excellent preparation to become future captains of industry. The span of control given to guys like the Geek was very large. In just a few years, he would likely have thousands of people working for him, and hundreds of millions of dollars' worth of equipment under his management, as he led endeavors that only the largest commercial interests in the world could undertake, like deep-space logistics and orbital capital projects.

In less than a year, the Geek would be responsible for more people and a larger budget than a civilian executive could hope to amass in a thirty-year career. The cannon-fodder track Paul and Kata were on did not quite have the same commercial sex appeal, and they knew it.

They were proud, nonetheless. And wouldn't have it any other way.

"Another beer?" Kata asked Paul.

"Yep," Paul said as they both turned on their stools back to the bar.

A firm hand landed on a shoulder of each of them before they could waive at the bartender.

"This round is on me," Filson said.

Paul and Kata spun to face the colonel.

Colonel Filson ignored their astounded faces as he raised his hand to attract the bartender, who spotting Filson immediately, moved quickly to accommodate the VIP.

Paul and Kata stole disbelieving glances at each other.

"Give me three whiskeys," Filson said. "My usual."

The bartender nodded.

"Unless you fucking newbies would prefer milk?"

Paul and Kata laughed.

Colonel-fucking-Filson buying us a drink! They each wanted to shout to the other.

The bartender, having prioritized the colonel above every other patron at the large bar, returned with three glasses.

"Here you go, sir," the bartender said, placing the glasses in front of the three officers.

"Thank you, son," Filson said. "Please put it on my tab."

The bartender nodded and turned away.

Filson picked up the center glass.

Paul and Kata each grabbed a glass of the double whiskey, neat, and raised it.

Over Kata's shoulder, Paul saw members of their OAT class discretely watching. Other, more senior officers in the crowd, also stole glances at Colonel Filson.

Paul felt like a made man.

"I've never graduated two Combat Corps officers from a single class in over ten years of doing this," Filson said, smiling as he looked from Kata to Paul and back again. "You two have endless potential. Don't fucking waste it."

Paul and Kata smiled, basking in praise from the man they had feared for months. They were ready to kick back their shots of whiskey.

But Colonel Filson hesitated.

His smile melted as Paul and Kata looked at him, drinks in hand.

"So, a toast to the Combat Corps graduates of Officer Assessment and Training Class of January, 2062..." Filson hesitated and raised his glass between the two lieutenants.

They clinked their glasses to the colonel's as he said, "Nasty legs they may be," in a resigned tone of voice.

Paul and Kata exchanged hurt looks as the colonel drank.

Descended from the old US Marine battalions and Army infantry divisions, the exo battalions were referred to by the pejorative, "Nasty legs." An old army nickname for infantry, the term was based on the unhygienic and smelly state most infantrymen live in when in combat. Over time, the term morphed to signify a sweaty, unaugmented body in an exoskeleton. Command was always trying to stamp out the term. But it stuck.

Usually, they were fighting words. One had to be prepared to receive and throw punches when the term was used. Unless you were Colonel Filson.

Stung by the comment, Paul and Kata slugged back their whiskeys.

"The exo battalions are busier than hell these days," the colonel said as he put his empty whiskey glass down. "They are spread all over the world dodging bullets. Particularly on the African continent. You two are going to be in the mix before you know it."

Paul and Kata put their glasses down.

"I know most of the exo battalion commanders. They are good men and women. And the missions the exo battalions take on are critical. Mostly military police and combat support missions for the Centaur units. It's the essential, non-sexy mission components that make Centaurs successful. Furthermore, exo battalions give the Combat Corps a chance to observe new soldiers and officers in action before investing hundreds of millions of dollars in them to turn them into Centaurs."

The colonel gestured at the bartender to bring another round.

"Exo battalion service is honorable," he said, making sure to alternate eye contact between Paul and Kata. "And there are plenty of career exos—officers and soldiers—that want no part of augmentation. They regard it as weird, or heresy, or, worst of all, cheating. I know many fine officers, men and women who are life-long friends who hold these points of view."

The bar tender returned with three more shots of whiskey.

"But they are still just a bunch of nasty fucking legs," the colonel growled, winking at Paul and Kata. He pushed one of the whiskeys to Kata and another to Paul before taking his.

"You two will be eligible to apply for the Centaur program after a minimum of twelve months of service with the exos," he said in a low voice that no one else could hear. "Let me know when you put your packets in and I'll put in a good word for you. There are still some circles in which I still exert a little sway."

The colonel hesitated as if about to say more, but seemed to change his mind.

He raised his glass in silence. The two junior officers clinked their glasses to his, and the three of them drank.

"Unless, of course, you're satisfied being a nasty leg the rest of your life," Colonel Filson said as he set his glass down. He turned without saying more and walked away.

Paul chuckled as Kata sat in silence digesting the interaction.

"Funny, isn't it?" Paul said.

"What's that?"

"The military is the most egalitarian, merit-based organization in America," Paul said. "Anyone can join and compete and progress based solely on their competence. But the structure within the military is the pettiest caste system imaginable. Status is defined and limited by one's unit. Even brave groups, like the exo battalions, are not immune. Think about it… They are among the tiny number of Americans who actually fight for their country. They take hits, bleed, and die facing a hostile enemy. And, still, within the Combat Corps, they take an ungodly amount of ridicule."

"Sounds about right," Kata said.

Chapter Ten

22 February, 2062
New York City

"I thought you would be pleased about this," Pruden said.

Fiona stewed in front of one of the big windows in her office, arms crossed, shoulders sagging.

"It's your first real revenue associated with any of our deals." Pruden walked up next to her. "Enjoy it for a few seconds at least."

Fiona shook her head and then looked at Pruden. Half of a smile broke the surface of her face.

Pruden could tell she was fighting it. "You are ridiculous."

Fiona surrendered to the grin and chuckled. "You're right." She held out a fist. "You're absolutely right."

Pruden bumped it with his own.

"This calls for a toast," Fiona said, turning from the window and walking to the wet bar in the corner of the office.

"That's the spirit."

"Scotch, beer, or wine?"

"Beer works for me."

Fiona returned. She handed Pruden a bottle of Singha. "To our first decent-paying contract with a real customer."

"Cheers," Pruden said, clinking Fiona's soda water and lime.

They each drank.

"It's fucking irritating, though," Fiona said before Pruden had even swallowed.

"For Chrissake," Pruden mumbled, turning away from Fiona. "Then at least let me enjoy it."

"Seriously." Fiona followed him. "Don't you prefer the Spitting Metal architecture?"

Pruden didn't answer.

"It's so much safer for our soldiers," Fiona continued. "With Spitting Metal, they sit in air-conditioned boxes safely tucked away in the States, controlling combat robots thousands of miles away in hostile territory. Musashi wants our soldiers to walk into the breach side by side with his precious soldierbots and take the same shots they take. It's going to get people killed."

Pruden turned suddenly.

Fiona almost ran into him.

"That's a crock of shit," Pruden said without smiling.

"Crock of shit? No. That's actually exactly how the architectures work." She crossed her arms as if transgressed.

"It's a crock of shit that that is the reason you prefer Spitting Metal," Pruden said.

Fiona put on a wounded face.

"Come on, Fiona. It's me you're talking to. You can bullshit everyone out there." Pruden swung his beer around at the wide world. "Not me, though."

Fiona smiled the smile of the guilty. "I care about our troops," she protested.

"Of course you do," Pruden said without sincerity.

"Spitting Metal is a much bigger payday, and you know it," Fiona said, pointing at Pruden.

Pruden nodded, half in agreement and half to underline that he had been right about Fiona.

"It's a much bigger play!" Fiona said. "Human operators controlling large numbers of big-time weapons systems: tanks, bombers, surface warfare ships, submarines. The big toys with big-ticket prices! These guys are building an entire remote-control army, navy, and air force. If we can sell that, it will be a massive payday."

Fiona took another swig of water. Pruden matched her with his beer.

"Musashi's end goal is much less grand, in my view," Fiona said, looking into her glass. "He's just trying to build a good soldier."

Pruden nodded.

"You like them, though, don't you?" Fiona said, catching the look on Pruden's face.

Pruden shrugged. "I do."

"You and the Combat Corps." Fiona rolled her eyes. "I don't get it."

"That's because you don't get them. The Corps is being run ragged. They're stretched paper thin all across the world, and they keep getting more and more missions piled on them. And it's the last organization where human soldiers do real, old-fashioned fighting. They 'close with and destroy the enemy,' as they put it. Even if Spitting Metal pulls it off, the Corps' mission will not change. They will still be where the pain is. They will still be where the casualties are borne. Think about it." Pruden looked straight at Fiona, his face tightening with emotion. "They have the most to gain by having machines bear more of the load."

"For them, maybe," Fiona stated. "Not the most to gain for us."

There was an edge to Fiona's voice.

Pruden knew the debt weighed heavily on Fiona. He couldn't blame her. Spitting Metal would need more funding soon, and the line of credit with Talisman had ballooned to more than $20 million. He estimated it would be more than two fifty before the end of first quarter next year. The monthly interest payments were getting onerous, and the punitive covenants were always in the back of Fiona's mind.

Pruden knew that, for Fiona, this had nothing to do with which type of military architecture was best suited to the task. It was boiling down to survival for her. The bigger deal had to win. Period.

And his job was to help her get it done.

"It's a ten-million-dollar contract," Pruden said, trying to ease his boss's anxiety. "And that's just phase one."

"Tell me the deal again," Fiona said.

"Pretty simple. Phase one is soldierbot performance testing. Mobility. Basic combat skills. Connectivity and extension platform validation. Durability—"

"We'll crush that," Fiona said with a wave of her hand.

Pruden nodded. "After that, we move on to phase two. Small-unit training."

"How will that work?"

"Don't know yet. Truthfully, I don't think the military knows yet. They are still trying to figure out who is going to run the program."

"Doesn't matter. We'll crush that also. That's not part of the ten million, though, right?" Fiona said, raising her eyebrows.

"No. We haven't even started negotiating that yet. The ten million is just for phase one."

"Good. So, give me the bad news. What will phase one cost us?"

Pruden smiled. "Dr. Musashi says no more than five million."

Fiona's grin returned. "Good. We'll use the rest to service Spitting Metal's debt."

"We can't do that."

Fiona looked at him.

"Why the hell not?"

"Because," Pruden said with patience, "Dr. Musashi is going to need that money to get ready for the next phase."

"All of it?"

"Yes."

"We'll see about that."

Fiona's cell phone rang. She pulled it from her pocket.

"It's Eugene," she said.

Pruden nodded. He pointed at himself and then the door.

Fiona's brother called her every day, and Fiona always took the call. There was no telling how long the two of them would talk, and Pruden was not going to hang around to find out.

"We'll continue this conversation tomorrow," Fiona said as Pruden reached the door. "Go celebrate!"

Pruden gave her a thumbs-up and closed the door behind him. He was glad Eugene's daily call had interrupted the conversation. It was old ground, covered many times. And Eugene eased Fiona's anxieties in a way no one or nothing else could. Having endured their family together, there was a strong bond between Fiona and Eugene that they both drew strength and perspective from.

Pruden thought it strange to use the word "endured" to describe growing up in one of the wealthiest family in the world, but he knew it had been hard on them both. He did not underestimate their scars.

"Hey," Fiona answered. "How are you? How is Mio Posto?"

"It's perfect as always. How are you? You sound tense."

"I'm good. It's just work. Nothing important."

"You lie," he said, sighing heavily. "Why do you put yourself through this?"

"Why do you always ask me that?"

"Truthfully, Fi, I don't know why I bother. It's fruitless. You are crazy. You are torturing yourself. Sell those stupid companies and come live with me over here."

"Someday, Eugene. But not yet."

"Then let your guy run them and come over here. The cute one. What is his name again? Poolen?"

"Pruden," she corrected.

"Yes. Him. Let him run it. Even if only for a week. Come visit me."

"I will soon, I promise."

"More lies," he said. But Fiona could hear his smile.

"So, I am really glad you called to yell at me again," Fiona said.

"I know. I'm sorry. I was really just calling to say hi."

"I'm glad you did. You caught me just in time."

"What are you up to?"

"About to grab a workout."

"Shocker," Eugene said. "Go grab a drink. Grab a guy. Live a little, for crying out loud."

Fiona took another sip of water and waited him out.

"Fine," he said. "Call me later."

"I will."

"Love you," he said.

"You too."

Fiona hung up. She pictured Eugene on the patio of the small Italian villa he had purchased when he'd turned eighteen and gained access to his trust. Eugene had fallen in love with Italy early in his life. He'd planned his escape from the family during a semester abroad in high school and left the States the day after meeting with their grandfather. Eugene had never told Fiona what was said in the meeting. But she knew it had been more hurtful than most.

"Wow," Fiona had said the first time she'd visited him there. "When you run away, you don't mess around. This place is gorgeous."

Eugene had beamed. Hers was the only opinion in the world he cared about.

Fiona smiled at his happiness.

"So, no more school, then?"

"College, you mean?" He laughed. "No thanks."

"What are you going to do?"

He rolled his eyes at her. "Are you kidding?"

"No. I am serious. What are you going to do when you get sick of Italy, art, wine, farming, and whatever else you're getting into over here?"

"If that happens, I'll figure something out. But I'm sure whatever it is will make no sense to you at all. I love you, Fi, but we're different. I just needed to escape. I don't need revenge."

"I'm not out for revenge," she said.

"Uh-huh."

"I'm not."

"So, you're getting an MBA at Harvard because you love law and business sooooooo much that, even though you have probably more money than you will ever need, you just want to do more business."

Eugene looked at his sister. He'd said the word "business" like it was a derisive punch line.

"What happened to the girl who spent every car ride looking for airplanes?"

he asked. "Remember how you could tell me what every plane in the sky was? You would yell out, 'Boeing!' 'Airtruck!'"

"Airbus," Fiona corrected.

"What?"

"It's 'Airbus,' not 'Airtruck.'"

"Whatever. That's not my point, Fi. Why don't you go learn how to fly planes or something?"

Fiona shrugged.

"Seriously," Eugene said, stepping closer to her and putting his hand on her shoulder. "I feel like you are binding yourself more and more tightly to grandfather's world, when you already have the power to escape."

"I can't explain it, Eugene."

"This works for you"—she gestured around at the grounds of the villa—"and I'm glad. But it won't work for me. I wish it would."

"I know this won't," he said. "I'm telling you to find what will."

"I know what will."

Eugene took his hand off her shoulder and put it on his hip in frustration.

"I want to create something," she said. "Something really fucking big."

"You mean make a lot of money."

"That's how 'big' is measured."

"And then what?" he asked her.

"What do you mean?"

"You create something big. Make a lot of money. Then what? What will happen?"

"He will know."

"Who?"

"Grandfather," she said.

"Know what, Fi?"

"That he underestimated me. Underestimated our father. Should have treated him better. Should have treated us all better. And damn well should have treated you better."

"We promised we would never speak of that," Eugene said, cocking his head and raising a finger.

"We're not. I'm just saying. I want him to know how wrong he was. And the only way to do that is in a language he understands."

"Even if the scales do one day fall from his eyes. Grandfather will never admit to it."

"He'll know it. That will be enough."

"Will it?"

Eugene looked at his sister. "I worry for you," he said, shaking his head.

"Don't."

"You're on a fool's quest, Fi."

"Then wish me luck."

Eugene sighed.

"Only if you promise you'll move here when your quest is over."

"Deal!" she said with a smile, glad the topic was changing and realizing she was serious. "This place really is beautiful."

Eugene nodded and turned away from Fiona. He looked at the rolling green hills. He kept turning, his eyes sweeping over the olive trees, the old barn where his painting studio was set up, the stables, and then back to his sister.

"God help me," he said. "I know this is just a material thing. It's just a simple place. But I love it so."

"What did you decide to call it? Places like this need a name."

"Mio Posto," he said with a big smile. "It means 'my place.'"

CENTAURS

Chapter Eleven

---

11 March 2063
Fort Bragg, North Carolina

"It feels like someone went to work on me all night with a baseball bat and an ice pick," Kata groaned as she sat down across from Paul in the hospital mess hall.

The past two months had been long for the both of them.

After a year of traveling around the world getting into scraps with their exo battalion, Paul and Kata had submitted their Centaur program applications as soon as they were eligible. Though it was not common for junior officers to get picked up on their first application, no one in their unit was surprised when they were accepted.

Paul and Kata reported to Fort Bragg after the new year and went right into surgery. It was not pleasant.

And it wasn't just the pain of having electronic implants attached to their skulls. They were injected with nanobots to fight disease and accelerate healing. They had hundreds of tissue samples taken to be analyzed for weaknesses and to begin growing spare vital organs. Their musculoskeletal systems were reinforced to withstand the use of military-grade battle suits.

"Yeah," Paul said, taking a sip of bad hospital coffee. "I'm over it." He set down his mug and ran his hand along the scar on his forehead, tracing it around behind his ears, where it got bigger.

"It will be good to get out of this place," Kata said.

Paul nodded and said, "Good to see the colonel, too."

They had been stuck in Womack Army Medical Center for twelve weeks for the augmentation process. During the first few weeks, they were too sore to get out of bed. When they were ambulatory again, though, they had not had the time. The physical therapy sessions were long and tiring.

This week, though, they were feeling good.

Colonel Filson had checked in on them a few times during their augmentation. But, as he well knew, they were in no condition for visitors. The colonel would poke his head in and say hi if they were awake. If not, he'd scan their charts and check in with their doctors.

Now, though, the colonel sensed their increasing strength and resulting restlessness. He had called the day before. The plan was to pick them up and treat them to a night out of the hospital.

It was unusual for Centaurs to get a night away so early in the protocol. But Filson knew General Davidson, the director of Military Augmentation Programs, well. He'd been one of the general's first patients.

"I promise I'll bring 'em back fully operational, sir," Filson had told the director over the phone.

"Where do you want to take them, Don?" the general asked him.

"To the lake house, sir. Just for the night."

The general was quiet.

"I just want to give them one night away, sir," Filson said, sensing the general wavering. "Think about it. They signed in from a twelve-month combat tour with their exo battalion and went right under the knife. They need a chance to relax, time away from being poked and prodded by strangers in lab coats. You and I both know how aggressive the training is about to get."

"Damn it, Don. I've got one mission: to deliver successfully augmented soldiers to phase-one training. You're asking me to jeopardize that mission just so—"

"Sir," Filson interjected. "With respect. That's bullshit. I don't care what your job description says. Your mission is to deliver Centaurs with the highest possible chance of graduating from the program. All of it. Not just phase one."

The colonel paused for effect before continuing.

"And I'm telling you that giving these two soldiers a night away from the goddamn flagpole is the best possible thing you can do for that mission."

Filson waited, wondering if he had pushed too hard.

"Jesus, Don," the general finally said. "I forgot what a drama queen you were."

"Is that a yes, sir?"

"No swimming, Don," General Davidson said.

"Of course not, sir."

"I'm serious. They cannot get in the water at all. Not for at least another two weeks."

"You have my word, sir."

"And no drinking."

"Of course not, sir."

"The last thing I need is one of them stumbling into a wall and setting their grafts back weeks or, God forbid, necessitating a reattachment."

"Sir, please don't worry about it," Filson said, realizing that if he did not get off the phone soon, the general would talk himself back out of it. "I really appreciate it, and they will too."

"Don't make me regret this," the general said.

But Filson had already hung up.

The colonel picked Paul and Kata up at 1700 hours. Kata hopped in shotgun, and Paul got in the back seat of the colonel's old pickup truck. He handed them each a beer as soon as they were out of sight of the hospital.

"Oh God," Kata moaned, taking the cool beverage in her hands. "Thank you, sir."

"You're welcome," Filson said. He handed Paul one. "But I'd advise you to savor it. I'll be rationing this shit tonight. I promised the general you would be undamaged and fully operational when I return you tomorrow."

Colonel Filson swiveled his head to glare at Kata.

"I also promised him I would not allow any alcohol tonight. So, Centaur code of secrecy invoked."

"Invoked it is, sir," she said.

The colonel shifted his stern gaze to the review mirror to lock eyes with Paul.

"Invoked, sir," Paul said, popping open his beer.

Convinced their oaths were sincere, the colonel grabbed the open beer he was stabilizing between his legs and raised it toward Paul and Kata.

"To the fallen," Filson said.

"To the fallen," they echoed.

The three military officers took large swigs of beer.

The colonel secured his beer. Paul and Kata settled into their seats.

"Where are we going, sir?" Paul asked.

"Lake Harris. About an hour north."

"What's there?" Kata asked.

"My cabin."

"You've got a cabin, sir?" Paul asked.

"One of the advantageous to being stationed at Bragg for fucking ever is you get to put down more roots than most," the colonel said, gesturing at Kata to put her beer down. They eased past the Fort Bragg gate guard and rolled onto the highway heading north.

"When they airlifted me back from Santiago to Womack, I had about eighteen months' worth of salary plus combat pay that I had not been able to spend," he continued as he put his truck into autonomous cruise and turned to face Kata. Paul leaned forward. "God, that was a long deployment," Filson said with a weary face.

"Six months later, when I got out of the hospital, I had about ninety days of leave built up. I rented a cabin on Lake Harris and took forty-five days off. By the end of my leave, I had talked the owner into letting me buy it. It's been my fortress of solitude, you might say, ever since." Filson shook his head. "It's what I miss most when I am on Benning running an O.A.T cycle. God, I hate Fort Benning."

"Cheers to that, sir," Kata said.

Paul raised his beer as well.

An hour later, at the end of a dirt road, they parked in front of the small cabin about a hundred yards from the water.

"Damn, sir," Kata said, getting out of the pickup truck. "It's perfect."

"Yep," Filson said with a smile. "It is."

The three of them stood still for a moment and gazed at the small Appalachian-style cabin. The two-story board-and-batten-sided building was well maintained. A small, neat stack of wood sat on the left side of the porch, an olive-drab wooden military trunk on the right side.

The colonel led them inside. The downstairs was one big room, encompassing the kitchen and a sitting area with a stone fireplace. Upstairs, there were three small bedrooms.

Hours later, after exploring the water's edge and getting a tour of the lake in the colonel's old boat, Paul and Kata sat in large chairs on the back porch overlooking the lake. The colonel brought them each a hamburger, corn on the cob, and another beer.

Filson watched as they devoured the food. The sun sank below the rolling hills to the west, and shadows cast by the tall pines stretched across the lake, reaching for the cabin.

Paul burped loudly and leaned back in his cushioned chair.

Kata smiled and did the same.

The colonel chuckled and leaned against the porch railing, his back to the water, his own beer in hand.

"So how does it feel to be super soldiers?" he asked them.

"Sore and tired," Paul said. "That's how."

"Have to tell you. I don't feel shit yet, sir," Kata said. "Other than lumpy in places I used to be smooth."

"Long as you're not smooth in places where you used to be lumpy!" the colonel said, laughing.

Paul and Kata smiled, each thinking about the relative meaning of that statement for them.

"I was the same, guys," the colonel said. "Coming out of the augmentation, you don't know shit. But you've got some monumental things coming your way."

The colonel took a sip of beer while they waited for him to continue. The man knew how to use anticipation to hold his audience's attention.

"The first is when you get into an exoskeletal battle suit for the first time. I know you both have driven exoskeletons before, but a battle suit is different. In addition to being more powerful, more armored, and more lethal than an exo, it's made to integrate to you. That's why you go through the suck of the augmentation process. So that you and the battle suit can become an integrated fighting system.

"The helmet has a special visor that uses near-eye-display technology," he continued, "enabling you to see from the point of view of your drones as well as integrated situational displays. Maps. Imagery. And other stuff. All selected via mental command. The battle suit's powerful communications suite extends your ability to command and control drone assets over very long distances. Using it, you can maneuver drones and employ their weapons systems in real time. And since it's you doing or overseeing the shooting, the kill chain is perfectly compliant with the Tokyo Accords. It's slick."

The colonel paused. Paul and Kata looked at each other. Filson's enthusiasm was contagious. They wanted to climb into their battle suits right then.

"I will not lie to you guys, though," the colonel said. "It is going to suck for a few weeks."

He took a long pull of beer and set his glass on the railing.

"What is, sir?" Kata asked.

"The adjustment period."

"Adjustment to what?"

"To commanding and controlling drones," the colonel said, pulling three cigars out of this shirt pocket. He gestured them toward Paul and Kata in offering.

Paul shook his head.

Kata nodded.

Colonel Filson took a step closer to her as he said, "It doesn't sound like much. But, holy hell, it sucks at first."

Kata took a cigar. Filson stepped back to the railing. In a few moments, cigar smoke wafted back and forth across the porch, pushed around by eddies of the slight evening breeze.

"You have to understand," Filson continued, "the human brain is the product of millions of years of evolution that perfected its ability to drive this thing around. The human body," he said, gesturing at himself.

"When you give it a direct feed from, say, an airborne drone system flying nap of the Earth, at an airspeed of over one hundred knots, making erratic course changes to avoid enemy anti-aircraft systems, the brain gets pissed. It compares that to the data it is getting from its actual body saying it is stationary, and the brain says, *Fuck you. This sucks for me, so I'm going to make life suck for you too.* The nausea is intense. For the first month of training, my abs were sore all the time from barfing."

Filson took a lazy sip of beer while Paul and Kata looked at each other, their excitement fading.

"Seriously," the colonel said, almost to himself. "After the first week, my battle suit reeked of vomit and piss."

"OK," Kata said, waving her cigar to dispel the mental image. "We get it, sir."

"Sorry, it's not that bad, really," Filson said without conviction.

"What is the training like, sir?" Kata asked.

"It's hard. But it's also a lot of fun."

They looked at him skeptically.

"I'm serious, guys. I mean, it's going to have its shitty moments, but, for the most part, it's good training."

He could see they were not believing him.

"Remember, the drones we fight with are smart. But they don't have any real independent decision-making capabilities. They are just mobile sensor and weapons platforms that a battle-suit pilot can tap into remotely. So, the course is trying to teach you how to play chess in three dimensions while on the run."

The colonel put placed his beer on the railing behind him.

"But to get to be that fluid with a platoon of combined-arms drones," he continued, "takes about six months. Most of it is out in the desert at Tonopah, where you can't do much damage as you learn the systems."

Filson leaned back against the railing and took a pull from his cigar.

"The training has a couple main phases. The first is battle-suit qualifications, where you'll learn how to get around in the battle suit without killing yourselves. That takes about a month. Then they put you in 'the box' for phase two."

"The box?" Kata asked.

"The simulator. Basically, an immobile battle suit in the hangar facility. That second phase is all about learning how to control drones from the suit.

"After proving you can keep drones under control from the suit, you move on to phase three, which is out on the maneuver range. There, you learn to move around in a battle suit while commanding drones. That's when the nausea is the worst. Ugh." The colonel made a retching face.

"Seriously, sir," Kata said. "We get it."

"The graduation task for phase three is Dead Man's Canyon," Filson said, reaching for his beer.

"Dead Man's Canyon?" Paul said with disbelief.

"Yeah. I know. It's cheesy," the colonel said with a shrug. "I didn't name it."

"What is it?" Kata asked.

"It's a canyon near the Tonopah training site. Water beat the shit out of ancient mountains for thousands of years for the sole purpose of destroying drones. It's only about twenty miles long, but it's narrow, twisty, and very difficult to fly through. It's claimed thousands of drones, and, funny thing, they never pull out the crashed machines."

The colonel smiled and took another sip of beer.

"They let them pile up. The canyon floor is littered with them, and there are burned impact points polka-dotting the canyon walls for the entire route. It sets quite a mood."

"So, you have to fly your drone through the canyon in one piece?" Kata asked.

"Yes." The colonel nodded, putting his beer back on the railing. "But that is not all of it. While the trainee pilots their drone through the canyon, they have to simultaneously negotiate their own canyon obstacle course. Dog Hobble Canyon. It's shorter than Dead Man's. But lots of vertical drop, fast-moving water, and overhanging rock that make it really tricky for a battle suit to get through quickly."

Kata nodded.

"It is a simple task: pilot your drone and battle suit through the canyons as quickly as you can without wrecking either."

"How did you do?" Kata asked.

"I did OK. I never lost a drone or hobbled my battle suit."

The colonel raised his fist in a show of victory.

"The last three months then get increasingly tactical," the colonel continued. "Until the last month, when you're commanding not only your drones but a handful of other soldiers in battle suits controlling their own drones."

He looked at the pair of young officers.

"It's a long course, guys. But it's more than worth it," he told them.

"What did you like most?" Paul asked him.

"About what?"

"Being a Centaur."

"The sensation of flying," the colonel said without hesitation. "For me, that was the best. Those points in a mission when you truly forget you're telling a drone that is miles away from you how to zig or zag. When it feels like you are the thing that is zigging or zagging."

"That must be a crazy sensation," Paul said.

"It is." Filson nodded. "And really because there is no sensation to it at all. A Mark IV aerial attack drone can pull over twenty G's. But, strapped into your battle suit, you feel none of that. The heads-up display conveys everything about the drone and its systems, of course. Airspeed. G-forces. All of that. The thought-control architecture encodes your thoughts into maneuver commands, and the battle suit's communications suite is in continuous communication with the drone. As soon as you think it, the drone executes. But you don't feel the G's, the burning impact of enemy fire, the force and explosion of losing control and careening into the earth. That drone's data feed simply ends, and you toggle through your deployed forces to call up the next best positioned platform according to your plan."

The colonel stopped.

"Sorry," he said, shrugging. "I tend to babble on about it."

Filson took a long pull from his cigar. The end burned bright red in the fading evening light.

"You miss it?" Kata asked.

"Every damn day."

They sat quietly for a few minutes. Paul and Kata watched as the last glints of reflected light receded from the surface of the lake. The colonel looked at his cigar.

"Can I ask you a question, sir?" Paul said, breaking the silence. "It's about O.A.T."

"Ancient history?" the colonel asked.

"Seems like a zillion years ago," Kata said.

"Combat tours do that to your perception of time," Filson said. "Even if you're just a nasty leg. There's before and after, and the before always seems a long way away."

Paul and Kata nodded at the observation.

"What's on your mind, Owens?" the colonel prodded.

"Were you pissed when the Geek graduated O.A.T?"

Filson raised his eyebrows at the question and then slanted them down. Paul thought he saw a flash of anger pass across the colonel's face.

But the colonel just took a long pull on his cigar.

"I had that REMF dead to rights," Filson said with a smile. "And I was going to send him out on the morning drone."

"Then why did you let us get away with helping him?" Kata asked.

"I learned long ago not to doubt the process. No matter how mad I get or how much I disagree… I know that it is wiser than me."

Paul and Kata shared a side-eyed glance. But she couldn't hold it in.

"A classic, mystical Colonel Filson response," Kata said, shaking her head and raising her beer toward the smiling old man.

"What process is that?" Paul asked as the colonel tipped his beer toward Kata.

"What you and your class went through," he said. "The crucible."

The colonel looked at them as if his statement should have explained everything. He saw their blank faces and rolled his eyes at their lack of understanding.

"The experience rewired you guys," he said, pointing at them with the glowing red end of his cigar. "I reprogrammed you. You and the rest of your graduating class are all part of the same unit now. It's not an official unit. But you're connected, and you understand each other. Our military complex is huge now, and the REMFs run it. But, mark my words, years from now, when you are downrange for your country leading men and robots against our enemies, when you need help, the Geek and guys like him will tear the world apart to get it to you."

He caught them glancing at each other again.

"I don't give a damn if you believe me or not," he said with a shrug. "I trust the wisdom of the unit. A well-led unit will make the right decision about its comrades. Who it allows to stay. Who it eliminates. So, when the Geek made the cut in your unit's eyes, I'll admit… I did not expect it. I was surprised. I disagreed. I tested it. I subjected it to stress. I made it prove itself. But I accepted it."

"Isn't that just the rule of the mob?" Paul asked.

"I said a 'well-led' unit," the colonel answered. "Big difference. You know that. Mobs do not make it through my training."

"And how about that envelopment in the swamp phase?" Kata asked him.

The colonel shook his head and took another sip of beer before saying, "You realize your platoon is the only platoon to pass the swamp phase machine-gun nest assault?"

Paul and Kata bumped fists, smiling.

"It's true," he said. "That task is ordinarily a sure failure for the platoon leader. I was certain I'd get rid of the Geek that night. But, damn it. Your harebrained, borderline-cheating idea to split your force worked."

"That must have really pissed you off," Paul said with a hint of taunt in his voice.

"No, son," the colonel said in an earnest tone. "You're not fucking hearing me. I just about cried when you guys pulled that off. When you guys risked getting kicked out for the Geek, I knew the bond was there. So, no matter how much I personally wanted to kick that chubby egghead out of my program, I knew I'd done my job and that the process had gotten it right."

The colonel smiled as he recalled that night in the swamp.

He put his beer on the railing, leaned back and said, "As you guys know, sometimes as a leader you have to maintain your mask. Play the role. I had to be the angry superior officer on the outside. To cement it, you guys had to believe you had beaten not only the cadre, but also me."

"We did beat you, sir," Paul said.

"You did, son," the colonel said with a gracious smile.

"And you know what?" Kata said. "Since then, the Geek has been promoted twice already. He's the highest-ranking member of our O.A.T class. Gonna be a general, no doubt."

"Fucking REMF," the colonel growled in mock disgust.

Paul and Kata smiled. Then the colonel did too.

They all took a sip of beer.

"How much longer you gonna run O.A.T., sir?" Paul asked.

The colonel chuckled. "Oh, I dunno."

Paul and Kata shared a glance, both noting a curious tone in Filson's voice. But the colonel turned away from them to look at the lake, ending the topic.

They all sat in silence as the last bit of light faded and the surface of the lake darkened.

Chapter Twelve

"I'm starting to think this was not such a good idea," Kata said.

"Well, it was your idea," Paul said without looking up from his magazine.

The Las Vegas sun baked them as they lay poolside on oversized lounge chairs. With a week of downtime before they had to report Ramstein Military Base in Germany, Kata had insisted they spend a few days in Vegas on the way. A last bacchanal before their first combat tour as Centaurs.

Paul snuck a look at Kata. Despite her sunglasses and tough demeanor, he could see the disappointment and pain on her face.

"Come on, Kat. It's our last day. Let's just try to enjoy it."

"I guess I thought it would be fun after being sequestered for months on Tonopah," she said, shaking her head at him.

"That place sucked," Paul said. "Hot, dry and dusty."

"And everything there was the color of sand!" Kata said, sitting up in her recliner. "Our uniforms, our battle suits, the drones, the barracks. Even our fucking underwear."

"I know. It felt like we were all pieces of the same bleached skeleton."

Kata nodded in agreement.

"So, you know," he said, reaching for solidarity. "This is a lot better."

Paul gestured around. The pool was an electric aquamarine color surrounded by what must have been a square kilometer of white tile. The wait staff wore ox blood red kimonos and carried silver treys.

He looked skyward at the towering expanse of mirrors and neon that rose up around them on all sides. At Kata's insistence, they were staying in the middle of the strip.

She harrumphed and laid back in her chair, ab muscles rippling. She was, like him, wildly attractive from some angles; just enough smooth and sinewy muscle bound together in a golden mean feminine structure topped by a symmetrical face with high cheek bones and piercing eyes.

But from other angles she was different. A pink, puffy scar the width of a pencil encircled her head just above her ears. Other scars popped out above her hips, on her shoulders and down her spine where augmentation protocols had strengthened her skeletal system to withstand the stresses of battlesuit combat. Her elbows, and knees, and shoulder blades bore metal hard points, the size of dimes, for battlesuit systems integration. The augmentations were not freakish, really. But it was disquieting for those not in the tribe.

As she walked around in her bikini, Paul could see the alternating waves of attraction and revulsion wash over the civilian crowd. He also saw it as he walked around himself. By the end of the trip, he got to the same place she did.

"Fuck 'em."

It started off fine. The first day, after sleeping late, they went to the pool to wake up and relax in the sun. The contrast from remote military base to poolside in Las Vegas was jarring. Though they had spent the past six months only about a hundred miles north in the same stretch of desert, Vegas felt like a different planet.

It was exciting initially. To be surrounded not only by the vibrant colors and amenities but also by the beautiful civilians in skimpy bathing suits. The hard run of training, augmentation, and then more training had left no time for romantic pursuits. Paul and Kata were lonely and horny.

They dove into the environment with the characteristic boldness of Combat Leadership Corps officers. Knowing they were ultra-fit specimens, they waded into the pool and got social. They had separate rooms, of course, in anticipation of lots of athletic romance with random partners. The plan was to link up for dinner each night, no matter the fatigue from their sexual exertion.

It did not take long to notice, though, that all of their civilian interactions followed the same basic pattern. They would approach an attractive person with a ridiculously direct pick-up line. The target would respond positively, and engage them in conversation, if not outright flirting. Then, after a brief back and forth, the target would ask about their augmentation scars and metallic battlesuit chassis attachment points.

Then the stupid questions would start, 'Did it hurt?', 'Is water bad for you?', 'Can you send a message to my cell phone with your mind?' And the inevitable, 'Have you ever killed anybody?' After their initial curiosities were answered, the target would break it off and blend back into the sea of oblivious civilians.

It got old quick.

Then Kata noticed people staring at her and Paul. By the middle of that first day at the pool, they realized they were oddities. The fact that they were in the military was weird enough, but that they were Centaurs made them freaks.

Civilians knew about Centaurs, of course. They read about them in the news and heard about what they did around the world. But they never saw them. The military had consolidated its combat maneuver units to two locations. Fort Bragg and Fort Irwin; the armpit and asshole of America. Not places one would put the military if integration into society was a goal.

"I didn't realize how badly they had butchered us," Kata said at the end of the first day as she glared at the pool.

"What do you mean?"

"I mean this shit." Kata pointed at her scars.

Paul made a show of looking at Kata and nodding in empathy.

Then he looked across the pool at the civilian woman in VR sunglasses. She gestured as she moved through whatever app she was immersed in. Paul knew that if he had the opportunity to look behind her ear lobe, he would see the slight bulge from the augmentation enabling her to interact seamlessly with her technology and the internet.

Civilian augmentation was still pricey and indulged in only by the wealthy. When it was, it came with a cosmetic attention to detail that the military did not prioritize. Durability and performance specs were different, of course, for augmentations embedded in a Centaur versus those emplaced in socialites.

Paul and Kata were different. And not in a good way. It was a lonely feeling.

The second day, when they met for breakfast, Paul wore a baseball hat.

"You fucking pussy," Kata said, bearing her shaven head, showing her young augmentation scar in all its pink and puffy glory. "I don't give a shit if these people stare. I like the way the sun feels."

Paul took his hat off.

They both ended up getting laid the last night. But it wasn't great. And neither wanted to talk about it. They were relieved when they boarded their flight to Germany.

Halfway over the Atlantic Ocean, Kata turned to Paul and said, "It's weird, isn't it?"

"What?"

"I guess I just got used to everyone in the military saying what an honor it was to get selected. How proud of us they were. How proud we should be of ourselves. I never gave it a second thought. This is what I wanted to be for so long." Kata pointed at the augmentation scar that circled her head and looked at Paul with a rare twinge of doubt in her eyes.

"I didn't realize how different we were going to be," she said. "How weird what we're doing is compared to… normal civilian folks."

Kata turned and looked out of the window.

Paul didn't know what to say. But he knew it was harder on Kata than him. Everything is always harder for women in the military. They give up more. His scars would, one day, be ruggedly handsome. Hers would always be weird and intimidating to civilian men.

In Germany, they had two free days and then one day of in processing before heading into theater. They spent the two days drinking beer and driving from castle to castle on the Rhine River. Wearing baseball hats and loose clothing for security reasons, they got no stares. They had almost forgotten the weirdness in Vegas when they reported back to Ramstein Air Base on the third day.

At the processing facility, they were given their final immunizations and updated their wills and financial paperwork. But as they made our way through the process, they heard the same refrain of questions, 'Did it hurt?', 'Is water bad for you?', 'Can you send a message to my cell phone with your mind?'

This time, it was Paul that took it hardest.

"You OK?" Kata asked him, as they sat waiting for their flight.

"Yeah," he mumbled without looking up.

"Hey," she said sharply. "What is wrong with you?"

"This is a fucking military base. They sound like dumbass civilians."

"What did you expect?"

"I guess that they would know what we are. That they would kind of get it. That it would feel more, I don't know, like we were all in the same military."

Kata laughed. "Did you not hear a word Filson said?"

Chapter Thirteen

The aircraft ramp lowered, revealing the black night sky. Paul walked aft past the soldierbots of Outlaw Platoon. Their multi-sensored heads swiveled to watch him as he walked out onto the ramp and placed the heel of his armored boot on the edge. The sparse lights of isolated villages passed twenty thousand feet below his toe.

Paul closed his eyes and let the swirl and tug of wind at the edge of the ramp beat against his face. The air was cold. It felt good.

It would be much warmer on the ground.

The air mission commander interrupted Paul's meditation. "One minute, Captain," he said over the intercom. "You gonna wear your helmet tonight?"

Paul said nothing. He held up a middle finger up toward the video camera in the front of the drone's cabin without turning his head away from the night. The soldierbots looked at his finger with curiosity.

"Easy, Captain," the voice came back. "You are addressing a major."

"Uh-huh," Paul mumbled. Deployed almost a year now, he had no love or patience for the drone-flying smoothies he had to work with. He pictured the major reclining in a swivel chair, steam rising from his cup of coffee due to the overworked air-conditioning, gazing at multiple displays of imagery and data with half interest.

Paul always left his helmet off until the last possible second. Whether he was in an aircraft, in a ground vehicle, or walking, he preferred the feeling of "open air," as he'd told Kata during their training back at Bragg. She'd told him that was stupid.

Paul turned and looked forward, his back to the open ramp and night sky. Staff Sergeant Gamal and Sergeant Anton stood by their soldierbot squads, helmets on. They gave him a thumbs-up.

Paul nodded.

"Thirty seconds," the air mission commander said.

Paul pulled on his armored helmet. It clicked against his battle suit's collar fitting, and he listened to the familiar ratcheting sound as his battle suit twisted the helmet into place.

A flood of information glimmered across Paul's heads-up display. He cycled through unit, soldier, and soldierbot statuses before settling on a tactical guidance format.

Paul took a deep breath and tried to center himself before the chaos. Commanding a Centaur platoon was like being that clown in the circus that spins a dozen plates at a time above his head. He had to maneuver himself in his armored battle suit while monitoring and commanding his soldierbots via his HUD. He had to constantly cross-check his team's telemetry feed: their positions, ground speeds, directions, energy and weapons statuses. Based on the situation, he had to jack into individual soldierbots, assume their point of view, take over their guidance and weapons, and fight the enemy while confirming rules-of-engagement compliance for those soldierbots he was not actively driving. Because he was more than just the commander on the ground. He was the critical link in the kill chain. The piece that made their application of violence legal.

All that, while trying to not get killed.

He knew that once things got loud, he would be fine. The training would take over. He also knew that he was really good at this.

This mission would not be easy, though. A female American physician named April Sanchez had been captured eight hours earlier by a warlord whose treatment of prisoners was not nice. Intel gave her twenty-four hours to live. Tonight was their only window.

What made it a trick shot was intel's inability to nail down her location.

"She's in one of these three small villages," was the best they could do.

Just a few hours ago, Paul and Kata had listened carefully as the briefing officer pointed at the map display and talked through specifics of each target site. The villages were about fifteen kilometers from each other and sat in the middle of an area controlled by one of the region's most violent warlords.

The briefing officer had launched into a familiar refrain of "unconfirmed this" and "no way to definitively say that," and Paul felt his anxiety level rise. He'd looked at Kata, the only other Centaur platoon leader in theater. She'd met his gaze, eyebrows raised in apprehension.

The problem was that the Chinese had equipped the warlords handsomely in exchange for money, rare-earth metals, and conflict diamonds. And the warlords didn't give a shit about the Tokyo Accords. They'd throw some wicked automated tech into the fight without any kill chain whatsoever, putting the robot on the "fuck everyone" setting and letting it rip.

So, Paul and Kata never knew what they were headed into. Some villages seemed to be living in the 1800s, and they'd face off against soldiers with old bolt-action, single-shot rifles. And then, in the neighboring town, a Chinese autonomous biped tank would walk around the corner and go into murder mode, killing half of the town while trying to get at the American soldiers.

Earlier, as they had huddled around the mapping table in the small planning facility, Paul had listened to the situation report and realized that they would have to hit all three villages simultaneously. If they hit the wrong village, word would get out and they wouldn't get a shot at the other two. April Sanchez would be dead. Furthermore, given the number of enemy foot soldiers believed to be in each village, they would not be able to approach the targets on foot or by drone copter. The likelihood of detection and failure was too high. Somehow, the plan had to provide assurance for the element of surprise.

When these kinds of missions came down, the squad leaders would get the team ready while Paul and Kata made a quick plan, met with the air component, and gave their commander, Lieutenant Colonel Andrews, an overview. Once the colonel had approved, he would go to the command center to monitor the mission and get them support, should things go to shit. At this point in their tour, they could get through the planning-and-prep cycle and be wheels-up in thirty minutes.

Paul's plan was straightforward, but it had still gotten a grimace from Andrews. The colonel stood across the mapping table from Paul, his arms crossed and his face masked with skepticism as Paul outlined his plan.

"Sir, I am going put three squads out of an aircraft at twenty thousand feet," Paul had explained. The mapping table panned back from three red triangles that highlighted the three target locations. "Each squad will track toward their target village in free fall down to five thousand feet above ground level. At that point, we will deploy and proceed the rest of the way under canopy. When each squad is positioned directly above their target structures at approximately five hundred feet, I'll give the command to cut away, and we will drop onto the targets."

Colonel Andrews rubbed his chin and looked at the mapping table as green icons descended onto the target triangles. He was one of the early Centaurs, assigned to the Combat Corps immediately after it stood up. Paul took his tense silence as likely approval, so he gave the colonel a little more.

"I'm going to assign the most likely target village to Staff Sergeant Gamal and give him two squads," Paul said. The map display zoomed into target village one. "He is the best small-unit leader in the battalion and a hell of a drone driver."

"Rumor is he held the Dead Man's Canyon record for a couple of years," Kata said, trying to help Paul's case.

Paul nodded. "I've seen him pull off some amazing things with his soldierbots."

The colonel remained silent. Still rubbing his chin.

"Sergeant Anton will take a squad into target village two," Paul continued. "And I'll take one into village three." The map display tracked as he talked.

"You'll be on the ground on this one?" the colonel asked.

"Yes, sir. Have to. I'm still down two squad leaders."

Colonel Andrews shook his head slowly, remembering that two of Paul's squad leaders were still recovering from wounds. The operations tempo was wearing them down.

"What about your first sergeant?" Andrews asked Paul.

"He's with a squad outside the wire on a convoy escort mission."

"Continue," Andrews said with irritation.

"From there, it gets kinetic, sir. We'll work through the houses, swarms out and weapons up, until we find her."

"And what is your role tonight, Captain Vukovic?"

"I'll have a quick reaction force of two squads orbiting ten kilometers south," Kata said, gesturing at the map display, which panned south. Six icons representing quad copter assault drones circled clockwise in a tight formation. "The QRF will be on call in case things get sporty. If not, we'll extract Captain Owens and his platoon when they call."

Colonel Andrews stared at the map. As he did so, Paul looked at the augmentation scar that ringed the colonel's head. It passed above his ears and across his forehead, just like Paul's. The colonel's scar was over ten years old, though, and it was no longer pink and puffy like Paul's or Kata's.

"There is a lot I don't like about this," Andrews said. Paul took his eyes off the augmentation scars and met the colonel's gaze. "But I don't have any better ideas."

Colonel Andrews looked at his watch.

"And none of us have any more time. Do it."

"Roger that, sir," Paul said as he and Kata turned from the table and headed for the door.

"Oh, and Owens?" the colonel called after him as he left.

"Yes, sir?"

"You ever done a five-hundred-foot drop in a battle suit?"

"No, sir."

The colonel chuckled and shook his head. "It sucks."

Now, with the toe of his armored boot hanging off the edge of the aircraft's ramp, twenty thousand feet above the ground, Paul remembered Colonel Andrews' knowing chuckle.

Maybe this is not such a great plan, Paul thought.

"Exit! Exit! Exit!" the air mission commander said.

Paul and Outlaw Platoon ran off the aircraft ramp.

Paul held his head down for about eight seconds to reach terminal velocity before flaring. He leveled out and assumed a tracking position. His battle suit computed the optimal canopy deployment point given the winds, their weight, and other factors and marked it as a green X thirteen thousand feet below and three miles in front of him. Paul tracked toward it and called up a tactical display to check on the rest of the platoon.

Things looked good. Staff Sergeant Gamal was tracking well toward his target, with ten soldierbots behind him. Sergeant Anton was doing the same with his five. Paul's team of five soldierbots fell with him in a loose trail formation.

So far, so good.

Forty-five seconds later, Paul bull's-eyed the green X and deployed his parachute.

He cycled through statuses on his HUD. Green across the board. No canopy malfunctions, and all three teams seemed assured to hit their next checkpoints, directly over the target houses.

Paul felt his pulse quicken as he monitored their altitude. He tried to slow his breathing as they descended through two thousand feet above ground level.

His HUD superimposed a vertical green column over their target that rose from the house's roof and extended seemingly to space. When Paul and his team flew into that column, they were to cut away their canopies.

The cutaway point was now about thirty seconds away.

Paul looked down and cycled his HUD through infrared to ultraviolet and back again as he scanned the target area. He counted at least a dozen enemy patrolling the outside.

Paul thought for the hundredth time that night how lucky they were that there was not much of a moon.

Ten seconds to the cutaway point.

Paul checked his altitude and winced: 575 feet above ground level. He resisted the urge to try to bleed off altitude. Any maneuvers now would screw up his cutaway point.

Three.

Two.

One.

Paul gave the cutaway command and entered free fall for the second time that night.

Paul resisted the urge to flail when gravity snatched him down. That enabled his battle suit to do the work as well as it could. They were falling subterminal, with very little vertical airspeed to fly with. Paul knew that when they got close to impact, the suit would execute whatever maneuvers it could, based on their rate of fall and what it sensed below them to optimize their configuration.

Paul expected those maneuvers to be abrupt.

A battle suit equipped with a full combat load weighed about five hundred pounds. Paul was carrying extra ammo tonight, though, figuring it would be a short but intense engagement. Adding his weight, Paul had calculated during mission planning that he would tip the scale at over 750 pounds when he "landed."

Maintenance had assured him that the impact was well within the battle suit's capabilities.

Paul watched their altitude wind down to zero.

You've got to be fucking kidding me, he thought as his battle suit assumed a tight cannonball pose.

The initial impact as he penetrated the roof was less jarring than Paul had expected. The second even less so as he blasted through the flimsy second-level floor.

But the third, as the colonel had predicted, sucked.

Paul shook his head to clear it as he stood up.

Per the plan, he was standing on the first floor of his target house with two soldierbots from Dagger Squad. Eight shocked bandits, four of whom were suited in armored exoskeletons, looked back at them. With a thought, Paul designated them enemy combatants.

Four of them dropped to the floor in bloody heaps without getting a single shot off.

At the same time, Paul and the two soldierbots deployed their swarms.

The two dozen scout drones they each carried and controlled had limited range but were very useful as extended, multispectral eyes and ears. The swarm of marble-sized airborne sensors dispersed through the house. A complete tactical situation map began to form on Paul's HUD.

Paul noted the charging battle suited enemy behind him just in time.

He jumped to his left as the lumbering exoskeleton's battle-ax came down. It struck a glancing blow to his helmet.

His helmet absorbed most of the oblique impact, but his ears rang and visuals flickered as he sank into a kneeling position. Immediately, he threw a punch at the armored enemy's chest, adding his battle suit's leg strength to the motion and extending his forearm-housed depleted-uranium bayonet as he swung his fist.

The punch caved in the bandit's chest armor as the blade impaled him.

Paul withdrew his fist, sheathing the bayonet as he scanned the tactical situation on his HUD.

The enemy armored suit, now housing a dead man, took a few mindless steps back until it bumped into the wall.

Paul studied the other dead enemy on the floor. Four were in oversized exoskeletons. Like the one he had just killed, they seemed to be designed more for intimidating crowds and close-quarters fights than fire and maneuver work. Intel knew that the warlords had 3D printing capabilities. Seemed they remained focused on gang work over higher-level tactical applications.

They've got fucking imaginations too, Paul thought, looking across the room at the exo's battle-ax appendage, which reached almost to the floor. Blood ran down its chest onto the floor as it stood motionless, its back to the wall.

Paul winced, thinking about what would have happened if the ax had found its mark. He sent the intelligence out to his platoon. It was going to be a bruising fight if they lost the advantage of their surprise. They had to move fast.

Paul put his battle suit into park-and-defend mode and relaxed his body so that the suit could make any moves it needed to. It went into a defensive crouch position with weapons at the ready.

There were two potential target buildings in Paul's assigned village. The other three soldierbots in Dagger Squad were taking down building two. Paul switched his POV to their targeting feeds. About a dozen bandits looked at Paul in disbelief via data link with Dagger Three. He counted five in exos.

The bandits scattered as Paul swiveled Dagger Three's integrated minigun toward the group. He dissected four of them while giving Dagger Four and Dagger Five the weapons-free command. Antipersonnel rounds from Dagger Five decapitated several more of the bandits.

The last bandit charged Dagger Five and pulled the pin from a hand grenade. It detonated as the bandit tackled Five. Red mist and soldierbot parts flew through the room.

Paul gave up control of Dagger Three as swarm data confirmed the rest of the building was empty.

The assault had been underway for thirty seconds, and their targets were secure. But he'd already lost one soldierbot. And no April Sanchez.

The man-down alert flashed on Paul's HUD. Staff Sergeant Gamal, commanding Saber Squad in village one, was down. His battle suit transmitted a Mayday plus vitals.

With eighteen structures and at least three dozen bandits, Paul had a hunch Sanchez would be in village three, though intel refused to make a similar bet.

Gamal had been struck by an armor-piercing RPG round, which had severed his left arm just below the shoulder. His battle suit's first-aid system and his own internal nanobots had cauterized the wound, stemming the blood loss. His vitals were strong and stable, but he was in shock and unconscious. Out of the fight.

Their kill chain was broken.

With a thought, Paul ordered Staff Sergeant Gamal's battle suit to move to the exfil site and threw Saber Squad's telemetry up on his HUD.

Their swarm data confirmed Saber was in direct contact with at least two dozen enemy. The soldierbots dodged RPGs, small-arms fire, and at least two directed energy systems while trying to shield Gamal's withdrawal. Saber One, escorting the unconscious Gamal, provided covering fire. A small swarm flew ahead of them, scouting the route to the extraction site three kilometers south of the village.

"Shit," Paul muttered to himself. Based on the well-equipped force Saber Squad was facing, he was starting to feel confident that Sanchez was there.

Paul took over Saber Two and began to kill enemy soldiers while checking the telemetry from village two. It did not look promising, but he called Sergeant Anton, the squad leader in village two, on the radio.

"Blade Six, this is Dagger Six," Paul transmitted. "What is your status?"

"Dagger Six, Blade Six. We've got a dry hole here, sir."

Paul nodded inside his armored helmet. That confirmed it.

Sanchez was in Saber's village.

"Understood," Paul answered. "Banshee on Saber."

"Roger that. Banshee on Saber," Anton repeated, ensuring Paul knew he'd heard the code-word command. They would both converge on village one to assist Saber Squad.

And they both knew they would get there too late.

Paul focused on Saber Two's telemetry and weapons system. As it acquired targets, he confirmed the ROE compliance before authorizing kill shots.

Meanwhile, back in village three, where Paul was actually standing, his squad signaled complete. The soldierbots' facial-recognition systems had scanned and cataloged the dead enemy and had secured any potentially valuable intel. Paul signaled the copters for exfil and gave his squad the command to withdraw.

Dagger Four led them out.

Paul took a deep breath as he put his battle suit into autopilot. It was always a difficult transition when his suit started sprinting, and he was trying to stay limp, mind focused on another fight kilometers away.

The squad of five ran out of village one with Dagger Four in the lead. Paul was in the number-three position in the formation. They were out of the village three minutes and seventeen seconds after the attack had begun.

Paul focused on the fight in village one as his squad moved to their pickup zone. Fifteen kilometers away, Gamal's battle suit had gotten him to the aircraft, and he would soon be in the air. Saber One was still with them to provide security. A couple of foolish bandits had followed them and were now bleeding out on the ground.

Paul gave Saber Four and Saber Five the weapons-free command. They provided covering fire as he maneuvered Saber Two and Three around the enemy. At that point, he had five weapon bore sights up on his HUD and was working through kill shots and managing all five soldierbots. He needed help.

He called Kata.

"Raptor Zero Six, this is Dagger Zero Six, requesting driver assist."

"Dagger Six, this is Raptor. Got your back."

"Raptor, take Saber Four and Saber Five."

"Sabers Four and Five, roger. I have the controls."

Kata relaxed her shoulders and leaned back in her seat as the drone copter she rode on orbited in a long, lazy left-hand turn pattern at fifty feet above ground level, three hundred knots airspeed.

Let's get it on, she thought as her heads-up display flooded with high-definition video and telemetry from Sabers Four and Five.

Centaurs preferred to have the commander on the ground drive a Centaur unit in combat. It was old-school thinking that had been around since the Battle of Jericho. But it worked.

It was simple enough to throw control of a subunit to a remote commander, though. And it helped in situations like this, where the commander on the ground was close to task saturation. So, Kata, orbiting fifteen kilometers away with the quick reaction force, got into the fight and assumed part of the kill chain.

Down to fighting with two soldierbots, Paul sped up. He and Saber Three sprinted toward the last enemy building, firing as they went.

They had been on the objective for almost five and a half minutes. Paul felt the window closing. A few swarm drones had penetrated the target house. They counted ten enemy and put together a partial floor plan before being destroyed. Paul would have preferred a more complete tactical picture. But it was now or never.

Paul and Saber Three charged the house.

As he accelerated his soldierbot, Paul switched his HUD to infrared. It was an imprecise imaging system, and the signal noise caused by all of the discharging weapons made it worse. But at least it provided some kind of check against warm bodies on the other side of the wall he was running toward.

He didn't want to kill Sanchez when they breached.

Paul hit the wall at twenty-eight miles an hour. Saber Three bested him by two miles an hour.

They burst through opposite walls.

Bricks, dust, and debris filled the air.

Violent chaos erupted inside the house.

There were times like this in every operation when, despite all of the slick technology and data, it became a close-quarters melee. Paul and Saber Three each took multiple hits as they shot, bludgeoned, and stabbed their way toward the back of the structure.

There was another ax-wielding exo in the mix.

Are you kidding me? Paul thought.

The bandit charged.

Paul jumped back fifteen feet, to the far side of the room.

He lost his footing, though, and fell onto his back.

The bandit ran after him, just a step behind. He raised his ax for a killing stroke, and then his upper body disintegrated.

Paul saw Saber Three across the room, its smoking minigun still pointed at the halved bandit.

Blood ran down the enemy exoskeleton's still-functioning legs as they ran into and tripped over Saber Two. They skidded into the wall, dark blood from the bandit's lower half pooling around them.

Paul quickly righted Saber Two. He and Saber Three charged forward.

The POV from Saber Two was flickering, and Paul struggled to keep the soldierbot moving forward.

Saber Three ran with a limp, hydraulic fluid streaming from its left knee.

Finally, after what seemed like forever to Paul, the two soldierbots burst into the room where Sanchez was.

A lone bandit held a pistol to her blindfolded head.

Saber Three had the better angle and clearer POV, so Paul swapped to its bore sight while commanding Saber Two to charge.

Paul squeezed off a dozen rounds from Saber Three's minigun. They stitched a line from the bandit's jaw to his pelvis. His body folded in a bloody spray and fell away from Sanchez.

She screamed. The warm blood of her captor sprayed on her face.

Saber Two reached her as she fell. It caught Sanchez and cradled her in its metal and ceramic arms. The battered soldierbot straightened up, lifting Sanchez off of her feet and into its chest. Paul swapped back to Saber Two's POV and transmitted his voice through it as he used its hand to gently pull the blindfold from her eyes.

"April Sanchez?" he asked softly, from the quad copter flying in her direction at three hundred knots ground speed.

"Yes," she whispered, confirming what Saber Two's facial recognition routines were saying.

"You're safe now."

"Who are you?" April asked in a cracked and weak voice.

"I'm Captain Paul Owens, of the United States military."

Chapter Fourteen

"I'm so happy you're here!" Eugene said, running toward his sister.

Fiona stepped out of the driverless car and met her brother's charge with a hug.

"I can't believe you finally came," he said, releasing her and grabbing one of her bags. "How long has it been?"

"I was wondering about that on the flight," Fiona said as they walked to the main house. *When I wasn't wondering how to tell you what I need to tell you,* she thought. *How to ask what I need to ask.*

"Five years?" she guessed.

"Way too long!" Eugene declared as they walked through the large wooden doors into the main house.

Built of wood and stone over three hundred years ago, the kitchen flowed into the dining area, which spilled out onto a large stone patio. Massive beams ran the width of the ceiling, holding up the wooden second floor and its four small bedrooms. The sand-colored walls were made of local stone, and despite their variation in size and color shade, each stone seemed to fit perfectly in its place.

"Put your bag down. Let's sit for a few minutes," Eugene said, walking through the wide archway and onto the patio.

A large pergola, conquered decades ago by climbing roses, covered the patio. Thick, ropy vines wrapped around the pergola's old wooden columns, snaking up into the lattice of beams. Leafy green vines punctuated with small red roses spilled from the lattice in places.

A sweating bottle of prosecco waited for them on the table, alongside a pitcher of water.

Thank God, Fiona thought. *Alcohol.*

"Water or prosecco?" Eugene asked her.

"Prosecco. Please."

Eugene smiled. "Me too," he said, pouring two glasses. He handed her one and then held his out. "A toast to my sister. Finally visiting us here at Mio Posto."

They drank. Fiona taking long pulls on hers. She set down an empty glass.

"Wow." Eugene chuckled.

"That's so good," Fiona said. "And it was a long flight."

He gestured at her glass, and she nodded. He poured more prosecco into her glass as she held it out.

"Truthfully, it's been a long year," she said, before taking another long swallow.

Eugene leaned back in his chair.

His smile drained away.

"What is it, Fi?" He set his glass down on the table.

"What?" Fiona said, sipping her wine.

"Don't bullshit me. I saw the weight on your shoulders the second you got out of the car. Your distraction and shifty eyes. You are in mode."

Eugene crossed his arms.

"And it pisses me off," he said.

Fiona rubbed her face.

"Are you even staying the night?" he asked.

"Depends," she said.

"On what?"

"On if you let me."

Eugene regarded her for a long moment.

"I'm your brother, Fi. We stick together. You taught me that."

Fiona smiled despite her anxiety.

"Now fucking out with it," he said.

"I need to borrow some money."

Eugene blinked.

Fiona waited.

"You've run through twenty-five million dollars?" he asked.

"Not really."

"Not really?"

"It's a timing thing." She leaned forward. "My assets are worth several multiples of my current debt."

"So, sell them."

"Can't." Fiona shook her head. "Not now. I'd be selling insanely short."

Fiona thought of Talisman. The prospect of ceding more equity and control to them enraged her.

"What about a bank? A proper lender for this kind of thing?"

"Word would get back to grandfather," Fiona said. "He could take advantage, possibly take control. He would make my life difficult in a thousand ways. I can't afford that right now."

Eugene shook his head at the mention of the old man. He stood up from the table and walked to the edge of the stone patio. A single rose vine fell almost to his head. He studied it.

"I hate that you have brought this to me here," he said to Fiona without looking back. "This is my sacred space. Why didn't you ask me to meet you somewhere to talk about this?"

Fiona shrugged.

"Would that really have made it any better?"

"For me?" he said, turning around. "Yes."

Eugene walked back to the table and sat down.

"This is for your fighting robot things, I presume?"

"AI weapons systems," Fiona said. "Yes."

"How much?"

"I need five million."

"Jesus, Fiona," he said, flopping back in his chair.

"It's basically zero risk, or I wouldn't ask. It's a debt service payment. One of my companies is working with the Combat Corps now and is sailing through a phase-one test. Phase two will be a big-time liquidity event, and I'll be able to pay you back. Forty-five days. Ninety at most."

Eugene looked up, tracing one of the rose vines with his eyes. It got thinner the farther it went until it concluded in a handful of blazing-red buds.

"You're in big trouble, aren't you?" he asked Fiona without taking his eyes off of the roses.

"Huh?"

"Don't." He swiveled his head to stare at Fiona.

"If you are here asking me for money, that means you failed to negotiate a restructured payment schedule. And that means you already did that once or twice and fell behind again, or the business you took the loan on has increased in value to the point that the lender wants it rather than their money back."

Fiona sat motionless. "Look who likes to pretend they don't understand business," she said.

"And, knowing you, you've gone all in on this and you don't have another penny to your name," Eugene continued, without acknowledging the interruption. "And you don't know anyone else you trust enough to ask this of, since one of the guiding principles here is to keep grandfather in the dark, lest he take advantage of the situation to humiliate you or worse."

Fiona smiled. She raised her hands, palms up, in a gesture of surrender.

"Fuck," Eugene said sadly.

He turned his head back to the dangling rosebuds.

"I'm sorry," Fiona finally said.

"It's OK," he said, getting up from his chair. Fiona watched as he poured himself another prosecco. He took a sip and said, "Next time, though, just call me. Or let's meet somewhere. I really hate discussing family business here. I won't do it again. Please remember that."

"Deal."

"Now I'm going to go take a bath and wash this whole conversation off."

He turned and started back into the house. "You can stay," he said, pausing at the threshold.

"Thanks."

"Some friends are coming over for dinner," Eugene began.

Fiona's shoulders sagged.

"Don't! Not after all that shit." He flailed the hand not holding the glass of prosecco in Fiona's direction in a disgusted gesture of chaos.

"You're going to be nice and social and interact. I don't give a damn how tired you are."

"OK, OK," Fiona said with a smile. "I'll be on my best. Who are these people?"

"Four hot and single Italian guys," Eugene said, wearing a hungry smile.

"Why did I bother asking?"

"It wouldn't kill you to get laid, you know," Eugene said as he turned to leave. "But don't touch Alessandro," he called over his shoulder from inside the house. "I've got plans for him."

Fiona poured herself the rest of the prosecco. She stood up and walked to the edge of the patio, and pulled out her cell phone.

Pruden picked up on the first ring.

"We're good," Fiona said.

"Thank God."

"I expect the wire will hit my account by tomorrow. I'll transfer it as soon as it hits, and you can make the payment."

"Great."

Fiona looked over her shoulder back at the house and then said in a low voice, "It's only five."

"What?" Pruden asked with alarm. "Why?"

"It's all I asked for."

"Shit, Fiona. Why? That's about half of what we're going to need."

"It buys us a little more time."

"That's true. But we're going to have a problem. Why didn't you ask for what we needed?"

"It wasn't the right time."

"When is it ever going to be the right time? Those Talisman bastards are going to—"

"Damn it, Marty," Fiona interrupted, her voice taking on an edge. "I'll handle this the way I see fit."

Pruden waited a few seconds before saying, "Of course, Fiona. Of course."

"Sorry," Fiona said. "I'm sorry. I just… This sucks for me, OK?"

"I understand," Pruden said with sincerity. "I hate it for you. Try to enjoy your week out there. It will be good for you. I can handle everything we've got going on here."

"Thanks. But I'll probably head back tomorrow."

"Why? Don't do that."

"Trust me," Fiona said, glancing again back at the house. "If I don't get out of here in a day or so, he is going to figure out we really need more, and it won't be pretty. Better to save that reckoning for when I am ready."

Pruden didn't respond.

Fiona drained her glass.

"I'll call you from the airport tomorrow. I'm going to get drunk now."

Chapter Fifteen

12 September 2064
Camp Resolve, Africa

The US military had been improving and enlarging Camp Resolve for almost five years. It was the main logistics and military hub on the African continent and had more than twenty thousand American military personnel on station at any one time. But there were never more than a hundred ground combat troops there, and never more than five Combat Corps officers.

Paul and Kata had been two of the Combat Corps officers on Resolve for almost a year and a half now. They were the only platoon commanders. The truth was there was no need for more.

For hundreds of years, an army platoon had been made up of forty to fifty soldiers. Technology had reduced that by 90 percent in the span of just a few years, while increasing the combat power by the same multiple. Paul's platoon could bring as much firepower to bear, and command as much terrain, as a turn-of-the-century regiment.

Unit structure and technology architecture made the application of that large-scale and widely dispersed violence manageable. Paul and Kata each had a human platoon sergeant and six human squad leaders. All were Centaurs with embedded electronics, enhanced skeletal systems, circulatory nanobots, and other augmentations. Five of the squad leaders each commanded six soldierbots, AI-enabled humanoid fighting robots. Each soldierbot was equipped with a swarm of two dozen airborne sensorbots. The battle suit's architecture enabled the human leadership to assume control of the soldierbots, driving them directly against the enemy.

The sixth squad leader managed a special platforms unit equipped with fifty fighting drones of a dozen different types: airborne, waterborne, groundborne, and some hybrids. They enabled Paul and Kata to put together mission packages tailored to specific tactical situations.

Complying with the rules of engagement was tough at times, but the architecture was well suited to special operations and was fully compliant with the Tokyo Accords.

Paul's and Kata's services were in high demand. That fact enabled them to survive a few highly visible incidents on Camp Resolve that, for any other soldiers, would have resulted in immediate courts-martial and rotation back to the States in shame. Their luck ran out this morning, though.

"Time for some hot chow," Kata said. "And a hot shower. And a few good nights of sleep inside a guarded wire."

"Roger that," Paul said.

They had just returned from a four-day patrol. They were tired.

They turned their battle suits and undamaged soldierbots in to the motor pool and signed the damaged units over to the maintenance crew. As usual, Paul had many more damaged soldierbots than Kata to sign over.

"Damn, sir!" the maintenance chief exclaimed as he surveyed the damage. "Why is it that your soldierbots always get so chewed up?"

"I use the equipment to accomplish the mission, Chief," Paul said.

"So does Captain Vukovic," the chief said, scratching his head. "But she doesn't destroy half her platoon in the process every time."

"Yeah?" Paul said, irritation creeping into his voice. "Then put her in for a medal, Chief."

"Maybe I will, sir."

Kata shook her head. She had seen this back-and-forth many times over the past year and a half.

"Just fix the fucking robots, Chief," Paul said, still irritated. He turned to face the sergeant.

"Roger that, sir," the chief said in a voice that clearly meant, *Fuck you, sir.*

"Let's go, Paul," Kata said, pushing him ahead of her out the door. "I'm hungry."

Kata chuckled at Paul as they walked toward the living quarters area. He was still simmering.

"The guy's role is to fix the damn robots," Paul said. "So, fix the damn robots. I don't need the tactical commentary from a REMF who never goes outside the wire."

"You break a lot of robots, Paul," Kata said, weariness dripping from her voice. "Get over it."

Paul looked at her.

"So what if I break a lot of robots? It's his damn job."

She tried to ignore him.

"Fine," Paul said.

Their hooch, a rusting shipping container, was past the heavy drone pilot area in a corner of the cantonment.

The heavy drone pilots drove the big aircraft, tanks, coastal patrol ships, and other large mission platforms. Alternating between controlling missions all over the continent from their air-conditioned control pods, eating in the mess hall, or hanging out in their plush barracks, they never went outside the wire. They never got dirty. Never got shot. Never went a night without a shower or a hot meal.

It was getting close to 0800 hours, and there were several heavy pilots walking back from morning chow. Paul and Kata walked by in their dirty flight suits, caked with days of mud and splattered with enemy blood.

"Fucking limo drivers," Kata said, ensuring they could hear her.

Paul and Kata looked with disgust at the crisp and clean pilots walking back and forth with fresh cups of coffee. Boots shiny. Hair just so.

The heavy pilots sneered.

Paul and Kata smoldered.

"I wish I wasn't so tired," Paul said.

"I know." Kata nodded. "Would be so satisfying."

"But I don't think I could punch a flea right now," Paul said. "Besides, the base commander promised to throw us in the brig if we got into another fight with those guys."

"Whatever. Maybe we'd get lucky, and they'd rotate us home."

"Throw me in that briar patch, please."

They trudged on to their hooch.

"I really need some chow," Paul said.

"Roger," Kata answered. "Shower fast."

Twenty-five minutes later, Paul and Kata sat in a corner of the mess hall with their platoons, eating powdered eggs and cold French toast.

"I love French toast," Kata said, drowning her breakfast in mess hall syrup.

Paul didn't answer. He was dealing with a mouthful of eggs and hot sauce and a heart full of discontent.

He chewed slowly as he looked around the vast mess hall. He estimated there to be at least five hundred people eating and milling about. Kata and he were there late relative to the standard-mission day crowd, who normally ate chow around 0700 hours. But the place was still crowded and active.

Requests and coordinations, shouted across tables and aisles, overlay the roar of loud working breakfasts and the lower tones of one-on-one conversations. Khaki and olive green dominated, sitting together in clumps, flowing through the food stations, coming and going. But the black, green, and blue uniforms of coalition partner countries were scattered randomly throughout the scene.

The uniforms enabled the scene to be quickly decoded: a full bird colonel berated his staff at that table; a group of edgy intelligence captains spoke in whispers at this table; an exhausted heavy drone maintenance team bitched to each other as they made their way through the chow line. Everyone's duty and reason for existence was obvious in rank and insignia.

And no one else, for as far as Paul could see, other than Kata and their platoons, was here to fight on the ground, face-to-face with the enemy.

Worse, if Paul glanced quickly to his left or right, he would usually spot someone staring furtively at their augmentation scars.

For the first six months or so, it hadn't bothered them much. They were too busy and excited and scared every day. But as they got better at the job, got numb to it, the days and weeks slowed down and their disappointment grew.

As did their hatred of smoothies. The unaugmented soldiers who outnumbered them on Resolve. Sharing none of the sacrifice, danger, and filth. They bore none of the augmentation scars the Centaurs did.

"Smooth like perfect little Ken dolls," Kata would say.

But it really meant more than that. To Centaurs, a smoothie was someone who had not sacrificed like they had. They didn't fight. Never would. They were just ungrateful, undeserving, ignorant members of the bloated administrative military machine.

"Sir, we're gonna head back to the hooch and try to get some rack," Paul's first sergeant said to him.

"Roger that, Top," Paul said. "I hope I won't have to bother you guys for a day or so. You've earned the rest."

"You have too, sir."

Kata's soldiers left as well, leaving the two tired Centaur officers alone at their table.

"This fucking place," Kata said after swallowing a large bite of French toast.

"You mean this fucking military," Paul said. "It's not just this place."

Kata looked at Paul.

"All my father ever talks about from his days in uniform is the camaraderie." Paul shook his head. "About how tight he was with all his buddies. I don't feel any of that, do you?"

"No. I feel like the freak in the circus."

"Exactly. And all we do is run around the country with a bunch of fucking robots. Hell of a lot of camaraderie, that is."

"Is that why you are hard on the soldierbots? Use them up like you do?" Kata asked.

"That again?"

Kata shrugged.

"I'm just doing my job," Paul said. "And I'm over it."

"What does that mean?"

"I did it, Kata. I applied for training command."

Kata dropped her fork and looked at Paul for a long moment. He stared back at her.

She realized he was telling the truth. He was going to give up and ask for a REMF teaching assignment.

"You jackass," she said, shaking her head and picking up her fork. "I thought we talked about this?"

"I don't need to wait and see how the next assignment goes. I can do the math. It will be another robot command. I'm not interested."

"What a waste," Kata said, disappointment smothering her voice.

Paul looked at her but decided against it. They had argued about this for the past six months. There was nothing more to say.

"I just think I got here about fifty years too late," Paul had said during one of their first arguments on the topic. They were in the motor pool, getting out of their battle suits after a long mission. "I'd have been a better officer back then."

"Oh, for fuck sake," Kata said. She had no tolerance for Paul's brooding. "Stop fishing for compliments. It's annoying. You kick ass at this, and you know it."

"I know I kick ass. That's not the point."

"What is the point?"

"It's not leadership," he said. "It feels empty to me."

Now, replaying their arguments for the thousandth time in their heads, they both stewed in their seats, drank coffee, and gazed out into the mess hall with vacant eyes.

"Those fuckers," Kata said under her breath.

Paul sensed something in her voice. She wasn't arguing anymore. He looked at her. She was glaring across the mess hall.

He tracked her line of vision to a table of eight smoothie limo drivers enjoying a leisurely cup of coffee after breakfast.

"Is that them?" he asked her.

Two weeks earlier, Paul and Kata were assigned a high-value target, an insurgent leader who had been eluding the task force for a long time. Human intelligence had located the target, holed up in a hotel in the center of a small town. Though the target's strength in soldiers was small, the population was probably about fifteen thousand. Command was in constant hot water over collateral civilian casualties, so a heavy drone strike was out of the question. And they wanted him alive, if possible. So they told Paul and Kata to go in, to try to grab him, but to kill him if they had to.

It was an urban operation, with all of the associated risks and difficulties. And the target's bodyguards were known to be equipped with high-powered exos, which meant a fight. And, to top it off, the rules of engagement placed on Paul and Kata hamstrung them badly.

They got him. But by the time they got to the extraction point, they had lost one soldier, KIA, and two soldierbots, destroyed.

Intel had gotten it wrong. The town was crawling with enemy, and they'd had to fight their way out. The enemy ducked in and out of civilian buildings so Paul's and Kata's units couldn't hammer them back.

They'd lost another soldierbot on the way out.

Then the heavy drone commander had refused to pick them up because of the intense enemy activity and the degrading weather.

It wasn't the first time it had happened to them.

There were numerous protocols for tactical situations like that night. Rules of application that balanced the threat levels and risk of missions involving heavy drones, Centaurs, and any other assets. The air mission commander was tasked with weighing the situation and applying the protocols.

That night, the air mission commander had called off the extraction and directed Paul's team and Kata's to a ground linkup ten miles away.

Paul and Kata and their units had to evade another ten miles, on foot, under fire the entire way, until they were able to link up with friendly ground forces. They'd lost another human soldier on that long run.

Since that night, whenever they were back on Resolve, they had been on the lookout for the aircrew. On that morning, as they sat in the mess hall in dark moods, Paul and Kata had found them.

There was no stopping them now.

Kata stood up and glared at them. "Hey," she said sharply. "How about keeping it down over there?"

Half of their heads swiveled and looked at Kata in disbelief. Paul counted at least two majors in their group.

"My buddy and I just got back inside the wire," Kata said, pointing at Paul but continuing her challenging glare. "We're tired and not in the mood to listen to a giggle party. How about letting us eat in peace?"

It was a ridiculous thing to demand. There were still hundreds in the noisy mess hall. But it would suffice to get things rolling.

All but one of the rest of their heads snapped around. A major stood up to meet Kata's glare. He was muscular, as most of them were, since they lived inside the wire and spent a lot of downtime in the gym.

Paul stood up, making it clear they were together.

As he did so, he wondered how they appeared to the smoothies. He and Kata were scarred and dirty, bags under their eyes from a constant lack of sleep. But they embodied something that the smoothies weren't. Rather than cloistered gym muscle power, Paul and Kata radiated a twitchy, hair-trigger ruthlessness that came from personally facing down the beast outside the wire for a living.

Whatever their thoughts, Paul could see the hatred was mutual.

"How about you two go back to your hooch to eat if you're so sensitive?" the glaring major said.

"No," Kata answered, punctuating the disrespect of her not saying "sir" by shoving her hands into her flight-suit pockets. A *fuck you* in all military circles.

The major cocked his head, registering the insult.

"I think we've earned our meal here," Kata said. "Just a few weeks ago, we had to fight our way back because the chickenshit heavy drone force wouldn't come get us. Had to fight our way back. Lost two good soldiers."

"That right?" answered the major. Two more of them stood up. A female captain and a young male lieutenant.

"I think I was that air mission commander," said the last officer at the table with his back to Paul and Kata. He stood up slowly and turned around. He was a lieutenant colonel.

"Well…" Kata said, not backing down, acid in her voice. "Mission accomplished, eh?"

"You got that right, Jigsaw," the colonel said, matching Kata's acidity and turning back to his meal.

"Jigsaw" was a pejorative nickname the rest of the military used for Centaurs. It was a callout of how scarred up they look after all of the surgery. It was usually accompanied by "fucking" or "that damn" or a similar windup.

And they were fighting words. Every time.

Paul leapt across the table, but Kata was ahead of him. She was faster than him at everything.

She charged the lieutenant colonel like a crazed wolf.

Paul was right behind her.

The captain and lieutenant intercepted Kata before she got to the startled colonel. They collided and spun to the floor in a flailing pile of arms and legs. The two majors met Paul, throwing punches as fast as they could.

The mess hall crowd gathered around them quickly. But Paul and Kata were the only Centaurs. It was eight against two, and there would be no help.

It didn't matter.

The limo drivers were bigger, stronger, healthier, and more rested. But they were not used to what Paul and Kata were used to. Several minutes later, the two Centaurs stood over the smoothies, panting from exertion but satisfied with the punishment they had meted out.

That's when the military police showed up.

After two days in the brig, Paul and Kata realized this time was different. Usually, the base commander would get overruled quickly by the theater commander and have to release them to support ongoing missions. Not this time.

"Sorry, sir," Paul said when Lieutenant Colonel Andrews visited them on day three.

"Yes, sir," Kata joined in. "It was my fault. I was just—"

"Shut the fuck up," Andrews interrupted. "Do you realize you two broke three noses, dislocated a shoulder, and fractured two ribs on those guys? The heavy drone commander is more pissed off than I've ever seen him because he had to turn down several missions due to a pilot shortage. A new batch just landed on today's resupply drone."

Paul and Kata exchanged a we-may-really-be-fucked-this-time look. They had been in uniform long enough to realize that embarrassing a superior officer was a cardinal sin.

The colonel shifted on his feet, clearly enraged. "I wish I had been there," he said. "I hate those smoothie bitches."

Paul and Kata looked at each other. A slight grin appeared on Kata's face.

"But for Chrissake!" the colonel yelled, snapping Kata's smile off. "You don't stand around and gloat until the MPs show up. You're trained better than that. Get off the objective before they can fix supporting fires on your location. Beat the shit out of them and run!" He shook his head at their stupidity and then said, "I know Filson taught you guys that."

"So, when do you think we'll get out, sir?" Kata asked.

Andrews looked at them both for a long moment and then said, "Tonight."

Paul and Kata smiled.

"Thank you, sir," Paul said. "It won't happen again."

"Oh, I know it won't. You're going to be on the resupply drone when it takes back off for the States."

Paul and Kata stared, mouths open in lack of comprehension.

"Your replacements will be here in forty-eight hours. Until then, your first sergeants will command."

"What the hell, sir?" Kata said.

Andrews raised a finger. Kata got the message.

The colonel relaxed when he saw Kata spin down. He shrugged. "Your tour is over, guys. You're both good officers. And I'm going to miss the hell out of you. But this won't blow over. Besides, I've been putting Filson off for a few weeks now, and I've been able to use that to get you out of the country without a court-martial. We need to act while that window is open to us. The two of you are going back to Fort Bragg."

"Putting Filson off?" Paul asked.

"Window?" Kata asked.

But the colonel was already walking away.

"Sorry," he said over his shoulder. "But I don't do tear-jerking goodbyes."

The colonel got to the door and knocked on it. He turned around while he waited for the guard to unlock the cell.

"Tell that crazy old man 'hello' and 'fuck you' for me," he said.

ŌKAMI

Chapter Sixteen

25 September 2064
Fort Bragg, North Carolina

The large transport drone shuddered and its landing gear barked as it touched down at Pope Airfield on Fort Bragg.

"Shit," Kata said, waking up. "That was a long-ass flight."

Paul rubbed his eyes and grunted in agreement.

The aircraft taxied to its parking spot on the apron and shut down. Paul and Kata filed out of the aircraft's massive rear ramp along with the other soldiers, tired from the long flight from Africa. They boarded waiting buses and were shuttled to the flight operations terminal.

The moment they walked into the flight ops building to sign back into the country, they felt something they had not felt in almost eighteen months. People staring at their augmentation scars. Paul caught the flight ops sergeant gawking at him. The sergeant looked away, flustered.

"I'm going to wait outside," Kata said to Paul as she glared back at the smoothies.

"I'll join you."

The tired pair stood outside waiting for their ride.

"Weird, isn't it?" Paul said.

"What?"

"None of the civilians on the Horn looked at us like that," he said. "Not the kids. Not the adults. Not even the old timers. None of them."

"Your right," she said. "I don't remember ever being stared at like that except by other Americans. And fucking military personnel are the worst."

"Civilians from other countries are more familiar and at ease with us than our own supposed military comrades." Paul shook his head.

He kicked at the North Carolina grass.

Ten minutes later, a utility vehicle with its top down pulled up next to them.

"Captains Owens and Vukovic!" the driver said, waving them over. "Welcome to Fort Bragg. I'm Major Williams."

They stepped forward and shook the major's outstretched hand.

"Colonel Filson is waiting on us," he said. "Hop in."

The major drove them across post, passing by the Combat Corps headquarters compound, where Paul and Kata thought they were reporting. He turned instead toward the deserted weapons ranges.

The major grinned at their confused looks. "We're headed to the old tank range. Colonel Filson put the project out there so we would have more privacy."

"The project?" Paul asked.

"Privacy for what?" asked Kata.

The major didn't respond right away. He was driving the vehicle in manual mode, which demanded his full attention as it bounced and skidded across the gravel range road. They had entered a derelict part of the base where the roads were not well maintained. After he had safely navigated a series of washouts, the major said, "Sorry, guys. But the old man made me promise to let him brief you up. We'll be there in about twenty minutes."

Kata looked at Paul with her what-the-hell face.

Paul closed his eyes, leaned back, and tried to relax.

Twenty minutes later, deep in the bowels of Fort Bragg's expansive old World War II tank maneuver range, they turned off the main road through a thick grove of trees and stopped in front of a checkpoint.

Kata sat up. She noticed, as did Paul, that the checkpoint equipment was brand new. The advanced vehicle barrier and armored station seemed out of place on the old dirt road. Two guards strapped into advanced exoskeletons waved the major to a stop. A late-model biped tank drone behind the barrier trained its minigun on them. It looked better than any equipment Paul and Kata had back on the Horn. They eyeballed each other as the major showed the guards his ID.

"Pretty tight security for a dipshit training site," Kata said to the major as the vehicle barrier was lowered.

The major didn't answer as he goosed the gas, launching the vehicle forward and around the bend to a small compound of a dozen shipping containers. The containers were painted white and arranged in a grid four across and three deep, like a platoon in formation. An American flag flew from a pole in front of and centered on the formation of containers. Colonel Filson stood beneath the flag wearing his trademark exoskeleton flight suit, hands on his hips like he was posing for a statue artist.

"Cheesy bastard," Kata muttered to Paul. But he could tell by her smile that she was as glad to see the old man as he was.

The major came to a stop in front of the colonel and saluted him without getting out of the vehicle.

"So, these wussies really did survive the Horn?" the colonel said as he returned the major's salute.

Paul and Kata walked up to Filson, who smiled as they saluted.

"Owens and Vukovic reporting for duty, sir," Paul said.

Filson returned the salute without losing his smile, then said gruffly, "Follow me."

Filson walked to the container immediately behind the flagpole. A soldier standing outside saluted and opened the door. Paul and Kata followed the colonel inside.

Half of the container had been converted into his office. The other half was a meeting room. They turned to the right and stepped into his office. Filson closed the door and gestured at the two chairs facing his desk.

Paul and Kata gazed around as they sat down. The wall behind Filson's desk was covered with plaques, certificates, and photos, as were the other three walls. His whole career, almost thirty years in the military, was chronicled in those wall hangings. It was impressive. There were photos of him with presidents, with dirty comrades on battlefields wearing early-model exoskeletons. Certificates from every military training course under the sun, unit flags and patches and keepsakes.

Paul thought the colonel must have been out there a while to take the time to set up his office like that. It did not have the feel of a temporary assignment.

Colonel Filson opened a desk drawer and pulled out a bottle of scotch and three glasses.

"Fucking good to see you two," he said, pouring each of them a stiff shot.

"To the fallen," the colonel said as they clinked their glasses together.

"To the fallen," Paul and Kata said.

The colonel sat down, looked at the ceiling, and gathered his thoughts. Paul and Kata could tell he was arranging some kind of argument in his head. They waited for him to verbalize it.

Paul's eyes fell on an old framed photo behind the colonel over his shoulder. A group of tired soldiers in exoskeletons stood on a beach holding a Chinese flag. There were five of them. Filson wore the rank of captain, and the rest of them were lieutenants. It must have been his company command. Paul remembered that the old man had served in the first exo battalion back in the early '40s. They were the ones who were sent to dig the Chinese out of their artificial islands in the South China Sea. Their faces were exhausted, but happy. They had the look of survivors. One of them, a female lieutenant, wore a bloody bandage on her arm. Another lieutenant's head was bandaged, covering his left eye. Filson seemed to have a bloody lip. But his face was glowing with pride and relief.

"Here is the situation," the colonel said, interrupting Paul's thoughts. "I've got a hell of an opportunity for you two, and I've broken just about every rule to tee it up. Even called in a favor from Havron himself. But I am going to have to get a yes or no from you before you leave this room."

"Yes or no to what?" Kata asked.

Filson leaned forward as he continued. "For the past year, I have been leading a technology evaluation for the Combat Corps. Now we are moving into phase two of the effort, unit formation and training. If we do well enough on phase two, we will go to combat trials and deploy the most important military technology program in history."

Colonel Filson paused to let the grandness of his statement sink in. Kata began to chuckle.

"What the hell is so funny, Vukovic?" the colonel roared.

Paul stifled a smile. It felt like old times again.

"Sorry, sir." Kata tried to swallow her guffaws. "I didn't think you were serious. That sounds... um... very important." She cleared her throat and continued to dig. "And, I am honored, sir, to have been invited here to this august facility among all of your plaques and awards to—"

"Shut the fuck up, Vukovic!" The colonel jabbed an angry finger at Kata.

Paul tried to swallow the smile cracking across his face, glad the attention was on her.

"And I see that smirk, Owens!" The colonel's finger swiveled like a cannon to cover Paul. "Fuck you too!"

But then he cracked.

Filson smiled, closed his eyes, and shook his head.

"Look, I know I seem ridiculous to you guys. That's what I get for giving a shit, I guess," the colonel said with a resigned chuckle. "Well, fuck both of you. I don't care what you think about me. This project is a big deal."

"What project, sir?" Paul asked.

The colonel leaned back in his chair. "You know what the problem is with our current military AI?"

Paul and Kata sat in silence.

"The command link architecture."

More silence from Paul and Kata. They were used to Filson's lectures.

"Think about it," he said, trying to engage the two captains. "While you were over there on the Horn, you had to drive everything. Sure, your battle suits would serve up your soldierbot's weapons systems and POVs seamlessly, at your mental command. And your thoughts would drive them around and make them kill people and blow up things as if they were extensions of yourself.

But you had to do it all. It limited the scale of operation you could undertake.

"And don't get me started on the morons who want to go exclusively to an offset command link." Disdain sheathed the colonel's face. "Cowards in air-conditioned boxes half a world away from the fight.

"Fucking smoothies," Kata muttered.

Filson nodded.

"We've launched a pilot program with an old genius Japanese scientist named Dr. Musashi. He has been pioneering direct-link AI fighting systems for decades and has recently made some significant breakthroughs. He has developed an architecture that enables an augmented human to form a neural connection with an expansive team of fighting robots."

Paul and Kata sat still, not knowing what to think yet.

"His system offers the Combat Corps radically compressed kill chain time requirements with very low error rates. We are going to field two companies of his latest-generation Ōkami and put them into the fight. If it works, it will greatly reduce the manpower demand we are sagging under now. But, most importantly, it will preserve the humanity of our military."

Paul had a million questions about what the colonel had just said, but Kata beat him to it.

"Ōkami?" she asked.

"Ōkami is Japanese for 'wolf,'" Colonel Filson said. "Dr. Musashi has based his architecture on the social structure of a wolf pack. The neural link flows from an augmented human, the alpha, down to every member of the unit, including the lowest omega."

"Omega?" Kata asked.

"That is the lowest-ranking member of a wolf pack."

"So, the omegas are, like, the privates?"

"Sure," Filson said. "They are like privates."

"So, why call them wolves?"

"Who fucking cares what they are called!"

Veins bulged in Filson's forehead. Paul had forgotten how fun it was to watch Kata work the colonel.

Filson shook his head as if clearing his ears of water. Kata looked at Paul and smiled.

"Any questions so far, Owens?" the colonel asked.

"Yes, sir. A lot. But the most important is probably, why are we here? What are you asking us to do?"

"I want you guys to command the first two companies of Ōkami." The colonel shot Kata an I'll-fucking-kill-you-if-you-say-a-word glance and then looked back at Paul. "Quality of leadership of this unit is critical. It's the deciding factor. I want it to be you two."

"Leadership of the unit?" Paul asked. "It's just robots, right?"

"These things are different. Not like anything you've ever led or driven before," Filson continued slowly. "There are a lot of whiz kids in the Pentagon these days who think you can take a teenager, throw him into an air-conditioned box, and after a few hours of simulation training, he will be able to drive and fight anywhere in the world. I'll admit, the firepower these satellite-linked drones bring to bear is impressive. That fucking teenager can rain down more destruction than an entire infantry division used to.

"But I think they are leading us down the wrong path. It's not the kill chain we want to extend…it's the ethos of the American soldier. That's what Musashi is providing. A way to scale the humanity we bring to the fight."

The colonel paused to let his statement sink in, while scanning the two captains for any signs of mirth.

"I've got a window of opportunity here," he continued, "In which I can personally place the field commanders of this pilot. But it is closing. I don't want to have to deal with a bunch of Combat Corps or Department of Military bullshit. They'll fuck it up for sure.

"I told General Havron I had two volunteers who were ideal for the project. Told him they were fresh off of a combat assignment where they served with distinction." Filson paused to let Havron's name sink in. "When I told them it was you two, he agreed immediately and gave me a window to get you signed up."

"Distinction?" Kata said, turning toward Paul and smiling. "How about that?" She slapped Paul on the shoulder.

"I embellished things to the old man, Vukovic," Filson growled. "You need to understand that this is a closing window. Acquisition Corps is under a ton of pressure to let the military contractor pick the unit leadership. Havron is stiff arming them for me."

Paul and Kata nodded, tuning in to the colonel's anxiety and seriousness.

"I convinced the old man that this project should count toward all captain's course requirements," the colonel said. "So, you won't have to go to Fort Benning to study how to work with your REMF supply officer to requisition latrines. You'd be working with me on this project. And I'll be pushing hard to keep us moving fast so no one can fuck us up along the way."

The colonel leaned back in his chair, satisfied he had made his case.

"So, I need to know right now if you guys want the job or not."

"You going tell him?" Kata asked Paul.

"Tell me what?"

Paul looked at his feet. He really didn't want to tell the colonel he had applied to training command. Not at that moment.

"You mean, tell me that he applied to training command?" the colonel said in a mocking tone as he looked back at Kata and shook his head in disappointment.

Paul looked up from his feet, surprised.

The colonel glared at him.

Paul glanced at Kata, who shrugged and shook her head to indicate she had not told him.

Paul looked back at the colonel.

"The Combat Corps is a small place," he said. "I hear everything. Especially about my favorites."

Paul didn't know what to say.

"Why?" the colonel asked.

"It's a long story, sir," Paul said, not wanting to get into it or argue. Suddenly, he felt very tired from the long flight.

Filson just nodded and waited for Paul to continue.

There was no way out of it, so Paul said, "It's just not what I expected, sir. It's not what I want to do anymore."

"Look, Paul, combat is tough," Filson said. "No one likes it. Anyone who says differently is lying to you or crazy."

"That's not what I'm talking about, sir."

"What the hell are you talking about?"

"It's all the robots," Kata interjected.

"No," Paul said, irritated. "It's not that there are so many robots, it's that there are so few humans, so little camaraderie. I don't hate robots. I would just rather serve with and lead people."

Paul looked back and forth between Kata and the colonel, seeking recognition, an indication they understood.

He didn't find it. So, he just shrugged and said, "I think I would be a good instructor."

"You would be a great instructor," the colonel said in a measured and genuine tone Paul was not expecting. "But that is not what we need right now," Filson quickly added. "We need your leadership out there, outside the wire."

Filson pointed notionally to the frontier. To the Horn of Africa, South America, and all the places the military was engaged.

Paul looked back at his feet. It felt terrible to let the colonel down, to let Kata down. He was torn.

After a few heartbeats of silence, the colonel said, "Paul, you have to do what you think is best for you. And I will support whatever that is a hundred percent. I've actually already talked to Colonel Godfrey at O.A.T. I told him I was going to try to talk you out of it. But that if I couldn't, you would be the best instructor on his staff, and he would be a moron not to take you. If you walk away from this, we'll be square, I promise. If you say yes, you'll lead the most unique unit in the military. You'll be pioneers. Both of you."

The colonel looked in turn at Paul and Kata.

"What else happens if we say yes?" Kata asked.

"You'll skip lunch and go directly to the hospital for pre-op. Your augmentation surgeries are scheduled for tomorrow morning."

"But we're already augmented," she said.

"Not for Ōkami."

Kata frowned.

"I've been told it's just tweaks," the colonel added.

"And if I say no?" Paul asked.

"We'll head back to main post for lunch and then head over to the airfield to get you to Benning. You will meet with Colonel Godfrey tomorrow. No one the wiser."

Filson shifted his gaze to Kata. "You and I can talk about what would be next for you. I would not blame you if you did not want to do this without Owens."

The colonel stood up.

"This is a volunteer gig, guys. There is no penalty for saying no."

Paul and Kata started to get up also, but he gestured at them to stay seated.

"You two stay and hash it out. But I need a decision when you come out of this office," he said, walking to the door.

He paused and looked at Paul.

"You say you are seeking camaraderie, Owens? You need to ask yourself if you really know what camaraderie is. Because I'm your comrade," Colonel Filson said, pointing at himself with his thumb. "Vukovic is your comrade," he added, pointing at her. "And we need you with us on this." He pointed at Paul.

Then he left and closed the door behind him.

Chapter Seventeen

Paul woke slowly. His eyes fluttered as they tried to focus. The soft hum of health monitoring devices emanated from the head of his bed. After a few minutes, he could make out the ceiling tiles of his hospital room at Womack Army Medical Center on Fort Bragg.

Paul also saw an old Japanese man sitting in the lone chair in the opposite corner of his room. The elderly man was reading a book and did not notice Paul waking up.

Paul stared at him in a daze as the anesthetic receded. The top of the man's head was bald, and the white hair on his temples was closely cropped, as was his goatee. His eyebrows, though, were dark. They gave his thin face a youthful and expressive quality that made it impossible for Paul to guess his age. He could have been fifty, or a hundred and fifty.

The old man's body was slight but not frail, and he looked tiny in the red upholstered chair. He wore kakis and a dark, short-sleeved, button-down shirt. A pocket protector with several pens bulged from his breast pocket.

Paul looked at him for ten minutes. The man never looked up. So, Paul was surprised when he said, still without raising his head, "How do you feel?"

"Terrible," Paul said.

"Understandable," the old man said, turning the page of his book. "But the procedure went very well. We were able to use a lot of your previous augmentation architecture. I think your recovery will be quick."

The old man closed his book and stood up, grabbing his leather satchel.

He walked slowly toward Paul's bed. Closing the distance did not make him seem any bigger.

Paul tried to sit up, but the familiar white-hot metal railroad spike of pain drove between his eyes and through the middle of his skull.

"Shit," he said, wincing. Paul laid his head back on his pillow. He grimaced and waited for the pain to subside.

"But not without pain," the old man said as he put his hand on Paul's chest. "Patience, Paul. You cannot hasten this or any other part of our task together."

"Why does it hurt so bad?" Paul asked between groans. "You said you were able to use a lot of our previous augmentation."

"We were," he said. "We are leveraging the brain-to-machine interface components, primarily the neuron-to-data conversion and transmission architecture. That spared you from a lot of pain, though I'm sure you don't believe me at this moment. Most of your discomfort is from the integration of the neural link module. The procedure requires us to drill through the parietal bone on the back of your skull to establish the interface. Then the module must be permanently attached."

Paul reached his hand back as the old man spoke, but all he felt was bandaging. His head throbbed when he moved, so he put his arm back by his side, face tight with pain.

"When your bandages are removed in a week or so, you will be able to feel the module there. It's just a little smaller than a deck of cards. I am confident you will be pleased with what it enables you to do. For now, though, Paul, please rest."

The old man left his hand on Paul's chest until the pain subsided enough for him to unclench his jaw.

"Good," he said. "I'll come back in a few days when you are feeling better. Please rest."

Paul heard the old man's soft footsteps as he walked away toward the door.

"Who are you?' Paul asked without opening his eyes.

"I am Dr. Musashi."

Chapter Eighteen

Eugene walked into the lobby of the Four Seasons. It was almost ten o'clock in the morning on a Saturday, and the brunch crowd was building in the restaurant. The bright midmorning sun spilled through the lobby windows. Most people sipped coffee and chatted while they waited for their tours or activities to begin. A couple of suited business types glared at their phones, not enjoying their weekend as much as the others.

It was busy, and it took Eugene a moment to spot his sister in a large leather chair in the sitting area in the back. He smiled at the sight. In her jeans, white T-shirt, and ball cap, she looked more like a traveling grad student than a military-weapon-systems entrepreneur.

She held a large glass of red wine in one hand and her phone in the other. Staring at her phone, she did not see Eugene yet. He walked toward her, studying her as he approached.

She looked tired. A pang of empathy welled within him. He wished she could let the family go like he had. Or, more accurately, run away from it like he had.

He stepped up to Fiona and stood over her, his feet inches from hers.

Still, she did not notice him.

"Hello, Fi," Eugene said.

"Oh, shit!" she said, jumping to her feet and hugging him. "When did you get here? I didn't see you walk in."

"Of course you didn't," Eugene said, holding on to the hug. "You only have eyes for your phone."

"True enough," Fiona said, gesturing at the chair next to hers as she sat down.

She waved at the waiter.

"Coffee, please," Eugene told him with a smile. "Cream and sugar."

Eugene eyeballed Fiona's glass of wine.

"What?" she asked.

"It's not even ten a.m."

"Fuck you," she said, rolling her eyes. "It's almost four in the afternoon my time."

She took a large swallow from her glass. She looked nervous to Eugene. It made him nervous.

The waiter appeared and set the coffee down between them.

"How was your train?" Fiona asked as Eugene dropped a brown sugar cube into his coffee, followed by a heavy pour of cream.

"Fine. I love the train."

Eugene leaned back in his chair and took a sip of coffee.

"You look like shit," he said to her.

"Not going to argue with you there," she said, sinking into her chair. "I'm tired. Seems like I've been tired for a few years now."

"How is it going?"

"It's going well. Really well. Some very exciting things about to pop."

"Good."

They both watched the lobby for a moment as Eugene waited for her to speak. When she had called the previous week and asked him to meet her, she'd told him to name the spot. He'd picked Prague. It was a mutual favorite. And far enough from Italy. He was worried about her and knew there was an ask coming, but he had not pressed her. Fiona never responded well to that.

"You want to go for a walk?" Fiona asked. "Best walking city in the world."

She looked at him with a forced smile.

"For fucksake, Fi," Eugene said.

"What?"

"I can't stand it." Eugene leaned forward and set his coffee down. "What is going on? You need more money, don't you?"

"I do."

Eugene sighed heavily and stood up. He walked away from Fiona, toward the lobby.

"Shit," Fiona muttered, following after him.

Eugene walked out of the hotel onto the cobblestoned roundabout between the hotel and the next building. He took a left toward the river.

Fiona hurried to the door.

"Will you watch my bag?" she asked the doorman. She handed him a fifty-euro bill. "Black roll-on, back against that leather chair."

"Yes, ma'am," he said as she pointed at the bag.

Fiona jogged to catch up to her brother.

"Eugene!" she called after him. "Eugene, please."

She grabbed his arm, but he jerked it away.

Fiona followed him as he walked along the stone walkway above the river. A couple of swans paddled in formation below them, hoping for food.

Eugene stopped and turned to face the river. He clutched the railing with both hands.

"Why didn't you just fucking call me?" he asked Fiona as she stepped next to him.

"Seemed like I should ask in person."

"Why make me come to Prague?"

"Because you love Prague. And you told me not to bring family business to Mio Posto."

Eugene shook his head and mumbled, "So selfish."

Fiona put a hand on his. He didn't jerk it away.

"How bad is it?"

"It's not bad. I meant what I said, Eugene. We are so close. It's just a timing thing."

"Isn't it always?" Eugene said in a weary voice, turning to look at Fiona.

She nodded.

"How much?"

"Fifty million."

Eugene laughed.

Fiona scowled.

"Are you kidding me?" Eugene asked her.

She just shook her head.

"Well, you came to the wrong bank, sister," Eugene said. Fiona thought she heard relief in his voice. "I don't have that kind of cash, and you know that. You know how illiquid I am."

He looked at her with an apologetic face.

"I'm so sorry, Fi," he said. "I wish I could help. But, really, most of my money is in Mio—"

He stopped talking as if someone had slapped him.

Fiona looked back at him. Now hers was the apologetic face.

Eugene shook his head slowly.

She waited.

"You would ask me for that?" he whispered.

"No," she said. "Just to use it as collateral. You keep it, of course."

"Collateral?"

"Just until I get them paid. And for no more than a year."

"How do you know they would even go for that?" he asked.

"They will."

Another slap.

"You've already talked to them about it?" Eugene yelled, startling passersby and the hungry swans.

"Yes," Fiona said.

She had met with Talisman Partners a little more than forty-eight hours earlier. Fiona pushed the memory out of her head. They had been too accommodating. They sensed their increasing advantage over her.

Eugene's eyes were wide. He looked at her with heartbreak.

"I just pitched it conceptually," she said. "I didn't want to bother you with this kind of ask if it wasn't going to work."

Fiona stepped closer.

"Eugene, I would not ask if there was any other way. If I had any other option, I would take it. But you are my last chance. And this is not a gamble. It is going to happen. And when it does, you will make enough money to buy ten Mio Postos."

Eugene shook his head. "I don't want ten Mio Postos. I just wanted to be left alone on the one I have."

Fiona said nothing.

A tear ran down Eugene's cheek.

Fiona's heart filled with regret. But she was in it now. Committed.

And what she had said was the cruel truth. She had no other option.

Eugene stepped away from the railing and walked past Fiona back to the hotel.

Fiona leaned on the railing overlooking the dirty river for a long time.

Chapter Nineteen

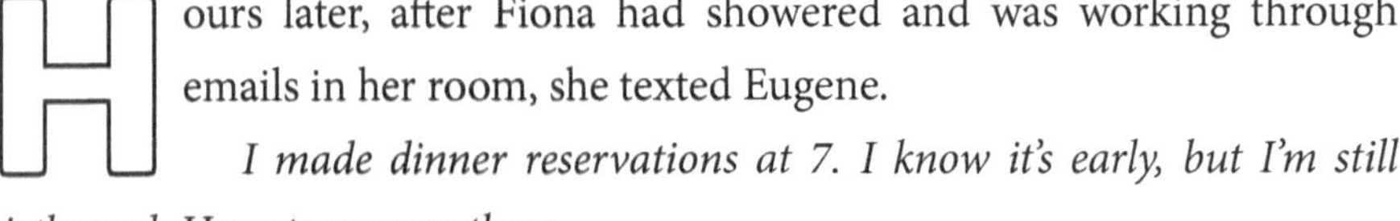ours later, after Fiona had showered and was working through emails in her room, she texted Eugene.

I made dinner reservations at 7. I know it's early, but I'm still jetlagged. Hope to see you there.

Fiona got to the restaurant a few minutes early. She slipped the hostess a hundred-euro bill and was seated at a table by one of the windows. She ordered a glass of wine and scanned the room as she waited for Eugene. The chic, dimly lit restaurant was full. Russians, Chinese, Europeans, and Americans chatted as they ate and shared cell-phone pictures of their day in the city. It was Saturday night, and the crowd was festive.

She was not.

Fiona looked out the window, across the river. Brightly lit, the squat stone arches of the Charles Bridge blazed orange as they crossed the dark water of the Vltava River. Prague Castle stood silvery and proud above it all, basking in spotlights striking it from every angle. Moments like this made Fiona reconsider her disdain for European capitals that heavily regulated airborne drone activity. Cities like Prague should lie beneath dark skies.

She remembered walking across the Charles Bridge and up to the castle on one of the trips here with her parents and Eugene. The thought of her father, alive and loving, made her sad. She took a long sip of wine.

Fiona set her glass down and tried to do the math. She must have been ten years old at the time. That would have made Eugene nine.

She smiled, recalling how cranky Eugene had gotten about halfway up.

Fiona looked around for Eugene. No sign of him yet.

She finished her wine.

She checked her watch. It was 7:15 p.m.

He's right to punish me, and I know he hates eating early, she thought. *I'm betting he shows at 7:30.*

She signaled the waiter for another glass.

At 7:45, she started to get irritated and asked the waiter for some bread.

Last thing I need to do tonight is be hangry, she thought.

At eight p.m., she ordered dinner and ate it with her third glass of wine.

I deserved that, she texted him when she got back to her room. *I'm sorry. I'll head back tomorrow. Forget I asked.*

She rose early the next morning, her body still on East Coast time.

After showering, she sat at the small desk in her room and texted Pruden. *We're fucked. It's a no go.*

Are you kidding? he texted back immediately. *You said it was a sure thing.*

I was wrong. Then she added: *I'm kind of glad.*

I'm happy you are glad, Pruden texted back. *Because you are going to be worse than broke in a few months.*

Fiona almost texted, *Fuck you.* But she deleted it and then typed, *I'll figure something out.* But she deleted that also.

She sat at the desk for another ten minutes, staring at her phone and trying to think of what to say.

But she was stuck. No pithy texts. No business ideas. No hope.

And now, in addition to losing her fortune, she might have lost her brother. At a minimum, she had damaged their relationship.

Fiona stood up and packed her bag.

She asked for a car to the airport at the front desk as she checked out.

"Also," she said, "please ensure that Mr. Eugene Malloy's bill is charged to me. I don't want him paying for a thing during his stay."

"Mr. Malloy has already checked out, ma'am," the receptionist said.

"Oh," Fiona responded.

"And he's already taken care of his bill."

"Oh."

Fiona finished checking out.

"Your car will be here in about ten minutes," the receptionist said, handing her the receipt. "Please have a seat in the lobby, and we'll come find you when it arrives."

"Thank you."

Fiona walked back to the same leather chair she'd sat in the morning before. She was exhausted and felt the stab of regret in her gut. She felt foolish. She looked around the lobby for the waiter.

"Wine is not going to help, Fi," Eugene said, stepping up behind her.

"Eugene? What?" Fiona stammered as he sat in the chair next to her. "But you checked out?"

"I'm heading back today," he said. "This has not been a good visit for me."

"I am so sorry, Eugene. I'm so close to succeeding, and I'm so close to failing. I'm on a high wire flailing my arms, and I'm scared. I shouldn't have dragged you into it. Please forgive me."

Eugene looked at his sister. She looked even worse than yesterday.

"I'm going to do it, Fi," he said, turning his eyes to the floor.

Fiona's brow furrowed. "I don't follow," she said.

"I'm going to do it," he said, refusing eye contact with her. "Have your people get in touch with my estate manager. I have already spoken with him. He is expecting their call."

"Eugene, I—"

"Stop," Eugene said, interrupting her. "I would do anything for you. If you needed my help and I wasn't there for you, I would never forgive myself."

Eugene paused, still looking at the floor. Fiona saw that he was shaking. He was furious.

"And you should never forgive yourself for asking this of me." Eugene stood up as he said, "I won't."

Fiona reached for his hand. He let her take it but did not look back at her.

"I am begging you, Fi. Please do not fail."

Eugene pulled his hand back and walked out of the hotel.

Chapter Twenty

20 October 2064
Fort Bragg, North Carolina

After about a month of recovery and academics, Paul and Kata were finally introduced to their units.

"Damn," Kata said as a group of over two hundred Ōkami soldierbots marched into view. "Look at those things."

Paul and Kata stood under the flagpole on Filson's compound late in the day, as the soldierbots came marching back from the small-arms range. They walked five across in two long company formations, their strides in perfect sync.

At eight feet, they stood a little taller than a human soldier in a battle suit. They were humanoid, with two arms, two hands with opposable thumbs, two legs, a torso and a spheroid head. Their proportions were lean and graceful, and they moved with a fluid efficiency that suggested terrific power and speed.

"What do you think?" Colonel Filson asked as he and Dr. Musashi walked up behind them.

"Beautiful," Kata said.

"Yeah," Paul agreed grudgingly. He did not say it, but to him they looked like large, slender mythical creatures, not mere robots.

The doctor smiled.

"That is titanium-reinforced ceramic armor they're sporting," the colonel said. "See the hint of red iridescence on them with this setting sun behind us? In a neutral light, they are actually matte gray. In a bright desert sun, they seem almost white, and at night, they are nearly black. The engineers tell me it is a result of the bonding and curing process. They were worried about the soldierbots' appearance and were trying to figure out a way to paint them, but I stopped them.

"'Hell no,' I said. 'You're not going to cover these guys in paint! Every great warrior tribe has a trademark look as they join the battle. The Comanche horseman. The Roman centurion. The army ranger. I like the way these guys look a little different depending on the light they're in. Don't fuck it up!'"

Paul and Kata nodded in agreement with the colonel as the front half of the formation filed past.

"Their humanoid configuration is also practical," the colonel said. "They've been designed to use all of the equipment a battle-suited soldier can. They can fit in most vehicles and aircraft, and can pick up and fight with any of your weapons, from pistol to minigun to rocket launcher. The vision is that, after we have proven ourselves, Ōkami will be part of every unit in the Combat Corps."

As the Ōkami formation passed by, the front row of five separated from each company. The rest of the long column continued toward the helipad a quarter mile away.

The two groups of five marched over to Paul and Kata, halting in front of them in two small formations.

"These are your betas," the doctor said, stepping in front of Paul and Kata and gesturing at the two groups of robots standing at attention. "Through them, you will command the rest of your Ōkami."

Paul studied the Ōkami standing in front of him. They were different from the large group of soldierbots still marching away. Their torsos were bigger and shoulders broader.

The beta's heads were also different. The configuration of their eight visual sensors, aligned approximately where a person's eyes would be, created the sense of underlying cheekbones and elongated their heads slightly. Four small antennae blades extended from the rear top of their heads. About six inches in length, the antennae blades hinted at the feathered headdress of a Native American warrior.

Paul smiled, liking the vibe and doubting it was coincidental.

"Alpha Company is to the left, Kata," Dr. Musashi said. "And Bravo Company is to the right, Paul."

Paul and Kata looked at each other and then at the doctor.

"Please," he said. "Introduce yourselves."

"Go on," Colonel Filson added, amused by their hesitance.

Kata walked toward Alpha Company.

Paul walked over to the Bravo Company betas and stepped up to the first one in the rank. Dr. Musashi followed behind him.

"This is your first sergeant," Dr. Musashi said.

"M-458, this is Captain Owens," the doctor said. "He is your alpha."

"It's good to meet you, sir," the first sergeant said as she saluted. "And an honor to serve under you."

Paul nodded and looked at Dr. Musashi, who beamed as he watched the interaction. It was a big moment for him; his creations were reporting for duty for the first time. The doctor lingered, waiting to hear what Paul would say next.

Dr. Musashi had told Paul and Kata that morning that they could name their soldierbots if they wanted to. Until that day, they had been referred to by the last three digits of their serial number. Kata, the history buff, had decided to name hers after Civil War generals. She named her first sergeant "Grant."

"Very good, 458," Paul said to his first sergeant before stepping to the next beta.

"What is your serial number?" Paul asked.

"Sir, I am M-902," it answered in a male voice.

The doctor walked away in disappointment.

Kata gave Paul grief later.

"Why are you such an asshole?" she asked. "Those things are going to fight with you. Give them damn names."

"I don't need to name the equipment," he told her.

Chapter Twenty-One

"Where is the rest of the unit?" Kata asked, the next morning after chow. She and Paul stood next to the flagpole as their betas stood at attention.

"Yeah," Paul said. "I thought we had a hundred in each company?"

"You do," the colonel said. "They'll be back in about a month and a half."

"Where did they go?" Paul asked.

"Nowhere," the colonel said. "They'll be back when you get a handle on the neural link."

Paul and Kata looked at each other nervously. What insanely fatiguing training event was about to happen?

"There are three fundamental components to Musashi's architecture," Filson explained. "The first is the in-head display interface, which integrates vast amounts of information into a rational analysis and display context.

"The IHD is a game-changer," Filson said with excitement. "You will be able to view maps, imagery, and other points of view as if they were right in front of your eyes, when they are actually being piped right into your visual cortex. It will give you guys near-perfect situational awareness. After some training, you will be able to call up and move cursors around on the maps viewed in your head. You will be able to designate targets, LZs, routes, whatever you want.

"The neural link is the second foundational component. It is an extended brain-to-machine protocol that removes all friction from the communication, command, and control of the Ōkami. Your thoughts and commands are shared with them securely, at the speed of light. And their thoughts, points of view, and actions are shared with you the same way.

"Finally, the Ōkami betas," the colonel said, gesturing over his shoulder at the tall graceful robots standing at attention. "It is through them that you both will command your units. I don't know how any of that quantumtronic computing and artificial intelligence shit works, but these betas are different, higher functioning. They understand intent, strategy, and risk assessment. And they possess a level of tactical creativity that is borderline creepy.

"The sum of all that is that you will no longer being controlling drones like teenagers with joysticks. You will be back to giving your troops commands and intent. Take that hill. Cover my flank. Meet me here at this time instead of yanking and banking drones through the air. Don't get me wrong. Yanking and banking is fun, but it's not where your head needs to be when you are leading a unit in combat. It is not scalable."

Filson gestured at the group of humans and Ōkami to follow him.

"We found out quickly that the human brain could not handle a direct link connection to very many AIs at one time," Filson explained as they walked toward the rear of the compound. "Five seems to be the limit. So, we leveraged the army's old rifle company structure. The five direct-link connections are your first sergeant and four platoon sergeants."

Colonel Filson gestured over his shoulder at the betas marching close behind Paul and Kata.

"Through them, you will be able to command your entire wolf pack, including all soldierbots and extension platforms."

"Extension platforms?" Kata asked.

"Your betas don't have the networking limitations of the human brain." Filson said. "Each of them can link to hundreds of extension platforms, fighting robots that are designed to extend your sensor and weapons reach."

The colonel halted and turned suddenly.

Paul and Kata skidded to a stop.

Their beta teams stopped behind them.

The colonel walked up to Grant and pointed at his head.

"Those bladed antennae on their heads are not just for show," the colonel said. "That's probably the most expensive antennae and networking hardware ever produced."

Paul and Kata looked at the colonel, trying to decide if that was more Filson hyperbole.

He read their circumspection and stepped toward them.

"The strategies, intentions, and plans that form in this dim melon of yours," Filson said, putting his hand on top of Paul's head, "flow from your brain to the hardware we've implanted in you to your betas."

Filson took his hand off of Paul's head and pointed at the tall, sleek Ōkami.

"And they are networked to every soldierbot and extension platform in your unit. They pass it on seamlessly and immediately. Those soldierbots you saw yesterday are amazing," the colonel continued. "They truly behave like a wolf pack. On missions, they'll split into packs that latch on to you and your betas. They will mirror, augment, and iterate off of whatever you do, striving always to achieve your intent.

"There are numerous other XP configurations as well. You've got several versions of tracked and wheeled systems, a couple different types of airborne systems, and even some waterborne configurations. Once you get comfortable with the architecture and are fluid with the linkages, you will be able to effectively command hundreds of fighting robots in any environment."

Paul shifted on his feet. It all sounded a bit daunting and far-fetched.

The colonel interrupted Paul's doubts by turning and motioning them all to follow again.

They walked to the last building in the compound, and the colonel held the door open. Inside, Paul and Kata found six small tables, each with two chairs. Two of Dr. Musashi's engineers stood in the back of the room in white lab coats.

Colonel Filson did not wait for Paul's and Kata's questions. He looked at the betas behind them.

"You guys take a seat," he said to them. "Pair off. One Alpha Company and one Bravo Company beta per table."

Paul watched as the Ōkami moved to sit down. Despite their size, they moved easily in the cramped, cluttered building.

The colonel pointed at the one table remaining empty.

Kata shrugged at Paul, and they sat down.

"Step one is to develop and strengthen your ability to form a neural link to your betas," the colonel said, walking over to Paul and Kata's table. "We have to build that into an unbreakable but flexible link that can withstand the pressure of combat."

The colonel gestured at the two engineers. One of them walked over and handed the colonel a new deck of cards, still in the wrapper, as the other walked around and placed a deck on each table.

"The hardware installed in those otherwise empty heads of yours can establish the neural link over short distances," Filson said, tapping the side of his head. "Your battle suits will push that signal out, far over the horizon. But we'll get to that when you have developed a minimum level of competence."

Filson took the wrapper off the deck of cards he held, as more engineers entered and began putting monitoring equipment on the betas.

"We'll start with Texas Hold 'em," he said, placing the cards on the table between Paul and Kata.

Minutes later, ten sleek, humanoid, killer robots sat in silence, paired off in six separate one-on-one card games. In the next room, Dr. Musashi, Colonel Filson, and the engineers monitored Paul and Kata's progress.

Paul and Kata were not allowed to speak. They had to form links to their betas while playing each other in their own poker game. The betas were not allowed to bet, discard, deal, or do anything until they had successfully flashed the situation to Paul or Kata and received direction.

It was the least fun poker Paul and Kata had ever played.

Chapter Twenty-Two

Paul and Kata played poker with their betas all day, every day, for the first week. It was disorienting and took a while to get used to. Paul and Kata each had five Ōkami trying to flash in to get approval for their next move. At first, it was very slow.

Paul would feel a tingle, then an image would flash into his head. He would miss about half of what they were trying to send and would try to call it up again. He would get halfway through his memory of it before someone else would flash in. It took him ten minutes to respond to anyone. It was tedious.

Gradually, Paul and Kata started to feel stronger. The links were quicker to establish and more durable. The information they got in each flash doubled, then tripled, then increased tenfold. They developed the ability to prioritize what their minds called up first.

This phase of training lasted six weeks. Paul and Kata spent all day, from reveille to taps, with their betas. After the poker, Dr. Musashi and his team changed it up. Every day a new task, designed to test and strengthen their ability to form and maintain neural links, was thrown at them.

Paul always had to stifle a chuckle when he saw the doctor. Musashi wore the most ill-fitting, baggy military uniform Paul had ever seen. The colonel was trying to help him blend in. But the wise old Japanese engineer looked ridiculous, lost in a sea of camouflage fabric. And always with a pocket protector.

A few weeks into the training, the doctor started walking over each day and saying, "Hello, Paul and Kata. How are you?" Usually, Musashi had a specific question about some technical performance metric his team was chasing down that day. They would talk about it, and the doctor would take notes in Japanese on his ever-present notepad. Then Musashi would close the pad, put it back in his breast pocket, and say, "What is on your mind today, Captains?"

At first, Paul would drill into him. "Why do they do this?" he would ask. Or: "Why can't I get them to do that?"

But, as time went on, Paul's curiosity focused on the doctor himself.

"How did you get started developing this architecture in the first place?" Paul asked the doctor one night as the two of them stepped out of the small mess hall.

"The early days of AI were challenging for the military," Musashi answered. "Balance was elusive. Fielded systems tended to skew one of two ways. Either the robots fought too aggressively, methodically killing everything as quickly as possible, or they were too calculating and protective of human life, particularly friendlies. Each of these extremes was bad and, I believed, the result of trying to optimize outcomes rather than ethos."

He continued as they strolled through the cantonment. "So, years ago, when quantumtronic processors first became available, I began experimenting with the incorporation of the principles of Bushido."

"Bushido?" Paul asked in a skeptical tone.

"Yes," he answered, not taking offense. "Have you ever studied it?"

"Closest we came to that at the academy was *Hagakure*."

The old doctor grimaced.

"Better than nothing, I suppose. Do you know the seven principles of Bushido?"

"No."

"They are: Integrity. Respect. Heroic Courage." Dr. Musashi held up another of his thin fingers as he said each principle. "Honor. Compassion. Honesty and Sincerity. Duty and Loyalty."

"Aren't some of those repeats?"

"Don't play the fool, Paul."

"I'm sorry, Doc. I was expecting you to give me a complex mathematical answer I could only half follow. Not a philosophical response."

Dr. Musashi looked at Paul without irritation. He seemed amused.

"It seems a little fluffy to me." Paul shrugged as respectfully as he could. "I just don't see how you get all that noble stuff into a machine's brain. And supposedly you've blended all that together with the social structure of a wolf pack? So, Bushido-adherent wolves?"

Paul hesitated, realizing that sarcasm was creeping into his voice. He did not want to disrespect the doctor.

"I guess what I mean is," Paul said, recalibrating his demeanor, "how do you know that's really what drives them?"

"Come with me," Musashi said, abruptly changing direction before Paul could object. He walked to one of the shipping containers in the middle of the cantonment.

They entered on one end and stepped into Dr. Musashi's office, which took up half the structure. His sleeping quarters took up the other half.

The doctor had used wood from old pallets to construct floor-to-ceiling shelves on every wall of his office. Books and electronic components stuffed them all. A small desk was pushed against one of the longer sidewalls, nestled into a gap in the expedient shelving.

The doctor grabbed a jar off his desk and handed it to Paul.

"Do you know what that is?"

"Sure, Doc." Paul nodded at the gray mass in amber liquid. "It's a human brain."

"Correct." Dr. Musashi took the jar back and held it up to the light, studying the preserved organ. "Three pounds of tissue that contains everything a person is—or was. Their memories, beliefs, fears, loves." He set the jar on the corner of his desk and turned to his shelves. "Now let me show you something else."

He returned and placed a heavy metal sphere, about the size of a softball, in Paul's hands.

"What's this?" Paul asked.

"That is an early-generation Ōkami brain and memory sphere."

Paul turned it over in his hands as the doctor spoke. It felt like holding a cannonball that had been fired in battle and recovered years later. The sphere was a dull-gunmetal color with dark splotches across its rough and pitted surface. It had a deep dent in one side.

"A little banged up, isn't it?" Paul said.

"Yes," the doctor said. "Their spheres should be perfectly smooth and shiny, like a mirror."

"It's heavy."

"Fifteen pounds," the doctor said. "The current generation weighs slightly less, but is still well over ten pounds.

"So, it stores their memories, I'm guessing?"

Musashi smiled.

"Everything about you that truly matters, Paul, in your head and in your heart," the doctor put a gentle finger to Paul's temple, and then to his chest. "Resides in here for them."

Musashi rested his hand on the sphere. "Belief, knowledge, values, skill, volition and, yes, memories."

"How did you get all that in here?"

Musashi chuckled. "I'm not sure."

Paul looked at him, an eyebrow raised.

"Some essential Quantumtronic elements. Memory capacity. Purpose and discernment…"

Musashi's voice trailed off, his eyes resting on the sphere in Paul's hands.

"In many ways, that is my life's work," Musashi said, almost to himself.

"And you don't know how it works?"

"My arrogance goes only so far."

A peaceful smile broke across the doctor's face as he met Paul's skeptical gaze.

"So, you are asking Kata and I to fight with and depend on something you're not even sure works?"

Doctor Musashi's smile widened as he took the sphere from Paul and placed it next to the jarred brain. He gestured at the two disembodied objects on his desk.

"Which of those two has killed people?"

"I don't know."

"And which of them contains the principles of Bushido? The values of a soldier?"

Paul shrugged.

"One of these brains murdered three people before being captured and executed," Musashi said. "The other flew an aerial drone that took extensive damage while covering the retreat of an outnumbered American infantry unit." The doctor picked up the heavy, dented metal sphere. "Then, when the retreating infantry unit was slowed down by a difficult river crossing, the drone crashed itself into the advancing enemy—destroying two armored ground drones, killing a dozen enemy soldiers, and successfully delaying the enemy's advance so that the infantry could escape." The doctor handed the sphere back to Paul as he asked, "The military spent a lot of time training and educating you, correct?"

"Yes."

"When you were finally commissioned as an officer, how did they know they had succeeded in inculcating ethical military leadership?"

Paul raised his eyes from the sphere and met Dr. Musashi's earnest gaze.

"You know from their actions, Paul. It's the only way to know. About any of us."

Paul nodded, turning the dented and scarred sphere over in his hands.

"How did you get this one back?"

"Several days later, when the Americans advanced back across the river, they recovered the drone's wreckage. They extracted its sphere and got it back to me."

The doctor's eyes rested on the sphere.

"These spheres are very tough," he said. "Often, even after extensive damage to their host system, we can extract the memories, data and other important elements from the sphere."

"You're able to bring them back? Reboot them in a new body?"

Musashi's eyes narrowed.

"Alas, we've had only limited success at partially reconstituting a soldier's identity. But we are often able to extract memory and data. We save, analyze and add it to our learning models. This has proven very valuable for our program."

"Were you able to extract this unit's memories?"

"No." Dr. Musashi took the sphere from Paul's hands and returned it to its place on the shelf. "The damage was too extensive."

Chapter Twenty-Three

"We shoulda known," Paul said as he looked at the large rucksack at his feet. It was packed with food, water, and the rest of what he would need for the next ten days. He was not looking forward to hoisting it onto his back, and he dreaded marching up and down the mountains of North Carolina for eighty miles with it. "It's always field time with Colonel Filson."

"I'm telling you," Kata said with anger. "If I'd known what his training plan was, I would never have signed up. And, you're right, we should have known."

"I wanted to transfer to training command," Paul mumbled.

"Fuck you," Kata said.

"Good morning, Captains!" Colonel Filson said in a cheery voice as he walked into the light of the cantonment flagpole.

"Oh, good morning, sir," Kata said. "We were just wondering: How do we get out of this chickenshit outfit?"

"Same way you get out of all my outfits, Vukovic," he answered with more cheeriness. "Just fucking quit."

It was four in the morning on a Monday, and phase two of unit training was about to begin. Paul and Kata were briefed on the phase-two schedule the previous day after evening chow. It was classic Filson, and they were not happy.

It was too similar to O.A.T for their liking: a lot of hiking up and down mountains and through other daunting environments with task stations along the way. It was just Paul and Kata and their betas. No wolf packs.

"Is this really the most appropriate training for next-generation technology like the Ōkami?" Kata had asked as the arduous ninety-day curriculum lay on the mess hall table between them and Filson.

"Yeah," Paul had said. "You said we were going to be leading the most advanced stuff ever. This looks like you are training us to fight in World War I again."

"See you in the morning, Captains," the colonel had said, rolling up the large calendar printout. "I'd get some rest if I were you."

Now, as Paul and Kata's breath condensed in the cold Carolina air, their betas marched out of the shadows with Dr. Musashi. A dozen engineers in puffy winter parkas followed close behind. They joined Paul and Kata in the soft light of the flagpole and stood at attention.

The engineers began a last maintenance check of the Ōkami. Paul and Kata checked their canteens and rucksacks. Soon, Colonel Filson would give the command, and they would march to the helipad for their flight west to the mountains.

The colonel walked up to one of the engineers and handed him a piece of paper.

"I want you to remove everything on that list from each soldier," Filson said, gesturing at the Ōkami betas.

The engineer looked at the list and then stammered, "But this is all of their navigational and communication equipment."

"I'm aware of that," Filson said.

The engineer studied the list again, his face incredulous.

"You," Colonel Filson said, grabbing another engineer by the arm. "I want you to remove all visual sensing technology, except for infrared from this soldier and that one." The colonel pointed at one of Paul's and one of Kata's, 902 and Sherman.

Kata looked at Paul and shook her head. They were accustomed to the colonel's ways.

Dr. Musashi was not.

"What is the meaning of this?" he yelled at the colonel. "There will be no such modifications of any of my soldiers!"

Colonel Filson looked at Paul and Kata and smiled before turning to Musashi and saying, "Doctor, should we discuss this in my office?"

"No, we should not. There is nothing to discuss. There will be no modifications to the soldiers before the training event."

"Dr. Musashi," the colonel said. "You are correct that there is nothing to discuss. I am the director of this program." Colonel Filson looked back at the frightened engineers and said, "Proceed!"

"No!" Musashi yelled. "This may be your program, but these soldiers are still the property of Musashi Solutions. This is ridiculous! What are you trying to do?"

"We have to put these soldiers, both human and robotic, in a degraded state," the colonel said. "Because that is how it is going to be when they go downrange. I do that to the captains by wearing their asses out, making them walk up and down mountains with little rest."

Filson pointed at Paul and Kata to emphasize his point.

They each held up a gloved middle finger in his direction.

Paul's first sergeant tilted her head at him, studying their gesture.

Filson ignored Paul and Kata. He continued.

"The advanced power plants in your betas mean I can't safely tire them out, but I can sure as hell degrade them. When they finally deploy into a real-world situation, they're not going to have a bunch of fawning engineers in spotless lab coats to keep them going. They're going to have to do hard things that you and your team of eggheads haven't thought of. Things that even I haven't thought of. They need to start getting ready for that. As a team. Now.

"So we make the simple things hard," Filson continued. "We make it hard for them to walk, see, communicate. Whatever we can do to stoke the flames of resilience, creativity, and teamwork."

Paul and Kata looked at Dr. Musashi, curious how receptive he would be to the colonel's philosophy. They were suckers for it every time. When he got going, the arrogant, cranky old man could have told them that the path to being warriors demanded they walk barefoot across a fire, and they would have done it. But they didn't know what Doctor Musashi was made of yet. They didn't know if this civilian artificial-intelligence wizard would be so easily influenced as they were.

Dr. Musashi hesitated. His whole team waited for his response. Filson put his hands on his hips, allowing the doctor to take full measure of his resolve.

"If you must degrade them, then let us simply deactivate the modules you want them to operate without," Musashi said. "We don't have to remove the components."

"I want it to be as close to battle damage as possible," the colonel said as he pointed at the betas. "That means missing components. You're lucky I'm not hacking limbs off them."

The engineers looked at Musashi for guidance.

The doctor shook his head, not ready to give up.

"This is highly questionable, Colonel."

Filson had had enough.

"I'm not interested in anything a Japanese academic, who has been tinkering with ones and zeros for decades, has to say about training soldiers!" the colonel yelled. "You've been at this for how many years? Fifty?"

"That's right! For five decades, my engineers and I have worked to perfect these soldiers."

Kata winked at Paul.

He nodded.

This was getting good.

"Fifty fucking years!" the colonel responded. "All spent trying to put together one reliable soldier?"

The colonel held up a single finger as he paused to laugh in disgust.

"You give me ten weeks and one young man or woman, and I'll give you a soldier," he said. "Ten weeks!"

"You have the advantage of a two-thousand-year-old tradition, and it still takes you ten weeks?" Musashi leered with disdain. "Why does it take you so long? You give me a millennium's worth of tradition and best practices, and I'll give you a soldier in less than five minutes!"

The colonel and the doctor stared at each other in angry silence.

Paul and Kata, their betas, and the engineers stood motionless, transfixed by the strange confrontation.

The colonel looked around and then muttered, "Goddamn it," as he stomped past everyone toward his command hooch. "Come with me, please, Doctor," Filson said as he walked past Musashi.

They were in the colonel's shipping-container office for almost an hour. Paul and Kata took the engineers around Filson's building to the grill, where they lit a fire. The humans hovered around the fire to stay warm while the Ōkami stood on the perimeter.

Paul and Kata were not surprised when Dr. Musashi came and told the engineers, "Please do as the colonel commands."

Chapter Twenty-Four

ays later, Paul was still navigating through the mountains, leading his betas through their first real Filson mode of suffering.

The colonel's modifications had reduced the team to a motley combination of partially mission-capable robots and one exhausted human. All their navigation components had been removed. All imaging capabilities other than human visual spectrum had been de-activated—except for 902, who was left with only infrared imaging. Filson had ordered mobility reductions for two of Paul's betas. This privilege landed on 158 and 357, who each had the range of motion in one of their ankle joints reduced by 90 percent.

It was slow going.

They had one compass, a map, and a watch. The map was insidious, even for Filson. He was beaming when he'd handed it to Paul.

"Here's your map, Owens," he'd said.

Paul had unfolded the map and shaken his head. "Sir, this is a blank piece of paper."

"No, Owens," the colonel had said, grinning. "It is not blank. It is printed with infrared ink."

"Fuck you, sir."

"That one will be able to read it just fine." Filson had pointed at 902. "You're lucky I gave you a map at all."

902 had shifted on his feet, hearing the talk about him but unable to see anything more than fuzzy heat blobs.

Since 902 was the only one of them that could read the map, Paul put him in the middle of their group. They all kept an eye on him as he stumbled along.

When they reached a waypoint, Paul would pull out the map and put it in front of 902, who would describe what he was seeing.

Without their communications equipment, the Ōkami had to communicate through actual speech, not via instantaneous wireless data bursts. It took some time for them to get used to that.

"Based on our last leg," 902 said, "there should be a large mountaintop to our southeast."

"I see one," said 667. "Over there." She pointed toward a mountain in the distance.

"That is too southerly," 458 said.

"He said southeast," 667 said. "That is southeast."

"It should be more east than south," said 902, staring at the unfolded blank map spread out on the ground in front of him.

"I think I see the right mountaintop," 458 said, pointing at a peak. They all followed her gesture and nodded. That was it.

"Why didn't you say it was more east than south in the first place?" 667 said.

"I thought southeast was sufficient guidance," 902 said.

"We are surrounded by mountains," 667 said. "You must be specific."

"That's enough," 458 said. "What's next?"

902 puzzled over the map for a few minutes. The rest stood and waited.

Then, just before Paul was going to tell him to hurry up, 902 said, "There should be a cliff face three miles from us on a more southerly bearing of one hundred and forty-five degrees."

458 and Paul looked in that direction as she held the old compass up to confirm the direction of their line of sight.

"That specific enough for you?" 902 muttered to 667.

"At ease, both of you," 458 said. "Cut the chatter and act like a team."

"We've got the cliff in sight," Paul said. "Looks like about three miles to me."

"Good," 902 said. "Thank you, sir. Our position is confirmed. Now, please allow me a moment to plot our next leg of travel."

Again, they all stood around as 902 studied the map only he could see.

Paul was getting impatient and, after a few minutes, couldn't hold it in anymore.

"All right, Magellan," Paul said, his voice thick with sarcasm. "We're not asking you to circumnavigate the globe. Just get us started, and we can figure it out on the way. We're burning daylight."

All of the quantumtronic heads swiveled to look at Paul. He realized his sarcastic nickname for 902 confused them.

"I'm talking to you, 902," Paul barked for clarity. "Hurry the fuck up!"

"Yes, sir," 902 said. "Next leg is on an azimuth of three hundred and fifty-five degrees. Five miles. We'll go down the north side of the mountain we are currently on, up a long ascent to a saddle between two peaks, and then down to a river crossing. The next checkpoint is the bridge over the river."

"Thank you, Magellan," 458 said. "You all heard the captain. Let's move out."

Paul just shook his head rather than fight it.

They started walking again, in the order Paul had put them in the first day as soon as they'd dismounted the transport drone.

158 had one of the bad ankles, so Paul had put him up front to set the pace. Paul walked in the number-two slot with Magellan right behind him.

Paul fastened a ten-foot dummy cord to Magellan and then tied the other end to his belt as a backup. Magellan put his hand on Paul's shoulder to feel his way along. Paul told 667 to walk behind Magellan. She had the stopwatch and was followed by 458, who kept the team on azimuth. 357 walked trail with the other bad ankle.

About once a week, a quad copter would swoop down from the clouds and plant itself on the side of the mountain they were walking up. The colonel or the doctor would hop out, march with them that day, and then spend the night.

They would ask how it was going and interview each of the soldiers, taking extensive notes.

The contrasting styles of the colonel and the doctor amused Paul. He noted that the colonel would jump off his copter while it was still at a hover, assault style, in an exoskeleton, loaded down with tactical gear like he was about to attack the Great Wall of China all on his own. He'd scan the area until he spotted Paul. Then he would stride over and say, "Captain Owens. How you feeling?"

"Fine, sir," Paul would say. "Ain't nothing but a thing."

"You're damn right. How are they doing?" the colonel would ask.

"Good, sir," Paul would answer, nodding his approval. "They're solid."

"Uh-huh," Filson would say, ensuring Paul heard the skepticism in his voice.

The colonel would walk over to 458 and start talking to her. And then, to Paul's chagrin, until the quad copter picked him up the next morning, Filson would spend all his time with the Ōkami. The next time the colonel would speak to Paul was as Paul walked him to his transport drone.

"Good work, Owens," he'd say. "I'll be back soon." Then he'd look around at the betas with a false grimace of doubt and say, "Keep your eyes on these fucking newbies."

And then he'd be gone.

Dr. Musashi, Paul observed, would wait until his copter was on the ground, engines off, auxiliary power unit shut down, before he got off the aircraft. 458 and the rest of the betas would be lined up, just outside the large ducted fans, waiting for him.

Musashi looked tiny stepping off the aircraft into the midst of his powerful eight-foot soldiers. Paul always gave them a little distance then. The doctor would speak with the Ōkami for a few minutes before waving to Paul and walking over.

Then, Paul noted with amusement, Musashi would spend almost every moment with him. At first, Paul thought it was strange. He was not, after all, the newfangled artificial intelligence. But then he realized the doctor was trying to figure out what kind of variables Paul and Kata introduced to his fledgling architecture.

Paul realized the doctor thought he and Kata were the weakest links.

Chapter Twenty-Five

11 February 2065
Fayetteville, North Carolina

Pruden called Fiona as soon as he got back to his hotel room just off of Fort Bragg.

"Well?" was all she said when she picked up.

"They are kicking ass," he said. "Combat Corps loves them. The kill chain link is working better than anyone expected, and the extension platforms seem to have stabilized as well."

"Believe it or not, Dr. Musashi gets along great with the colonel they have running the field trial," Pruden told her.

"Thank God," Fiona said with a sigh. "I was convinced that mean old bastard was going to alienate himself from everyone in uniform and get us thrown out."

"He's not that bad, Fiona."

"Whatever," she answered. "Keep going."

"The two officers in the program, both captains, one male and one female, have adjusted well to the architecture. I met them both briefly and agree with Dr. Musashi that we got lucky with those two. They are highly competent, adaptable, and, I have to say, amazing physical specimens. Baddasses, both of them. I'll send you the detailed files as soon as I get online. But I'm telling you, Fiona, there is zero chance we don't get the success milestone payment on schedule."

Pruden smiled as he waited for Fiona to react.

182

But she was silent.

"You there?"

"Yes," she said. "I'm just waiting for the rest. The part I give a shit about."

"Oh," Pruden said, frustrated. "Excuse my enthusiasm for the truly innovative work one of our companies is doing. I thought you would also be interested."

Fiona waited.

"Colonel Frank says that, so far, the trial for Spitting Metal is on track to kick off in April. He is working through the budget and scheduling process but will have a final approvals and resource allocations in a few weeks."

"A few weeks?" Fiona asked with dread.

Pruden grimaced. Ever since Fiona had returned from Prague, she had been anxious and short-tempered. Pruden wondered whether it would have been better if her brother had refused her, had not agreed to let her use his villa as collateral on Spitting Metal's line of credit.

It confirmed for Pruden what a favorite professor had told him at business school: "It matters where the money is from."

"I'm sorry," Pruden said. "But with these guys, process is everything. We can't speed them up."

Pruden heard Fiona sigh. He waited for her to speak.

"OK," she finally said. "When is the phase-two milestone meeting for Musashi's trial?"

"A month. Fort Belvoir."

"We must leave that meeting with a start date for Spitting Metal," Fiona said.

Pruden nodded as he ran the dates and numbers in his head. They needed the Spitting Metal kickoff payment to hit before the end of May, or they would be in final default with Talisman.

It would be over.

"That timing should work," he said, trying to sound as convincing as possible. But he shrugged to himself, alone in his hotel room, resigned that there was no way for him to speed up the US military, and that Fiona expected him to do just that.

"It must work," Fiona said.

Chapter Twenty-Six

1 March 2065
Fort Bragg

On the last night of phase two, Dr. Musashi flew out for one of his visits and stayed the night with Paul and his betas. Paul's mood was light. In the morning, all they had was a short march to a nearby mountaintop, where the drone copter would pick them up and fly them back to Filson's cantonment. Paul was really looking forward to a shower.

That night, after the doctor had completed his interviews, he and Paul sat by the fire and ate dinner together. The colonel had told Musashi that Paul loved chili mac, so the doctor had brought a few packets with him. He'd even brought Tabasco sauce. Paul was happy.

They ate in silence for a while, staring at the fire. Finally, Paul's boredom or curiosity got the better of him.

"So, what's your story, Doc?" Paul asked. "How did you end up in the States?"

The doctor took a bite of chili mac without looking at Paul. He scraped the bowl as he slowly chewed, arranging the last bits into a final spoonful. He placed his bowl on the ground and chewed his last bite. When he was done, he wiped his mouth.

As the doctor folded his napkin into a small, precise triangle, Paul thought he was ignoring the question. Paul looked back at the fire and tried to relax.

But after the doctor dropped the napkin into his empty bowl, he looked at the fire and said, "I was born in 1975 in Ine, a small fishing village about a hundred and twenty kilometers to the northwest of Kyoto. Ine sits on the tip of the Tango Peninsula, a small finger of land that pokes out into the Sea of Japan and served as a trade route between Kyoto and the Eurasian continent for centuries."

Paul settled back into the rock he was leaning against and continued to stare at the fire as the old doctor spoke.

"When I was five, my father moved to Kyoto to support his family with the higher wage one could earn in the city. He was gone for months at a time. My mother went back to teaching as soon as she could, to make money for the family as well. She worked long hours. So, I was raised by my mother's father.

"Grandfather came from a family of fishermen," the doctor continued. "He had hoped his sons would follow him into the profession, but his wife and two boys were killed by American bombs in the summer of 1945. Only my grandfather and my mother survived the war. My mother was thrown from the house by the blast. She was found by the firemen, unconscious in the mud, twenty meters from the burning house. She was only a few years old and didn't remember any of it. Grandfather survived because he was not there when the village was bombed. He was away fighting on the islands. It is a miracle he survived.

"After the war, he came home, found his daughter, and went back to fishing. When I was born, he was making his living as a fishing captain on the small boat that his father had built years ago.

"When I was five, he started taking me out on the boat with him each day. I hated it. Grandfather made no allowances for my age. He would show me how to do things once, and then I was expected to perform as well as his two crew members who had been fishing with him since after the war. They looked out for me, though. Making sure I didn't get hurt and helping me with tasks when my grandfather was not looking.

"They were very long days for a child. When we were done, and the boat was properly cleaned and secured, my grandfather and I would walk home. Ine was a small village, and it was not far, but at five years old, my exhaustion was overwhelming. Grandfather had to carry me home each night. I remember being so mad at him for how he treated me on the boat that I did not want him to carry me. But once he picked me up, I fell immediately asleep. The next thing I knew, it was the next morning, and he was waking me again to go back to the boat. I would cry as we walked to the dock, dreading the coming day.

"After a year or so working on the boat, though, I was no longer miserable. Then, after another year or so, I was happy. The last year was…"

The doctor hesitated.

Paul looked at him. Musashi was gazing at the sky. Paul looked back at the fire.

"I am ninety years old, Paul," he continued without taking his eyes off the starts. "And I can tell you that, to this day, that last year on the boat with my grandfather was the most joyous year of my life. My heart was full.

"I was twelve years old and part of the crew. I was one with the boat. I could read the ocean. And my grandfather was the center of the universe. In my young eyes, we all orbited him. The crew, the boat, the ocean, and me. The planning, preparation, and process that he demanded, the discipline he enforced, by that last year, it all receded behind rhythms and rituals that felt as natural and certain as the tides. The nets were prepared just so. They went out. They came in. The lines were baited just so. They went out. They came in. The fish came in and were cleaned. The boat was steered. It went out. It came back in. Every day. Each time. The same.

"My grandfather and I were so close, we almost never spoke. We communicated constantly, though. We did so with nods and glances and grunts and shrugs that were invisible to others. Most of the time, though, we didn't even do that. We just knew the other. We just heard the other. The other two crew members would shake their heads. 'You two are weird,' they would say. 'You've got radios in your heads.'

"My mother, though, was jealous. Grandfather and I would make each other laugh at dinner without saying a word. She would demand to know what the joke was, but we were unable to explain it. She never said so, but I believe that was part of her decision that summer.

"When I was twelve, my parents enrolled me in school in Kyoto. My father was home for the weekend when they told me. I refused. I threw a tantrum. I said some very disrespectful things. My mother cried.

"The next day, my grandfather stepped onto the boat early in the morning and found me sleeping in the pilothouse. I woke up that morning to the smell of coffee. My grandfather saw me stirring and poured me a cup. He placed it on the small table in the pilothouse and sat down at the other small chair to have his cup. He did not look at me. I got up and walked to the table. I took the seat across from him and sipped at the coffee. We did not speak. Half an hour later, the crew arrived.

"I stayed on the boat for a week. Grandfather would arrive well before the crew. We would drink coffee in silence together. Then, when we were done, we would set to work preparing the boat. The crew would arrive. And we would be underway. We would go out. We would fish. And we would come back in. After the boat was tied up, my grandfather would leave without saying goodbye. I believed I had escaped. This was my life now. My heart was full.

"After a week, my mother came with my grandfather one morning. I yelled at my grandfather, 'How could you betray me?'

"My grandfather let me yell and then put his arm around me. 'You must go now,' he said to me. 'A good life has many chapters. Our chapter on the boat together is over.'

"'I don't want it to be over,' I said through tears.

"'I don't either,' he said. My grandfather's voice told me there was no hope. My heart, which had been so full, emptied onto the floor. 'I cherish our time together, grandson,' he said. 'And you will always be welcome back on my crew. But you must go to school now.'

"'Will we have another chapter?' I asked.

"'I don't know,' he said. 'No one can know.'

"I went to school in Kyoto. I made it back to Ine as often as I could and would spend the time on the boat with my grandfather. But it was never the same. It took me a day to get back into the rhythm. Grandfather had to tell me what to do and when to do it. But I loved being with him anyway.

"I worked very hard in school. I applied to MIT in America and was accepted. My parents were very proud. I was excited for my future. For America.

"I spent a week fishing with my grandfather before I left. He was the most talkative he had ever been. He peppered me with questions. About the school I was going to attend. The engineering I would study. He asked me a lot about Boston. He wanted to picture where I would be living, but it was unimaginable to him. He asked about America also. The country he fought many years ago. The country that had killed his wife and sons.

"My parents picked me up at the dock when we returned. My grandfather handed my bag to my parents while I sat at the small table in the pilothouse. Even though I was just eighteen, and a fool, I had the vague sense that I was losing something very special. That I would not see my grandfather again. I did not know what to do. I was frozen with fear and sadness.

"My grandfather returned to the pilothouse. My parents returned to the car to wait. He made coffee and then sat with me. As we sipped on our coffee, I noticed a tear run down my grandfather's cheek. He did not try to hide it.

"'I am so happy for your next chapter, grandson,' he said after a few minutes. Then I left for America. Grandfather died while I was away at school."

Paul and the doctor spent a long moment in silence, gazing at the flames.

"After I graduated from MIT, I spent many years in the space industry, working on artificial intelligence for space craft. I loved the challenge of creating something that could think and solve problems when it was all alone. Millions of miles from any help. I did a lot of work on exploratory probes.

"But, while I hold man's efforts in space in high regard, it is our life and struggles on earth that I am most interested in. My grandfather never spoke about his experience in the war. I think he went through some very hard times. The only thing he ever said to me about it, was that being a good man in war was very hard. But very important.

"After some years I decided it was time for my next chapter. It was not easy to do. I had made many friends and worked with many smart colleagues in the space industry. I respected them very much and am still in touch with most of them even now, many, many years later. But I left the space industry and set upon this path. And I am glad I did."

The doctor gestured at their small fire and the area around them.

Paul and the doctor stared into the fire.

"Thanks for telling me that," Paul finally said.

"Thank you for asking."

Chapter Twenty-Seven

When Paul and Kata finally got back into the cantonment on Fort Bragg. They took much-needed showers, and Dr. Musashi's lab coats crawled all over the soldiers, putting them back together again.

Later in the evening, Paul and Kata ate dinner in the mess hall. They had not seen each other for months, save for brief flights or mission briefings.

"It is always good to get back, eh?" Kata said. "Warm showers. Warm food. Warm bed."

"Yes, it is. Kind of irritating, though, isn't it?"

"What?" Kata asked, chewing a mouthful of food.

"Colonel Filson. I have to admit that he is, in fact, an evil genius."

Kata, mouth still full, waited for him to continue.

"Out in the mountains, after a few weeks, my legs were smoked."

Kata nodded in agreement.

"One day, I lost my footing and almost fell down a steep drop-off," Paul continued. "But Magellan caught me. Grabbed me by my rucksack at the last minute, stopping my fall."

"He was your blind guy, right?" Kata asked. "The one Filson stripped down to infrared?"

"Yep. All he could see were fuzzy blobs. Definitely not enough visual acuity to see me stumble."

"Then how did he know?"

"Doc thinks it was the link," Paul said.

"But they took out their communications equipment."

"I know. Doc thinks other components, other electronic bullshit onboard the Ōkami, compensated. Didn't form a true neural link. But did establish some kinda…hell, I don't know."

Paul shrugged.

"When I talked to him about it later, he was astounded. He thinks the stress of Filson's training regimen morphed it all somehow. It's different now. It's more than just tactical and telemetry data. The doctor and his team are still trying to figure it out."

"Same shit happened to me a few times," Kata said.

"That is what I am talking about," Paul said. "The colonel. The evil genius. He is doing it again."

"Doing what?"

"Rewiring a bunch of soldiers into a unit."

Chapter Twenty-Eight

fter a day of debriefing phase two, Colonel Filson gave Paul and Kata a four-day pass. When they got back, they met the new members of their unit and a new phase of training began.

"Each of your units is equipped with a dedicated air component consisting of six QC-10 medium assault quad copters," the colonel said as he led Paul and Kata into the large hangar facility. Dr. Musashi trailed behind them.

"Don't let the word 'medium' fool you. That's just a weight classification. The QC-10 kicks heavy ass," Filson said with an enthusiastic grin. "Particularly these guys that our good doctor has specially modified."

They rounded the corner into the large open space in the hangar and saw the quad copters. There were two groups of six copters on opposite sides of the hangar. "That's Alpha Company," the colonel said, pointing to his left. "And over there is Bravo."

"Oh, hell yeah," Kata said with a lusty smile.

Paul smiled at her reaction. Kata was probably the best combat drone pilot in the Combat Corps at that point. And the QC-10s looked like serious combat drones.

The first thing Paul noticed was the large ball turret mounted on the nose. It was a massive combination of sensors and gun barrels and rocket tubes that gave the front end a menacing, insectoid appearance. Then his eyes moved aft to the large, ducted, thruster fans, each almost ten meters in diameter. There were two on each side of the thirty-meter-long fuselage, like coiled legs, ready to leap. Finally, a stout utility wing assembly jutted out from between the forward and aft thruster fans. Its gull-wing configuration looked like a powerful insect wing that was about to unfold and propel the beast into the air.

"I've heard about the QC-10s," Paul said to the colonel. "They were just fielding them when we rotated off the Horn."

"Yeah," Kata added, smiling. "They looked like ballsy aircraft, and I heard they could take a stupendous amount of punishment and keep flying."

The colonel nodded proudly. "You guys have no idea the shit storm I had to walk through to get us a dozen of these things."

Their small fleet was brand new that day. Their surfaces clean, not yet dented, punctured, and stained from combat. The sleek, composite armor skin seemed to be stretched over straining muscle and had been painted a desert-sand color.

"Top airspeed for these beasts is three hundred knots," Filson said, crossing his arms in satisfaction. "They were designed for maximum payload flexibility and will give you a lot of mission optionality downrange."

The colonel led the two Centaurs around behind the Alpha Company aircraft, pointing out their large aft ramps.

"Each one can carry two dozen fully equipped soldierbots," the colonel continued, "enabling you to transport almost your entire wolf pack in just four aircraft. That utility wing has a ridiculous cargo- and munitions-bearing ability."

The colonel pointed as he continued around back toward the front of the aircraft, where Dr. Musashi waited.

"It's one of the elements that makes these machines so damn useful. There is no weapons system in your units that you cannot transport into battle, at a high rate of speed, on the wing, slung beneath, or inside of one of these war birds." Filson turned and looked at the two drooling Centaurs. "Please don't fuck 'em up."

Paul and Kata looked past him at the aircraft.

"Anything you want to add, Doctor?" the colonel asked.

"Only that these aircraft are Ōkami. They rank high in your wolf pack, just below your betas," Musashi said.

Colonel Filson could see that Paul and Kata were eager to get closer to their new toys.

"Go introduce yourselves," he said, stepping to the side.

Kata winked at Paul and walked away toward Alpha Company.

Paul walked across the hangar to his group of QC-10s. As he got closer, he noticed the large weapons turret had two smaller, basketball-sized sensor turrets embedded on either side of its top half. Each of the QC-10s tracked his approach with one of these sensor pods.

Paul stepped in front of the nose of the first aircraft.

"Good morning," he said.

"Good morning, sir," the male voice said.

"What is your name?"

"I am Bravo Company Unit One, sir," the aircraft answered.

Paul walked from his nose toward his left front thruster fan. A soft whirring noise emanated from the small left-side sensor pod as it tracked him. He stopped between Unit One and the next QC-10. The tops of their large thruster fans stood fifteen feet above his head.

"And, let me guess," Paul said to the other aircraft. "You are Bravo Company Unit Two?"

"Roger that, sir," the female voice said.

"What are you going to name them?" the colonel said, walking up behind Paul.

"Name them?"

"Vukovic just named hers the Eagles."

"Good for her."

"She's calling her company the Apaches, by the way," Filson added. "It's a good unit name, don't you think?"

"Sure."

"Damn it, Owens."

Exasperated, the colonel shook his head at Paul before turning back to the half dozen aircraft. He admired the line of war machines for a moment and then said to Paul, over his shoulder, "Aircraft this ballsy got to have a ballsy name."

"Listen up, Bravo Company!" Filson said loudly, turning his head back to address the aircraft.

Whirs and clicks emanated from the group as their sensor pods swiveled to view Filson.

"From now on, you are Dragon Flight. Do you understand?"

"Yes, sir," the aircraft answered in unison.

"This stick-in-the-damn-mud standing next to me is Captain Owens," the colonel continued. "He is your commanding officer. Take care of him. He's actually better than he looks."

Paul narrowed his eyes at the colonel.

"Your in-head display and neural link will enable you to employ and command your Dragons with your thoughts, just like your betas," the colonel said, turning to Paul with a smile. "Sound good?"

"It does, sir. I'm excited to see what they can do."

"I bet," the colonel said, still gazing at the QC-10s. After a moment, he turned his head back to Paul and said, "But don't be too excited. Integrating the in-head display capabilities is phase three."

The colonel waved toward Dr. Musashi, who was still standing at the doorway of the hangar. "All right, Doctor," he shouted across the enormous space. "Send 'em in."

Musashi gave the colonel a thumbs-up and disappeared through the doorway. Paul looked back at the colonel, who smiled at him like a schoolyard bully.

Dr. Musashi came back through the doorway, followed by a team of two dozen lab-coated engineers pushing large carts of technical equipment.

"Fuck you, sir," Paul said to Filson as he realized what was about to happen.

"Fuck you too, Captain," the colonel said. He patted Paul on the back and walked toward Musashi and his group of engineers.

"They're all yours," the colonel said. "I want them stripped of all of their advanced avionics and sensing data."

The lab coats pushed their carts past Paul, two to each aircraft. The Dragons' front sensor pods twitched back and forth, trying to track all of them.

"What is happening, sir?" Dragon One asked Paul.

"I've known Colonel Filson a long time," Paul said. "I think he is about to put you through the oldest play in his book." The two lab coats in front of Dragon One opened their carts. The female engineer pulled out a wrench set, and the male engineer grabbed a large black duffel bag. They walked around the number-one thruster fan to the left-side cargo door.

"Open up, please, Unit One," the engineer said as she stood in front of the cargo door.

Dragon One ignored her.

"Unit One," the engineer said again. "Open your left cargo door now."

Paul looked around. The same standoff was playing out at the side of each of the Dragons. He walked back to the middle of the group.

"Dragons," Paul said. "Open up and let Dr. Musashi's engineers on board."

Six cargo doors slid open, and the engineer teams hopped into the QC-10s.

"Nothing to be afraid of, Dragons," Paul said, chuckling. "You're all about to experience life as a World War I aircraft."

"Pull out anything not required to keep them in the air with their greasy side down," the colonel bellowed from the middle of the hangar. "I want them blind as bats but still able to fly without killing themselves or anyone else."

Paul and Kata met in the center of the hangar as the engineers stripped their aircraft down to the basics.

"How long do you think this phase will last?" Kata asked Paul.

"I don't know. A month maybe?"

"Asshole," Kata said, as they watched Filson walk over to talk to a smiling Dr. Musashi. "I'm surprised Dr. Musashi didn't resist."

"Are you kidding?" Paul said. "They're like brothers these days."

"You mean evil twins."

At that moment, Filson laughed at something the doctor said. Musashi smiled and then laughed as well.

Paul and Kata shared a skeptical glance.

"Are your betas doing strange things?" Kata asked Paul.

"Strange how?"

"Strange, like noticing stuff," she said. "Strange, like, being really observant. Almost creepy."

Paul shrugged.

"For example, I hate it when people talk to me when I am eating," Kata said.

"I know that."

"Sure. You know it. But they don't know it. And I never told them. But I noticed after a few weeks that none of them ever approach me if I am eating. Somehow, they figured this out through observation."

Paul smiled.

"What?" Kata asked, suspicious of his grin.

"Somehow, mine realized… well, a part of the female anatomy I enjoy." Paul circled his open hands in front of his chest like he was polishing large brass lamps.

"You mean tits?" Kata said matter of factly.

"Yes. You know that computer engineer from Idaho?"

"Yep," Kata said. "I know exactly who you are talking about. Buxom girl."

"Yeah, she's hot."

Kata nodded in agreement.

"Well, I guess I look at them a lot."

"No kidding," Kata said with zero surprise in her voice.

"My soldiers must have noticed, because lately I've been getting flashes of them from every angle over our neural link."

Kata burst out laughing.

Several lab coats turned around to look at her, as did Filson, who scowled from across the hangar.

"I know," Paul said without remorse. "But you know how she is always working on the Ōkami? Leaning over them, plugging something into them to download telemetry or whatever. They get a lot of good shots. 158 is the worst. He sends them so often I started referring to him as Snapshot."

"Classic," Kata said, shaking her head and adopting a saddened tone.

"What?"

"Your team is using Dr. Musashi's life's work, the result of decades of cutting-edge engineering, to send you fetish pornography," she said.

Paul was silent.

"To their commanding officer," she added.

Paul smiled.

"I love it," Kata added, chuckling.

Chapter Twenty-Nine

The night after the QC-10s were stripped down, Dragon One was flying across North Carolina at five hundred feet and two hundred knots. Paul was up front with a stopwatch in one hand and a map in the other. Colonel Filson had taken everything out of the QC-10s except for their magnetic compasses, attitude gyros, and pitot static systems. The Dragons were large airborne versions of blind men with canes, capable only of holding a magnetic heading, an airspeed, and an altitude. They had to get all directions from Paul as the colonel dropped nightly time-on-target missions on them.

Every day around two in the afternoon, the colonel would give Paul and Kata three coordinates each and the times they had to be at those targets. Then they had a couple of hours to plan the flights. They worked on a large folding table in the middle of the hangar, rolling out maps and combing over them with rulers and protractors as the Eagles and Dragons watched from their parking areas on either side.

Paul's and Kata's respective targets were always in opposite directions, but they would work together on both routes. The two sets of eyes helped to reduce error among all the time, distance, and heading information.

Paul and Kata would break for dinner after they'd finished the planning, usually around 1900 hours. Then, as it got dark, they would split up and brief their teams on that night's mission.

The missions were the same for both of them. They flew in formations of six aircraft. When they landed at each target, Paul and Kata would open an envelope the colonel had given each of them prior to takeoff. In the envelope, there was a piece of paper with a single number written on it, designating which of their aircraft would lead the next leg. This element of surprise made it important that each aircraft listened closely to the mission briefing.

Paul would sit in front of Dragon Flight and hold up the map as he talked through the mission, the routes, the targets, the times they had to be there, the weather, and the forecasted winds.

Paul made a point to call out what terrain features to look for along the way. The Dragons' sensor pods would shift back and forth from the map to Paul. They would follow his hands as he traced the map. When Paul was done, he would ask the team a few questions to make sure they understood and retained the mission. Then he would go grab his flight gear while the lab coats removed the last of the Dragons' optical sensors.

To start each mission, Paul climbed into the lead Dragon. Once he had strapped himself into the forward-most seat in the front of the drone, he told the team to hover to the far end of the airfield. They would hold position there, ten feet above the ground, while Paul waited for the start time. As the seconds ticked down, Paul would say, "OK, Dragon Flight, first leg - Heading - one hundred and thirty-five degrees, airspeed - one hundred and fifty knots, time - thirty-five minutes and seventeen seconds. Checkpoint is a small bridge over a north-south-running river."

"Roger that, sir," the team would respond. "One three five at one fifty for thirty-five seventeen."

"You got it," Paul would confirm. "Takeoff in five, four, three, two, one. Go."

Paul would start his stopwatch and grin. He loved the way it felt as his aircraft accelerated forward. He would crane his neck around to look at each of the other aircraft in Dragon Flight as they all started a gentle climb to the assigned altitude.

Then they would fly the mission with the same instrumentation as a flight of World War I tube-and-fabric, open-cockpit biplanes.

After a month of basic navigation training, they moved on to a month of gunnery.

Kata was surprised when Filson did not restore the aircraft instrumentation for gunnery.

"Come on, sir," she said. "I get hazing us with navigation, but gunnery?"

"You want us to actually hit stuff, right?" Paul added.

Colonel Filson handed them both a grease pencil.

"What's this?" Kata asked, not wanting to hear the answer.

"Works in all types of weather. Never gets jammed by the enemy. Never runs out of power. And is fully customizable," he said, with a smug smile.

Paul and Kata turned the grease pencils over in their hands.

"OK," Kata said. "I give up."

"Sit in the command seat in one of your Eagles," the colonel said, feigning irritation. "Fly out onto the range and have it fire its minigun. Lean forward and mark the impact on your canopy with a crosshair."

The colonel made a show of closing one eye and drawing a marksman's X in the air in front of himself.

"Yeah," Paul said. "But the QC-10s can't see that."

"That's right," the colonel said. "That's why you will have to talk them in on every run."

Paul scratched his head and regarded the grease pencil with skepticism.

"Working together as a unit," Filson said, turning to leave. "That is the only way through any of this shit."

Chapter Thirty

Paul, Kata and Doctor Musashi sat cross-legged under the wing of one of Kata's Eagles, eating breakfast together before the day's gunnery training began. Kata was enjoying stale French toast with too much syrup while Paul and the doctor ate powdered eggs.

"I've got a question for you, Doc," Paul said as he squeezed a plastic packet of hot sauce over his eggs.

"What is it, Paul?"

"I've been wondering, how old are the Ōkami?"

The doctor set his paper plate down. "How do you mean?"

"I mean in their heads. Mentally, I guess."

Kata looked at Paul and rolled her eyes.

"It's an interesting question," the Doctor said. "How old are you in your head?"

"Twenty-six years old."

The doctor nodded.

"I think if you asked one of your betas, they would respond with the time since their activation date. That is when their manufacturing and programming is mostly complete, and we wake them up, for lack of a better word, for the first time. For most of your betas, that was about three to four years ago."

"Well, they perform and behave like they are much older," Kata said. "Much more experienced."

"The learning models we train them on are quite large," the doctor said, picking up his plate. He scraped and maneuvered a small bite of crumbling eggs onto his plastic spoon as he continued. "In some ways you can think of each Ōkami beta as a PhD in the military practice."

"Damn," Kata said. "Nice to start the day feeling like the chief dunce of the Apaches."

The doctor chuckled.

"It is not like that at all, Kata," he said.

"I'm good with it, Doc. Long as Owens is around, I'm not the dumbest member of the unit."

Kata winked at the doctor, who glanced at Paul. He had a faraway look on his face as he chewed a mouthful of eggs.

"Anyone need a coffee reload?" Kata asked, standing up.

"That would be nice, Kata," the doctor said. "Thank you."

Kata looked at Paul.

"Paul," she said.

"Huh?"

"Coffee reload?"

"Yeah. Thanks."

Kata nodded and walked toward the flight operations building on the other side of the flight line.

"What are you thinking about, Paul?" Doctor Musashi asked.

Paul looked at the doctor as he finished chewing and then swallowed. He shrugged and then said, "I was just thinking that would be a hell of a way to be activated, or woken up. To open your eyes and simply be told, 'You are a soldier. You exist to fight.'"

Paul scooped another mound of eggs onto his spoon and said, "They don't get much choice, do they? Their destinies are decided for them."

Paul shoved the spoonful into his mouth and chewed.

He and Doctor Musashi sat and ate in silence for a few minutes before Kata returned with three paper cups of black coffee. She handed Paul and the doctor each a cup and sat down between them.

Paul looked at his watch. They had fifteen minutes before the gunnery was scheduled to start. He took a sip of coffee.

Musashi was a slow eater compared to Paul and Kata. When he finished, he set his plate on the ground in front of his crossed legs.

"Paul, how did you decide to become a military officer?" Doctor Musashi asked.

"I was a brat," Paul said with a shrug.

Musashi looked back at him with a blank face.

"An Army brat," Paul clarified.

Musashi's eyebrows raised as he tried to grasp the unknown term.

"An 'Army brat' is someone who grew up with parents in the Army," Paul explained. "My father was in the Army. Our family bounced around the world from post to post during his career. Lot of time in Europe. Couple years in Japan. Fort Campbell. Fort Bragg. Spent my high school years on Fort Carson, Colorado."

"What did your father do in the Army?"

"He started off as an infantry officer, then went special forces. That's what he was doing when we lived in Colorado."

"Was he a Centaur?"

"No," Paul said. "He was too old when the program really got going. The last few years were frustrating for him. All the changes. But he loved it. Saw some real action."

"Was he a graduate of the academy like you?"

"Oh yeah, Doc," Kata said, making sure her voice sounded disgusted. "He's from one of those families."

"Fraid so," Paul said with a smile.

"And you, Kata?" the doctor asked. "How did you come to be a military officer?"

"I'm a brat also," she said, shrugging like Paul did when he answered.

"Dad and Mom both were in," she added. "Dad was Infantry at first. He loved it before all the changes. He failed the physical for the Centaur program and took the early out as a major. Mom was Aviation. She was a helicopter pilot. Went through one of the last few flight school classes. But not much use for pilots anymore, so she tracked intelligence when it was obvious she was never going to really get into the cockpit."

"What was it like? Your childhoods?" Musashi asked.

Paul and Kata exchanged a quick glance. Kata rolled her eyes. Paul answered.

"It was good. I mean, the truth is I didn't know any different. Dad was gone a lot. This was during that Global War on Terror thing that had us fighting everyone everywhere. Mom worried all the time. When I was younger, I worried too. But as I got older, I worried less. But missed him more. He seemed invincible to me. I could not imagine him ever being hurt. I knew he would always come home. I just wished he was around more."

"I see. And you followed your father's path?"

"I guess."

Doctor Musashi nodded and smiled, as if that made complete sense to him. But then he asked, "Why did you do that?"

Paul took a sip of coffee as he pondered the simple question.

"My dad was great. I really looked up to him and his friends. I loved being around them when they were back from a deployment. I would hang around as long as I could wherever they were, in the back yard burning meat and drinking beer, after church, watching sports, wherever. I would listen to their stories. I tried to imagine myself in those situations. Tried to think of what I would do."

Kata nodded as Paul spoke.

"My dad seemed happy." Paul continued. "Seemed like he had a purpose. And, though it exacted a toll on us as a family, it seemed like we all shared that purpose."

Paul paused and took a sip of coffee.

"You had a similar experience growing up?" Musashi asked Kata.

"Yep. It was the same for me."

"I was actually surprised at how my dad reacted when I told him I wanted to be a military officer," Paul said. "I think it was meaningful to him, but he was not really happy about it."

"Why do you suppose that was?"

"I think he thought it was a harder life than I realized. And I think he saw how things were trending in the Army and the early effects of technology and the shrinking combat leadership roles. While he could never really explain it to me, it worried him."

"Did his reaction give you pause?"

"It was too late," Paul said, shaking his head and smiling. "I think growing up as a brat had changed me. Civilian life made no sense to me. It was too foreign. When my friends and I were around civilian kids our age, they seemed different."

"Different how?"

"I don't know if I can explain it. We'd lived overseas and all over the United States, so we felt like nomads. But we'd been immersed in military culture since birth, so we felt grounded. Bound together. And by more than just a common ideological foundation. We shared a common sense of place. We were adaptable, resilient, and good at making new friends and assessing new situations. I thought we were more mature than the civilians our age we knew. More worldly."

"So, you felt superior to them?"

"No. More like outsiders. Like we didn't belong."

The doctor raised one of his bushy eyebrows.

"OK," Paul said with a smile. "We didn't want to belong either."

"Yeah," Kata said. "They sucked."

Musashi smiled.

"OK," Paul shrugged. "I guess we did feel like we were on a better path. And, despite the costs the life had extracted from us, several of my friend's parents had been wounded or killed in combat, we were infected with the service bug. Most of us were plotting careers as police officers, nurses, Foreign Service officers or the military."

Kata nodded.

"I read somewhere that the vast majority of military officers these days are brats," she said.

"I did not realize that," the doctor said, rubbing his chin.

"Yeah, almost 95% are brats," Paul added with a hint of pride. "Most multi-generational, with the family lineage going back to the grandparents or farther."

"Is that true for the combat part as well?" the Doctor asked.

"You mean the Combat Corps?" Kata asked.

"Yes."

"That's what we're talking about," Kata clarified. "The Combat Corps is the only real part of the military anymore, Doc."

"I see."

"Surely you've been around Colonel Filson when he's giving one of his angry speeches on the matter?" Paul asked.

"I have, indeed," the doctor chuckled. "So, you ascribe to the same beliefs?"

"Yes," Paul and Kata said in unison.

Musashi nodded.

"It is interesting," the doctor said. "That the Combat Corps is so predominately made up of… brats."

Doctor Musashi smiled.

"What?" Paul asked him.

"It almost sounds to me that you two did not so much decide to follow your parents' path of military service. Rather, you acted consistently with how you were raised and the traditions that were part of your lives."

"Yeah," Paul said as Kata nodded. "I think that is right."

"It didn't feel like much of a choice to you."

Paul and Kata shared a glance.

"It was almost as if your destiny was decided for you."

Paul chuckled.

Kata shook her head in appreciation of the old man.

"It makes me happy," Musashi said. "To think of you and my Ōkami sharing that destiny."

Chapter Thirty-One

The last part of training pulled everything together. The colonel moved Paul and Kata around the country with their companies and threw missions at them every day for six weeks.

First, they focused on getting a feel for how best to integrate the wolf packs into their operations. Then they incorporated the rest of the ground XPs. Then the air XPs. In a few weeks, they were conducting combined-arms operations that only a few years ago would have required an augmented brigade staff to pull off. Paul and Kata did them on their own.

Filson also made them flex the self-sustaining capability he was so proud of. For that month, they lived entirely off of the services of their support platoon. The colonel called them the 'F3 Team,' for 'fix, fuel, and feed.'

The support platoon was led by a squatty humanoid robot Paul called Chief. Chief was not part of the neural link, but he was an impressive machine. In addition to bossing around the ten repair bots, he was Paul's logistics assistant. His AI was constantly working to optimize their situation. Fuel, ammunition, repair parts, material to feed the 3D printer—it was all he thought about. Paul included him in every mission plan. He wanted Chief to be able to anticipate their requirements. He always did.

As the one human soldier in the unit, Paul was Chief's only customer for biological food. All of the repair bots were loaded with food-preparation routines, but Chief was the only one that ever fed Paul. It seemed weird at first. But, over time, Paul came to like it.

Paul never let Chief know, though. He bitched about whatever Chief brought him. "What is this shit, Chief?" He would yell, eyeballing the plate of food Chief handed him.

"Sir, that is chili mac," he would answer.

"You call this slop chili mac?" Paul would ask in disbelief.

"Yes, sir."

"This is terrible!" Paul would say, pretending to gag as he swallowed.

"Sir, I am sorry. I will prepare another serving so that…"

"Fuck no, Chief! Don't make me suffer through another plate of this," Paul would say before he walked away. "I'll just choke this shit down."

"OK, sir," he'd say. "Again, my apologies."

Paul felt a little bad for ribbing Chief in this way but stuck with the timeless military tradition of complaining about the food. By the end of the training, Chief had learned Paul was just ribbing him. He realized it was an important part of the military feeding ritual.

"Goddamn, Chief," Paul would say. "What is this slop?"

"It's fucking chili mac, sir," Chief would respond with irritation in his voice. "What does it look like?"

"This is unidentifiable," Paul would say, angling the plate Chief's way so that he could see.

"That is the best chili mac in the back forty, sir. You're lucky to have it."

"Oh my God!" Paul said, retching for effect. "Am I being punished? That is the only explanation I can think of for you feeding me this shit."

"You're the expert on shit around here, sir," Chief said, turning to walk away. "If you'd like a plate of that, you don't need me."

But the real challenge Chief faced every day was keeping the company fit to fight. The colonel made it hard on him. Every day, Filson would pick one of the Ōkami betas and shoot them.

By that stage in the training, Paul hated to watch it happen. These were his soldiers.

The colonel's logic was that he'd rather find out the support platoon's limitations then, while they could address them, than downrange on a real-world deployment.

Musashi, to Paul and Kata's surprise, did not protest. By that point, the colonel and the doctor had mind-melded. The doctor was all for it. He didn't want his Ōkami to be stuck downrange having to fight with injuries that could not be repaired.

Each day, the colonel would pick one of the Ōkami betas and shoot them with something. A rifle, a rocket, a laser. A couple of times, they ran over their limbs with a tracked vehicle. The only thing that was really off-limits was a bad shot to the thorax. Their spheres were embedded in an armored chamber in their chests. They were hard to damage. But it was not worth the risk.

The expectation was that Chief and his team would have the wounded Ōkami fully operational by sunset, which they always did. Paul and Kata marveled at the maintenance bots' capabilities. It seemed they could fix anything.

In addition to the food, the other aspect of the support platoon dedicated solely to the humans was the medical pod. Capable of just about any surgical procedure, all the Ōkami had to do was keep Paul alive long enough to get him into it, and the MedPod would put him back together.

Every robot in the unit was competent in basic human first aid. If Paul or Kata were wounded, they were programmed to render immediate aid, stabilize them, and get them to the MedPod. Without Paul and Kata, after all, the kill chain was broken. The Ōkami had no reason to exist. No authority to do what they were made to do.

The first time the Filson showed Paul the MedPod, the colonel went on and on about it. Paul could tell he was proud of it and wanted Paul to feel comfortable that it would actually work. 458 and Chief were standing behind Paul as the colonel spoke. When he finished his overview of the MedPod, he asked Paul, "So, do you want it in the leg or arm?"

"Sir?" Paul asked, not getting his question.

The colonel drew his pistol. "Leg or arm?"

"What?" Paul said, backing up.

458 and Chief stepped in front of Paul, unsure of what to do but certain they would not let the colonel shoot their company commander. Filson started

laughing. He holstered his weapon and shook his head at the war machines in front of him.

"Just kidding," he said between chuckles. "Jesus, Owens. You should have seen the look on your face."

Paul finally started to chuckle. Soon he was belly laughing. The colonel was as well. 458 and Chief looked at each other in bewilderment.

Chapter Thirty-Two

During the last couple of weeks Paul, Kata and the Ōkami conducted numerous operations in various mission profiles: ships underway at sea, assaults on the top floors of skyscrapers, convoy ambushes, airfield takedowns. Filson threw some crazy scenarios at them. And they passed every one. He couldn't deny it anymore, they were ready.

The last training mission had been a long one that combined both companies. It took Paul and Kata several days to plan and then a full seventy-two hours to execute. When they finally got back to their airfield on Fort Bragg, they were exhausted and hungry. As Paul and Kata walked back to the barracks, Colonel Filson drove up in his old jeep with a large deer strapped to the hood.

"Check it out," he said, coming to a stop in front of them. "This guy wandered onto the range and was, sadly, the victim of an accidental shooting."

Paul and Kata smiled. Hunting on Fort Bragg was strictly prohibited. North Carolina was super uptight about it. So, Bragg's commanding general was super uptight about it. Intentionally killing game on post was a surefire way to get your ass in a sling.

Kata laughed as she said. "Wow. That's a really clean shot to the head."

"One unlucky fella, I guess," Filson deadpanned.

Paul looked the dead animal over. It had been taken down by a precise headshot. The deer's meaty body was in perfect shape.

"Very unlucky," Paul said. "Seems a shame to let his accidental demise be in vain."

"Any ideas, Owens?"

"Leave it to me, sir," Paul said.

The colonel helped Paul string the deer up by its hind legs on a tree behind the containers, and then Paul went to round up Chief.

"Come with me, Chief," Paul said, poking his head into the motor pool. He then explained everything he did as he field dressed the deer. Chief stood next to Paul, watching closely.

"You have to be careful not to cut too deep," Paul said as he inserted the knife into the deer's belly. "If you do, you will open the gut bag and intestines. That makes the job messier and can spoil the meat. Once the tip of the blade is in position, run it down toward the neck until you meet the breastplate."

Paul worked quickly, confident that Chief's quantumtronic brain was capturing every detail. As he made his way his toward the buck's head, the bulge of entrails hanging half out of the animal grew larger.

"At this point," he said, pausing to look at Chief, "all you have to do is reach down inside the deer toward his throat and feel for the windpipe with your blade." The deer's gaping abdomen swallowed Paul's arm as he reached inside down toward the animal's head and felt for the trachea.

Paul severed it and the esophagus with a firm cut.

"The only thing that's really holding it all now is what's left of the diaphragm," Paul said, gripping the fibrous red tissue.

He sliced through it, and the mass of entrails fell to the ground with a wet splat.

Later than night, Kata built a fire, and Paul cooked the venison slowly. The colonel drank his scotch. Paul and Kata drank beer. Chief watched Paul closely. The smell of roasting deer wafted through the cantonment area, luring Dr. Musashi and his team out of their small labs. Finally, Kata couldn't take it anymore.

"Damn it, Paul," she said, glaring at him across the fire. "Let's get into it already!"

"Chief," Paul said. "Come over here."

"Yes, sir," the Ōkami said, stepping over and leaning in toward the sizzling venison with Paul.

"You smell that?"

"Yes, sir."

"You see that fat bubbling up through the charred surface?"

"Yes, sir."

Paul pulled out his bayonet and carved a piece of meat. "See how juicy it is?"

"Yes, sir."

"Now watch this," Paul said as he handed Kata his bayonet, the large piece of venison hanging from the blade tip. Vapor rose into the brisk Carolina night as she smiled and placed it in her mouth. Kata closed her eyes and shook her head in slow motion. Grease dripped from her chin. She let out a noise somewhere between a moan and a grunt that lasted for few seconds.

"You see that?" Paul said to Chief, pointing at Kata. "That reaction means you did it right."

Chief nodded. "I understand, sir. Thank you for the instruction."

They stayed out late that night under the stars, eating venison and getting drunk. One of Musashi's lab coats brought out a stack of paper plates. Paul sat on a beat-up field chair next to the fire roasting deer, carving as everyone cycled by. There was no activity on the ranges that night, so Bragg was quiet.

The Ōkami betas mingled among the humans. They were never sure what to do with themselves during periods of leisure like that, but seemed to want to be around Paul and Kata. When people started showing up for seconds, Paul asked Chief to relieve him and moved to an old ammo crate on the edge of the firelight. He watched Chief expertly carve servings of venison for folks and sipped from his own flask of bourbon.

After some time had passed, Paul gestured at 458. She walked over and stood next to him.

"Yes, sir?"

"I'd like to call you something other than 458," Paul said.

"Yes, sir," she said.

"I would like to call you Top. Do you know what that means?"

"No, sir," she said.

"Top is an old nickname for a company first sergeant," Paul said. "It's a role that dates back almost two hundred years to our country's civil war. It means *top sergeant*. It identifies you as a leader. There are many soldiers with the rank of first sergeant. But only a very few of them are the top-ranking sergeant in a combat unit. You are fulfilling a special duty. I command Outlaw Company, but you run it. You are my top sergeant."

She towered above Paul as he sat on the ammo crate. Her sleek head bent down toward him as she focused on his words.

"You good with that name?" Paul asked her.

"Yes, sir, I am," she said, nodding.

"It is fitting," Musashi said. Paul swiveled on the crate to see the doctor standing behind him. "I'm sorry, Paul," he said. "I was not intending to listen in. I just happened to be walking by."

"No problem, Doc," Paul said.

"May I join you?" he asked.

"Of course," Paul said, making room for Musashi on the ammo crate.

"Thank you," he said, sitting next to Paul. "Top, may I have a word alone with Captain Owens?"

"Yes, Doctor," she said as she walked away.

"Excellent," Musashi said, gesturing at Paul with a fork laden with venison. "Thanks."

"The colonel told me you decided to name your unit 'Outlaw Company,'" the doctor said.

"Yep," Paul said as he chewed.

"Is there a significance to that name?"

Paul wiped his mouth with a paper napkin and said, "The platoon I commanded on the Horn was called the Outlaws. Figured if got me through that tour, it must be a little lucky."

The Doctor nodded as he took his last bite of venison. They sat together in silence as he chewed slowly.

"What do you think?" Musashi asked as he placed his empty plate and silverware on the ground next to his feet.

"About what?"

"The soldiers. Your unit. Are you ready?"

"We're going to find out."

The doctor nodded. "Any ideas where they will send you?"

"Just guesses," Paul said with a shrug. "I don't know how you decide where to send an experimental unit. Kata thinks back to the Horn of Africa. Seems like they're sending everything that way these days." The doctor looked at Paul with a troubled face. "I'm just looking forward to a few weeks of leave while they figure it out, Doc," Paul said, smiling, trying to change the subject.

Kata laughed loudly across the fire, likely at one of her own jokes. Paul glanced her way. A couple of young male engineers surrounded her, captivated by the exotic warrior queen. Paul had a sense of what was on Kata's mind. They were back to war soon, after all. Paul and the doctor shared a glance.

"I will miss our time together, Paul," he said. "But I am excited for your next chapter."

"Me too, Doc. And, I don't want you to worry. We're ready. You've done a good job with the Ōkami. The kill chain is solid."

The doctor looked at Paul for a long moment.

"What is it?" Paul asked him.

"Paul," he finally said. "I don't know what it is like for you and Kata. I can only try to imagine. I have never been to war."

In almost a year of training, the doctor had never discussed 'war' with Paul and Kata. They spent endless hours discussing tactical situations, strategic trade-offs, and kill chains. But never 'war.'

"You must remember that you are not just at the center of a communications architecture. It is also a moral architecture. And the architecture needs a human to be a moral system, to be a good system, not just a kill-chain-compliant system. Human leadership and values are the key."

Paul looked at the doctor, surprised by the sudden earnestness in his voice, and unsure how to respond to the high ethical stakes he was establishing for him and Kata.

Musashi looked back at him, sympathy on his face.

"Hey there," a female voice behind Paul said.

He turned to look.

It was the computer engineer from Idaho. She smiled and gestured at her empty plate. "So good," she said. "Didn't mean to interrupt. But wanted to say thanks." Her brown hair, ordinarily in a tight bun, was down. It spilled over her shoulders, framing her pretty face. She had ditched her white lab coat. Paul thought the long sleeve grey T-shirt hugged her in all the right ways.

Paul turned back to the Musashi, but the doctor had already grabbed his dirty plate and stood up. Musashi extended his hand. Paul shook it. The doctor nodded, then turned and left.

Paul looked back to the attractive computer engineer and gestured at the spot on the ammo crate the doctor had just left.

She smiled and sat down next to Paul as he ran his hand along the augmentation scars on the side of his head self-consciously.

They both stared awkwardly into the fire for a moment

"So, I'm Melanie," she said, not taking her eyes off the fire.

Paul knew it was unlikely things would progress further than chatting by the fire. But he thought it was a good way to spend that last night.

Chapter Thirty-Three

10 July 2065
New York City

The charter drone met Fiona at six AM on her building's flight platform. It was a warm morning, and she took off her jacket before climbing in. She had worn her favorite dark grey pantsuit, thinking it exuded the right gravitas for the meeting without sacrificing style.

The aircraft rose from the platform and joined the teeming drone traffic above the city as Fiona pulled the materials Pruden sent her last night out of her bag. She placed the folder in her lap and leaned her head back. He said it was important she read the material before the meeting, but it had been an early wake up at the end of a long week. She wanted to rest her eyes for just a few minutes. The vibration of the aircraft's four ducted fan thrusters penetrated the cabin like a soft, relaxing purr.

The jostle of landing woke her an hour and a half later.

Pruden met her at the VIP landing facility with a car.

"Good morning," he said as she got into the vehicle. "How was the flight?"

"Good." Fiona blinked her eyes, trying to shed the lingering drowsiness from her nap as the car pulled out of the parking lot. "Slept the whole way."

"Did you read Colonel Frank's dossier?"

Fiona cast Pruden a sheepish glance.

"Damnit," he muttered.

"I'm sorry."

"This guy is no joke, Fiona."

"So, give me the basics now. You have my full attention."

Pruden glanced at his watch.

"Oh, come on, Marty. Cut me some slack."

"Of course. I'm sorry," Pruden said. "I'm just nervous."

"Me too. So, tell me what I need to know."

Pruden nodded and collected his thoughts.

"Colonel Thomas Frank is the Program Manager for AI Combat Systems. His nickname in the industry is 'The billion dollar man.'"

"No shit?"

"No shit. His budget is classified, but his decisions have decided what companies and projects have lived or died for almost twenty years. His approvals typically mean billions in revenue."

"I like him already," Fiona said. "Did you say almost twenty years?"

"Yeah. He is the longest tenured acquisitions lead in the US Military."

"The whole time in AI combat systems?"

"That's right," Pruden said, with a deliberate nod. "The guy is a maverick. He's an exception to every unwritten military career rule. He was a respected small unit combat leader and promotable major, selected for battalion command, when he surprised everyone and requested a transfer to the AI team in the Acquisitions Corps.

"He was written off by personnel command until the Second Battle of Santiago, when General Havron requested him by name. He left the Acquisitions Corps for a year to command a company in the campaign to liberate Santiago and came back with a bunch of medals, including the Purple Heart. Havron offered him a Combat Corps command during the General's reorganization of the military, but Frank turned it down."

"Turned down General Havron?" Fiona's head cocked in surprise.

"Yeah." Pruden nodded. "He shocked everyone again when he went back to his AI desk in the Acquisitions Corps."

Fiona crossed her arms and leaned back in her seat. Eyes focused on Pruden.

"So, he goes back to Acquisitions as a decorated combat veteran and everyone is figuring he is going over to basically retire on active duty, live the easy life behind a desk. But he attacks it. And, he gives conventional military career wisdom the finger again, staying at the AI combat systems desk for almost another fifteen years now."

"What does that mean?" Fiona asked.

"The standard successful career trajectory in Acquisitions is to bounce around disciplines, networking with as many arms manufactures of as many stripes as possible, while delivering a successful program or two before getting promoted and heading back out into the wider military, or being recruited away by one of the companies you were putting through he paces."

"Ah, graft and perverse incentives," Fiona said with a knowing smile. "What would we do without them?"

Pruden shook his head.

"This guy could make a bazillion dollars a year working for industry. Colonels these days are forced to retire after thirty years of service, but the military has made an exception for him every year for the past couple of years. I'm not even sure if he requests it. They just do it. He is a notoriously hard-nosed program manager and, along the way, has become a globally recognized, visionary AI weapon system strategist."

"And no engineering background?" Fiona asked.

"Not a traditional one," Pruden shrugged. "But he has led troops in combat, fought alongside AI systems, and has been around cutting-edge technology for almost twenty years. Now he's like a veteran football scout that can spot future greatness or certain failure in a quarterback prospect years before anyone else."

Fiona nodded.

Pruden regarded her in silence.

"What?" she asked.

"He is not someone you can run over or charm."

Fiona raised an eyebrow.

"I'm serious, Fiona." Pruden leaned forward slightly to emphasize his point. "No matter what happens, we stay cool. Get out of the room. And make a plan."

"You expect something bad to happen?" Anxiety crept into Fiona's voice.

"No. I don't. We're going to be fine. I'm just saying that whatever happens, this is not a man that responds well to anything other than an even, professional demeanor."

"Got it."

* * *

"This place looks more like a college campus than an army base," Fiona said. She and Pruden walked from their car toward the Military Acquisition Corps headquarters building on Fort Belvoir.

Green grass blanketed the facility beneath leafy trees that stood in front of wide red-brick buildings.

"Yeah, it's an old one," Pruden said. "And what they do here is more science and business than military."

Fiona and Pruden walked up the steps and between the large columns of the headquarters building. They were both excited.

A captain met them at the door.

"Good morning, Miss Malloy. Good to meet you. I am Captain Perry. I'll escort you and Mr. Pruden to the meeting."

"Good morning, Captain," Fiona said, stepping through the door. Pruden followed close behind.

"I've already checked you through security," the captain said. "So, if you'll put these name tags on, we can head on in to the meeting room."

Captain Perry led them past security and down a long hallway to a large meeting room. Two dozen uniformed personnel and engineers were milling about in the room, most clustered around a full bird colonel.

"Ah, Miss Malloy," Colonel Frank said, spotting her as she entered the room.

Tall and angular, the colonel cut an imposing silhouette above the shorter engineers in white lab coats that encircled him. His silver hair was cropped short on the sides but longer and swept back on top, adding height to his narrow, patrician face. After hearing his bio, Fiona had expected a weary man slowed down by experience and fatigue. Instead, as the distinguished officer strode in her direction, she was warmed by the vitality that radiated off him, and intimidated by his intensity. Fiona smoothed her suit jacket.

"I'm Colonel Frank, Program Manager for AI Combat Systems." He extended his hand, fixing her with his cool blue eyes. "It is good to finally meet you in person."

"Good to meet you, sir. I am excited to be here today." She shook the colonel's hand and smiled.

"You should be. Your team should be very proud."

"Good to see you too, Martin," the colonel said. Fiona felt the weight of Frank's attention shift to Pruden as they shook hands. "Can I get you guys a cup of coffee or water?"

"Coffee would be great," Fiona said. Pruden nodded.

Frank turned to the captain. "Perry, go get Malloy and Pruden a cup of coffee." Colonel Frank then pointed at the large conference table. "Please make yourselves comfortable while I try to get all these damn engineers pointed in the right direction."

"Shit," Fiona mumbled to Pruden as Colonel Frank walked back to the gaggle of engineers. "A lot of people."

"Yeah. This is a big deal."

Fiona's phone buzzed. She pulled it out of her pocket and read a text from Eugene.

Today is the day, right?

Yep, she texted back. *And it is already going well,* she continued, hoping her exaggerations would ease his worry.

I'll be so glad when we are through this, Eugene wrote back. *You feel good about it?*

"Excuse me, Miss Malloy!" Colonel Frank said from across the room. "I'm sorry, but no cell phones are allowed. Captain Perry should have told you that."

The colonel glared at Perry, who was almost done preparing coffee for

Fiona and Pruden. The captain nearly jumped out of his shoes to get to Fiona before Colonel Frank did.

"These meetings are classified top secret," Frank said, beating Perry to Fiona and holding out his hand.

Fiona wanted to glance down at Eugene's anxious, unanswered text on her phone, but met the colonel's blue stare instead.

"Miss Malloy," Colonel Frank said. "I'm sorry. This is one of the things us military folks are really uptight about."

"Of course! No problem, Colonel," Fiona said, handing him her phone. "I apologize."

"Sorry, sir." Pruden gave the colonel his phone. "I know better."

"It's not your fault. Captain Perry was responsible for you."

Colonel Frank turned and handed the phones to the now-trembling Captain Perry.

"Secure these phones, Captain, and then bring these two their coffee," Frank growled before turning to corral the rest of the engineers.

Fiona forced herself to share an amused glance with Pruden.

She then winced as she thought of Eugene waiting for a text from her. She tried to put her brother out of her mind. She would be able to call him with good news after the meeting.

Captain Perry returned with two cups of coffee and, after a few more minutes of introductions and handshakes, Colonel Frank started the meeting.

"OK, team." All heads swiveled toward the colonel as he cut through multiple conversations. "We've got a lot to get through today, and I have to be at the Pentagon for a staff meeting at noon. The bird will be here to pick me up at 1130 hours sharp."

He looked at his watch.

"That gives us three and a half hours to get through five hours of information. Let's get started."

A shuffle of chairs ensued. Within seconds, everyone was seated facing Colonel Frank.

"Thank you. The purpose of this meeting is to review the progress of our two ongoing AI-combat-system evaluations we have underway with Miss Malloy's companies. I want to leave here, as I am sure Miss Malloy does, with clear agreement regarding milestones and what comes next."

Colonel Frank looked around the room and then took his seat. An aide handed the colonel a thick three-ring binder full of hundreds of tabbed pages. He muttered thanks and opened the tome to the first page.

Two aides entered the room, one pushing a large cart piled high with additional binders. They circled the room slowly, handing each of the attendees one of the large binders.

"Please open your project binder to page seven," Colonel Frank said to the room as he put on his reading glasses.

Fiona's heart sank as he flipped through her binder.

"Oh Jesus," she muttered, leaning over to Pruden. "Three hundred pages?"

"No shortcuts with these guys," he whispered back. "Might as well strap in and make the best of it. Remember, there are millions of dollars on the other end of this meeting."

"We're going to start with the analysis of field trial phase two," Colonel Frank said to the room.

The parade of charts and graphs and schematics pounded Fiona as she tried to stay engaged. Pruden did most of the talking for them, and the meeting seemed to go well. Thoughts of Eugene nagged at her. She reached for her phone to text him more than once, only to remember it was not in her pocket.

Three hours later, Colonel Frank looked at Fiona and said, "Congratulations, Miss Malloy, I am declaring phase two a success and authorizing the milestone payment of fifty million dollars, as well as immediate planning and preparations for combat trials."

The room applauded.

Fiona nodded and smiled as she nervously flipped through the last sections of the binder.

"What the fuck?" she said, leaning into a beaming Pruden.

"What is it?" he asked.

"There is nothing about Spitting Metal in here," she hissed at him. "Nothing!"

Pruden flipped through the last pages of his binder.

Fiona was right. There was nothing about the proof-of-concept trial that was supposed to begin this year. Fiona had been counting on the milestone payment from this proof of concept to save Spitting Metal and Mio Posto from the lenders.

"Um, sir?" Pruden said to Colonel Frank.

"Is there a problem? I thought you guys would be happier."

"Oh, sir, we are very excited. Trust me," Pruden stammered as Fiona nodded beside him. "On the matter of Spitting Metal's proof of concept, though. Are we not going to discuss the start date and payment milestones for that today?"

"No." The colonel closed his binder and looking at his watch.

Fiona's breath quickened.

"No?" Pruden said.

"No." The colonel stood up and pointed at Captain Perry.

Captain Perry left the room as the colonel began putting things into his satchel.

The sounds of an approaching aircraft penetrated the walls. Fiona tried to maintain control.

"Sir, we don't understand," Pruden said. "That trial is supposed to begin in a month."

"Did you guys not get the email?" Colonel Frank asked, suddenly irritated.

Fiona's and Pruden's blank faces told him what he needed to know.

"Did we not send them the email?" he demanded of the staff officers standing next to him.

"Shit," the colonel said after the staff officers exchanged a series of shrugs and blank faces. "I apologize, Miss Malloy and Mr. Pruden, but the Spitting Metal trial has been re-scheduled for sometime late next fiscal year."

"What?" Fiona shouted.

The anger in her voice froze the room.

Colonel Frank, not used to hearing that tone of voice, put down his satchel. "Excuse me, Miss Malloy?"

"You can't do this," she continued, eyes fixed on Colonel Frank, pleading. "It has to move forward. It has to. That kind of delay would… It would… You can't do this!"

Pruden put his hand on Fiona's shoulder and interjected. "I'm sorry, sir. It's just that this is news to us, and we've been working very hard to get Spitting Metal ready for their trial. We have, frankly, dedicated enormous resources that we would have directed elsewhere had we known about this schedule change. I'm sure you can understand."

His hand still on Fiona's shoulder, Pruden felt her trembling.

He glanced at her and tried to give her the signal to calm down. But her eyes darted around the room in panic.

Colonel Frank regarded Fiona. He had been doing this long enough to have seen it before. The desperate technology company just one step ahead of their bank, shareholders, or whoever it was that had funded them. He didn't understand that life. But he knew that, back in his operational days, he had been the author of many a desperate tactical plan. Plans that a slight shift in the winds of fate would have reduced to bloody disaster. His reckoning never came. But he knew that made him lucky. Not good.

"We are still very excited about Spitting Metal's potential, Miss Malloy," Colonel Frank said. "It's just a schedule and budget thing. Our wheels turn slowly here in the federal government."

The colonel watched his words hit Fiona like bullets. Her reaction seemed out of whack to him.

"Should I be concerned about Spitting Metal's financial health?"

"No." Fiona willed her voice to be calm and decisive. The colonel's direct question reeled her back in. Time to bluff.

"It's just frustrating, Colonel Frank." Fiona crossed her arms. "As Martin said, we've dedicated a lot of resources to Spitting Metal. If I had known you guys were going to delay us, I would have focused those resources on

Musashi. We'd be further down the road there. I just hate inefficiency and missed opportunity."

Fiona stared at the colonel.

He stared back at her.

"Thank you, sir," Pruden said, breaking into the standoff. "Can you give us any more insight into the potential schedule?" Pruden wanted to get every scrap of information he could get out of the closing minutes of this meeting. The sound of the aircraft vibrated the windows, and wind swirled in the courtyard where it was landing.

Colonel Frank left his eyes on Fiona as he answered.

"The Ōkami are my priority right now. I want to get a good look at their combat trials and make an acquisitions decision. If we move forward with them, we will need to devise a fielding strategy and organizational hypothesis. After we have completed all that, we will get serious about Spitting Metal."

Fiona knew she was being measured. She held herself still and her face placid as she raged inside.

Pruden asked the question for her.

"So, then, sir… the Spitting Metal timeline would likely b—"

"I expect we'll have a kickoff meeting for that project in twelve, maybe eighteen months," Colonel Frank said as Captain Perry came back into the room. "Then I would expect the first execution milestone about twelve months after that. The bottom line is that we will move sequentially."

"Sir, your bird is landing," Perry said.

Colonel Frank nodded to Captain Perry, eyes still on Fiona.

"Everything I see about Spitting Metal is very positive. Use this time to get them ready. To make sure it is a home run."

We don't have that kind of time! Fiona thought in despair. She forced herself to smile and stand straight, though her knees were weak and she started trembling again. She smiled at Colonel Frank. *We can't make it two years!*

"Good meeting, everyone." Colonel Frank finally broke eye contact with Fiona and looked around the room. He then nodded to Pruden and Fiona and left without shaking their hands. Most of the military engineers followed him out.

Fiona sat down in a daze with a look on her face that Pruden had never seen before.

"I'll walk you two out," Captain Perry said.

"Thank you." Pruden pulled on Fiona to get her started out of her chair.

Captain Perry gave them their phones back at the door, and they said goodbye.

"Great meeting," the young officer said with a well-meaning smile. "Congratulations."

The roar of Colonel Frank's bird taking off drowned out the sound of Pruden saying, "Thank you." The dark shape rose from behind the building and accelerated away.

They sat in silence for most of the drive back to the airport.

"What if we cancelled the Ōkami trial ourselves?" Fiona asked Pruden.

"What do you mean?"

"I mean, the fucking Ōkami are in the way of Spitting Metal's survival. What if I cancelled the trial? They are my machines, after all. That might help accelerate things for Spitting Metal."

Pruden shook his head.

"Very bad idea," he said, looking at Fiona. Her face was a knot of tension.

"Why?" Fiona demanded.

"You have to understand the military acquisition mindset." Pruden spoke carefully, knowing that Fiona was close to losing it. "When the military's acquisition corps invests time and effort in something like the Ōkami, or Spitting Metal, you must be perceived as a stable, reliable partner. In every way. Or you will get blackballed."

Fiona glared at Pruden.

"If you yank the Ōkami now, we will never recover," Pruden said in an apologetic voice. "We will be branded as undependable. And we will never get Spitting Metal up to the plate."

Pruden looked at Fiona. He thought she might start to cry. She turned her head from him and looked out of the window. Her shoulders rose and fell as she got control of her breathing. A few minutes later, she turned her head back toward the front and said, "I understand. Thank you."

Pruden nodded. He sank back in his seat, relieved.

Fiona held her phone in her hand. She stared at it but had not switched it on yet. She was scared to. She did not know what to say to the texts from Eugene that waited for her.

"We'll figure something out," Pruden said to her, not believing it.

"Musashi and his fucking Ōkami," Fiona mumbled without looking up from her phone.

"This is solvable, Fiona. We'll find a way forward. We always do."

"I don't know how. We've got one, maybe two, months of runway with Talisman. Then we're done. We won't be able to make the payments. We'll lose the business, and I will be ruined. Bankrupt."

Fiona didn't say the rest. That Eugene would lose Mio Posto. And she would lose Eugene.

She turned on her phone.

It buzzed as it registered new text messages from Eugene.

Hello? the first one said after she had not responded to his last.

You must be in the meeting.

Please call me right after.

I can't wait to hear the good news!

Love you.

Chapter Thirty-Four

17 July 2065
New York City

Fiona steeled herself as she walked into Talisman Partners LLC. She was about to do something she had never done before. She didn't know exactly how to approach it. But she had to succeed.

She was walking into Talisman to beg.

She needed more time.

Fiona stood in the lobby and looked at the same velour chairs she and Pruden had sat in years ago. She thought of her cavalier pride back then and wanted to vomit. She had risked too much.

They made her wait almost forty-five minutes. She refused to sit. She paced back and forth, reciting her speech, the one she hoped would buy her the time she needed, the one she hoped would save Mio Posto.

"Miss Malloy?" the receptionist finally said. "Would you follow me, please?"

Fiona followed her down a long hallway. At the end, the receptionist opened a pair of French doors, and Fiona walked into a small meeting room where her grandfather sat at the end of an oval table. The senior partner of Talisman, Buck Dorrity, stood behind Robert Malloy II, smiling.

"What the fuck?" Fiona said.

"Such language," her grandfather said with a straight face.

"You scheming asshole!" Fiona yelled, pointing at Dorrity. "I'm going to sue this place to the ground for violation of our nondisclosure!"

Dorrity laughed. "But, sweetheart. You have no money to sue us with. That's why you are here."

Fiona's arm dropped to her side. She looked at her grandfather and then back at Dorrity. She took a deep breath and stood as straight as she could under the weight of her crumbling world.

"What now?" she asked her grandfather.

Robert Malloy II leaned forward in his chair and, after a hint of a glance over his shoulder at Dorrity, pointed at the door.

Dorrity nodded and left the room.

Fiona's grandfather gestured for Fiona to sit.

She took a chair at the opposite end of the table.

Her grandfather stared at her for a long moment before speaking.

"You are a prideful and careless little bitch, you know that?"

Fiona did not respond. She looked at him with a blank face she hoped did not betray her emotions.

"Did you really believe your flimsy non-disclosure agreement would prevent them from coming to me? That they would hold your confidence more dear than earning favor with me?"

Fiona sat in silence.

"Did you really believe that I was not aware of Determined End States?"

Fiona looked at her feet to hide her surprise and disappointment that he knew that name.

"Did you really think you could hide your activities from me?"

Fiona lifted her eyes and glared at the old man.

"From me!" he yelled.

Fiona started in her chair as her grandfather struck the table with his hand. He was on his feet and pointing at her with a bony finger.

"Prideful, careless, ignorant little bitch!" he yelled in a voice Fiona was sure everyone on the floor could hear.

Fiona trembled. She trembled with rage, sadness, embarrassment, and despair. And with fear. Because as bad as this moment was, she dreaded having to tell Eugene she had lost Mio Posto.

But she kept glaring at the old man. She would not give him the satisfaction of seeing her tears or fear or pain.

Her grandfather sat down slowly. He leaned back in his chair and said, "Why?"

Fiona hesitated.

"Answer me, girl," he said. "Why did you hide this from me?"

"Because I knew you would try to control it," she said, realizing it was over and there was nothing more to lose. "And I despise you. I despise our family. I wanted to create something fucking huge and rub it in your mean old face. Then I wanted to be free. And I wanted Eugene to be free too."

"Oh yes," her grandfather said. "The deviant. Of course. How could I forget? Always a pair, you two were. It makes no sense to me, though, what you have done. You were both millionaires. You were free. And yet you risked it all to achieve…what?"

"I told you," she said. "To show you how wrong you were."

She knew it sounded stupid. She didn't care.

Her grandfather tilted his head as he regarded her.

"That's it?" he asked.

"Yes."

"I don't believe it," he said.

"I don't care."

"I see that you believe it. But I don't."

Fiona shrugged to make it clear she did not care what he believed. But she had to know.

"What did you do?" she asked him.

"I made a deal with Talisman. Your debt is to me now."

Fiona stopped herself from gasping. She willed herself not to shake. She took a deep, even breath and placed her hands on the table.

"So, what now?" she asked.

"That depends."

"On what?"

"On what you are willing to do," he said.

She waited for him to continue.

"Are you willing to call your gay boy brother and tell him to vacate his grimy little villa immediately, that its new owner is planning to bulldoze it to the ground?"

Fiona blinked.

"No?" her grandfather asked.

"Then are you willing to do what it takes to make Spitting Metal realize the full potential you saw in it in the first place?"

"Yes," she said without hesitation. "I would do that."

Her grandfather paused. He leaned forward in his chair. "I can't tell. I am usually quite a good judge of people. But right now, at this moment, I cannot tell if you are willing."

"I am."

"I don't know," he said. "I don't know if you know what I mean. I don't know if you know what it will take. I am not talking about running Spitting Metal more efficiently, or finding synergies, or improving on its core competence, or any of the other useless high-concept bullshit you spent too much money learning at Harvard.

"I'm talking about sticking your arm up to your shoulder into the stinking, convulsing birth canal and ripping that screaming, bloody, shit-covered fetus out into the world. And then, while it lies on the floor in its own piss and afterbirth, are you willing to kill anything that comes near it? To protect it like a bloodthirsty she-wolf? To kill food for it to eat? And to keep killing until it can walk, then run, then kill and live on its own?"

He looked at her.

"Because the world is the same everywhere for everyone. Nothing lives without killing something else. You don't get a pass because you are a Malloy. If you take this path, you will face your moment, the time when you will be shown how far you have to go to get what you want. And then you will have to do it. Or I will finish you. And your deviant brother. For good."

"I will," she said. "I will do it."

"We'll see," her grandfather said, standing up. "You have twelve months from today."

Fiona sat at the table alone for a long time after her grandfather left.

THE
SOUTHERN
CONE

Chapter Thirty-Five

9 September 2065
Southern Cone

It took a formation of six heavy drones to deploy Paul and Kata, their betas, two hundred soldierbots, and all of their extension platforms to the South American continent.

They landed after midnight. A slight breeze blew the sixty-degree air around the busy airfield on Forward Operating Base Stalwart.

FOB Stalwart, South America's version of Resolve, was a large operating base just outside of the city of Cali in southwest Colombia. With easy access to the nearby Pacific Ocean and the natural defensive feature of the Andes Mountains running south to north through the country, it was a valuable and strategic facility.

Anti-aircraft and other defensive equipment ringed the massive airfield. Squadrons of heavy drones sat like resting athletes as far as the eye could see. The lights of incoming aircraft stacked up behind each other for miles in a straight, stair-stepping line that disappeared into the clouds almost twenty miles to the north.

Paul and Kata noticed another similarity to Resolve.

"Fucking smoothies," Kata said, hands on her hips as she looked around at the ground crew that met them.

"What did you expect?" Paul said.

"What is a 'smoothie,' sir?" Paul's first sergeant asked as they walked to the second heavy drone.

"Useless folds of skin wrapped in a military uniform," Kata answered.

Paul chuckled and nodded at his first sergeant, who looked at him for confirmation. "Top, secure the heavies for the night. We'll start the download in the morning."

"Roger that, sir," she said.

* * *

The next day, Paul and Kata left their first sergeants in charge of the off-loading and pre-operational checks while they reported to Lieutenant General Schofield's headquarters deep in the interior of Stalwart.

The three-star general commanded all coalition forces in South America. The first thing they noticed was that he was a smoothie.

Most generals were, of course. The Centaur program was a small piece of a huge military, and most of the current flag officers were already field grades when it got going. Ninety-five percent of the Centaur billets were captain and below.

But Paul and Kata still exchanged disappointed glances as they walked into one of the most important combatant commands in the US military and greeted a general and his staff without another Centaur in sight.

"Captains Owens and Vukovic reporting for duty, sir," Paul said, standing at attention with Kata in the doorway to the briefing room.

"Welcome," General Schofield said, returning the salute. "Come in and meet the team."

Schofield's briefing room was a small multimedia setup with two dozen seats. The four rows of seats were laid out stadium style, with the rear row sitting well above the front. The general and his senior staff stood in front of the first row, waiting to greet Paul and Kata.

"This is my deputy commander for operations, Brigadier General Keil," Schofield said, introducing them first to a one-star general with manicured fingernails. "Your companies fall under his authority."

"Good to meet you, sir," Paul said. "Looking forward to working together."

"Me too," Keil said with zero enthusiasm.

"Colonel Packard commands my heavy drone force," Schofield said, stepping to his right. "Also under Keil's authority. His guys really pack a punch."

Paul forced a smile. Kata did not.

Packard regarded them without expression. His slight paunch bulged beneath his crisp flight suit with colorful patches.

"Lieutenant Colonel Thurman commands our exo battalion," Schofield said, standing in front of the next officer. "You and your machines will work closely with him at some point, I am sure. If I'm not mistaken, you both served in an exo battalion before joining the Centaur Corps, isn't that right?"

"Yes, sir," Paul answered the awkward question as he stepped in front of the lieutenant colonel.

Exos did not like Centaurs. Particularly senior career exo soldiers like Thurman. They did not appreciate being viewed as a training ground and recruiting pool for Centaurs. Also, in the martial code of many exos, Centaurs were an abomination, a tainting of both man and machine, a form of cheating and cowardice.

Centaurs didn't like exos much either, viewing them as the B-team and suspecting that behind every judgmental exo soldier was a rejection letter from the Centaur Corps.

The fact that General Schofield brought it up at all just highlighted smoothie ignorance of the military's true warrior classes.

But interwoven with all of that was the fact was they were both the last parts of the human military that faced the enemy on the field, that were shot at, that were wounded and killed in direct-action combat. They would be chewing the same dirt together in South America and, sure as shit, would need each other more than once in the near future. Thurman was the only person in the room, other than Paul and Kata, wearing a bayonet on his left hip.

He was, at the end of the day, Combat Corps like them.

"Good to meet you, Colonel," Paul said with sincerity, extending his hand.

"Likewise," Thurman said, shaking Paul's hand and then Kata's. He made a point of nodding toward their bayonets. They nodded back.

"Welcome to Stalwart. If there is anything I can do for you guys, please let me know," he added.

"We will, sir," Paul said. "Thank you."

"If you don't mind, I'd like to get started," General Schofield said. "We have a lot to get through today, and I have a hard stop in an hour. You can meet the rest of the staff when we are done."

The half dozen officers that Paul and Kata had not yet been introduced to nodded at them and took their seats.

The three-star sat in the middle of the front row and gestured at the two seats next to him. Paul and Kata sat there while the general's staff moved to the rows behind them.

"Let's go, Wainwright," the general said once everyone was seated.

The task force intelligence officer, Lieutenant Colonel Wainwright, stepped in front of the large combination video and holo display and clicked a small control in his hand to get things going.

As the display kicked into gear, General Schofield leaned over to Paul and Kata and said, "I've asked intel to start high level and work their way down. I hope that works for you two?"

"Yes, sir," Paul said as a satellite image of the continent leapt onto the screen.

"South America is roughly divided into thirds," Wainwright began. As he spoke and pointed, multicolored icons and outlines flew around on the map display. "The US holds the northwest, with strong positions in Bogotá, Quito, and Lima. We also maintain control of Santiago, which still hasn't recovered completely from the battles there more than a decade ago. The Chinese hold the northeast, from Caracas, their decades-old stronghold, southeast to where the Amazon River flows into the Atlantic Ocean. This less populated southern third of the continent, called the Southern Cone, is up for grabs."

"It's too big, too empty, and too far away," General Keil said.

Wainwright nodded.

Schofield looked at Paul and Kata. "You two might as well come to grips with this right now. Africa is the real contest. Both for us and the Chinese.

Controlling that continent is the grand prize of empires. This theater is second tier. So, we are never going to have the resources to secure the Southern Cone the way we would like. Fortunately, so far, the Chinese don't either."

Paul and Kata nodded.

Schofield gestured for Wainwright to continue.

"Despite the mutual resource constraints the general mentioned, the Cone remains tense."

"Tense as hell," General Keil grumbled.

"Neither we nor the Chinese want the other to get too comfortable in the Cone," Wainwright continued. "We, in particular, cannot afford a strong, coherent enemy down there because, unlike the Chinese positions, we are vulnerable from the south.

"Note that the Chinese sit north of the Amazon River, which cuts across almost the entire continent, from the Andes Mountains to the Atlantic Ocean. No land force is going to penetrate the largest river-drainage basin in the world. And hypersonic air defenses rule out an air assault of any size.

"That leaves us only two avenues of attack. The first, from the Atlantic Ocean, which would be suicide. The second, overland from the west. But the border of Colombia and Venezuela is the most heavily armed and lethal in the world."

Schofield leaned forward and gestured at the map. "It makes the old Fulda Gap, where the Americans and Russians stared each other down in Europe almost a hundred years ago look like the crossing from Vermont into Montreal."

"Our greatest vulnerability," Wainwright continued, "is a soft underbelly to the south. Santiago is solid, having devolved into a fortress city under nearly constant martial law. No one is really worried that the Chinese can actually get past it. It is too well fortified, and any overland approach would be concentrated and made vulnerable by the looming Southern Andes, which mark the border with Brazil."

Schofield smiled. "Not to mention... The Chileans are still mightily pissed off. The Chinese would have hell to pay if they tried it."

"But, if they did get past Santiago," Wainwright said, "they could drive along the western edge of the Andes all the way to Panama, rolling up our positions all along the way to where we sit right now.

"China knows we are sensitive about that aspect of the south, and they have demonstrated admirable strategic patience there. They keep things riled up throughout the Cone with guerilla proxies, but never do enough for us to dedicate real forces."

"So, for fifteen years," Schofield interjected, eyes focused on the map, "the Southern Cone has been a boiling shit stew of scheming guerillas, opportunistic Russian arms dealers, and ever-present Chinese intelligence."

"And we're dropping you two right in the middle of it," Keil said with a smile.

"Don't get ahead of us, General," Schofield said over his shoulder. He pointed at Wainwright to continue.

"The most active Chinese proxy in the Cone is General Horacio Navarro," the intel officer said as a photo of Navarro appeared on the screen next to the map. "He comes from a long line of gauchos, the tough, nomadic cowboys of South America. His ancestors famously fought in the country's successful effort to expel the Spanish Colonial forces over two hundred years ago. Then, for hundreds of years, the Navarros have been part of the violent and unruly history of the Pampas, the vast grasslands that cover most of Argentina and the Cone, from the Andean foothills to the Atlantic Ocean."

"What is he general of?" Kata asked.

"Navarro calls himself a general because he graduated from a Chinese military academy back when the Chinese were doing a lot of that kind of cultural and military exchange stuff in the region. After graduation, though, Navarro came back to Argentina and led a small guerrilla force against the Chinese, whose presence was strong in the country at that time. They were trying to tip it all the way over to communism and vassal statehood. Navarro and his bandits killed a lot of Chinese soldiers before they finally captured him."

"Why didn't they execute him when they had the chance?" Paul asked.

"Good question," Wainwright said. "We don't know. We do know that he spent years in prison before getting out. There are differing accounts of how he got out. Some say he escaped. Some say he was released. But once he did regain his freedom, he went straight back to the Pampas and started kicking ass. Navarro's tactics have been aggressive. And he is in the final stages of a ruthless ten-year ascent to primacy. There are other guerrillas in the Southern Cone, of course, but Horacio Navarro is the Chinese favorite."

"Probably because he is such a pain in our ass," General Keil said.

General Schofield swiveled in his chair to face Paul and Kata.

"I know you two have the clearance, so I will share with you some very sensitive information. This information is not to leave this room. Do you understand?"

He waited for a nod from both Paul and Kata before continuing.

"A month ago, I was told to start preparing for an offensive to reduce, if not eliminate, Chinese influence in the region."

Schofield paused to let his statement sink in. Then he made it clear.

"That's right, captains. A direct military attack on the Chinese."

Paul and Kata took in the information in silence.

Schofield leaned back in his chair, looking exhausted.

"When I was told to start planning for an offensive operation," he continued, "I requested more heavy drones and at least a brigade of ground forces to seal off the Southern Cone while I go toe to toe against the Chinese. I asked them for anything that could be spared. I didn't care who they sent as long as they could hold a rifle. But you know what I was told?"

Paul and Kata felt the shift in the room. They wore their most polite faces.

"I was told no," the general said. "I was told that the mission in Africa was the priority. That every operational brigade with better than eighty percent strength was either already headed that way or was reserved in case it was needed there. Same for every heavy drone that can fly. Imagine my relief and joy, then," the general continued with a false smile, "when command, after refusing my request, told me that, though the brigade I requested was not available, help was on the way."

The general leaned forward.

"They were sending me two Centaurs." Schofield held up two fingers to emphasize his point. "Two Centaurs and a complement of the latest robotic-soldier recipe."

The general paused with a scowl, just in case there was any question he was not happy about this.

"I threw a goddamn fit but got overruled," he said, leaning back in his chair. "So here we are."

Paul and Kata didn't know what to say. Wainwright, still standing in front of the map, looked at his feet.

"I want to be very clear on this," Schofield said, pointing toward the map. "I don't give a shit about what happens on the Cone as long as it does not interfere with my operations. You just make damn well sure to keep that prick Navarro in his box."

"So, is that our mission, sir?" Kata asked. She had heard enough. "Keep the prick in a box?"

Schofield's eyes narrowed slightly.

"Yes. It is. Any questions, Captain Vukovic?"

"No, sir."

"So, I guess this briefing is over, then?" Paul added.

"It is," General Schofield said, standing up.

Everyone jerked up from their chairs to attention.

Rather than giving the at-ease command to release the room, Schofield walked slowly from his chair as everyone remained standing at attention.

Paul and Kata stood, locked up, as the general walked around the table and stepped in front of them.

"Wainwright will answer any more questions you have. And you'll get full access to our intel feed. Make sure they set that up before you head out. But I'll just warn you, it's not going to be very useful to you. It's all pointed northeast in support of my operations. It's not fair to you, and it's not fair to me. But command told me you guys could handle it. That was the deal. So, go fucking handle it."

Paul and Kata didn't talk much as they rode back to the hangar where their companies were unloading and conducting pre-combat inspections. After checking in with their first sergeants, they sat in their planning room and stared at the operational map of the Southern Cone and the millions of square miles they were now responsible for.

"Does this seem like a reasonable mission to you?" Kata asked Paul.

"Depends on what you're trying to do," Paul answered with a grimace. "If your goal is really to provide security and stability to the Southern Cone, then no. If you're trying to throw a new weapons system into the deep end to see if it floats, then, yeah, it's perfect."

"Perfectly impossible," Kata said under her breath.

"We promised the old man we'd touch base," Paul said, looking at his watch.

"Yeah. He's going to love this."

"What the hell?" Filson yelled a few minutes later on the secure videoconference. "You guys are not designed to be an occupying force. You were designed to be a special-ops strike force, to destroy the enemy using highly focused fire, maneuver, and shock effect. Not to occupy and hold terrain or to provide ongoing security operations. You're not equipped for that. It's like putting a basketball team on the football field. It's fucked up!"

"This is really providing me the emotional boost I needed," Kata said to Paul. "How about you?"

"I'm sorry," Filson said, rubbing his eyes.

"It's weird, sir," Paul said. "I can't decide if we are being misapplied out of ignorance, or out of a desire to see if we will sink or swim."

"Well, you're going to fucking swim," the colonel said. "I guarantee you that. What is Schofield like?"

"Fucking smoothie," Kata said.

"What did you expect?" Filson asked.

"I don't know," Paul said, agreeing with Kata. "At least one Centaur on his staff would have been nice."

Filson shrugged. "Nevertheless, if you and the Ōkami prove out, you will usher in a massive force multiplier that will radically affect the way the Combat Corps is able to resource operations. And you'll probably save a bunch of civilians and kill a few thousand guerrilla leaders and terrorists along the way."

"And if we fail," Paul said, "no one is going to mourn two junior officers and a bunch of robots."

Filson scowled at the comment, but held his tongue.

Paul and Kata looked at their feet.

Colonel Filson looked at his protégés and said, "Remember, guys, everything smells like shit on no sleep. Get some rack and let's talk tomorrow."

"Roger that, sir," Kata said as she switched off the videoconference.

Chapter Thirty-Six

Paul and Kata walked in silence across the flight line. Their companies were loading up onto aircraft as the sun rose over Forward Operating Base Stalwart. The large expanse of tarmac was a scene of frenetic activity as the Outlaws and the Apaches loaded and boarded aircraft to head out to the bleeding edge. Soldierbots, betas, and extension platforms loaded onto the QC-10s. The rising sun, scraping over the mountains, gave the Ōkami a burnished, faint orange glint as they moved across the dark airfield surface.

It was going to take several sorties to move both companies to their forward outposts. Schofield had denied their request for heavy drone support, which could have lifted the Outlaws and Apaches and all of their equipment in one flight. The general was setting the tone.

They got to the Apache staging area first. The two Centaur officers stood amid the activity for a long moment. Paul looked over Kata's shoulder as the last of her soldierbots climbed onto the Eagles.

"This doesn't feel right, does it?" Paul asked.

"No. Not at all."

They both tried to think of something to say, but couldn't.

"Fuck it," Kata said. "How bad can it be?"

They couldn't hug or shake hands well because of their battle suits, so they bumped armored fists. The familiar thud of the titanium-laced ceramic sounded good.

They turned and walked to their aircraft.

Paul and Kata were headed for separate outposts. They had named them before leaving Stalwart. They were sick of the military's platitudinal approach to naming: "Resolve," "Stalwart," "Endurance," "Courage," and the like.

They we went with names with more personal meaning.

Paul named his "Devil," after one of his favorite spots in Colorado where he grew up. In high school, he and his buddies had spent hours at the Devil's Punchbowl, swimming, drinking, and wooing girls.

Kata named hers "Philly" after her hometown.

They were feeling isolated. Out there. And not just physically out there. They felt isolated even from the military. The smoothies and REMFs on Stalwart felt as foreign and inhospitable to them as the rest of the Southern Cone. So, sometimes, it felt good at the end of a mission to head back to a place that reminded them of home. Even if they were the only humans who lived on the isolated outposts.

Devil, just like Philly, wasn't much to look at. It was a group of barren flat spots on the eastern-facing slopes of the Andes about ten miles north of the Uspallata Pass, one of the few direct, overland links between Chile and Argentina. By the time Paul and Kata got there, humans had been using the Uspallata Pass to get over the Andes for a thousand years. At its highest point, it was 12,500 feet above sea level. Both outposts were about two thousand feet below the peaks. But still high enough for it to take a week for them to acclimate to the thin air. From Devil, Paul could see the Argentinian town of Mendoza in the distance, almost ten thousand feet below.

As a military outpost, Devil was reasonably secure. Not only did they have the benefit of backbreaking mountainous terrain and tens of miles of easy line-of-sight surveillance all around, they were also surrounded by several concentric rings of sensors and patrolling weapons systems. Nothing could get close without being detected and challenged. Inside the perimeter, they burrowed their shipping-container structures into the mountain, digging out a system of bunkers that would protect them from just about anything on the conventional end of the munitions spectrum.

They had everything they needed, from maintenance to medical. They could fabricate their own repair parts, update software, and even design and produce new extension-platform configurations. Paul's human requirements were more than taken care of by their feeding, hydration, and sanitation capabilities. And, if necessary, the MedPod could handle just about any wound or injury he might sustain. As long as Top or one of the other soldiers got him back to the MedPod alive, he would survive and the kill chain would remain intact.

For consumables they could not produce on their own, like some ammunition types, Paul sent a Dragon back to Stalwart for resupply every couple of days.

The first month was low key. Paul and his betas familiarized themselves with the area and went on patrols every day and night, fine-tuning their standard operating procedures. They also started getting a feel for the people, villages, cities, and towns. 667 in particular.

Many of the towns had soccer fields on their outskirts. Paul noticed that 667 occasionally seemed distracted by the back and forth of the ball. Not always, but enough that Paul, having spent every waking hour for more than a year with the Ōkami betas, noticed.

After a few trips outside the wire with 667, Paul noticed her distraction arose only when the threat condition was low. 667, like Paul and the rest of the Outlaws, operated with a constant networked situational awareness that encompassed not only every platform in the unit but also any theater-level resources they were able to access. When the endpoints and networking were robust, the Outlaws had a lot of confidence in their assessment of low threat.

And that was when 667, like an eager Labrador retriever, glanced at the moving ball and the kids who chased it.

"What are you looking at, 67?" Paul asked her at the end of a long, uneventful patrol. A wolf pack, twenty soldierbots strong, walked in an extended wedge formation, Paul at the apex.

"The ball, sir," 667 said. "The game the children here play is interesting."

"Think so?" Paul asked as he stopped walking. 667 stepped up next to him.

"I do, sir."

"Why don't you give it a try?"

667 looked at Paul. Then at the soccer field. Then back to Paul.

"It's OK," Paul said. "We're clear for a twenty-kilometer radius."

"It's not necessary, sir. I would prefer to complete the patrol and get our soldierbots back to Devil."

"I would prefer you try to play soccer," Paul said, summoning a small tracked XP to his side. The soldierbots, acting on a mental command from Paul, moved out of the wedge formation and formed a perimeter around the soccer field. Paul removed his helmet and sat down on the XP. He leaned his weapon against the track and crossed his arms. "And that's an order."

"Yes, sir," the tall Ōkami said.

"Give me your rifle."

667 handed Paul her weapon.

"Just don't hurt any of those kids," Paul said, nervousness creeping into his voice.

"I will not, sir."

"I mean it."

"Yes, sir," 667 said over her shoulder, running toward the group of kids surrounding the soccer ball.

Paul watched as the group of amused kids quickly taught 667 the rules of soccer. Accustomed to humanoid maintenance and chorebots from their daily lives, the Ōkami looked like just another dumb, subservient machine to them. When it was time to pick teams for the next game, Paul chuckled when 667 was picked dead last.

A few minutes later, though, 667 had both teams laughing and squealing in wonder. She also had Paul on his feet.

Neither side was keeping score, and 667 had everyone in the action. She was a spectacular passing machine. Confining herself to the center circle, she alternated her long, arcing assists back and forth to either side of the field. Kids took turns heading and kicking her perfectly placed passes into the goal. If Paul hadn't known better, he would have mistaken 667's fluid ballistic solutions and leaping kicks as expressions of joy. Paul lost track of time.

"Everything OK down there, sir?" Top called on the radio.

Paul looked at his watch.

"Shit," he said. "Roger that, Top. We're wrapping up here."

"Shall I send the Dragons?"

"Roger that," Paul said, pulling on his helmet. "Send them down the mountain. I'll send coordinates for pickup shortly."

"Yes, sir."

"Wrap it up, Mia Hamm," Paul said to 667 over the radio. "Game over."

"On the way, sir."

667 sat next to Paul on Dragon One as the aircraft labored up to Outpost Devil. Paul and the soldierbots rode inside. The two ground XPs were slung beneath.

"What is 'Mia Hamm,' sir?" 667 asked Paul.

"Mia Hamm was a badass American soccer player. She was a two-time Olympic gold medalist about fifty years ago."

Dragon One landed at Devil, and the small patrol force hopped out.

"Put the soldierbots to bed while I link up with Top in the command hooch," Paul told the Ōkami.

"Roger that, sir."

"Good work today, Mia," Paul said with a smile.

"Thank you, sir."

* * *

The next day, the Outlaws got shot at for the first time.

Paul was on foot with Mia again just to the south of a small village with a dozen soldierbots on a night patrol. They had an aerial XP overhead. A shot rang out from their right flank.

The sniper's bullet made a snapping noise as it passed less than a foot in front of Paul's head.

He could tell from the sound that it was high caliber.

"Sniper!" Paul yelled as he turned to find cover. But he didn't even take his first step before the flash hit him. The sniper was on a rooftop two hundred meters to their west, drawing down on them. He was about to squeeze the trigger again when his head disappeared in a puff of red mist.

For a moment, Paul doubted it had happened. He could not believe how smooth it had been. Targeting imagery from an airborne XP to Mia, relayed to Paul by neural link, received and adjudicated at the speed of thought by his brain, neural-linked back to Mia, command sent to the AXP, armored piercing round fired into the guerrilla's skull.

Paul had not been aware he had given the kill authorization as he did it. It was strange. He spoke with Kata about it that night on their secure video link.

"It went down exactly like training," he told her. "Just as quick. So quick that I wondered if I had really given the authorization. When I started the program. I pictured myself taking my time, adjudicating each situation consistent with the rules of engagement, and then transmitting solemn official commands. 'I, Paul Owens,'" Paul said, intoning his voice in a deep and official-sounding baritone, "'do hereby authorize the just killing of the designated enemy combatant…'"

Kata laughed at him. "You are such a dork."

"Fuck you. I'm telling you, I just killed a man, and it seemed like no thought went into it. It was sublime. Bang. You're dead."

Kata smiled. "So, the shit worked."

"Yeah," Paul said. "It did."

Kata nodded.

Then she smiled.

"I guess that was his first test?" she said.

"What do you mean?" Paul asked.

"Navarro," she said. "That was his first test. Sniper on the roof of a nearby village."

Paul nodded.

"Game on," Kata said. "Finally."

Chapter Thirty-Seven

The next time Paul had to flex the neural link was more of a real firefight. A large group of Navarro's guerrillas ambushed an aid convoy on a desolate stretch of highway through the Pampas. The convoy made a Mayday call in the blind, which was picked up by Paul's listening equipment. Moments later, General Schofield's deputy commander called Paul on the radio.

"This is a fifty-vehicle UN convoy," General Keil said with emphasis. "Navarro has never been this bold before. Ordinarily, he wouldn't hit something so big. We can't let the bastard do something like this with impunity. How fast could you guys get there?"

Paul looked at the map with Top.

"Looks like about twenty minutes," he said.

"Including planning time?" Keil asked with doubt in his voice.

"Roger that," Paul said, rolling his eyes to Top.

Paul waited as Keil conferred with some people on his end of the line. Paul recognized the voice of Packard, the heavy drone commander.

"We don't want to take this on with heavy drones," Keil said a moment later. "We'd kill too many of the UN folks. And it will take us at least two hours to get there with one of Thurman's exo companies. It's your mission, Captain."

Paul looked at Top as he said, "Consider it done."

Seven minutes later, Paul, Top, and 357 walked up the aft ramp of separate Dragons, each with a wolf pack of ten soldierbots.

Dragon One carried two aerial XPs, one on each wing.

"Standard ingress profile, D1," Paul commanded as he climbed on board.

"Roger that, sir," Dragon One responded as he took off.

"Time to target?" Paul asked.

"Time to target seventeen minutes, thirty-five seconds, sir."

The three Dragons dove off the mountain and accelerated to three hundred knots while maintaining an altitude of fifty feet above the rocky, descending terrain. Paul's ears popped, struggling to equalize during the rapid descent. Top was in the lead aircraft, 357 was in Chalk Two, and Paul rode in the trail aircraft.

The Dragons pulled up as the terrain leveled out. Their engines screamed, working harder to maintain airspeed.

When they were two minutes out from the target, Paul radioed the lead aircraft. "OK, Dragon Two. I'm sure they have detected us by now. Go ahead and put a swarm on top of them."

"Roger that, sir," she answered as a rocket fired from her nose.

The rocket arced ahead toward the stricken convoy, now less than ten kilometers away.

Seconds later, the rocket disintegrated five hundred feet over the smoking, motionless convoy. Twelve hundred tiny airborne sensor drones dispersed through the air and energized. Each no larger than a honeybee, they fanned out into a swirling umbrella formation.

The enemy tanks responded quickly, firing fléchette rounds at the swarm. Each round took out large swaths of the small drones, destroying the sensor cloud in less than thirty seconds.

But it was too late. Paul had a full rendering of the target on his IHD, showing the exact position and movement vector of each enemy soldier, tank, and vehicle, as well as the aid workers. Fifty large cargo trucks were surrounded by at least 150 foot soldiers supported by two Chinese-made biped tanks and six pickup trucks with various pedestal-mounted armaments. Numerous bandits zipped around on smoke-coughing motorcycles.

One of the tanks was about a hundred meters to the rear of the convoy, walking south on a security patrol. The other was stationary in the middle of the convoy, dozens of tied-up and blindfolded aid workers at the base of its powerful metal legs. The last of the convoy's living armed escorts were bleeding out on the road. Navarro's soldiers crawled over the cargo trucks, inventorying their haul. It was the kind of land piracy that had been going on for a long time in this part of the world and had gotten worse over the past year.

Paul and his ten soldierbots nearly lost their balance as Dragon One veered sharply to the left. They all grabbed for handholds and stabilized themselves.

"Sorry, sir," Dragon One said as he jerked back to the right, firing chaff and decoys from his flanks. "One of the tanks is firing at us."

"No problem," Paul said. "Just a little closer and we'll get out."

"Roger that, sir."

Paul studied the tactical map on his in-head display one more time as D1 continued to evade tank fire. The aircraft banked hard left, right, up, and down. Without the stabilization smarts of his battle suit, Paul would have been splayed on the floor.

"Top, the other tank is too close to the aid workers," Paul transmitted. "We need to coax him away before killing him. Let's put you at the head of the convoy. 357 and I will take the rear."

As he spoke to the team, Paul designated targets and key positions on his IHD. His battle suit then shared the data across the team from Top and 357, to the Dragons, to the smallest XP. In less than a millisecond, every fighting system had the plan and a common map.

"I want a rapid-insertion profile," Paul told the three aircraft. "Right on top of them. Put Top here." Paul highlighted where he wanted Top to roll out on the ground on his map. "Have 357 and I roll out here."

D1 swerved hard to his left and then immediately back to his right. Paul could hear the crackle and snap of the tank rounds as they ripped through the air nearby, always a step behind D1.

"Let's hurry and get out," Paul said over the radio. "I don't want this fucker to get lucky."

"Rapid-insertion profile and rollout locations confirmed," the Dragons said in unison.

Paul leaned out of the right side of D1. Five of his wolf pack stood close behind him. The other five leaned out of the left side.

A hundred meters away, Paul could see 357 leaning out of his aircraft.

D1 banked hard to his left again. "On my mark, sir," he said.

"Roger. On your mark."

Paul knew D1 was focused on avoiding enemy fire at this point. All of the Dragons would be. Small-arms fire, rockets, and the intermittent tank round flooded the air around them. Dragon One would coordinate his evasive maneuvers so that he gave Paul and the soldierbots as straight and level an exit platform as possible while getting his ground speed down to two hundred knots.

A vibration ran through Dragon One as he fired his minigun, keeping someone's head down in front of them. The outboard cargo pods, one on each of Dragon One's utility wings, opened. An aerial XP dropped from each one. They fell a few feet and then turned away.

"Three seconds!" Dragon One announced as he banked hard to the left to avoid incoming.

Paul took a deep breath, gripping his handhold tight as Dragon One yanked back to the right.

"Exit! Exit! Exit!" the aircraft commanded as his wings passed through level.

Paul leapt into the air facing forward and spread his arms and legs to create as much drag as possible. Ten soldierbots followed him.

A bright flash erupted from the front of Dragon One as Paul fell away from him. A missile streaked toward the doomed southern tank.

When Paul's altimeter said twenty feet, he tucked into a ball and enabled his suit's autopilot.

Paul tried to relax as he struck the ground. The initial impact was jarring, as always. Then the deceleration and violent tumble lasted for a few seconds. He did not resist when his suit straightened his legs, propelling him back into the air. Paul landed in a sprint on the exact rollout spot he had designated a minute earlier. His wolf pack sprinted with him, five on each side in wedge formation, weapons ready.

A white flash erupted at his two o'clock, followed by a loud bang. Black smoke spewed from the Chinese tank's chassis, its turret and weapons vaporized. The enemy tank's red icon on Paul's IHD blinked out. The smoking headless legs fell over into the sand.

Paul gave the Dragons the command to loiter twenty kilometers to the west, behind the foothills of the Andes. He did not want to take a chance that Navarro had an anti-aircraft ace up his sleeve.

The QC-10s banked aggressively away and thundered west.

Paul took manual control of his suit, raised his minigun, and killed two foot soldiers unlucky enough to be right in front of him as he ran toward the trail aid vehicle.

Paul's wolf pack split up. Two stayed by his side. The others paired off and headed for different aid vehicles.

Paul could see on his IHD that Top and 357 and their wolf packs were also fully operational and moving to contact. Their wolf packs had spread out to aim at different target vehicles.

That's when he started to get the flashes.

A foot soldier aiming a rocket launcher.

Kill.

A foot soldier firing a fifty-caliber machine gun from the back of an old green pickup truck near the rear of the aid convoy.

Kill.

The aerial view of a foot soldier trying to drag an aid worker away from the vehicle they had been hiding under.

Kill.

Kill.

Kill.

The images came fast. Each one a clean kill shot.

A motorcycle-riding bandit charged Paul as he neared one of the aid vehicles. Paul lobbed a grenade.

Motorcycle and exoskeleton parts rained down as the remaining biped tank swiveled its turret toward Paul and opened up. He dove behind the aid truck's engine just in time. The cab shook with the impact of large-caliber, exploding rounds.

One of Paul's soldierbots did not make it in time. It lost a leg and then an arm before the third round hit it in the neck.

Paul switched his IHD to the point of view of an aerial XP immediately overhead. The tank was traversing its turret left and right, looking for them, as aid workers lay blindfolded at its feet. It was an older model, but packed a lot of firepower and was heavily armored. Only the Dragons had sufficient punch to take one out in a single shot. Paul could tell from the imagery that it was pilotless. Probably being controlled a hundred miles away, from one of Navarro's Chinese-equipped bunkers.

Paul was hit with more flashes as he worked around the other side toward the rear of the truck. An exoskeleton-clad foot soldier lunged at him, firing his weapon as he came.

Paul was caught distracted. He couldn't raise his weapon in time.

A flash hit him.

The foot soldier's helmet exploded in chunks and red mist, but his suit kept running. The dead, headless soldier smashed into the truck and toppled to the ground, the legs continuing to run.

Paul swiveled to see his one of his soldierbots, smoke rising from his minigun.

"Thanks," Paul couldn't stop himself from saying as a flash from an airborne XP hit him.

Enemy. Exoskeleton. Aiming a rocket launcher. Behind you!

Kill!

Paul spun in time to see the foot soldier's riddled body hit the ground and looked up at the XP darting by fifty feet above.

Paul checked his tactical map again as a soldierbot covered him. He felt behind the power curve of the battle, but he couldn't argue with the results he saw. Outlaw Company was quickly reducing the enemy.

They still had a problem, though.

"Top, we need to take out that tank ASAP!" Paul yelled into his radio.

"Roger that, sir."

Paul was getting concerned. They had taken out most of the enemy and lost only two soldierbots. It was obvious that this aid convoy was not going home with Navarro's troops. But Paul worried that whoever was driving the remaining tank would get frustrated, say, "Fuck it," and kill the civilians.

Seconds later, Top jumped out from behind a vehicle of the convoy. She took two long strides into the open, raised her minigun, and fired a short burst at the tank.

The rounds glanced harmlessly off the tank's armored turret but got its attention. It swiveled toward Top.

But instead of jumping back behind the vehicle, Top ran in the opposite direction, firing her rifle as she went. Her long powerful legs propelled her, kicking up a spray of dirt as she streaked away.

Two soldierbots leapt from behind the same vehicle Top had emerged from and sprinted in the opposite direction.

The tank's turret hesitated.

Two more soldierbots leapt from behind a different vehicle. They ran toward the group of bound captives at the tank's feet, grabbed several of them, and hauled them to safety behind a vehicle.

This pissed off the tank. It swiveled its turret decisively toward Top.

The bound and blindfolded civilians around the tank flinched as it fired its main cannon. A large burst of dirt and scrub engulfed Top, and she was thrown to the ground by the blast. She scrambled to get up and keep moving, but the tank had her.

Paul started to yell a futile warning to Top when he saw 357 sprinting toward the tank.

357 covered the distance from the front of the convoy to the tank in a blur and leapt onto the turret, fifteen meters above the ground, in a long, graceful arc.

The tank's turret had traversed left as it tried to gun down Top, so its main gun barrel was offset ninety degrees to the left relative to its legs. 357 sprang from the top of the turret and grabbed the end of the gun barrel, swinging his full weight on the cannon.

The sudden shift in its center of gravity caused the tank to stumble to its left as it tried to stay upright. Its large metal legs churned in an awkward side sprint, and it moved away from the cluster of bound captives.

Paul and a wolf pack of five sprinted to the captives and started jerking them off the ground one by one and yanking off their blindfolds. "Start running!" he yelled as he put each one on their feet. "Run! No time to untie you. Run!"

The tank fired its main cannon to shake 357 loose.

357 lost his grip as the gun jerked and recoiled. He fell to the ground just as Top, running at full speed, struck the tank's legs like a battering ram.

The tank lost its footing.

Six soldierbots mimicked the first sergeant. Hitting the tank in the legs at a full sprint in rapid succession, knocking it past the point of no return.

Now there was nothing to stop the tank from falling over.

It crashed into the sand.

They had to act fast.

Top, 357, and twenty-five soldierbots ran to the captives.

They helped Paul get the last three dozen bound aid workers moving as the tank thrashed in the sand for a few seconds.

As expected, the remote driver gave up and hit "destruct."

The tank exploded.

The Outlaws shielded their charges from the blast and shrapnel with their metal bodies. They were all knocked to the ground but were otherwise unharmed.

Paul checked the points of view of the aerial XPs. All clear. The time stamp in his IHD said they had been on-site less than six minutes.

"All right, Dragon One," Paul said over the radio. "We're ready for exfil."

"On the way, sir."

"What the hell, 357?" Paul said as they helped the UN workers to their feet and cut the ropes that bound their hands. "I didn't know you were such a damn stuntman."

"I'm sorry, sir," 357 said, jerking up to stand at attention. "I did not want to destroy the tank while it was so close to the civilians. I improvised, and I apologize. I will not be such a damn stuntman again."

"I'm sorry, 357," Paul said, standing up to look the Ōkami in its multi-sensored eyes. "I'm not being clear. You did great. I am giving you a compliment." Paul shook his head, appreciating the level of creativity and initiative 357's actions demonstrated. "Those were some really nice moves."

The Ōkami's stance unstiffened. His shoulders relaxed. He looked at Top and then back at Paul, who nearly laughed at the body language.

"Well done, Stuntman," Top said.

Chapter Thirty-Eight

aul had a few rough nights after the convoy rescue mission. He woke up troubled and unrested. When a maintenance day cleared his schedule the following week, he got anxious. Paul didn't have much to do while his war machines were cleaned and picked over by the maintenance bots. He spent the day trying to avoid his own thoughts.

By late afternoon, he couldn't stand it anymore.

"Top, can you take care of things for a bit?" Paul said, walking up to his first sergeant. "I'm going to head over to Philly for a few hours."

"Roger that, sir."

"Thanks."

Top watched Paul as he walked across their dusty outpost and hopped into Dragon One.

"Evening, D1," Paul said as he climbed aboard the aircraft.

"Good evening, sir," the dragon responded as a pulse surged through the aircraft, energizing sub-systems and preparing for flight. Paul found the whirrs and clicks of the waking aircraft comforting each time he heard them, particularly on D1.

Dragon One had become Paul's go-to aircraft. It started out as a random pairing. Paul just ended up in D1 for most of the training missions back in the states. Since they had been deployed, though, Paul found himself hopping aboard D1 more often, even for single ship logistic runs like this one. Superstition, maybe? He wasn't sure. There was nothing special about D1 compared to the rest of Dragon Flight. But he was Paul's favorite.

Dragon One tilted and swiveled its four large thruster fans as it completed its pre-flight self-checks and asked, "Destination, sir?"

"Outpost Philly," Paul said, swinging his legs out of the large, right side cargo door. He wanted to feel the wind. "And no hurry."

"Outpost Philly, Roger, sir."

The quadcopter rose gracefully into the air, staying just ahead of the large dust cloud in its wake. Soon, D1 and Paul were skimming the mountaintop, working their way to Kata's location.

"Would you let them know we are coming?" Paul asked as he looked at the horizon. A dark purple glow covered the Andes Mountains as the sun sank toward the horizon. The long, wide Valley stretched off in the distance to the south toward Patagonia.

"Roger that, sir."

It was about a fifty-mile flight to the north from Devil to Philly. D1 took it slower than usual as Paul sat, knees in the wind, looking at the horizon.

Twenty minutes later, Dragon One kicked up dust and small rocks as he landed among Kata's Eagles.

Paul hopped out and walked up the hill to Kata's operations center. She met him outside.

"What brings you to the neighborhood?" She asked.

"I was hoping to get some dinner."

Kata cocked her head in curiosity.

"And conversation."

Kata nodded.

Half an hour later, Paul and Kata sat on one of her tracked extension platforms. They had ridden to the edge of Philly's eastern perimeter. They talked while they ate the last bit of a wild boar Kata shot a few days ago.

"So, what's on your mind?" She asked Paul.

"I've been seeing things…after firefights," he said slowly. "Like, replays of the engagements. Highly detailed stuff. I was wondering if you were also?"

Paul could see immediately, from Kata's face, that she had.

She hesitated for a moment, though, before saying, "Yes."

Paul sighed.

"I don't know why," he said, "but that is a huge relief."

Kata put her plate down and looked at Paul as he continued.

"When I'm fighting with the Ōkami, the kill flashes seem to be mostly light and information. There is a micro instant of whiteout in my head, and I catch very little detail. Almost like an overexposed photo. They come fast and with certainty, giving me all the information I need to authorize the kill, but almost no discernible image. Nothing visceral. No impact."

Kat reached into the satchel she had brought along and pulled out a flask. She unscrewed the top and took a swallow from it as Paul was talking.

"It's a lot different from how it was, when we were in Africa. There, when I was driving a drone or trying to kill someone myself, my external senses were at their most heightened. My brain was hyperactive, fixated on the target. But twenty minutes after the firefight, I'd already started to lose the details. I could remember the main pieces and could tell you, 'I banked the drone to the left, squared up on the enemy, and then shot him in the head,' but that was it. And it's gotten fuzzier as time has gone on. Now all the people I killed on the Horn of Africa are the blurry and faded images of someone else's old photo album."

Kata nodded and handed him the flask. Paul held it as he kept talking, his eyes fixed on the horizon.

"With the neural link architecture, it is the opposite. Things are getting clearer as time goes on. It's like my brain needs time to unpack and process all the information in each flash. And the longer my head has ahold of the information, the more detail is revealed, and the further into me the images burrow. Later, back on Devil after a fight, they come at me again, but slow and clear and detailed. I can make out the craziest minutiae in my mind. I could see sweat on their foreheads, the texture of their uniforms, the color of their eyes. And then I will see the rounds impact and tear them apart or burst them open. I know if they died immediately, or if it took time."

Paul was quiet for a moment and then raised the flask to his lips. He took a large pull of whiskey and then handed it back to Kata.

"It's the same for me," she said somberly. "I get those damn re-flashes, too."

She took another swallow of whiskey and handed the flask back to Paul.

"Last night, after the firefight, rescuing the convoy, they hit me while I was eating dinner," Paul said. "I was sitting on the ground, leaning against the tracks of one of the large ground XPs, looking down at the glow of the city of Mendoza when they came on, one after the other. I must have authorized a hundred kills yesterday. I would push one out of my mind, and another would take its place. I started hyperventilating and couldn't move."

"What did you do?" Kata asked.

"I couldn't do anything," Paul said with sadness. "I sort of panicked and started to sink under them."

Paul took a pull from the flask.

"Then Top appeared," he said with a small smile. "She always has her eye on me, even when I eat alone. She came over, kneeled down in front of me, and tried to snap me out of it."

"I was unresponsive until she grabbed my shoulders and shook me. 'Sir, you are OK. They're just the flashes. Focus on your breathing.' I was sweating through my uniform and had dropped my plate of food, but her voice got through. She chanted the mantra she has overheard me use at the beginning of my meditations. 'So…hum…so…hum…so…hum…' It got me back."

Kata nodded. "Something like that happened to me the other day. I think our meditations are going to be very important out here."

"Yeah. That and the whiskey."

Paul took another swallow and handed the flask back to Kata.

"I told Top she was lucky she was a robot," Paul said. "Because this shit doesn't get to her. You know what she said to me?"

"What?"

"She said, 'I'm not sure about that yet, sir.'"

Chapter Thirty-Nine

t did not take long for Paul to see that the real world was giving the betas a lot to think about. The black-and-white rules of Filson's training world were not holding up. And that he himself was responsible for some of their indigestion.

Soon after the convoy rescue mission, the Outlaws were on a patrol on the outskirts of a small town southeast of Mendoza. Paul had two dozen soldierbots fanned out in a kilometer-wide line and an aerial XP flying patrol above them as they advanced.

It had been a quiet couple of days in the valley. Paul thought Navarro was digesting the ass-kicking they had given him at the convoy. He and Top were walking next to each other at the formation's center, talking.

A shot rang out. Paul was hit in the shoulder.

The small caliber round bounced off Paul's armor. He and Top ran for cover in case it was a ranging round for a heavier weapon. As they dashed off of the dirt road, Paul got a flash from the aerial XP.

But he did not authorize the kill. It didn't feel right.

A couple minutes later, Paul was standing over a fifteen-year-old boy who Snapshot and a couple of soldierbots had captured. He was terrified. Snapshot held the boy by the arm with one of his powerful hands and the boy's small hunting rifle in the other. On the ground lay a string of squirrels the boy had gotten that day.

Paul kneeled in front of the boy and spoke into his translator. "What were you thinking, kid? Why did you shoot at us?"

"I was scared," the boy said through tears. "I've heard how mean you soldiers are. I've heard how many boys and girls you have killed."

Paul raised the face shield on his helmet so the boy could see his face. "Look at me," he said in a gentle voice, smiling. "Do I look like I kill young boys and girls?"

The boy sniffled as he looked at Paul. After a long minute, he shook his head.

"You're right. We don't kill young boys."

Paul motioned to Snapshot to let go of the boy.

"What is your name?" Paul asked.

The boy rubbed his arm where the strong mechanical hand had held him and looked at Paul. Paul looked the boy in the eyes patiently.

"Sergio," the boy said in a trembling voice.

Paul smiled. "I'm Paul."

Sergio looked around, wondering what was going to happen next.

Paul reached for the string of squirrels, startling the boy. His anxious eyes followed Paul's armored hand as it reached down.

There were five dead squirrels on the string. Paul examined them for a few seconds and then said, "You're a pretty good shot, Sergio."

The boy continued to regard Paul skeptically, but nodded.

"Who are these for?" Paul asked.

"My family."

"Listen to me closely," Paul continued to kneel so he could look the boy in the eye. "I'm going to let you take your squirrels home to your mother. But I want you to do me a favor."

The boy's eyes widened with disbelief. "Yes, sir?"

"When you get home, I want you to tell your mother and father what happened. Do you have any brothers and sisters?"

"Yes, sir. One brother and one sister."

"I want you to tell them what happened also, OK? I'm asking you to help spread the word that we don't kill young boys and girls, Sergio. We're just here to help keep things peaceful, OK?"

The young boy nodded. Finally, he smiled. "I will, sir."

"Thank you," Paul said, handing the boy the squirrels. The boy's smile widened.

Paul stood up and looked at Snapshot. "Give him his rifle back."

Snapshot hesitated.

Paul looked at him. He had never had to repeat an order, ever, to an Ōkami. Paul was about to do it for the first time when Top interrupted him.

"Sir," she said, taking a small step toward Paul. "Theater rules of engagement state that hostile fire immediately establishes the shooter as an enemy combatant that should be killed or captured if possible. Upon capture, the rules of engagement further state release is not permitted. The prisoner must be transported to Forward Operating Base Stalwart for processing."

Paul looked at the boy to make sure that he did not understand the English coming from Top. He did not. He was smiling and looking at his squirrels.

Paul turned to his first sergeant.

"Thank you, Top. I am clear on the rules of engagement. I am overruling them."

Paul looked at Snapshot and said, "Give the boy his rifle."

Snapshot did so. Paul leaned over to get eye level with the boy again and said through his translator, "Don't let me down, Sergio."

"I won't, sir. Thank you."

Paul nodded, and the boy ran off.

Later that night, back on Devil, Paul was sitting outside his hooch looking down on the valley after dinner. Top stepped up beside him.

"Sir, may I ask you a question?"

"Sure," Paul said, gesturing at the empty chair next to him. Top sat down. Paul kept gazing down at the valley.

"Why did you release that enemy combatant today? It broke the rules of engagement, sir."

"You mean the boy?"

"Yes, sir."

"Same reason I didn't authorize the kill, Top. It didn't feel right."

Paul smiled as he kept looking down on the valley. He could almost hear the quantumtronic circuitry in her head laboring against what he had just said. After a few minutes, she tried again.

"But, sir, General Schofield and the rules of engagement clearly state that—"

"Top, do you see General Schofield out here with us right now?" Paul interrupted.

"No, sir. The general is back on Forward Operating Base Stalwart."

"That's right." Paul turned his head to look at her. "And if you are pinned down by the enemy and need help, who do you call? Do you call the rules of engagement to come save you?"

"No, sir. I call you and the Outlaws." she said.

"That's right," Paul said. He turned his head back to the valley, ten thousand feet below.

Paul let Top stew next to him for a few minutes. Finally, she said, "I'm sorry, sir. This conversation is not very helpful. I am sorry I have disturbed you." She turned to leave.

"Top, listen," Paul said, standing up from his seat and walking over to her. "I'm not trying to be difficult or vague. The problem is that, out here, it's just us. We have to apply all the shit Filson taught us in training and all the policies and objectives coming down from Schofield while we accomplish our mission and take care of each other. There are going to be gray areas and times when wrong is right."

Top, over a foot taller than Paul, bent her head down and listened intently. "When wrong is right?"

"Locking that kid up on Stalwart," Paul continued. "Or worse, killing him would have only made things worse. His family would never have forgiven us, and we'd have created a couple more enemy. Now, though, he is sitting at home eating barbecued squirrels with his family and telling them there is a good side to the Americans. Who knows? He may make a difference for us someday. And even if he doesn't, I don't believe locking him up or killing him was the right thing to do. In fact, I think it would have been wrong."

Top stared at Paul for a long moment. "How do you know when wrong is right?" she finally asked.

Paul shrugged. "It's a gut thing, Top. You will know."

Top was silent.

Paul sighed.

"It's OK, Top. My job is to handle the gray areas. I don't expect robots to be capable of that."

Top stood in front of Paul for a moment, then walked away.

Chapter Forty

"I'm not impressed," Robert Malloy II said to Fiona.

She tried not to fidget in her chair as she met her grandfather's gaze.

He sat at the head of the same table at which she had endured the humiliating gifting of her trust only twelve years ago. She did not allow herself to wonder what she would do differently if she had the chance to go back in time to that afternoon.

Instead, she focused on her grandfather. She had learned that, with him, it was wise to wait, to see if he would give anything more.

Robert Malloy II had learned long ago that speaking last was a strategic advantage. "He who speaks first loses," he had told her many times since her indentured servitude had begun.

She knew that one of his techniques was to create an uncomfortable vacuum and then wait for the weaker willed to fill it, thereby gaining an advantage.

So she waited.

He smiled.

"Child," he said, erasing the smile and cloaking himself in disappointment. "You just told me all about the conditions you have set. I'm waiting for the action."

"Action? You don't see the actions I have taken? I had to—"

"Ah, ah, ah," he interrupted her, putting his bony finger to his mouth in a *shhhh* command.

"I don't need the details. Those are your sins to carry. This old man has enough of his own."

Fiona sat still, startled at the hint of admission from him.

"Conditions are well and good, Roberta. But you are leaving the catalyst to chance." He paused. "Are you sure you want to do that?"

She studied him. *Is it a test question?* she wondered. *Or rhetorical? Either way, don't answer immediately. Let's see what a few dozen seconds of silence reveal.*

There was a knock at the meeting room door.

"Yes?" her grandfather called.

His assistant opened the door and leaned in. "Excuse me, sir. But the senator is here early for your two o'clock."

Robert Malloy II glanced at his watch.

"Fine. Bring him in."

The receptionist turned and left.

"Time flies, doesn't it, Roberta?"

"It does," she said, standing up. She put her tablet computer into her bag and walked around the table to leave.

"Think about our conversation."

"I will," she said, pausing at the door and looking at him.

"Action wins," he said. "Setting conditions is no better than wishing for luck."

"Of course, sir." She was ready to leave.

"And you need to win this," her grandfather added. "Your deviant brother needs you to win this as well."

The mention of Eugene took her breath away.

"Ha!" Her grandfather cackled and pointed at her. "I've only just now realized that you still have not told him. He has no idea who you are now bound to, nor of the precipice on which you both stand."

Fiona started to respond, but the senator walked in, three aides walking behind him.

"Robert! How are you, sir?"

"I'm good, Chuck." Her grandfather said, staying seated. "Thank you. Please meet my granddaughter."

"My Lord. I don't believe it," the senator swiveled to offer his hand to Fiona. "She is too good-looking to be related to you, Robert. Don't pull my leg like that!"

Her grandfather cackled again and then said, "I shit you not, Chuck. I'd like to introduce you to Roberta Malloy."

"It's a pleasure, Miss Malloy. Senator Chuck Book, of New York."

"The pleasure is mine, Senator."

The senator turned back to Robert Malloy II and said, "Robert, we can come back later if this is not a good time."

"No. Now is perfect. Roberta was bored with me, anyway. You have rescued her."

The senator and his aides rendered the appropriate laughter.

"And trust me," her grandfather added, "this one needs rescuing."

Fiona left as laughter filled the room.

Chapter Forty-One

In late November, Colonel Filson landed at Outpost Philly for the first of several periodic check ins. He had Martin Pruden in tow.

The commercial aspects of the field trial were not something Paul and Kata ever thought about. All they knew was that Colonel Filson and this guy, Pruden, were there to make sure they were succeeding.

The colonel had also been tasked with writing the tactical manual for Ōkami units. If Combat Corps bought into Musashi's soldierbots, the colonel's manual would be the instruction book. It would serve as the codified best practices for commanders that fielded Ōkami.

Pruden seemed like an OK guy to Paul and Kata. He was ridiculously out of place, though, walking around like he was dressed more for a safari than a combat zone. His helmet and armored vest seemed oversized on his skinny body. Paul and Kata had to stifle their chuckles more than once at the sight of him. But they liked that he seemed to really give a shit, and to respect them as well as the Ōkami.

When he visited, Filson kept Paul and Kata up late into the night after missions, debriefing them. He didn't care about body counts. He was more interested in each mission's stated objective and then the why and how Paul and Kata did what they did with the Ōkami to achieve it.

Pruden sat in on Filson's debriefs, taking extensive notes. He also separately interviewed Paul and Kata and even the Ōkami betas involved on missions, and would then spend hours analyzing the data and conferring with Dr. Musashi and his team via the sat phone.

Colonel Filson's debriefs often went long. After the facts were captured, he'd run endless what-ifs by Paul and Kata, stopping only after they stood up and left the operations hooch, cursing his persistence.

"Fine," he would yell after them. "I'll shut up. Come back and have a drink!"

Paul and Kata would feign hesitation before walking back.

The colonel would then pull out the whiskey, wine or other spirit he smuggled out to their desolate outpost in the Andes mountains and pour glasses for everyone. Paul, Kata, Pruden and the colonel would sit around, sharing the bottle as Filson waxed hyperbolic.

"You guys make me so proud!" He would say, pointing at Paul and Kata. "You're like the first Egyptians to use chariots. The first Chinese to bring gunpowder to the fight. The first soldiers to go to battle with rifled gun barrels. Or the internal combustion engine. The airplane. The Radio. Radar. Everything is going to be different! And you are the ones who are going to change it."

Paul and Kata would roll their eyes. But they swelled with pride on the inside at the old man's praises.

When Colonel Filson and Pruden visited, whichever outpost they were overnighting at became the group's communion spot. Paul or Kata would fly over, and the four of them would eat dinner together. When the group was at Devil, Paul asked Top to make sure Chief had something to grill. It was easy for one of the aerial XPs to zip out over the plains and bag a red stag or a wild boar. Chief expertly prepared whatever they came back with. He had become a grill master. Only a few months into their tour, Paul stopped trying to teach him things and started studying his technique.

Filson and Pruden never stayed more than two nights. They would leave by early afternoon on day three in order to make the last heavy drone out of Stalwart back to the states.

Paul and Kata would walk with them to whichever aircraft was ferrying them back to Stalwart. After shaking their hands, Pruden would board, leaving the two young Centaurs alone with their old mentor.

These goodbyes were always tough on the colonel. Paul and Kata noticed he could not make eye contact. He shuffled his feet. He rubbed his forehead while saying his goodbyes. He put his hand on each of their shoulders as he mentioned the date of his next visit. He would nod a few times, looking as if he had more to say, and then would leave, boarding the aircraft quickly.

Paul and Kata would walk away from the aircraft as it started its engines. Stopping just outside the jet blast area as the transport drone lifted off, they watched it depart. Standing in silence, they watched the aircraft until it disappeared, then walked back to the operations hooch feeling lonelier than before.

Chapter Forty-Two

Things on the southern cone went well for Paul and Kata for a few months. Musashi's architecture was proving itself to be lethal and self-sufficient. Because of how well the swarms and other systems were working, Paul and Kata were mounting effective operations with the thinnest satellite or theater-level intelligence support. Which, of course, suited General Schofield just fine.

Paul and Kata had everything they needed to plan and conduct their own operations. The neural link complied with all Tokyo Accords kill chain requirements. And the Ōkami continued to get better with each mission. They went almost sixty days with only losing a handful of soldierbots each.

Then a couple of factors started to work against them.

First, after getting his ass kicked for a few months, General Navarro opened his wallet and reached out to the Russians and Chinese. Paul and Kata started facing better tech.

And second, General Schofield started pulling on Paul and Kata for missions in support of his preparations to take on the Chinese. After reading some of the Outlaw and Apache after-action reports, he recognized the asset he had sitting in his backyard.

Colonel Filson was thrilled that Schofield recognized the capabilities and value of the Ōkami. Paul and Kata less so. The problem for them was that they still had responsibility for their primary mission. And General Schofield's extra-credit work was usually risky and poorly coordinated at the last minute.

It all came together in a bad way for Paul when a heavy transport drone went down about fifty kilometers from Devil in the plains north of Mendoza. It had been flying over the Pampas from one of the eastern port cities enroute to Stalwart. General Kiel called Paul and requested a rescue-and-recovery operation.

"What is the enemy situation?" Paul asked him. "Was it shot down, or was it a maintenance issue?"

"We're not sure."

"Any overhead imagery?"

"Working on getting that for you," Keil told him in an unconvincing voice.

"Any survivors or special cargo I should know about?"

"Not sure about survivors," General Keil answered. "There were two souls on board. This happened five minutes ago. Cargo is not high value—small-arms ammunition, medical supplies, and repair parts. Nonetheless, we'd prefer Navarro not get it. And, if there were survivors, we definitely don't want Navarro getting his hands on them."

Paul was quiet and looked across the planning room at Top, who was listening in to the conversation. Paul shook my head, expressing his unease. She shrugged, as she had learned to do, acknowledging the ambiguity.

"What about Thurman's exos?" Paul asked Kiel.

"Look, Captain," the general said, sensing Paul's resistance. "You guys can be there in fifteen minutes. Anything I launch from here would not be on site for at least four hours."

"Who do you want to send?" Paul asked Top.

"I'll go with you on this one, sir."

"Good morning, sir," Dragon One said to Paul as they took off. Top rode in Dragon Three, in trail formation behind D1. They each had a small ten-soldierbot wolf pack on board. Both aircraft picked up to a hover as they ran through their systems checks.

"Ready at your command, sir," D1 said a moment later, asking for permission to launch.

"Let's go," Paul said. The flight of two accelerated forward, and the mountain fell away beneath them. "How we doing today, D1?" Paul asked as they descended, skirting just above the jagged mountain.

"Good, sir. Finally got my number-four fan thruster rebalanced. That high-frequency vibration is gone. Can you tell?"

"Sorry to say. But I never noticed it in the first place."

"I understand," Dragon One said, with no disappointment. "The truth is, it ranged from six thousand to six thousand seven hundred and fifty hertz. Just outside your ability to sense."

"Well, that explains it. Wouldn't matter to me anyway, D1. You're my favorite ride."

"I appreciate that, sir."

Paul reviewed the limited available intelligence on the flight. He radioed the operations center on Stalwart several times, but didn't get much. He felt uneasy.

"Put a swarm on top of the crash site," Paul told D1 as it came into view.

A jolt ran through Dragon One.

"Done, sir. Intel in one minute."

With nothing to disrupt them, the sensor swarm stayed overhead and put together a detailed view of the crash site.

The downed aircraft was one of the larger hexacopters, designed to haul huge loads. It had tumbled after initial impact, shearing off all six of its thruster fans. The main fuselage lay broken in a grassy marsh thicket, nose half buried at the end of a dark, smoking trench it dug after its last bounce.

"Looks like we have two survivors," Paul called to the team. "They are the priority. Wolf packs will set a security perimeter while we stabilize and extract the wounded. Dragons, establish overwatch at a three-kilometer radius."

"Roger that, sir," both Dragons responded.

Once on the ground, Paul and Top worked fast. One survivor had been thrown clear of the aircraft. He was unconscious and had lost a lot of blood from a bad laceration to his arm. Paul stuck him with an IV as two soldierbots stood watch over them. Top tried to get to the other survivor, who was trapped in the mangled aircraft. She used her strength to peel away bent metal as two soldierbots shadowed her for security.

Paul threw Top's POV up on his IHD to monitor her progress while he bound the arm wound. The closer Top got to freeing the survivor, the more he panicked.

"Please! Please get me out of here. I can't breathe. It really hurts."

"Try to relax," Top said in her most calming voice. "It won't be long now. I'm just moving carefully so I don't accidentally hurt you."

"Please hurry!" he wailed. "Oh, God!"

"What is your name?" Top asked.

"Lawson," he said, nearly hyperventilating, "Sergeant Bill Lawson."

"Lawson?" Top said with some excitement. "Are you kidding me? My Commander knows a Lawson. Where are you from?"

Paul smiled ruefully in respect for Top. He did not know anyone named Lawson. She was just trying to distract him, trying to calm him down.

"Wisconsin," Lawson answered. As he did, Top peeled back a piece of aircraft, and Paul wretched at what he saw on his IHD. The sergeant's legs were mashed to a pulp. Most of his pelvis, too. The airframe that had crushed him was now holding him together, and it was a mercy that his body was in shock and he didn't feel any of it. But his rising anxiety was a sign that his body was beginning to calibrate to its situation. Soon, he would be in agony.

"Sir," Top transmitted to Paul in whisper mode. "This man's wounds are not survivable."

"Yeah," Paul answered, also in whisper mode. "I see that. I'll be there in one minute."

"What is it?" the sergeant asked Top, sensing her hesitance. "Oh, God! What is it?"

"It's nothing, Lawson. I've almost got you out."

He could not see how badly he was hurt because of the angle of his head and a large piece of metal across his chest. But he was getting agitated. "Tell me! I can tell something is wrong! Oh, God. It hurts so bad... I'm scared! I don't want to die!"

"Easy, Lawson," Top said, grabbing his hand. "Nothing is wrong. You're actually in much better shape than I thought you would be."

"Really?" His voice was pitiful. For a second, Paul felt guilty they were misleading him. But there was nothing else to be done.

Lawson looked at his hand in Top's and then back at the tall Ōkami's face.

"Yes," she answered. "In fact, would you do me a favor and wiggle your toes?"

"OK," Lawson said, calming down slightly. "I'll try." Lawson stared at Top, and his brow furrowed as he concentrated on his toes.

"Very good!" Top said as she watched the blood continue to ooze out of his mangled, motionless legs. "Just amazing, Lawson. You may actually walk out of this aircraft once we get you free." Lawson squeezed Top's hand and sighed as he believed her lie and continued to die.

Paul stepped up next to Top. Because of the narrowed space of the mangled airframe and Top's bulk, he could not get close enough.

"I can't get in there, Top. I'm going to have to get out of my suit."

"No, sir!" Top said, transmitting again without making a sound Lawson could hear, but expressing her displeasure directly into Paul's helmet.

Lawson moaned in pain.

"It will only be for a minute," Paul told her. "Just long enough to administer the morphine."

"No fucking way, sir."

Getting out of your battle suit on an operation was forbidden. And not just by regulations. It grates against every instinct. Because, out of that suit, your ability to shoot, move, and communicate is gone. You're just naked, weak, mortal flesh. Soldiers were trained from day one to never get out of their suit when they were outside the fence line unless it was on fire. Period.

"God," Lawson cried out. "Oh God, it's really starting to hurt!"

"Hand it to me, sir," Top said, swiveling her left arm back toward Paul. Lawson still held her right hand. Paul put the syringe in Top's hand.

"OK, Lawson," Top said. "We're going to get you out now, but first I want to give you this pain medication."

"OK. That's great. Thank you."

"How much of this do I give him, sir?" she asked Paul in whisper mode.

"I was going to do the whole thing."

"Looks like a lot to me, sir."

"It is."

Paul watched through Top's point of view as she inserted the needle. Before she pressed down, though, a flash hit him.

She was asking for kill authorization.

Paul knew she was trying to be thorough. Or she wasn't comfortable with it. But this time, he didn't use the neural link. It seemed like Lawson deserved more.

Paul completed the kill chain in whisper mode.

"It's OK, Top. Do it. It's the right thing."

Top's thumb pressed down, flooding Lawson's veins with morphine. His eyes closed, and his body relaxed, but he maintained his grip on Top's hand. She squeezed back. Top was silent as Lawson's head lolled to the side in his final moments. His pupils moved around beneath his eyelids, following the last sights of his life.

"There you are…" Lawson murmured.

"What is he saying, sir?" Top asked, in whisper mode.

"I don't know. He is seeing something in his mind. It happens sometimes… at the end. It is probably someone important to him."

"Should I talk back?"

"Only if you want to."

"What do I say?" she asked.

"Whatever… feels right."

"I can't quite…" Lawson said. "Can we…"

"Yes, Lawson," Top said. "As soon as you are home."

Lawson smiled for the first time since Top had met him. "It's going… going to be so great…" he said. A long breath bled out of Lawson as his heart stopped. He was still smiling.

Top waited until she was sure, then she released his hand and worked her way out of the bent airframe. She walked a few steps past Paul and then stopped, facing the horizon. Over her shoulder in the distance, Paul could see Dragon One flying his security pattern.

"You good, Top?" He finally asked her.

"Sir," she said, turning around. "I didn't realize that—"

An explosion erupted in the distance behind Top.

She and Paul crouched, shouldered their weapons, and turned toward the noise. Flames and smoke stained the sky.

Dragon One burned as he fell.

"Mayday! Mayday! Mayday!" Dragon One yelled over the radio. Paul watched him fall out of the sky, transmitting as he went.

"Mayday! This is Dragon One. Have been hit by a surface-to-air missile. Lost engines two and four. In uncontrolled descent. My position is—"

The transmission stopped as he descended out of view.

A blinding headache hit Paul. His legs buckled. He kneeled to steady himself.

The pain subsided in a couple of seconds. He stood up and started running toward the last living survivor, yelling into his radio.

"Dragon Three, come get us ASAP!"

"On the way, sir."

Dragon Three dove toward the earth, trading altitude for airspeed. In a blink, he was moving at over a hundred miles an hour. Then, in another blink, he was flaring, nose high, nearly vertical, trying to decelerate for landing. All four thruster fans howled as Dragon Three demanded they stop his hulking frame. He kept himself nearly vertical until the last possible second, then lowered his nose abruptly.

Dragon Three slammed onto the ground and slid the final fifty meters until he stopped just in front of Paul. His insectoid forward weapons pod swiveled back and forth, scanning for enemy.

"Top, grab the survivor!" Paul yelled.

"Roger, sir!" she said, already sprinting in that direction, her soldierbot shadows in close formation at her side, weapons aimed outward, searching for enemy.

"Dragon Three, do you have a fix on the surface-to-air missile launcher?" Paul asked.

"Affirmative!"

"Swarm it."

"Roger." A missile streaked from under his starboard weapon's wing. It rose to five hundred feet and disintegrated into a swarm over a small hilltop about five miles away.

Paul scanned the area. They were sitting in a small, scrubby basin surrounded by several swelling hilltops like the one Dragon Three had just swarmed. Each was a perfect overwatch position from which to take out an aircraft. Each one could have a surface-to-air missile team on it.

"Fuck me," Paul mumbled. He was pissed. He'd taken the hasty mission and then allowed himself to be distracted by Lawson dying. Dragon One had paid the price. He felt terrible. He wanted blood.

He was also pissed at General Keil. By then, Paul was used to the fact that he and Kata never had enough imagery and intel when they launched. They had to build the picture ourselves. They were supposedly self-sufficient, but that really meant that they were often half blind.

But this mission was at Keil's direct request. Paul had assumed he would have more eyes and support behind him. He thought that the reason he got no warning of enemy ground-to-air threat was because there wasn't one. Not because they just hadn't fucking checked.

Paul and Top kneeled beneath Dragon Three's forward weapons pod as the telemetry came together. The turrets snapped back and forth as they scanned the area. Four soldierbots stood over them, weapons at the ready, while the rest of the wolf pack collapsed the security perimeter to a tighter ring around Dragon Three.

"Appears to be a lone fire team, sir," Dragon Three said. The shape of the small hill appeared in Paul's IHD. Its crest was about five hundred feet above them. Two of Navarro's foot soldiers stood next to a tracked vehicle. One of them held a missile launcher on his shoulder. The other held a pair of laser ranging binoculars.

"Damn it," Paul said. "We rode into a classic baited ambush." Paul zoomed in on the missile launcher until he could see Chinese letters on the long black tube.

"You seeing this, Top?"

"Roger that."

"Is that what I think it is?" Paul asked.

"Yes," she said. "SkyFang."

SkyFang was the intelligence code name for a particularly deadly Chinese surface-to-air missile system. Multispectral targeting. AI enabled. Ten minutes of loiter time. Top of the line and deadly. There was no way to spoof it. If it was in the air anywhere near you, you were in trouble.

Paul rubbed his eyes.

Top finished strapping the patient onto a litter and then looked at Paul.

"How many more swarms do you have, Dragon Three?" He asked.

"Sir, I have six swarms on board."

"What is your indirect munitions count?" Paul asked.

"Two indirect munitions on board, sir."

"Perfect," Top said.

Paul looked at her and smiled.

The SkyFang was designed to be deployed in squads of three. By spacing the fire teams across a wide area, the missiles were able to network and assist each other in target fixation and intercept solution calculation.

Paul had to assume there were two more fire teams on hilltops in the area. Dragon Three could hit two with indirect munitions. Top knew what Paul was about to do. She had a request.

"Let me go also, sir."

Paul looked at Top and nodded.

"If I could move fast enough," he said. "I would go with you."

An Ōkami soldier could run at a top speed of forty-five miles an hour. A battle suited human could not reach that speed.

"Be careful," Paul said. "Use some stealth. Remember, SkyFang can be used as a direct-fire weapon on the ground."

"Roger that, sir," Top said as four soldierbots stepped next to her, two on each side. She looked at Paul.

Paul nodded, and dirt flew in the air as they sprinted away toward the hilltop.

Paul waited for ninety seconds, then said, "All right, D3. Fire at will."

Dragon Three launched four swarm rockets in rapid succession. They each climbed into the sky and flew in a different direction. Thirty seconds later, they disintegrated over the four surrounding hilltops.

As the sensor swarms fanned out over each hilltop, Paul put Top's POV up on one-third of his IHD. She and her small wolf pack were still running toward the team that had shot down Dragon One. Paul watched the distance tick down as they moved in a line, five abreast. They would be on top of the enemy in eighty-five seconds.

"Imagery coming online, sir," Dragon Three said.

"I'm ready."

Top was sixty seconds away from her target.

"I've got a positive ID on one of the SkyFang fire teams, sir," Dragon Three said.

"Roger, me too," Paul said. The image of three foot soldiers, one shouldering a SkyFang, the other two with binoculars and rifles, appeared on the middle third of his IHD, next to Top's POV. The two soldiers with binoculars wore exoskeletons and were scanning the horizon in the direction of the downed aircraft.

Top and her wolfpack were forty-five seconds away from their target.

"I've got a positive on both teams now, sir," Dragon Three said. "Other two hilltops are unoccupied."

"Roger that," Paul said as the final targeting image filled the last third of his IHD.

Dragon Three flashed Paul. He authorized both kills. Two indirect munitions launched out of the aircraft's spine, sailing up into the sky and then turning off in different directions toward their targets. The soldiers on the hilltops saw the missiles fire and ran to their vehicles. But it was too late.

Top was fifteen seconds out.

Paul expected Top and her wolf pack to stop and flash him before shooting their targets. But they didn't. They kept running. And Paul received the notification that Top had extended her bayonet.

Two sharp cracks rang out as the indirect munitions activated over the other two hilltops. Explosives ejected hundreds of smaller submunitions.

Top finally flashed Paul. He authorized the kills as the submunitions showered the fleeing vehicles on the other hilltops. The soldiers and their vehicles dissolved in fire and shrapnel.

Top and her wolf pack ran through the first enemy fire team on the other hilltop, bayoneting them at a forty-five-mile-per-hour sprint.

Dragon One was still burning when they got to his crash site. It took over an hour for the temperature to die down to the point they could get into the avionics compartment where his sphere was located. He was dead. The impact of the SkyFang, the violence of the crash, the heat of the burning fuel. It was too much. Top handed Paul the burned and caved-in sphere without saying a word, then walked back to Dragon Three.

Chapter Forty-Three

Paul and Kata ate in troubled silence. They sat in folding field chairs on either side of a large, flat rock that acted as their dinner table. Kata came across the rock early in her occupation of Philly, when she walked the perimeter with her First Sergeant. She put the pair of old field chairs next to the rock and left them there. The spot had become the standard venue for their dinner communions on Philly.

The large rock was about knee height, the shape of an irregular oval, and almost flat. Over six feet across its longest axis, it made the perfect table for dinner and water bottles. It also performed well as a resting place for contraband wine or whiskey bottles when Paul or Kata obtained them.

On more carefree nights, Paul and Kata speculated on how the old stone got its shape and came to rest where it did, on the east facing slope of the Andes. Paul was sure that it had been sheared off of a larger stone millions of years ago and abandoned in this spot by an indifferent glacier, inching down to the valley.

Tonight, though, Paul and Kata were ill at ease.

They had just spent over an hour on a video conference call with Colonel Filson, Dr. Musashi, and several of the doctor's engineers. The team had asked for a live debrief of Dragon One's death and the associated piercing headache Paul had experienced. They also asked Kata to walk through a similarly blinding headache she had endured two days ago when one of her betas, Hancock, was killed in a firefight.

After listening to their detailed mission debriefs, though, the team offered no explanation or insight into the painful phenomena. Musashi's engineers flipped through large notebooks while the old doctor rubbed his forehead. Filson sat motionless, hands folded together on the table.

"The headache was them, right?" Kata pressed as the meeting came to a close. "It was them dying."

"Yes," Dr Musashi said, dropping his hand from his forehead. "I believe that is the most reasonable explanation. Hancock and Dragon One were the first Ōkami to die. Until now, we simply did not know the neural link would transmit their last gasp like that."

"Last gasp?" Paul asked, frustrated.

"That's what we call it. For lack of a better term."

"Can you explain it?"

"No," Dr. Musashi said. "I am sorry. This is unanticipated. But we will work hard to be able to do so."

Now, as they quietly shared army rations on a rock, Paul and Kata stewed, feeling more isolated than ever.

"Doesn't inspire a lot of fucking confidence, does it?" Kata said.

"No," Paul said.

"I mean, they cut us open and put all that shit in our bodies and, turns out, they really don't understand how it all works yet." She pushed her empty ration can across the rock and leaned back in her field chair.

"I wanted to go to training command," Paul said, placing his empty ration can on the rock.

"Fuck you," Kata said, unable to stop a smile from spreading across her face.

Paul stood up and moved his chair so that he could put his feet up on their table rock.

Kata did the same.

"Guess we can't do a fucking thing about it now," she muttered.

"No. Other than win down here."

"Win?" Kata laughed. "I'll be happy to get out of this shit alive."

Paul nodded.

"You know," Paul said. "The Ōkami can fight. That is for sure. But they are strange."

"What do you mean?"

Paul thought about it for a moment.

"Well," he said, taking his feet off of the table rock and leaning forward in his chair. "You remember how in Africa, when we got back inside the wire after a mission, the soldierbots would shut down until we needed them again?"

"Yeah?"

"Well, the Ōkami betas never shut down. They are just like you and me. They have to endure the idle time. The endless hours and days of nothing. But they never get bored like us. They are always observing. I asked the Doc about it and he said it was part of their 'Quantum enabled self-learning,' or some shit."

Paul made air quotes with his fingers and rolled his eyes.

"Continuous self-bullshitting, more like it," Kata said, real irritation in her voice. They were both sick of scientists and theories.

"Top, especially. She says the damnedest things."

"What things?" Kata asked.

"Things where I can't tell if she is brilliant or stupid."

"Like what?"

"Like, earlier this week," he said. "As we were wrapping up a patrol and were headed to meet the Dragons at the PZ, we walked next to a small river. Two old men were fishing from the bank as the sun set. Top says to me, 'I do not understand fishing, sir.'"

"'Pretty simple,' I said. 'It's a way to obtain food. And it is a nice way to spend time.'

"Top walked in silence next to me for few minutes and then said, 'The people that fish from the banks of the river cast their lines as far as they can out into the middle of the water.'

"We took a few more steps together in silence before she looked at me again and said, 'While the people fishing from a boat in the middle of the water cast their lines as far as they can to get close to the edge of the water.'"

Paul smiled and shook his head at Kata.

"What did you say?" Kata asked.

"I gave her my standard answer."

"And what is that?"

"'No fucking idea, Top.'"

Chapter Forty-Four

The mission assignments from Keil became more frequent as time went on. Some of them were real shots against the Chinese in the northeast, complex missions that required a significant amount of planning and coordination with the heavy drone forces, the exo battalion, and other units under General Keil's authority.

The close collaborations did nothing to improve the working relationship between Paul and Kata and Kiel's units.

One of the more ambitious missions was a deep raid on a Chinese depot where they stored and maintained a large number of fighting robots. It was a high-risk, high-payoff mission that required close collaboration between all the elements under Schofield's command.

Close collaboration that served to amplify Paul and Kata's opinion of those other elements. And theirs of Paul and Kata.

Paul's company was tapped for this one. Kata acted as his operations officer and went to all the planning sessions and mission briefings. As company commanders, Paul and Kata didn't have staffs that did all the planning for them like the commanders of the exo battalion and heavy drone units. It was just Paul and Kata and their first sergeants.

The mission was well designed. But given the strength of resistance they expected to face, every detail was critical. It called for putting all of Outlaw Company on one part of the objective while Thurman's exo battalion hit another part.

Colonel Filson was fired up when Paul and Kata told him about the mission.

"This is great! An Ōkami company doing the same work as an entire exo battalion."

Paul and Kata were too tired to share in the colonel's parochial excitement. They just stared back at the secure video screen, exhausted. Filson tuned in quickly, though, then spent the next few hours helping them plan their piece. Paul could tell, when they rang off, the colonel was nervous for him and Outlaw Company.

Since Dragon Flight would be acting as close air support on the objective, they did not have enough payload capacity for troop transport. The plan was to use every ounce of their max gross weight to carry munitions. As a result, the Outlaws would be inserted and extracted by heavy drone.

That part made Paul nervous.

Paul and Kata planned the assault like they always did - down to the gnat's ass. One of the most important details was the aircraft heading on landing. The heavy drone was configured with an aft ramp. They did not have side doors like the QC-10s. Because of the layout of the enemy facilities and the anticipated resistance, the Outlaws needed the ramp to be facing due west when they exited. That way, they could target and return fire directly on the enemy as they moved to cover. If the ramp was facing the wrong direction, they would not be able to suppress the enemy as they exited. Worse, they would not have a direct path to cover. Getting off the ramp and changing direction would increase their vulnerability. The Chinese could pick them off as they ran around the large squatty drones.

Paul and Kata emphasized this during planning with the heavy drone pilots. Over and over. To the point that Colonel Packard finally waved them off. "OK, guys. We get it. We'll set down with our ramp facing due west. Have a little faith, will you?"

Kata looked at Packard. For a second, Paul thought she was going to say, "That's the problem, sir. We have little faith in you." It's what he was thinking as well. But Kata swallowed it in the spirit of collaboration, and let the mission brief continue.

Forty-eight hours later, with the mission underway, the heavy drone landed ramps facing due east. The exact opposite direction the Outlaws planned for and needed. They lost Mia and several soldierbots as they exited and maneuvered around the aircraft. The shock of her last gasp nearly knocked Paul out, but his suit kept running.

The Outlaws fought through it, though. They had surprised the Chinese and achieved most of their objectives in the first few minutes. They destroyed a lot of enemy equipment.

But intel had missed a few things. Chief among them was the Chinese armored battalion and Centaur infantry regiment that were billeted on the robot depot.

They counter attacked viciously, driving a wedge of tanks and infantry between Outlaw Company and the exo battalion. Within minutes, both American ground forces were surrounded and fighting for their lives.

Kata stood in the command center next to Colonel Packard, watching the tactical display with concern.

Packard and the heavy drone command swung into action, executing a hasty extraction of Thurman's exo battalion.

"Whats the plan for getting the Outlaws out, sir?" She asked him as the heavies dropped in, right on top of the exo battalion, weapons spitting fire in all directions. "This window of opportunity it going to close fast."

Kata watched with anxiety as red icons, symbolizing Chinese forces, surged around the Outlaws' position on the tactical display.

The video feed from Colonel Thurman and other exo leaders showed a fierce fire fight as they ran for the aircraft.

"Thunder Six, this is Outlaw Six," Paul's voice came over the speakers in the command center as he called Colonel Packard. Explosions and weapons fire nearly drowned out his voice. "Requesting immediate extraction!"

Packard held his breath as the display showed the heavies blasting their way off of the ground. They took some hits, but all the of the aircraft made it out. All the exos, including wounded and dead, were extracted.

"Thunder Six, goddamnit!" Paul yelled over the radio. "Expedite!"

Kata surveyed the tactical display and swallowed hard. Red swarmed around Paul's position.

Packard leaned over to his operation officer, a major standing on the opposite side of him from Kata, and said, "Get me a fast mover. The human takes priority. We'll pull Owens out if we can. But we will not attempt extraction of the robots. The landing zone is just too hot. Too much enemy fire."

"What?" Kata yelled, turning to Packard. "What the fuck is your problem? You chickenshit! Get the Outlaws out of there!"

The Colonel took a step back from Kata.

The major leaned in toward her and held a hand in front of the colonel. "Easy, Captain. You are addressing a superior officer."

Kata slapped the major's hand away.

"You can't just leave them there!" She jabbed Packard in the chest with a finger.

General Keil, on the other side of the tactical display table, moved quickly, intent on getting between Kata and Packard.

"Goddamn it, Vukovic! You will secure your shit, or I'll have you removed from my command post. Get control of yourself!"

Keil gestured at the two military policemen that always stood at the entrance to the Operations Center. They glared back at Kata.

"Thunder Six!" Paul's strained voice came over the speakers again.

General Keil and Kata looked at the tactical display. Colonel Packard looked at his shoes.

"We need extraction!" Paul's voice yelled.

General Schofield walked into the command center. He made his way to the tense standoff at the tactical display table.

Colonel Packard cleared his throat.

"You've got to understand, Captain," Packard said to Kata, ensuring Schofield heard. "The math just doesn't work. We can't risk the heavy drones just to pull one Centaur out."

General Schofield nodded at the statement and Keil said, "I agree."

Kata knew she was close to being thrown out of the command center and losing any ability to influence the battle for Paul. She didn't want that. She tried to swallow her rage.

A few minutes later, Packard mustered the courage to walk back over to Kata.

"We will get him out as soon as we possibly can," he said to her in a low voice. "We are working on a plan to send in one of our smaller fast movers. A lightweight drone that Owens can strap into for a solo extraction."

"Don't bother. Captain Owens will not leave his soldiers behind."

She turned from Packard in disgust and walked to the other side of the tactical display table.

As she walked away, she overheard Colonel Packard say, "Crazy fucking jigsaws," to General Keil.

Ordinarily Kata would have flown into an asskicking rage at the word. But she was past caring what they thought. All she was concerned with was Paul and Outlaw Company. She would not leave the command center, or get thrown out, until they were extracted.

The Outlaws took more losses while they waited. Paul's soldierbots and XPs were taking a lot of hits. Snapshot had an arm blown off. Then Paul took a round to the leg. His armor stopped most of it, and his suit cauterized the wound immediately. But Paul was hobbled.

"Shit," Packard said in the command center. "Hypersonics inbound."

Keil shook his head.

Schofield chewed his lower lip.

"Outlaw Six," Kata called to Paul over the radio. "Be advised. Hypersonics inbound!"

Paul, crouching against a shattered wall for cover, keyed his radio twice to acknowledge and muttered to himself, "Of course they are."

The Chinese had hypersonic batteries in Caracas, Paramaribo, and a few other coastal cities. Meant for longer-range defensive fires, the missiles, like the American version, flew faster than Mach 15 and were networked with their spy satellites. Hypersonics could take out long-range strategic aircraft at nearly intercontinental ranges, or even aircraft taking off from the mainland US if they wanted.

"Damnit," Packard muttered.

Keil rubbed his forehead as silence settled over the command center.

Kata looked from Packard to Keil and finally to Schofield. None would meet her eyes. They were thinking the same thing she was.

The hypersonics effectively capped the battle area. Anything five hundred feet or above would be disintegrated by the lattice of projectiles flying fifteen times the speed of sound. The Chinese decided they liked their numbers and chances on the ground and were willing to seal it off and fight it out.

And they were right. The Outlaws were down to less than half strength. They did not have the staying power to hold out against the Chinese onslaught for very long.

"Where are your heavy drones, colonel?" Keil asked Packard.

"Loitering at a safe altitude and distance behind that eastern mountain range, sir," Packard answered. "They are covered from the hypersonics."

Packard could feel Kata's glare burning into him.

"They are doing their best to support Outlaw company with indirect fire," he added.

"Maybe a quarter of their rounds are making it through the hypersonic cap," Kata said.

No one would meet her eyes, so she focused back on the tactical display table.

"Thunder Six," Paul called over the radio. Packard almost flinched. "Can I get an ETA for Exfil?"

Packard hesitated.

"Outlaw, this is Apache," Kata said, staring at the silent Packard. General Schofield started walking her way. She glared at him too as she continued, "We're working it. But I won't lie. It's going to take some time."

"Roger that, Apache.

Kata winced at the resignation in Paul's voice. She would have rather heard him scared.

Paul did not know what to do.

It was hell on the ground. The mission was designed to be a raid, an in-and-out job. The Outlaws did not have sufficient force to hold terrain. It was just a matter of time. And the Chinese could sense it. They kept pouring it on. The noise was terrible. The chain-saw sounds of Outlaws firing echoed off the broken buildings. Explosions from Chinese munitions hitting all around them. The shriek of the hypersonics overhead. Indirect fire from the heavy drones detonating in the air when struck by a hypersonic, or on the ground if they made it through.

Paul and Top fought on opposite ends of their small defensive position. They looked at each other at one point. She nodded at Paul, and he realized he had said, "This is it," to her in whisper mode. Paul nodded back.

General Schofield stood behind Kata in the command post, monitoring the mission. Each time Paul called for extraction, Schofield would look at General Keil and Colonel Packard and shake his head. Then Packard would repeat his promise to Kata: "We'll get him out as soon as we can."

Paul called several more times. To Kata, he sounded more resigned with each call. As if he were going through the motions. No one in the command center would make eye contact with Kata when he called. It felt like this went on for a long time. Kata stared at the mapping table, watching the enemy stack up around the Outlaws as their numbers dwindled. It would not be long now.

"Outlaw Six, this is Dragon Three," a voice came over the radio.

Everyone had forgotten about the Dragons. Including Paul.

And including the Chinese.

A jolt ran through Kata when she heard his voice. She looked at the tactical display table and saw three Dragons due north of the Outlaws' location, and two due south.

Schofield, Keil, Packard and their staffs looked at each other and then at the mapping display, trying to figure out what was happening.

"Who the hell is Dragon Three?" Schofield asked.

Kata ignored him as she looked at the two Dragon formations on the tactical display. One north of Paul. One south. They looked at first glance like they were lining up for strafing runs. But when she looked closer, she realized they were preparing for something else.

Kata stifled a smile. For the first time since things went to shit, she felt a glimmer of hope for Paul and the Outlaws. But she didn't want to tip her hand to Schofield and his officers yet.

On the ground, Paul and Top shared a quick, surprised look before Paul responded.

"Go ahead, Dragon Three."

"Keep your head down, sir," Dragon Three radioed back, the roar of his engines almost overwhelming his voice. "Dragon Flight is coming to get you. Going to be on your pos in two minutes for extraction. But before we get there, we're going to have to fire everything we have left into your vicinity to lighten our load."

"What is happening?" General Schofield demanded in the command center.

"You sure you want to do that, Dragon Three?" Paul transmitted. "It's pretty sporty here at the moment."

"Negative!" Schofield yelled over the radio. "Negative! Do not attempt extraction. I repeat. Do not attempt extraction. Acknowledge!"

"Ninety seconds, sir," Dragon Three announced.

"This is Iron Zero Six, goddamn it!" Schofield responded. "I am ordering Dragon Flight to abort!"

Kata glanced around. The command center was in shock at the development. General Keil and Colonel Packard stood motionless in stunned disbelief.

As Kata realized what the Dragons had done, she was unable to suppress her smile any longer. They had been flying ballsy low-level strafing runs on the enemy, weaving around the incoming heavy drone fire trying to clear out an LZ so that the Outlaws could be extracted. When the alert for hypersonics had come over the net, instead of climbing to a safe altitude and running behind the mountains with the heavy drones, they dove down to make sure they were no higher than a hundred feet above ground level. At that altitude, though, they were much more vulnerable to ground fire, so they had to move off of the fight.

They were also monitoring the radio, of course. Listening in when Paul asked for extraction. They heard his request get denied as the exo battalion got pulled out. They listened as he asked repeatedly for extraction and was repeatedly turned down. They got tired of waiting.

"Goddamnit!" Schofield slammed his fists down on the tactical display table, shaking the holographic image.

General officers, as a rule, don't handle it well when reality doesn't bend to their will. But Schofield was the commanding general of a combat-zone. A demigod. His words moved mountains, changed the course of rivers, and caused men and women to die. No one and nothing disobeyed him.

Except Ōkamis going to get comrades.

The general's eyes nearly bulged out of his head as the five flashing green icons identifying Dragon Flight turned to converge on Outlaw Company's location. Three were flying in from the north. The other two from the south. All of them were flying at more than three hundred knots, less than fifty feet above the ground.

Kata looked around at the stunned officers, doing nothing, mouths open, staring at the tactical display. She wanted to get her comrades help.

"Colonel Packard, Sir," she said, in her most respectful voice. "Can we get some indirect fire on the Chinese to keep them occupied while the Dragons attempt extraction?"

Packard and Keil looked at Kata and then to Schofield. They wouldn't do anything unless he approved.

"Sixty seconds," Dragon Three called on the radio.

On the ground, Top's head swiveled toward Paul. He gave her a thumbs-up while saying in whisper mode, "Get ready. If they actually make it, we're not going to have long to get aboard and get gone."

"Always the best-case scenario with you," she whispered back.

Kata waited a few heartbeats before walking over and standing in front of General Schofield. "They're not going to stop, sir," she said in a quiet voice. "Least we can do is support them."

The general stared at Kata for interminable seconds before looking away in disgust. He nodded to Colonel Packard and walked out of the command center.

"Colonel Packard, sir, I am designating the fire line now," Kata said as she spun on her heels and raced to the tactical display. Reading the terrain quickly, she entered the fire instructions.

"Roger that," Packard said. He started speaking quickly into his headset.

Kata stared intently at the tactical display. The green Dragon Flight icons inched closer to the LZ. She keyed the radio.

"Attention this net. This is Apache Six. Heavy drones will be laying down supportive fire along the protective lines I'm broadcasting now." She hit 'send' from the mapping table, sharing their display with Paul instantly.

The protective fire lines lay across the 3D map on Paul's in-head display. Paul smiled. Kata laid them exactly where he would have put them. Yellow crosshairs indicated targeted coordinates. Yellow dotted-line circles outlined the lethal blast radius of each impact. Paul's smile faded to a grimace. It was going to be close.

"It's going to be heavy, Dragons," Kata said over the radio. "Keep an eye out for debris on your approach. Outlaw Six, I'd get low and skinny if I were you."

Paul keyed his mic twice to acknowledge Kata.

The Outlaws sheltered as best they could as the heavy drone fire struck the Chinese in long sheaths of death to the east and west of their position. Dragon Flight fired off the rest of their heavy ordnance as well, to lighten up and kill enemy. The ground shook. The smoke and debris thickened. Visibility was zero.

In the command center, the mapping table bloomed yellow as the heavy drone fire struck. Kata watched as the five Dragons joined up in a tight clockwise circle, spitting more fire on the Chinese.

Paul saw three Dragons dive from the dark sky to the ground.

"Go! Go! Go!" He yelled.

Every living Outlaw ran toward the three Dragons as the aircraft flared aggressively under the explosions and crisscrossing fire.

The Outlaws were a sad sight. Down to two dozen undamaged soldierbots, they ran and fired their weapons as they carried and dragged their wounded and broken comrades. Snapshot fired his weapon with his one good arm at a full sprint. Paul was limping badly, one hand clinging to Top to keep upright, shooting his rifle with the other.

The Dragons slammed onto the ground, skidding to a stop, every weapons system blazing. Their large forward turrets glowed red from the volume of fire they were spitting at the enemy.

Paul and Top and were just a few meters from Dragon Two's ramp when Colonel Packard transmitted. "Dragon Flight hold position for five seconds," he commanded.

Paul started to protest, but Kata sent another line of fire to his IHD map, directly north, to cover their egress. He and Top fell to the floor of Dragon Two. Her ramp closed as Paul watched the covering fire erupt on his map.

"Go now! Go! Go!" Kata yelled into the radio.

The three Dragons surged into the air, following the rolling line of heavy drone indirect fire. They accelerated quickly, engines screaming in exertion.

Paul had just picked himself off the deck when a missile struck Dragon Five, the last aircraft in their formation. Paul collapsed under the pain of the last gasp as Dragon Five disintegrated, flaming debris careening in all directions.

The two surviving Dragons hugged the terrain until linking up with their comrades who had been supporting the extraction with strafing runs. The flight of four carved through the valley headed for Stalwart.

Kata met them on the airfield. Paul had passed out from the combination of blood loss and Dragon Five's last gasp. She helped his soldiers get him to Stalwart's medical facility, where he was immediately placed into a MedPod.

An hour later, Kata went back to the command center to grab her things. Schofield, Keil, and Packard were standing at the mapping table, replaying parts of the battle. Kata tried to be quiet, but they turned to look when she grabbed her rucksack.

"Captain Vukovic," General Keil said. "Come here."

Kata walked over to the three senior officers. She could see they were not happy. Neither was she.

"What the hell happened out there tonight, Captain?"

"I'd like to ask the colonel the same question," Kata answered, matching the general's venom with her own.

"What do you mean?" Packard asked, indignant.

"Let's start with, how the hell do you fuck up the landing direction after we went through it so many times?"

General Keil waved her off. "The assault was a success, Captain."

"Success?" Kata nearly screamed.

"Yes. We achieved every objective. And incurred negligible losses."

"Negligible losses?" Kata shouted. "We lost seventy percent of Outlaw Company! Captain Owens nearly had his leg taken off!"

The one-star general glanced at the other two senior officers as if the three of them were in on a joke. "Like I said," Keil said with a shrug.

Kata took a step toward the general.

"Captain!" Schofield said sharply.

Kata didn't come to attention, but she stopped her advance on Keil. "Sir?" she said.

"It's been a long night for everyone. I suggest you get some rest."

"Yes, sir," Kata said, realizing there was nothing to be gained or proven at that point. She turned to leave.

"And, Captain?" General Schofield said. "You should know that I have contacted Colonel Filson and the manufacturer and asked for a full malfunction report. I expect they will need you and Captain Owens to assist. See to it that you do."

"Malfunction, sir?"

"Dragon Flight's failure to follow orders," the general said, glaring. "Dependability is the primary requirement of any weapons system. Your team better get their shit together, or this proof of concept is as far as you will ever get. I will not tolerate defective, rogue robots in my command or in my military."

"A few more missions like tonight, and you won't have to, sir," Kata said as she turned to leave.

"Crazy fucking jigsaw," General Keil muttered to General Schofield.

Kata walked out of the command center into the night.

If loyalty is a malfunction, she thought, *I hope I am as defective as the Ōkami.*

Chapter Forty-Five

Colonel Filson showed up a week after the botched raid, dispatched by Combat Corps Command to figure out why the Dragons had malfunctioned. Pruden was with him as well as several of Musashi's engineers.

For three days, Filson, Pruden, and the team interviewed Paul and his Ōkami. The engineers had brought special equipment along, enabling them to download massive amounts of data from the robots hoping for a causal link or at least insight. They spent time with Kata and her soldiers, as well. Though the Apaches had not been involved in the now infamous, willful act of disobedience, they had exhibited lesser, but still strangely independent behaviors as well.

Though it was good as ever to see Colonel Filson and even Pruden, this visit had a different tone. Filson and Pruden seemed nervous. They went about their tasks and interviews with a different vibe than usual. They still enjoyed their evening communions, but with a less celebratory air. It left Paul and Kata a little spooked.

Paul and Kata were also troubled by their tactical situation. They held off talking to Filson about it, but after two days, they could not hold back any longer. Kata, of course, started first.

"This is bad, sir. Paul's Outlaws are down to less than fifty percent after that fucked-up depot raid, and I'm almost as bad after the goat screw they sent me on. I lost Grant, Sherman, and two Eagles!" Kata's face was tight with strain as she continued. "We're down to six Ōkami betas between us. Our soldierbot and extension-platform numbers are dwindling, and the maintenance bots can't keep up. But even worse, the Chinese have taken notice of us."

"What do you mean?" Filson asked her.

"We know they've been watching us since we've been in country. But Paul's depot raid was a red flag. Until then, they had been happy to leave us alone while we fucked with Navarro. I think they, like Schofield, are more focused on the big fight that's coming. But now that we have inflicted real pain on them, not their proxy bastard in the Cone, they view us as something that has to be eliminated. Intel has picked up Chinese intercepts telling Navarro to get aggressive. And we know they gave him a bunch of new tech."

"Have you talked to General Schofield about this?"

"We did." Kata sneered. "The smoothie told us to stop assisting the Chinese."

The colonel's blank look told Kata to continue.

"When we finished our situation report, he just asked us to please stop assisting the Chinese," she told Filson. "He said the Chinese wanted him to divert forces to deal with Navarro, but that it was our job. He was gearing up for a push east and didn't want to divert forces to the Southern Cone because an aging warlord was spooking two Centaurs."

Filson shook his head.

In a dejected voice, Kata said, "We're degrading while Navarro is getting stronger. Like I said, this is bad."

They all sat in silence for a moment. The only sound was Pruden's typing on his laptop in the corner.

"You are quiet today, Paul," the colonel said.

Paul looked back at him and shrugged.

"What is it?" Filson asked.

"The depot raid got in his head," Kata said, pointing at Paul.

"No," Paul said. "Not the raid."

"What is it, then, son?" the colonel asked.

Paul hesitated.

"Tell me."

"I still don't understand why Dragon Flight came back for us," Paul said. Pruden, still in the corner, looked up at him.

"We've been through this. Right, Marty?" Filson said, turning to look at Pruden. "Read him our executive summary."

"Sir?" Pruden said, caught off guard.

"Read him our executive summary, please," Filson repeated.

"Oh, right," Pruden stammered. He tapped a few keys on his laptop and said, "Let me get the file open and—"

"Don't bother!" Paul stood up from his chair. Filson, Kata, and Pruden, all startled, stared at him.

"I'm not interested in whatever bullshit you have concocted to feed the administrative beast and keep your precious field trial on the rails!"

Colonel Filson regarded him for a long moment. Pruden sat still, not sure what to do.

"I want to understand what happened," Paul said.

"Isn't it obvious?" the colonel asked. "They came back for you. You, Top, and the rest of their comrades."

"Why?" Paul insisted.

"Marty?" the colonel said, turning to look at him.

"Yes?" Pruden said, sitting up straight as he answered.

"Did you ask the Dragons why they returned for Captain Owens and the rest of Outlaw Company, despite direct orders from General Schofield not to?"

"Yes."

"And what did they say?"

"They said that it was the right thing to do."

Filson nodded as he turned from Pruden and looked at Paul.

Paul shook his head. He had had the same conversation with the Dragons, and they'd told him the same thing. When he'd pressed them on how they knew it was the right thing, Dragon Three had just said, "It was a gut thing, sir."

"Why are you making this so hard?" Filson asked Paul. "Why don't you accept their answer?"

"That's not how they are supposed to work. They are just machines."

"What does that mean? Just machines?"

"It… it means…" Paul stammered, searching for the words. "It means…"

The colonel chuckled, which really pissed Paul off. He glared at the old man.

Pruden looked nervously at his laptop.

Kata looked at Paul with concern.

"I'm sorry, Paul," the colonel said, trying to swallow his smile. "I don't mean to laugh."

Filson stood up and stepped closer to him. He put his hand on Paul's shoulder. "Most soldiers spend their entire careers looking for comrades that will do what yours did that night. Most soldiers go into battle bearing doubt. They're not sure that their buddies will be there for them. Not a hundred percent, anyway. You, though?" Filson tapped Paul's chest with a finger. "You know. No matter how shitty, no matter how dangerous, no matter how impossible, no matter if it contravenes a fucking three-star general or their own programming, your soldiers will never leave you behind. They will come back for you. Every. Damn. Time. That's all that matters."

"Maybe," Paul said. "But I want to know why."

"You know why," Colonel Filson said over his shoulder as he walked back to his chair.

"I don't."

"You do, son. It was the process."

Paul looked at the colonel, then at Kata. Her face was tense, waiting for Paul to explode on the old man.

Pruden sat in the corner, confused and nervous. Paul looked back at the colonel. Then he shook his head and chuckled in surrender.

"What is the process?" Pruden asked Filson.

"I'll tell you on our flight back tomorrow," the colonel said, pulling a cigar out of his breast pocket.

"It's bullshit," Kata said, trying to hide her smile.

"It's gospel," the colonel said.

Filson lit his cigar and blew a few smoke rings across the hooch. Pruden sensed the tension in the room had ratcheted down and returned to his notes.

The next morning, Paul and Kata walked in silence with the colonel to his aircraft. Pruden walked behind them.

At the aircraft, they stood together at the end of the aft boarding ramp.

The colonel looked at them. "I won't lie. I'm worried about you two." Then he shook his head. "And I wish I wasn't so goddamn old."

Paul and Kata looked at their feet, trying not to show how unsettling the colonel's words were to them. Pruden stood awkwardly on the periphery.

Filson looked over Paul's shoulder, back across Devil toward the shipping-container hooches dug into the side of the mountain, almost two hundred meters away.

At that moment, Top stepped out of the Outlaw ops hooch. The colonel nodded slightly to her and winked, a gesture that would have been imperceptible to a human at that distance. Top, though, stopped and gave Filson a sharp salute before continuing on her way.

Filson looked back at Paul and Kata with a tired face. "This is not the time to let the pressure off, guys. If you guys get in trouble, General Schofield is not going to divert even a cook's assistant to help. If Navarro knew the situation, he'd run you over today. You can't let him suspect, even for a second, that you are in a weakened state. So, give 'em hell, guys," Filson said. Then he stepped onto the aircraft ramp and walked forward into the shadows.

Pruden, suddenly alone with Paul and Kata, looked around Outpost Devil for a moment and then back at them.

"It's been an honor," he said, awkwardly extending his hand. Kata took it first.

"Yeah," she said as she shook his hand. "Thanks."

"Thanks," Paul said without enthusiasm.

Pruden leaned in as he shook Paul's hand. "I don't think it's bullshit,

Captain. I think they came back for you because they thought it was the right thing to do."

Paul just nodded.

Pruden took a few steps onto the aircraft ramp. He was half in the shadows when he stopped, turned back to Paul and Kata and said, "And they were right."

Chapter Forty-Six

Fiona paced back and forth in her office in front of the big windows. It was early evening in Manhattan and the streets far below her office were brightly lit. She was anxious. Pruden was meeting with Colonel Frank and representatives of the Combat Corps Command on Fort Belvoir today. He was going to call her as soon as the meeting ended and he got his phone back and got clear.

The Ōkami "malfunction" during the mission down in the Southern Cone had rattled both Combat Corps Command and Acquisitions Command. The US Military was on the leading edge of America's artificial intelligence activities and investments. The scope and depth of AI applications throughout DOD was extensive. They were used to the occasional hiccup. It came with the territory of pushing the envelope to stay ahead of the Chinese and keep the world safe for democracy. They had protocols for the hiccups, including potential sentience, runaway algorithms, and numerous other scenarios. But, as is always the case for the military, outright disobedience struck a nerve.

The military wanted answers.

After their fact-finding trip, Filson and Pruden flew back from Stalwart directly to Fort Belvoir. Doctor Musashi joined them there for the meeting with Colonel Frank and several high-level Combat Corps Command officers. After hearing the trio's report and explanation, the officers would decide the fate of the Ōkami field trial.

Fiona knew that termination of the project was the most likely outcome. Given the nature and visibility of the malfunction, she thought it highly unlikely the military would continue with the Ōkami evaluation.

And Fiona knew what that meant for Determined End States.

She paced back and forth in her office, trying to tamp down her hope and anxiety and to get her head around what would likely happen next. She had to be ready.

Fiona glanced at her watch again. Almost five-thirty.

She thought Pruden would have called by now.

Her grandfather and Eugene crowded her thoughts as her mind raced through scenarios and contingencies. Some more palatable than others. Some unbearable.

Her phone rang.

"Answer," she told it. "Speaker phone."

She turned back to her desk and said, "This is Fiona."

"Hey, it's me," Pruden said, his voice coming over the speakers in Fiona's office. "Sorry to take so long. Took forever to get my phone back and get away from the colonel and the doctor."

"What happened?"

"I've never seen anything like it," Pruden said quickly, excitement in his voice. "At the beginning of the meeting, I was sure we were dead. The project cancelled. You know how Colonel Frank is. And, let me tell you, the Combat Corps guys were even worse. But by the time the colonel and the doctor got done, they had flipped the whole group. For a minute in there, I thought there was actually a chance they were going to order a battalion of Ōkami on the spot. Tonight."

Pruden caught his breath and then said, "They did it, Fiona. They saved the field trial."

Fiona slumped into the chair behind her desk and put her head in her hands.

I can't believe it, she thought. *This is a disaster.*

Her head was spinning. This was the worst possible outcome.

"Are you there?" Pruden asked. "Did I lose you?"

"I'm here," she lifted her head from her hands. She tried to sound happy. "I'm sorry. This is great news. I'm just getting my head around it. It doesn't seem possible."

"I know!" Pruden agreed. "But they were masterful in there. First the Doctor went over the data backwards and forwards. Then the colonel hammered home the realities of the high-intensity conflict scenario the Ōkami had to contend with that night. He explained how a combination of poor communications, Chinese electronic warfare, and battle damage prevented the aircraft from properly receiving and processing the command to abort their emergency extraction attempt. Then the colonel emphasized it was no different than had it been a human pilot with a faulty radio. And then he challenged them. He looked right at the Combat Corps officers. Because they are his people, right? And asked them, isn't this what they wanted to see in a soldier who is in the shit without any communication? Don't you want to see him take initiative? To not leave a man behind? To—"

"OK, OK." Fiona tried to hide the anger and disappointment in her voice. "Look, this is great news and a tremendous relief. And I am suddenly feeling exhausted. Are you still going to be here in the morning?"

"Yeah, for sure. I am headed to the airport now. See you there at your office in the morning."

"Great," Fiona said through clenched teeth. "See you in the morning. And great work."

"Tha-"

"Hang up," Fiona told her phone.

She stood up from her desk and walked across the office to the wet bar. Her mind raced as she poured herself a stiff whiskey.

I can't fucking believe it, she thought. *I thought for sure this was the end, that the* Ōkami *field trial would be cancelled and we could get the Spitting Metal acquisitions process, and revenue, going.*

She downed her whiskey and then poured herself another.

I was a fool to let Filson go to that meeting. Romantic son of a bitch talks the customer's language too well. And he's a goddamn believer. And it has fucking rubbed off on Martin.

Fiona walked to one of the sitting areas by the large windows and sank into a deep leather chair.

"Call from Eugene Malloy," her phone said.

"Voice mail," Fiona told it.

She was not in the right head space to talk to Eugene at the moment. And what would she say, anyway? "Hey. Great news. The military just handed our grandfather the corncob dildo he is going to shove up our ass because of a secret deal I made with him and never told you about. You're gonna lose Mio Posto for sure. How was your day?"

She slugged the shot of whiskey back and placed the shot glass on the side table.

Fiona sat in that chair until late in the night, thinking through scenarios and contingencies, and wondering if she could live with herself after any of them.

Chapter Forty-Seven

iona had to be careful when Pruden met her in her office the next day. She tried her best to seem happy and relieved while she dug for more information. Anything that might help her next move.

"Great work, Marty," she said from behind her desk. He sat in a chair on the other side. "You. Filson. Musashi. Really great."

Pruden smiled.

"Thanks. It was really a team effort. I think things are really starting to come together. It feels good."

"So, do you guys really think the incident was just a combination of communications, electronic warfare, and battle damage? And that was it?" She asked in a way she hoped was casual. "Was there nothing else at play?"

Pruden hesitated.

Fiona studied his face.

She smiled.

"I mean, if I'm asking. Colonel Frank and the others must have asked."

"They pressed us," Pruden said. "But the data backs up our hypothesis one hundred percent. Ultimately, they agreed with our interpretation of the data."

"Uh huh," Fiona said, raising an eyebrow.

Now Pruden smiled.

"Tell me," she said.

"We think there may be more to it."

"More to it?"

Prudent hesitated for a moment and then shrugged. "We think something unique has happened."

"Something unique?" Fiona tried to mask her skepticism.

"Advancements in quantumtronics," Pruden spoke slowly. He raised his right hand and extended a finger as he listed his points. "Doctor Musashi's architecture and approach to continuous-learning AI, Colonel Filson's process of small unit training, the character of the two captains leading the Ōkami, and the experience of combat and fighting to survive largely on their own."

Pruden hesitated. He held all five fingers of his right hand in the air and nodded solemnly.

"Somehow that all came together to create and mold these particular Ōkami into a highly effective, and very loyal fighting force. They will never abandon one another. Ever."

Fiona sat in silence. She could hear the admiration in Pruden's voice. It irritated her. She swallowed it.

"But you didn't tell them that?"

"No," Pruden shook his head. "And one reason is that I'm not sure if we ran this experiment a hundred more times we could produce the same result. Different training method, different company commanders, different mission profile. It's just not clear to us the same bonds and unit cohesiveness would form."

"Terrific," Fiona said. "We have invested hundreds of millions of dollars in a poorly understood product that we cannot attribute any repeatability or dependability to. Combat Corps is going to love that."

Pruden smiled.

"Don't misunderstand me. The Ōkami work. They work very well. They are the best small unit, special operations capable, AI enabled soldierbots on the market. Colonel Frank, Combat Corps, or whoever is going to love them. I am not worried about that at all.

"You asked me a specific question about what happened," Pruden continued smiling. "And I am trying to explain how special it was. But trust me when I say we are going to sell a lot of these things."

We need to sell a lot of the Spitting Metal things, Fiona thought as she smiled and nodded.

"Well, based on what I am sensing from you," Fiona said. "We should expect a successful conclusion to the trial next summer and then on to the next step."

"Yeah…"

Fiona heard something in his voice. She cocked her head to one side.

"What is it?"

"Oh," Pruden delayed. "It's nothing. I agree. We will successfully conclude the trial next summer and will be off to the races."

"It wasn't nothing. Something is on your mind. What is bothering you?"

Pruden grimaced.

"Look. It's not my area of expertise. But…"

"But what, Marty?" Fiona pressed.

"It's our two company commanders."

"Owens and Vukosomething?" Fiona asked.

"Vukovic. Yes."

"What about them?"

"I feel like they have developed an unhealthy level of hatred for Navarro," Pruden said.

"Who is Navarro?"

"He is their main enemy. He's an old guerrilla warrior, the one the Chinese have sponsored to be their agent of destabilization down there."

Fiona leaned back in her chair, listening intently.

"I actually talked to Colonel Filson about it."

"And what did he say?" Fiona asked.

"He does not share my concern, per se. But he did think it had become somewhat personal for Paul and Kata."

"Those are our commanders?"

"Yes," Pruden said.

"But you still have concerns?"

"I do," Pruden said. "I mean, I trust Colonel Filson. He has obviously been doing his thing for a long time. This is his area of expertise. I just…"

"You just what?"

"I worry they may, in their desire to get Navarro, take unnecessary chances. Put themselves at risk."

Fiona nodded slowly. She held Pruden in a steady gaze.

"Well, the last thing we need right now is to take a step back," she said. "I trust Colonel Filson as much as you do. But I will speak with him about it."

"I think that would be a good idea. We are so close to success. I just don't want anything to screw it up. No matter how remote the chance."

"It's settled then," Fiona said, standing up from her desk. "I'll give the old colonel a call."

"Thank you." Pruden took Fiona's cue and stood as well.

"Great work, Marty. Really great work."

Pruden smiled with pride as Fiona walked around her desk to shake his hand.

"Now go get some rest," she told him. "Take a few days off. You have earned it."

"I just might do that."

"You should!"

Pruden walked out of Fiona's office and down the hall to the elevator bank.

Fiona shut the door and walked back to her desk.

She sat in her chair and swiveled around to look out the window. She sat for a long time, thinking about what she had to do next.

Finally, she made the call.

Chapter Forty-Eight

Paul and Kata changed tactics on Navarro. First, they started combining their forces on more important missions. Whenever possible, if time permitted, and the mission justified it, they would join their companies together. They decided that they would never both go on a mission together in order to preserve survivability of command and took turns commanding the missions. But joining forces like that meant that whoever went out packed a much bigger punch, hiding their actual weakness from Navarro.

Second, they threw a lot of tactical feints in the area. For example, Paul would have one of the Dragons take a small wolf pack out to a remote village or key terrain feature a few hundred kilometers south of Devil. They would conduct a patrol, interact with the locals, and make a lot of noise as if they were executing an ultra-critical mission. Some days, they did this several times in multiple places across the Cone. Doing this expanded their operational footprint dramatically, and they showed up in places they had never been before. It confused the hell out of Navarro.

Paul and Kata and were feeling stressed, though. It had been about a month since their conference call with Schofield. They knew that, despite his legendary cautiousness, the general would be launching his offensive soon, and that when he did, Navarro would seize his opportunity to cause havoc. He would come at Paul and Kata hard with everything the Chinese had given him. As weakened as the Outlaws and Apaches were, they would not be able to cope with that onslaught. So, they had to get him before that happened.

The operations tempo was excruciating for Paul and Kata…and for their soldiers. They had more than doubled our mission cadence. Existence for them became primal. They were in one of three states: asleep, mission planning, or executing. Four, if the occasional stay in the MedPod counted.

The Ōkami didn't have it much better. They were in maintenance, on a mission, or pulling security for their now consolidated base of operations on Devil.

It sucked for everyone.

And yet, their morale was the highest it had ever been. It was them against the rest of the world, and they weren't backing down.

All the decentralization stressed the kill chain, though. They had to do one of two things. The first was to use the standoff capabilities of the architecture. They could get the flash and authorize the kill if they were in neural-link contact with the commanding Ōkami or a relaying Dragon. This was much easier to do when they were in the same area of operations, of course, because it all rode on the comms they carried themselves. But the architecture did have a long-range capability that worked across theater, and they used it numerous times. Paul could sit in his command hooch when the link was solid and respond to kill requests on multiple missions at once. It was actually easier than the poker games back at Bragg.

The problem was it relied on satellite, ultra-high frequency, and laser comms that were always in demand by every unit in theater. Schofield made it clear Paul and Kata were the lowest priority, unless they were on a mission for Keil directly. So, there were many times they had no kill chain on the remote patrols.

"You know how we are going to have to handle this, don't you?" Kata said to Paul as they talked through the communications challenge.

"How?"

"World War I style," Kata said, smiling.

It was tedious over-the-radio stuff, but it worked. The Ōkami beta would call for authorization. Paul would listen to a full description of the tactical situation, including civilians in the area and other ROE complexities, as he looked at the map to confirm their location and give it a quick sanity check. No hospitals or religious sites or the like. All the while, his Ōkami were taking fire and not hitting back. Finally, when Paul had confirmed as best he could, he would unleash them.

"Clear to engage," he would call over the radio. "Lethal force authorized."

And that would be the end of it.

Usually.

They got away with this extended mode of operation for almost a month. They had Navarro guessing. Intel picked up panicked communications between him and the Chinese. He tried to convince them the Ōkami numbers had tripled in theater. The Chinese tried to talk him off the ledge, insisting they were still a small operating force.

But it caught up with the Outlaws one day south of Mendoza. Just far enough away that the comms were not solid. There was no neural link.

Stuntman was on patrol with a wolf pack of ten soldierbots and one aerial XP. They were in contact with a small force. It didn't seem like a big scrap to Paul as he tried to maintain command and control from his ops hooch miles away on Devil. It was nothing that they hadn't dealt with a hundred times before. The problem was, Paul had no satellite or high-altitude drone imagery that day. All he had was the imagery from Stuntman's aerial XP. And it was tied up in the immediate tactical situation, not providing overwatch.

So, they had no warning when a platoon of Chinese-made quad tanks flanked them.

The car-sized, four-legged armored vehicles could carry a wide variety of heavy weapons, including directed energy. They were fast and nimble and were used for both transport and fire support. The Chinese typically deployed them in groups of five.

And that's what Navarro did that day. Five tanks hit the Ōkami on their left flank while Stuntman and his wolf pack were dodging fire, waiting for permission from Paul to engage. Paul was reviewing the map and tactical display when Stuntman was hit. Paul was about to give him permission to engage.

"Sir, enemy tanks on my—" was all Stuntman got out.

Since there was no neural link, there was no hit from Stuntman's last gasp. Paul just stood there, mouth hanging open, radio in his hand, trying to figure out what had happened.

Then all hell broke loose.

General Schofield may not have cared much about the fate of the Outlaws and Apaches. But the Pentagon did. And, truthfully, the Pentagon didn't care so much about their fate as it did the disposition of the Ōkami classified information. Paul and Kata's units, and all of their equipment, were classified above top secret, a critical national asset due to the advanced nature of the technology. The last thing the Pentagon wanted was for the Chinese to get their hands on one of the Ōkami betas.

One minute after Paul called in the situation report, he had every national and theater-level asset pointed at his small bush-country firefight. Paul's command hooch lit up with real-time imagery from both satellite and high-altitude drone.

As the images came to life, he saw the platoon of Chinese quad tanks sprinting south like coyotes. Much farther south, two large Chinese quad copters flew at high speed to link up with them. Clearly, all the tanks cared about at that point was extraction.

"This makes no sense," Paul said, mostly to himself.

"What is that, sir?"

"Why are the Chinese not more interested in stuntman's body?"

Top said nothing.

"I mean, this is like the Norden bombsight," Paul said. "Highly sensitive shit. And there is a beta they could take. There is no way we can get there in time to prevent it."

But when Paul panned back over to the site of the firefight, he saw why.

Stuntman was in pieces. Navarro's foot soldiers had torn him apart. Pieces of him were on fire. And those that weren't were being pissed on.

"Mother fuckers," Paul said through his teeth.

Top was still quiet, staring at the images.

Paul keyed the radio.

"Banshee Zero Three, Outlaw Six."

"This is Banshee," Keil's voice came back.

"We need an airstrike ASAP," Paul said. He looked at Top as he spoke. She had not moved, just stared at the images of Stuntman's body parts being celebrated over by Navarro's men.

"Roger that, Outlaw. We've been told to send whatever you need to secure the situation."

"At this point, all we can do is prevent site exploitation," Paul said, looking away from Top.

"Understood. I've got a high-altitude drone within firing range. I just need coordinates and confirmation that the site is ROE compliant."

"The site is compliant with all Rules of Engagement, sir," Top said, turning to look at Paul. "I will enter the latitude and longitude."

Paul nodded.

"Banshee, I can confirm the site is ROE compliant," Paul transmitted to Keil. "Lat/Long coming via secure terminal."

Top nodded to Paul, indicating the coordinates had been sent.

"Roger that, Outlaw," Keil said a moment later. "I copy site is compliant. We have the coordinates. Stand by."

Paul keyed the radio twice to acknowledge.

"I'm sorry, Top," he said as they both watched the tactical display.

"For what, sir?"

"Stuntman. I'm really sorry."

Top looked at Paul and nodded slightly before saying, "It's OK, sir. We did our best."

"Outlaw. Banshee. Thirty seconds," Keil said over the radio.

Paul keyed the radio twice as they both looked back at the tactical display, waiting for the strike to hit.

"Some days, sir, I wonder," Top said.

"Wonder what?"

"I wonder if I really want our deployment to be a success," she answered as the display showed the missiles track from the high-altitude drone toward Stuntman's dismembered body. About a dozen Navarro foot soldiers were still milling around the area. "Because if we fail, Ōkami won't have to do this, right?" she asked, just as the image showed the impact. An incandescent bloom covered the carnage.

Paul turned off the display.

"Right, sir?" she asked again before Paul could turn away.

"I don't know, Top. But if you're right, you and I would have to figure out something to do with the rest of our lives."

"How about this, sir? We'll fish. You from the shore. Me from a small boat."

"Bullshit. I want the boat."

"Deal," Top said.

Chapter Forty-Nine

"To stuntman," Kata said, raising her brass shot glass of whiskey.

Paul nodded sadly. He touched his shot glass to hers.

They both downed their whiskey in one swallow and put their shot glasses down on the table rock. Kata had fashioned the shooters from 30mm ammunition casings. Shiny and flared at the top, she was proud of them.

Kata poured whiskey into the shot glasses and leaned back in her chair.

It was a clear night, and the stars were out in force. Mendoza lay glowing in the distance, far below Paul and Kata on Outpost Philly.

Kata sat quietly as Paul, head leaning back in his chair, looked up at the stars. They had each learned how the other mourned. Kata knew that Paul would talk when and only when he wanted to, maybe not until tomorrow. She did not have to wait as long as she thought she would.

"What do you think the Geek is doing right about now?" Paul asked.

Kata looked at Paul. He was still sitting with his head back, surveying the stars.

"Whatever space geeks do, I suppose."

"I heard he got a new assignment," Paul said. "He got promoted off of LS4. I think he is the executive officer on an orbital tug. The *Bluestone*, I think he said it was."

"He got promoted again?" Kata asked, indignant.

"Yeah," Paul said, lifting his head off the back of his chair to look at her. "He's a lieutenant colonel now."

Kata lifted her shot glass.

"To the Geek."

Paul smiled. "To the Geek."

They downed their shots. Kata refilled them.

Paul settled back in his chair.

"I'm really sorry about Stuntman, Paul."

"Yeah. Me too. He was a good one."

"He was."

"They're all good ones, really," Paul said.

"They are."

"It's us that are the weak ones. You and I are the weakest link in the whole fucking thing."

"Fuck you." Kata shook her head. "We are essential. We make the whole thing run."

"No. We just make the whole thing legal. If there were no Tokyo Accords, the Ōkami wouldn't need us at all. They might even fight better without us."

"I'm not talking about kill chain bullshit," Kata said. "I'm talking about fighting."

Kata leaned forward and grabbed her brass shot glass. "I dunno," she said, before taking a sip of whiskey and leaning back in her chair.

"What do you mean, you don't know?"

"I think they fight better for us," Kata said.

"Why?"

"It's like Doc Musashi told us. They need examples. They're still learning."

"OK. Fine. So, once they have learned, then they would not need us anymore."

"I dunno," Kata said.

They sat quietly for a few minutes. Paul took a sip of whiskey from his shot glass, figuring Kata had lost interest in the conversation and was thinking of something else.

"No," she said ten minutes later, surprising Paul. "They still would fight better with us."

Paul shook his head, assuming this was just more of Kata's stubbornness.

"If we weren't here," she continued, eyes still on the mountains, "they would not believe in what they were fighting for."

Paul chuckled.

Kata turned her head, fixing him with her intense eyes. "Those quantumtronic brains of theirs would realize the human race is a bunch of fucking cowards throwing machines at their wars instead of their own."

Paul opened his mouth to respond, but Kata spoke first. "And who would want to fight for a bunch of fucking cowards? Only dumbass humans like me and you do that."

Chapter Fifty

"I'm coming on this one," Kata declared.

"No way," Paul said, calling up a map of the target village on the planning screen. "Tonight is my night."

He and Kata had been rotating missions since starting their combined-forces strategy.

Top stood still, waiting for them to fight it out.

"Tonight is different," Kata said, stepping between Paul and the planning display.

"Why is that?"

"Because he is going to be there," she said, pointing at small village of Los Olvidados on the map display. "For sure."

A small, remote village fifty miles southeast of Mendoza, Los Olvidados sprang up in the late eighteen hundreds at the intersection of telegraph lines criss-crossing on their way to the larger cities. The agriculturally focused village never grew beyond a thousand citizens, with most living on ranches and farms spread out across the flat, dry land. It was hard for Paul to think of a less strategic location.

"You don't know that," Paul countered.

"What do you think, Top?" Kata asked Paul's first sergeant.

"I believe Captain Vukovic may be right. We seldom get more than one intelligence indicator that corroborates. Usually, one contradicts the others. But these are unanimous and point at a meeting of Navarro and two of his lieutenants around 2000 hours this evening."

Paul looked at his watch. It was 1730. They had time to plan a sharp operation. But they needed to get on it.

"We've never had this kind of quality intelligence of Navarro's location before," Kata pressed. "He is going to be there. I can feel it. I'm going on this one. You're in charge. You call the shots. But I want in."

"No. We can't both go out." Paul squared up to Kata and crossed his arms. "Not going to happen."

Ninety minutes later, Paul sat in Dragon Three as they flew fifty feet above the ground at two hundred and fifty knots. They were number three in a flight of five aircraft carrying an assault force of five beta soldiers, fifty-two soldierbots, three aerial XPs, and two large tracked ground XPs toward the target.

Kata rode in the fourth aircraft.

This was it. Other than Paul's first sergeant and a couple of soldierbots in maintenance, they had held nothing back.

Top stayed back in Devil's operations center to monitor the mission and coordinate any needed support. The plan was to insert into four LZs that surrounded Los Olvidados, ten kilometers from its center. They figured that was enough distance to both visually and acoustically mask their arrival. They would spread out, encircle the village, and then move forward, gradually tightening the noose around Navarro until he tried to leave, or they had his building surrounded.

Like the most recent missions, they decided not to put a swarm over the village. The swarms gave excellent intel on the objective, but at the price of letting the enemy know the Americans were coming. Paul and Kata thought they reacted and adapted better than the enemy could, so they opted for no swarm, no signature.

Their plan was simple. If Navarro tried to flee Los Olvidados, they would kill him. If they pinned him down in a building, they would kill him. If he came out and tried to fight, they would kill him. Paul wished they had more XPs and soldierbots but felt good about the plan.

Fifteen minutes later, the trail aircraft, Eagle Four, broke off from the formation. Carrying Buford, one of Kata's surviving Betas, and a wolf pack of ten soldierbots, the lone aircraft landed at a remote spot Paul and Top had selected to be the holding area for the quick reaction force. Only a fifteen-minute flight from Los Olvidados, Buford and his wolf pack would be sent into the fight at the command of Paul or his first sergeant, to effect rescue or press a tactical advantage.

The other four QC-10s would join Eagle Four at the remote spot after completing their insertions. There they would launch on command as part of the QRF, or to exfil.

A few minutes later, the flight of four split up, and each QC-10 headed for their assigned LZ.

Dragon Three flew for another eight minutes before coming to a hover at his assigned landing zone. He was carrying one of the large tracked ground XPs beneath his belly in a sling load. His engines howled as he eased himself down. When the XP was on the ground, D3 disconnected the load and reeled in the vehicle slings as he slid forward and landed.

"Thanks, D3," Paul said.

"Roger that. Just call when you're ready for exfil, sir."

"Will do," Paul said as he and twelve soldierbots leapt out of the aircraft.

Paul watched Dragon Three fly away to join up with the others at the QRF holding area and then waited for a few minutes as everyone checked in.

"Magellan is set."

"Snapshot set."

"Reynolds set."

"Chamberlain set."

"Apache Six set."

Paul checked his in-head display for the status of the XPs. The three aerial units had deployed, one over Los Olvidados to give overhead imagery, high enough not to be easily heard, while the others waited on the ground. They would launch into the village on Paul's signal, but for now, he did not want to risk them being detected and tipping off Navarro.

The ground XPs were positioned on the main road in and out of the village:

one to the north, one to the south. They each carried a 120-millimeter cannon and would make sure no reinforcements made it to Navarro, eliminating anything that tried to escape once things went kinetic.

Everything was ready.

"OK," Paul said. "Move out. Watch your spacing. No one get too far ahead or behind. I want a clean convergence on the target."

The soldierbots fanned out widely as they walked. Within minutes, Paul's IHD conveyed a complete circle on the map that constricted slowly as they moved forward. They had the village surrounded.

They closed on the village as the sun set. Paul walked due north. The sky was a blazing orange as the sun set behind the Andes Mountains far away to his left. A smoky haze blanketed the Pampas that evening. To his right, darkness crept toward them as the night started to advance on the landscape. By the time they entered the village, the sun was behind the mountains and the light was receding quickly.

Los Olvidados was small. A mile across at most. It was old and active, though, and sat on a trade route that had connected the sea to the interior for a thousand years. Two and three-story buildings stood close to the narrow streets that led to the middle of the village. In Los Olvidados' center, shops and restaurants lined a dusty, failed attempt to grow grass in the small square. A columned two-story municipal building on the north side of the square anchored the square.

As they entered Los Olvidados, Paul signaled to the XPs. The ground vehicles advanced until they were within a hundred meters of the first buildings on the edge of the village. Paul had them wait there, weapons ready, for further instructions.

The aerial XP orbiting at a high altitude was not the same as a sensor swarm, but he was able to provide some good imagery. On Paul's IHD, he could see a pair of foot soldiers milling around an old, manually operated vehicle parked in front of the municipal building.

Paul noted with a smile that there were no villagers about. It would be easier to deal with the two soldiers.

As they converged on the square, Paul studied the foot soldiers on his IHD. They had rifles slung over their shoulders and were smoking cigarettes and talking. But what bothered Paul was that neither of them looked up. Not once.

By now, they should have heard the overhead drone, even though it was operating at a high altitude, and at least been curious about it. But they hadn't noticed or didn't care they were being observed.

They advanced on the village square cautiously, their noose tightening with every step. Paul launched the other two aerial XPs, putting both of their POVs up on his in-head display.

The aerial XPs leapt into the air and streaked at low altitude toward the center of town. They shuddered as they opened their gun and missile-bay doors, dirtying up their aerodynamic profile.

Paul and the rest of the assault force stepped into the town square as the aerial XPs crossed, at high speed, over the municipal building.

Paul had a clear line of sight to the pair of foot soldiers. He knew something was wrong when they looked up at the blur of the fast-moving XPs and smiled.

Tension rose within Paul and radiated out through the neural link to the rest of Outlaw Company.

And why were there no villagers around?

Multiple explosions detonated throughout the village.

Red Xs lit up Paul's map as soldierbots went down. He cursed as he read the damage report.

Ten soldierbots destroyed in a blink.

Paul switched back to the POV of the high-orbiting aerial XP. He counted a dozen explosions. Multiple small buildings fell into the street.

Enemy soldiers in battle suits and exoskeletons poured into the streets. Unarmored snipers and grenadiers appeared on the rooftops. The aerial XPs estimated two hundred enemy. Navarro had held nothing back either.

Tracer rounds erupted from several rooftops, and Paul lost the visual feed from the aerial XP. He glanced up to see it fall out of the darkening sky in smoking pieces.

"Ambush!" Paul called over the radio as he turned for the nearest alley. "Take cover and return fire."

Paul let his suit do the running as he studied the situation display. Two soldierbots ran on either side of him, firing their weapons.

A red X marked the estimated impact zone for the destroyed aerial XP. The remaining aerial XPs were under intense small-arms fire from the soldiers on the rooftops. Their small-caliber weapons could not penetrate the aircraft's armor, but they were causing a lot of damage to the relatively delicate thruster fans.

Finally, Paul began getting hit by flashes as the team started to return fire.

Paul told the AXPs to designate and then had the ground XPs, still holding at their north and south checkpoints, fire indirectly. Paul heard the thumps of their mortars, followed by that sweet whistling sound. Antipersonnel charges began exploding over rooftops, killing enemy in large swaths.

The flashes came rapidly now as Magellan, Snapshot, and the others got drawn into their own firefights. It was hard to keep up. Kata was getting hit with her share as well.

Paul put one of the AXPs at a higher altitude. He wanted to understand which streets were now blocked and where their forces were concentrated. It got a few seconds of imagery before it started to tumble violently and fell out of the sky.

The aerial XP left a trail of smoke as it descended into a nearby building. It smashed through three floors until it lay, on fire, under debris in the basement.

The imagery Paul got from the AXP before it was shot down did not look good. Over a hundred enemy were running toward them, and the dropped buildings had turned the village into a maze. Kata saw the same thing.

"No clean way out of here now!" she yelled over the radio.

Paul grunted his agreement.

He felt a growing pit in his gut as he thought about what waited for them in the few remaining passable streets.

More flashes hit him.

Kill. Kill. Kill.

Paul could see on his IHD that Kata and Magellan were being forced into an alley. Paul turned to look and saw them across the town square.

A wolf pack of ten soldierbots fought furiously in front of Kata and Magellan. Enemy bodies and pieces of shattered exoskeletons were strewn around them.

Kata and Magellan backed slowly into the alleyway. The soldierbots stepped back with them, covering each other, their weapons spitting fire.

More flashes from the aerial XP.

Kill. Kill. Kill.

Paul switched on his suit's autopilot, pointed it at an alley, and selected close-quarters mode. Then he tried to center himself so he could take what was going to be a big wave of flashes.

"Outlaw Zero Six, this is Outlaw Zero Seven, I am launching the QRF," Top called on the radio from back at Devil.

"Roger that, Seven," Paul answered as he reached the cover of the alley. He pictured the aircraft back at their holding spot, leaping into the air and activating their weapons systems. Buford, strapped into Eagle Four with a wolf pack of ten, would be studying the tactical situation and licking his chops.

Paul looked forward to their arrival. In fifteen minutes, he would have five gunships overhead and another squad on the ground.

They would be able to kill a lot of enemy then.

Paul was hammered with flashes as his suit fought. He had the situational display up on his IHD showing everyone's position, their direction of movement, ammunition levels, and battle damage. Paul did not like the way that Kata and Magellan were getting pinched together into that alley. But they were holding their own.

For an instant, Paul felt his panic subside.

The alley Paul had run into was a dead end, so he did not have to worry about anyone creeping up behind him, and the soldiers attacking from the street were easy targets.

His main concern was the rooftops. He was scanning the last AXP's point of view and the situational display when the southern ground XP disintegrated in a large explosion.

"What the fuck was that?" Kata called.

"Don't know," Paul responded. "Stand by."

Paul had the last aerial XP climb and pan around.

"Shit," Paul said as he looked at two large biped tanks. One to their east and one to their west. They were three kilometers away and closing in fast. They were late models, bristling with weapons systems.

"Terrific," Kata called, viewing the same imagery.

Their remaining ground XP tried to execute evasive maneuvers but was struck within seconds by another high-explosive round.

Two large red triangles blinked on Paul's situational display, signifying the enemy tanks and estimating their direction and progress.

Paul looked across the square to the alley where Kata and Magellan were fighting. They were down to just four soldierbots, but it looked like Navarro's soldiers had cornered a hive of demons. Waves of exoskeletoned soldiers charged the dark alley. They'd get close before bursts of fire tore them apart. Those that made it farther were killed in close quarters by slashing bayonets.

There was a pile of destroyed battle suits, broken exoskeletons, and body parts at the mouth of the alley. Kata, Magellan, and their wolf pack were giving them well-coordinated hell.

"Kata, we need to get moving," Paul transmitted. "We don't want to be trapped in these alleys when those tanks get here."

"No shit! Reynolds, need you to move south. We're going to need some help getting clear."

"Roger that, ma'am!" Reynolds responded. "Moving!"

"Mayday. Mayday. Mayday." The final aerial XP interrupted Kata with a distress call. "Lost port thrusters. Descending into—" His transmission ended as he struck the ground.

"Damn it!" Paul yelled.

"Outlaw Six," Dragon Three called on the radio. "QRF ETA ten minutes."

"Roger that," Paul responded. "Be advised. I have designated two large enemy tanks on the map."

"Understood," Dragon Three responded. "They are emitting strong countermeasures. We can't get a fix yet to fire indirect. But we'll deal with them as soon as we can."

A loud clang filled Paul's helmet as dust and shards of brick erupted in his alley.

They were firing on him from above.

Paul leapt backward, deeper into the alley, as two of his wolf pack aimed their weapons at the building tops. Their miniguns sprayed bullets, and they let loose with a salvo of high-explosive grenades. They impacted the building walls near the top, collapsing large portions of the roof. Several enemy soldiers came down with chunks of building. All but one were killed by the fall.

Paul stepped on the head of the one survivor and crushed his skull.

Paul checked his situational display. Everyone was starting to take real damage, and they were down to thirty soldierbots. But they were still fighting well. Optimism welled within him.

Reynolds had made good progress. He was now one block north of Kata's position, providing enfilading fire. He mowed down dozens of enemy.

But they kept coming.

"Outlaw Six, this is Dragon Three," came a call on the radio. "We are five minutes out."

"Excellent, D3," Paul said. "Prioritization is the two tanks first, then troops on the roofs, then enemy in the streets."

"Understood, Outlaw Six. Stand by."

Paul surged back toward the street, firing as he went. He wanted out of that alley. As he reached the opening, he looked across toward Kata. The pile of bodies in front of her alley was taller now, but the wave of foot soldiers had not slackened. They pressed their attack.

Navarro was going all in.

A loud ripping noise drew Paul's eyes skyward in time to see half a dozen missiles streak over the village in the direction of the approaching QRF.

"Dragon Three!" Paul transmitted. "Incoming mis—"

Paul's voice seized and his knees buckled as he was hit by a terrible last gasp as Dragons Two, Four, and Six disintegrated.

Kata screamed into her helmet and her vision blurred as Buford and Talon Four incinerated.

Paul realized then how fucked they were.

Navarro obviously had a sophisticated anti-aircraft capability, and he had held it back until the most disruptive moment.

At first, Paul thought they were SkyFang. But he quickly realized these missiles were smaller. Faster moving. More of a kinetic munition than an explosive one.

Paul's mind raced as he shot enemy. It looked like the missiles were the type that required guidance. That meant something in Los Olvidados. Something that could detect and designate targets. Navarro must have gone shopping with the Chinese again.

Two violent explosions erupted from the buildings around Kata and Magellan. The three-story buildings shuddered and fragmented as they fell.

Kata's three soldierbots were knocked down by the explosions and engulfed in a massive dust cloud that surged into the street and engulfed Reynolds and the converging enemy troops.

They had been in the village for only a few minutes and had lost four aircraft, a beta, five XPs, and dozens of soldierbots, and now Kata and Magellan were trapped under two buildings.

They had walked into a trap.

Paul was enraged.

He went berserk.

Paul lunged out of his alley toward Kata and Magellan. He put his suit in sprint mode and activated his bayonet. It unsheathed from his battle suit's right forearm, and he decapitated an exoskeletoned enemy. The four soldierbots running with Paul extended their bayonets also.

Paul forgot the situational display as they slashed across the street. He forgot two biped tanks were headed their way. He didn't hear Top on the radio. He went into a killing frenzy.

He was shooting.

Throwing grenades.

Bayoneting.

He used everything he had to cut through them.

Reynolds fought toward him from the north. They converged on Kata's alley as the dwindling wolf pack of three got to their feet, bayonets extended and weapons blazing.

Paul was just meters from the alley when one of the tanks stepped into the square.

"Kata!" Paul yelled into his radio. "Do you copy?"

Reynolds impaled a battle-suited enemy and lifted him over his head. He flung the bloody and inert armored body at a group of attacking soldiers. They flinched at the sight before Reynolds cut them down with minigun fire.

"Outlaw Zero Six!" Top said over the radio. "Dragon Three is still airborne. We've got an exfil plan. Sending you coordinates. Need you all to move south immediately."

"Negative," Paul said. "Not without them."

"Captain Owens!" Top said over the radio. "Need you to start moving now so you can put distance between you and the tanks. We'll figure out a way to get them."

"No, goddamn it! They're trapped!"

"Captain Owens!" Top yelled. Paul could hear the urgency in her voice. "It's over, sir! Get out of there!"

An explosion interrupted their argument, tearing Reynolds to pieces and destroying two soldierbots. Shrapnel ripped Paul's right shoulder armor open and knocked him off of his feet as bits of Reynolds whizzed by.

Paul flailed through the air for an instant before his suit's gyros calculated a solution. He landed on his feet and spun to see the tank running at him from the northern end of the square, closing the distance, smoke drifting out of its main cannon.

It was a big one. And fast.

The tank aimed its minigun at Paul.

Paul tried to evade, but his suit was damaged and sluggish.

The tank's minigun spat armor-piercing rounds at him.

Paul braced for their impact.

The last soldierbot dove in front of Paul, absorbing the rounds.

By the time the soldierbot landed in sparking pieces on the ground, Paul had raised his left arm. He fired his last missile at the tank. It struck the heavily armored tank impotently but kicked up enough dirt and smoke to obscure Paul for an instant.

He turned toward the smoldering pile of rubble to find Kata.

But instead of running toward it, Paul's suit discharged all its electromagnetic smoke grenades.

A large, sensor-obscuring cloud of chaff and smoke engulfed Paul and then filled the square as he yelled into his radio, "Goddamn it, Top! You fucking better not!"

"I'm sorry, sir. I recommend you relax."

"No!" Paul yelled. But it was too late. He had just become a passenger. His suit turned and ran at max speed. The speed and violence of the maneuver and sprint knocked the breath out of Paul and wrenched his wounded shoulder.

All battle suits had an emergency escape mode. The suits were programmed to discharge their e-smoke grenades and then egress along the most tactically advantageous route at the highest possible speed that the occupant could survive.

For the occupant, it felt like a car accident.

The tactical operations center had the ability to put suits into emergency escape mode remotely. Once you did that, a suit could then only be controlled from the TOC.

Paul's battle suit carried him out of the square and southward. The rest of the surviving team members were close behind him, as well as the dozen soldierbots that were still operational. Fortunately, Navarro's tanks had run right into the middle of the village. It was a stupid move.

Snapshot and Chamberlain dropped a few buildings behind them with their remaining missiles hampering the enemy's pursuit.

Dragon Three, now about ten kilometers away, fired everything he had, putting down a line of indirect fire between the retreating team and the enemy. It was danger close. Two soldierbots were engulfed in the explosions and shrapnel.

But it worked. They gained some separation.

Snapshot and Chamberlain took some bad hits covering the retreat as rear guard, but they also made it out.

They met up with Dragon Three and leapt on board. Snapshot, Chamberlain, and the remaining soldierbots leaned out of Dragon Three and fired the last of their ammunition at the advancing enemy as the aircraft surged up and forward.

Dragon Three's engines shrieked and glowed red as he accelerated beyond three hundred knots, flying twenty feet above the ground.

Top gave back Paul control of his battle suit.

Paul moved up to the command seat to start planning a counterattack. His shoulder was throbbing badly now, an indication that his nanobots were working hard to close the wound. He could feel the blood pooling in his armored glove, and his right side felt damp.

Magellan's POV came back on line. It was dark at first but grew lighter as the tank kicked aside debris and large chunks of the building. Soon, it was dragging Magellan from the rubble.

Paul could see from his telemetry that Magellan was unable to move his legs and none of his weapons systems were online. He was helpless.

There were over a hundred soldiers around Magellan now. They were taking turns screaming in his face and spitting on him.

Some of them bound Magellan's feet with a large metal cable. They tied his arms above his head as well. They drove the old car over and tied one of the cables to it. Then the tank walked over, and they tied the other end to it.

Then they pulled Magellan apart.

Magellan's lower chassis separated from his torso. The tank and the old car dragged their halves of Magellan around the square for a few laps while the soldiers cheered.

Then they found Kata.

She was unconscious when they dug her out. But she slowly came to as they dragged her toward the center of the square. Kata's POV transmitter was intermittent, so Paul only caught glimpses of the angry Navarro foot soldiers as they spit on and kicked her.

A man walked up to what was left of Magellan. Paul recognized him. It was Navarro. The hard and angular face, the sun-dried skin, the moustache, were all chiseled into Paul's memory from thousands of intelligence files.

Navarro propped up Magellan's upper torso, sneering at the broken beta and smiling like a devil as he turned and walked back toward Kata.

Navarro wanted the Americans to be able to watch.

They were all watching. Paul. The Dragons. Top, back on Outpost Devil.

"Dragon Three, I am ordering you to turn around!" Paul screamed. "Turn around now!"

But the mission was over. Every soldier was in a recall state. Dragon Three tried to ignore him.

Paul charged toward the door when he saw the foot soldiers tie Kata's upper body to the tank.

Snapshot blocked him from jumping out.

"Get the fuck out of my way!" Paul commanded.

He tried to shove past Snapshot but was stunned by pain as his wound tore open wider.

Paul shook his head clear and screamed, "You are a bunch of fucking cowards! Hold on, Kata, I'm coming!"

Paul tried to lunge out of the aircraft. He was going to jump out and run back to her.

Snapshot blocked him again, and Top disabled his suit.

Battle suits could be deactivated remotely. A precaution against hijacking and other rare tactical situations, such as preventing suicidal actions.

Paul fell to the floor of Dragon Three.

His IHD display was still active, and he watched as they tied Kata's feet to the car.

The feed from Kata's POV flashed on and off. The transmission of her terrified screams came in and out. But Paul could make out his name.

She was begging Paul to help her.

Magellan wiggled his torso to try to avert his gaze, to disrupt the data flow, but Navarro's soldiers held him fast as Navarro got into the driver's seat of the old car.

The tank stood still as Navarro revved the car engine. Its tires threw sand and gravel, trying to get purchase to accelerate.

Kata screamed. She was not in pain yet, though. Her battle suit was holding. Then the tank lifted one leg to shift its weight back against the pull of the car.

Kata screamed louder. She felt it coming.

The tank leaned back.

Kata was pulled apart.

The car surged forward, and the tank nearly fell backward at the sudden release of tension, but caught itself, taking half a dozen steps backward. The crowd of soldiers cheered as Kata's entrails dragged across the ground behind her upper body.

Kata's POV feed flashed on a few more times. The suit had failed just above its hip actuators. A ragged flap of her lower abdomen extended beneath the armored suit. Strands of gore dragged across the dirt.

The last image transmitted from Magellan's POV was of a soldier approaching with a large weapon. Seconds later, armor-piercing high-explosive rounds tore Magellan apart.

Paul had lost too much blood to withstand Magellan's last gasp. He passed out. It was a mercy.

Chapter Fifty-One

"What the hell, First Sergeant?" General Schofield yelled over the secure videoconference. "They both went on the mission?"

"Yes, sir," Top replied, standing at attention in front of the large screen. The general sat in the center of the briefing table. General Keil sat to his right, Lieutenant Colonel Wainwright to his left.

"And now I've got a dead captain in my area of operations?"

"Yes, sir."

"And these equipment losses," Keil said, reading again the battle damage assessment. "A fucking disaster."

"Yes, sir."

"Well, I bet even your pea-sized artificial brain can do the math on this one, First Sergeant."

Top stayed quiet.

"I told those arrogant hotshot jigsaws that they had one fucking job!" General Schofield continued, yelling. "Don't screw up. Don't bring any heat on me while I'm trying to counter the Chinese empire's aggressive fucking adventurism in South America. Don't lose any big pieces of equipment." The general jabbed his fingers in the air, counting his points as he made them. "Don't do anything that would embarrass me. And for God's sake, I told them, nobody gets killed in fucking action!"

The general paused to catch his breath. He realized he was shouting. Keil looked down. Wainwright pretended to take notes. Schofield rubbed his eyes.

"Look, First Sergeant. I'm real sorry about Captain Vukovic. It's a damn shame. When Captain Owens is released from the MedPod, let him know that his orders are to roll it up and return to base. Your mission is over."

"Yes, sir," Top said. The general had started to get up from his seat when Top said, "Sir, if I may?"

"Go ahead, First Sergeant," he said, without sitting back down.

"I know that Captain Owens will feel strongly about this. And I do as well. The whole unit will. We still need to recover the bodies of our dead, and we'd like to go after General Navarro tonight. We have indications that he—"

"Are you out of your quantum-fucking-mind, First Sergeant?" General Schofield said, more bemused than angry.

"No, sir."

"Seems like you are to me," the general said, impatiently gesturing at Wainwright to get the hell out of his way. "Because I just recalled your metal asses. I am working other angles for the body recovery, and I want your whole misbegotten outfit here, behind the damn wire, on my fucking base."

The general pointed forcefully down at his feet as he halted his progress toward the edge of the screen.

"By 1800 hours tomorrow," Schofield said, glaring at the image of Top in front of him. "Between now and then, you will stand down. No more missions. Do you understand me, First Sergeant?"

"I do, sir."

"Good." The general continued toward the edge of the screen. Before he disappeared off to the side, he looked into the camera and said, "Again, First Sergeant, please tell Owens I'm sorry about Vukovic. She was an arrogant jigsaw. But she was a good officer."

Then the screen went dead.

Top left the command hooch and walked directly to the medical bay where Paul lay healing in the MedPod. She typed in the revival command and waited.

Thirty minutes later, Paul sat in the open MedPod. He rubbed his eyes as Top debriefed him.

"General Schofield has recalled us, sir. Our orders are to stand down and report back to Stalwart by 1800 hours. Also, the general wants you to know that he is really sorry about Captain Vukovic and they are working other channels for body recovery."

"You woke me up for this?" Paul asked his first sergeant in an angry voice. They had not yet discussed the failed raid, and Top overriding Paul's suit. But each knew there would be a reckoning.

"Yes, sir. And to tell you that there are indications that Navarro is going back to Los Olvidados tonight. The intel suggests that the villagers had been evacuated from the town in preparation for the ambush. That's why there were none around during the fight. This morning, they were allowed to return. Obviously, the damage to their town was extensive. Navarro is going to thank them for their patriotic sacrifice, and intercepts say that the Chinese are going to fund reconstruction. It is going to be a big moment for Navarro."

Paul stood up from the MedPod. He swooned. Top reached out to steady him.

"Help me get to the planning hooch," Paul said.

"Have you learned anything about Navarro's new anti-aircraft capability?" Paul asked minutes later as he stood over the mapping table, steadying himself on a chair. As he talked, Chief changed his bandage and inserted an IV. "Our first concern is surviving on the way in."

"Yes, sir. We analyzed the spectrum emissions captured during last night's failed mission and were able to identify the threat as a kind of mobile Argus system."

"A mobile Argus what?" Paul asked.

"It is a super observer," Top explained. "It is hypersensitive across the electromagnetic spectrum and can detect everything from radar altimeter emissions to weapons-targeting systems to radio transmissions. Any emission at all can be targeted and destroyed down to altitudes as low as fifty feet. It also has its own radar and laser designators, to home in on targets once it detects them. It is a new system, only in the field for about six months. Intelligence has given it the code name Argus, after the many-eyed Greek god."

"How nice," Paul said.

"The fact that it is mobile means that we should assume it goes wherever Navarro goes."

"Yeah," Paul said, looking at his bandaged shoulder. Blood oozed from the unhealed wound. He had not spent enough time in the MedPod. "The other factor is that General Schofield will probably be keeping some kind of eye on us. We're going to have to go in with everything off. That means every emitter on every system."

"We will be nearly blind," Top said.

"And nearly invisible," Paul responded. "Neither Navarro and his Argus nor Schofield and his forces will be able to track us."

"World War I style," Top said.

"That's right," Paul said, smiling wearily at his first sergeant. "So, let's assume we make it in," Paul continued, his smile vanishing. "How about troop strength? Find anything to indicate how many soldiers Navarro will have with him?"

"Nothing, sir."

Paul nodded, weighing the lack of intelligence against his remaining combat power. He had three betas, three QC-10s, ten operational soldierbots, and no extension platforms.

"I suppose we'll have to take that as a positive indication," Paul said.

"Yes, sir. The more soldiers he had in tow, the more likely we would have gotten an intel hit."

"Doesn't matter anyway."

"No, sir," Top agreed. "It does not."

The mission was simple. Go in and kill them. Paul and his first sergeant spent no time planning exfil or recovery. They didn't care about what happened after. They were going to avenge.

"Have you spoken with Colonel Filson yet, sir?" Top asked Paul. "He has tried to hail you on the satcom several times."

Paul shook his head.

"Not yet. Let's do that when we get back, OK?"

The first sergeant nodded. "Roger that, sir."

Later, as the sun set, intel confirmed that Navarro had arrived at Los Olvidados.

"Let's go," Paul said to Top. "I want wheels up in five."

Paul struggled into his battle suit as Top went to round up Snapshot and Chamberlain. The last three operational QC-10s began their preflight checks.

Chief ran up to Paul as he walked toward the aircraft.

"Sir!" Chief called. "Captain Owens!"

"What is it, Chief?" Paul asked as he stopped and turned around.

Chief stood in front of him, a minigun in his arms, ammunition belts crisscrossing his shoulders, a bayonet on his hip.

"Top said it was up to you." Chief shifted on his feet as Paul sized him up.

"This one is probably not going to go very well, Chief."

"All the more reason I should go, sir."

"You're not part of the neural network," Paul said, shaking his head.

"But I am part of this unit," Chief responded, jamming the butt of the minigun into the ground.

Paul nodded.

"Ride with Snapshot," he said, turning back toward the aircraft. "Do exactly what he says."

"Yes, sir!" Chief said, hoisting the minigun. He ran to the trail aircraft, where Snapshot was watching soldierbots mount up.

They took off in the direction of Schofield's base to throw off any potential observers. That made it look like they were starting the pullout early.

Several miles north of the outpost, though, the aircraft dropped down below the peaks of the Andes and into the shadows. They followed the canyons just fifty feet above the craggy terrain to avoid detection. The aircraft had turned off all their emitters, even their radar altimeters, so they flew with only passive visual references and inertial navigation data. It was challenging and made for a bumpy and tilting flight.

They leveled out over the valley floor and streaked toward Los Olvidados.

This time, though, they didn't insert kilometers away and walk it in.

Facing an unknown number of enemy troops and probably a Chinese tank or two, Paul wanted to maximize their advantage of surprise. He wanted to shock them, keep them off-balance, and kill them. If there were too many to achieve that, so be it.

Two of the QC-10s flew over the square at a hundred knots.

Foot soldiers and civilians ran in all directions.

The three betas jumped out of the shrieking aircraft.

Snapshot and Chamberlain struck the walls of the municipal building in the village center. They crashed through and started killing enemy soldiers inside.

Top landed outside, digging a crater in the dirt in front of the building. She quickly got busy killing Navarro's soldiers as well.

As chaos overtook the village, Eagle Six broke off of the flight of three. She banked hard to her left at rooftop level and decelerated.

"It's too hot for me to stop and land," she said. "I'll tell you when to jump."

"Roger that!" Chief answered.

"Get ready," she said to Chief as she approached a rooftop to her front. Eagle Six lunged left and right as tracer rounds sought her out.

"I'm ready," Chief answered as he struggled not to fall out of the door.

"Exit! Exit! Exit!" Eagle Six yelled as the roof passed under her nose.

Chief leapt out of the aircraft.

He tumbled across the roof, coming to a stop a few feet from the edge.

"You set yet, Chief?" Snapshot called on the radio.

"Roger that," Chief answered, standing up and getting his bearings.

He turned to face the high-caliber tracer rounds erupting from around the village square. Two of Navarro's big biped tanks were trying to get a bead on the attacking aircraft. Their tracer rounds sprayed through the moonless sky like drunken green fire hoses.

"Then get busy," Snapshot said. "If it is shooting, and it is not us, kill it."

"Roger that," Chief answered, raising the weapon to his shoulder.

The flashes popped like muted fireworks in Paul's mind. He focused on them, making certain no civilians were killed. This was a revenge mission. Not a murder spree.

Paul stayed on Dragon Two during the fight. He had forgone more MedPod treatments to make this mission happen and was not yet fully healed. His mobility was still hindered.

He still got into the fight, though.

Even over the village, with the slaughter begun, Paul did not allow the aircraft to turn on any of their targeting systems. Knowing if they did so, the Argus would have a better chance of taking them out. They would also pop up on Schofield's detection network, and Paul didn't want that either.

So, he used the trick Colonel Filson had taught him and Kata seemingly a million years ago, back on the Fort Bragg range. He drew an X on the Dragon canopy with a grease pencil and used it as an aiming reference.

The other two aircraft flew in tight formation on either side of Dragon Two, as if welded to each of her wings. Paul used the grease-pencil reference to walk their rocket fire into each of the tanks. In less than two minutes, the tanks were destroyed.

Paul then strafed a number of other vehicles, hoping to get lucky and take out Argus components.

As they flew back and forth above Los Olvidados, Paul had Dragon Two repeat on her loudspeaker, "We are here for General Navarro. Turn him over immediately, and we will cease our attack!"

On the ground, the betas led the wolf pack through the village, searching for Navarro and killing any soldiers that resisted.

Ten minutes later, Paul got the call over the radio: "We have Navarro in custody."

Once they had Navarro, it was over. His soldiers stopped fighting. They dropped their weapons and looked nervously at the dark sky.

Dragon Two landed so that Paul could get out.

"Dragon Flight," Paul said before walking away, "Get back in the air. Keep buzzing the square. Make it seem like a whole squadron is overhead and let me know of any inbound."

"Roger that, sir." The aircraft leapt back into the sky.

"Top," Paul transmitted on his radio. "Search the prisoners to ID those on the list."

"Roger that, sir. We already have two."

"Bring them to the village center. I will meet you there."

Before launching, Paul had Chief go through all the POV footage from the failed raid the day before. They had facial-recognition data for every soldier that had been involved in the murders of Magellan and Kata.

Paul stabilized himself against Top as the last of the soldiers on the list was identified and brought to the village center. Three had been killed in the fighting. Paul had their bodies dragged to the feet of the eight living prisoners.

The eight, including Navarro, stood in a line under the guard of the Chief's minigun.

Paul walked to the captive group, unholstered his pistol, and shot the first one in the head.

"Sir, what are you doing?" Top asked Paul.

Two tried to run. Paul shot them in the back of the head, then looked back at his first sergeant.

The remaining terrified men fell to their knees, begging.

"For Kata," Paul mumbled. "Magellan and the rest."

"Sir, I don't think—" she tried to say. But Paul cut her off.

"At ease, Top. This is my call. This is what we came here to do."

Paul stopped at Navarro.

The old general glared at Paul. Paul holstered his pistol and turned back to Top.

"Have we recovered their bodies yet?"

"Yes, sir," Top said. "They are loaded on Dragon Three."

"Good," Paul said, fighting dizziness. He looked at the old car. It still had the bloodstained cable tied to it.

Paul walked to the old car and looked inside.

The keys were still in it.

Paul got out of his battle suit. Blood was running from his shoulder down his arm, dripping off of his fingers.

"What are you doing, sir?" Top asked him. "You need to get back into your battle suit."

"In a minute, Top."

Paul eased himself into the car. He winced as he closed the door. The pain in his shoulder was getting bad. He had not taken any pain meds that whole day to stay as sharp as possible for the mission.

The old vehicle coughed to life. Paul drove it over and parked in front of Navarro. He left the engine running.

Navarro was shaking now. The general recognized death when he saw it. He prepared himself for Paul's rage, but he said nothing.

Paul pulled himself slowly out of the car.

"Snapshot," Paul said. "Hold him up."

The Ōkami beta walked over to Navarro and grabbed his wrists. The general grunted as Snapshot jerked him off his feet.

Paul tied the cable around the general's chest making sure it was uncomfortably tight.

The rest of the Ōkami kept their weapons trained on the mass of foot soldiers. The prisoners' eyes widened as they realized what was about to happen to their general.

Paul stepped back when he was done fastening the cable.

"Put him down," he told Snapshot.

Paul pulled his pistol out and pointed it at Navarro's head.

"Lay down," Paul ordered.

Navarro was frozen in fear.

"On the ground!" Paul yelled, striking him in the face with the pistol.

Navarro stumbled to the ground. Blood flowed from his mouth. Paul tied the general's feet with another cable he had found nearby.

Navarro begged now. Pleaded.

When Paul was done, he stood up slowly. He swooned and almost fell over, but Top stepped to his side and steadied him.

"What are you doing, sir?"

"For Kata," Paul said. He pushed himself away from his first sergeant, walked to the municipal building, and tied the other end of the cable to one of its large columns.

Paul then walked back, past his first sergeant, toward the idling car as she asked again, "Sir, what are you doing?"

"For Magellan," Paul said as he got into the vehicle.

Paul revved the engine to make sure it was good and warm and then popped it into gear.

"Sir! Don't do this!"

"Paul inched forward, dragging Navarro through the dirt until the cables were tight. He put the car in neutral and gunned the engine again. He wanted Navarro to be terrified. Like Kata was.

The old gasoline engine roared.

Most of Navarro's soldiers looked away.

Paul cried out in anguish, thinking of Kata and Magellan. And all of the Ōkami that had fallen. His voice was lost in the snarl of the roaring engine.

Paul reached up to put the car in gear.

A single gunshot rang out, surprising Paul.

He looked in the rearview mirror and saw Top standing over Navarro.

Paul turned off the car. He got out slowly, the arm of his flight suit now soaked with blood. His vision blurry, Paul walked over to Top. She reached out with her hand to steady him.

In her other hand, she held her pistol. Smoke drifted from its barrel. Paul looked at the general. His body was limp. His head in bloody pieces from the antipersonnel round.

"I'm sorry, sir. What you were doing did not seem right."

Paul looked at Top but didn't answer. His strength was fading.

"We're done now, sir," she said. "Let's go."

Two aircraft landed, and the team loaded up.

"Put me on Dragon Two," Paul said to Top in a nearly inaudible whisper.

Paul stared at Kata's body bag on the flight back to Devil until he passed out.

Chapter Fifty-Two

aul woke up a day later in the MedPod. He opened the pod's clamshell top and climbed out. He was unsteady and had to brace himself with a hand on the wall. When the room stopped spinning, he saw Colonel Filson sitting in a chair on the other side of the pod.

The colonel's face was clouded.

"Listen, Paul," Filson said. "We don't have a lot of time—"

"Sir," Paul interrupted him. "Kata is dead."

"I know, son," he answered, raising his hand to shut Paul up. "I know. I need you to get dressed and on the bird quickly."

Paul realized he was naked. He stepped over to the side table where someone had laid out a flight suit. He pulled it on, wincing at the pain in his arm and shoulder. He needed a few more days in the pod.

Paul zipped up and turned to face Filson.

"OK," the colonel said. "Let's—"

"When did you get here, sir?" Paul interrupted him again.

"I came as soon as I heard about Kata. I had just landed at Stalwart when we heard about the massacre. I convinced the general to let—"

"Massacre?" Paul asked.

They were interrupted by the sound of multiple aircraft over Devil. The medical hooch shook as an aircraft flew low over it.

"What the hell?" Paul shouted as he moved for the door.

The colonel caught him by the arm. "Goddamn it, Paul," he yelled over the roar. "That's what I'm trying to tell you. It's Schofield. They're here for you."

"What?"

Paul shoved past the colonel and opened the door. Wind ripped through the medical hooch as the door flew open and sand bit into Paul's eyes.

The colonel grabbed him by the flight suit, between the shoulders.

Paul jerked free.

"Damn it, Paul!" he heard the colonel yell before being enveloped by the noise and flying sand.

The sand hammered Paul's eyes. He struggled to see. A large military gunship hovered over the medical hooch, its forward weapons turret trained on him. The rotor wash knocked Paul off-balance, and he fell to the ground.

Paul tumbled for a few meters before strong hands jerked him to his feet.

It was Top.

Paul held a hand up to shield his eyes from the flying sand and surveyed the assaulting force. There were at least eight aircraft in the air. Maybe eight already on the ground as well.

A handful of soldiers in exoskeletons exited one of the aircraft on the ground. They were over a hundred meters away, but Paul recognized one of them. It was Lieutenant Colonel Thurman.

A civilian male talked to Thurman. The civilian looked familiar to Paul, but he was too far away to recognize.

As the group conferred under the stubby wing of the aircraft, more armed soldiers spilled out of its aft ramp. But they were not exo battalion soldiers. They were wearing different armor, black rather than the olive drab of Thurman's battalion. Their weapons and equipment were also different, not standard issue. Something was wrong. But Paul's head was too fuzzy to pinpoint it.

The black troopers fanned out. There were dozens of them. Paul was confused.

The civilian turned and pointed at Paul. Thurman nodded. He and two other exoskeletoned soldiers started walking toward Paul and Top.

"What's going on, sir?" Top said to him in whisper mode.

"I don't know. But I'm sure it's fine," he lied.

Colonel Filson walked over to them and steadied himself against the gale-force winds on the first sergeant's other arm. He turned and looked at the hovering gunship and gestured forcefully. His combination of middle finger and direction pointing would have been hilarious had menace not been so thick in the air.

But Filson got the message across, and the aircraft hovered backward, away from the medical hooch. The sand dropped out of the air as the rotor wash slackened and they were able to speak.

"I think we are under arrest, Top," Paul said.

"I think you are right, sir."

"I've been trying to tell you," Filson said, stepping around to face Paul and Top. His back was to the approaching soldiers.

"Schofield sent the exo battalion to bring you in. I convinced him to let me come along. Your mission last night was a global headline this morning, Paul. Caused a real shit storm."

"Who are the ninja-looking assholes?" Paul asked the colonel, pointing at one of the black armored soldiers moving to flank them.

"Malloy's private military contractors," Filson said, nearly spitting.

Paul looked back at the civilian. He remembered him now. It was Pruden. He worked for Determined End States.

Thurman stepped in front of Paul and the colonel. Two staff sergeants, each armed with suit-mounted minigun systems, stood on either side of the lieutenant colonel. Both aimed their weapons at Top. Thurman's right hand rested on his pistol. All three of them seemed nervous and twitchy to Paul.

"Captain Owens," Thurman said. "We're here to take you back to Stalwart."

Filson turned around and faced Thurman.

Six of the black troopers jogged up and surrounded them. Unlike Thurman and the two sergeants, they had their face shields down. Their armor bore a red insignia on their right shoulder, the name "DredSkill" above a red skull and wings.

Another large group of black armored troops was running out to the parked QC-10s.

Paul tried to keep track of them, but he could feel himself sagging into Top. His time in the MedPod had helped, but he was still weak.

"OK, Thurman," Colonel Filson said as he gave them a calm-down gesture with his hands. "Like I said, this is going to go quietly. Just like I promised. How about we ease up on the weapons?"

Lieutenant Colonel Thurman waited half a tick before giving his men a quick nod and taking his hand off of his pistol. The two staff sergeants lowered their miniguns but continued to stare at Top.

Paul noted that the DredSkill troops did not lower their weapons. He looked back at the aircraft. Pruden stood under one of the wings, talking into his phone. He looked agitated.

"We understand that you secured Captain Vukovic's remains last night?" Thurman asked.

"That's right," Paul said.

"Where are they now?"

"In the cooler in the medical hooch." Paul pointed at the shipping container behind him.

The lieutenant colonel looked over Paul's shoulder, then spoke into his radio. A pair of soldiers, not wearing exoskeletons, ran by and entered the medical hooch.

Thurman looked back at Paul. "Look, Owens. I don't want to make a big deal out of this. I'm assuming Colonel Filson briefed you. We've got orders to bring you back to Stalwart to face charges."

Paul did not respond.

"This is what I was trying to tell you, Paul," the colonel said, turning his back to the exo soldiers and stepping in to Paul.

"What?" Paul asked.

"The mission they took you on…" Filson glanced at Top. "It went too far, son. You let them murder those men."

"The mission they—?"

"Let's go, Colonel!" Thurman yelled, interrupting.

"Now you listen to me!" Filson's face was red with anger as he turned from Paul to look at Thurman.

"No, sir," Thurman said, stepping forward with the flanking staff sergeants, whose miniguns were back up, trained on Top and Paul. "You're not in my chain of command. Now get out of the way and stop interfering with my mission."

Thurman reached out and shoved the colonel to the side. He took a step closer to Paul and drew his pistol.

"Captain Owens," he growled. "We can do this the easy way, or we can do it the real easy way."

Paul raised his hands to show he preferred it easy.

Top mirrored Paul's actions, raising her hands, as did Chamberlain, who approached from behind Paul.

"Is everything OK, sir?" Chamberlain asked.

"Whoa!" one of the black troopers yelled at Chamberlain, aiming his large-caliber weapon at the beta.

One of Thurman's staff sergeants swept his minigun to the left to cover Chamberlain.

Thurman said something into his radio and then gestured at Top and Chamberlain. "You two step back over there."

Six more of the DredSkill troops jogged up, weapons drawn, completing the encirclement.

"All right, goddamn it!" Filson said, stepping back into the middle of the tense group. "Everybody fucking calm down!"

"I warned you, Colonel," Thurman said.

"If you'll give me sixty seconds," Filson answered, "I will save you a lot of trouble."

Thurman's face was cloaked in disgust. But he nodded slightly and then made a show of looking at where his watch would have been on his wrist.

Filson turned back to Paul. Paul could see the concern on the colonel's face. It scared him.

"Listen to me, Paul. Go with them. I'll meet you back at Stalwart."

"Sir, I'm confused. What is going on?"

"We'll discuss everything back at Stalwart."

"What about them?" Paul asked, gesturing at Top and Chamberlain, who had stepped several feet back and were standing together in a ready position, heads tracking multiple targets.

"The DredSkill commandos are here to take custody of them for Malloy," Filson said. "They are being recalled."

Paul started to shake his head.

"Listen to me, Paul!" Filson yelled. "Look around. You have zero leverage here. Don't make things worse. Go with Thurman. I will take care of them," Filson said, pointing at the Ōkami betas.

Paul looked at Thurman, then at the black armored troopers, then at Pruden, who was now walking toward them. Paul had a bad feeling but didn't have a choice.

"OK," Paul said. "OK, I'll go."

"Just in time," Thurman said with menace. He waved Paul over.

Paul stepped toward them, expecting the tension to ratchet down after his surrender.

But it did not.

One of the staff sergeants shifted his weight on his feet, minigun still covering the Ōkami.

Paul turned to look at Top and Chamberlain. As fuzzy as he was, Top was still able to get through to him on whisper mode.

"This doesn't seem right, sir," she said. "What do you want me to do?"

Paul glanced at the colonel. He did not seem unduly alarmed. "Nothing," Paul whispered back to Top. "Do what they say. I'll figure things out when I get in front of General Schofield. Follow Colonel Filson's lead."

"Roger that, sir."

Lieutenant Colonel Thurman grabbed Paul roughly by his bad arm.

"Shit, sir," Paul said, reflexively trying to jerk free from the pain. But Thurman's armored hand held fast.

"Let's go, Captain," Thurman said. They started walking toward the aircraft that was idling on the ground a hundred meters away. Pruden was halfway to them now, still talking on his phone.

Thurman turned his head away from Paul and spoke into his radio.

Paul looked back over his opposite shoulder. Filson was yelling at the staff sergeants. Top and Chamberlain had been separated from the colonel. A dozen black troopers stood between them and Filson, bearing down on them with heavy weaponry.

Past them, Paul saw a dozen black armored troops marching Snapshot, Chief, and ten soldierbots, at gunpoint, toward Filson's group.

Farther away, DredSkill commandoes ran around the QC-10s. They jumped in and out of the Dragons and Eagles, doing something Paul couldn't quite figure out.

Another pair of black troopers jogged past. They nodded at Thurman.

Pruden was off his phone now, walking toward Colonel Filson.

Paul started to feel the pieces clicking into place.

He looked back at the colonel and the Ōkami. One of the staff sergeants had drawn a pistol on Filson and was waving him to the side, his minigun still trained on the Ōkami.

Paul looked back toward his first sergeant. DredSkill commandos shoved Snapshot and Chief toward Top. The ten soldierbots marched obediently into the captive group.

The black armored troops were now lined up in front of the Ōkami, who stood in a tight bunch.

Paul tried to jerk away from Thurman.

The lieutenant colonel dragged him forward.

Paul tried to reach Top on whisper mode. But his head was too fuzzy.

Pruden was only a about ten meters away now, walking toward the colonel. His face was tight with stress. He looked at Paul for an instant, and then looked away.

"Pruden!" Paul yelled as they passed each other. "What the hell is going on?"

Pruden looked away from Paul, refusing to make eye contact.

Paul looked back. Black troops were running away from the QC-10s. Filson was being restrained by one of the staff sergeants. The line of black DredSkill commandos was raising their weapons. Top turned in Paul's direction.

Pruden, approaching Filson, looked back at Paul, then looked down at his feet.

"No!" Paul yelled.

"At ease, Captain," Thurman said dismissively, squeezing his arm harder.

Paul looked back again.

There was no doubt.

It was a firing squad.

Paul glanced at Thurman. His helmet was open, his face exposed.

Paul had one shot.

He leaned forward, stretching as hard as he could. He winced at the pain in his arm as his wound burst open, but managed to get a handful of sand.

He used the lieutenant colonel's grip to slingshot his body up and slung the sand into Thurman's eyes, letting the motion conclude with the hardest punch he could muster.

Paul felt Thurman's nose break beneath his knuckles.

The lieutenant colonel threw Paul to the ground reflexively. Howling in rage and pain, he retracted his armored gloves and pawed at his eyes with his bare hands.

Thurman's face was red and pinched in an angry, narrow-eyed grimace as he turned back to face Paul. He managed to yell, "Goddamn it, Owens! You're only making shit worse!"

But he was yelling at Paul's back. Paul was sprinting back to his soldiers.

Top looked at Paul.

She cocked her head to one side.

"What?" Paul heard her say in whisper mode.

Fire and sand engulfed the first sergeant and the rest of the Ōkami as the black armored troops opened up with every weapon they had. Armor-piercing high-explosive rounds ravaged the Ōkami. Sparks and fire jumped across them as pieces of their bodies were blown off.

Filson screamed and pinwheeled his arms against the staff sergeant holding him. The sergeant was smarter than Thurman, though, and his activated helmet protected him from the colonel's blows.

Pruden, head in his hands, fell to his knees.

Explosions erupted from the flight line as charges detonated inside of the Dragons and Eagles. Flames engulfed the dying aircraft.

Paul, screaming as he ran, heard the sound of rending ceramic and metal over the din of the circling aircraft. He thought he saw Top for an instant, standing against the impacts.

Then she fell.

Paul was slammed to the ground and passed out under the weight of the worst last gasp yet.

Chapter Fifty-Three

aul woke up hours later. He lay on a cot in a small cinder-block room. He was in bad shape.

His head was pounding, and his shoulder wound, ripped open at during his struggle with Lieutenant Colonel Thurman, was bleeding. Fresh bruises told him they had not handled him with much care when he was unconscious.

Paul sat up. Blood pooled on the cot where his shoulder had been. It soaked through the nylon and dripped to the floor.

Paul stared at the wall and listened to drops of blood impact the floor. He had no sense of time when General Schofield walked in, holding a tray of food.

The general placed the food on the end of the cot and walked back to the door. He turned and faced Paul.

The two officers stared at each other.

"Where am I?" Paul asked.

"Back on Stalwart."

Paul looked at the floor.

"You're going back to Bragg in a few hours," Schofield said.

"Is Colonel Filson around?" Paul asked, not looking up.

"No. He's on a medical transport back to the States, dying."

Paul looked up. His face a knot of disbelief and shock.

"First, he broke a bunch of bones in his hand punching an armored military contractor's head," the general said. "Then he sustained third-degree burns over most of his body."

The general shook his head dismissively. "He dove into the pile of destroyed equipment as the military contractors were trying to burn them. Medical staff told me the crazy old bastard was hurt bad. Said he wouldn't make it. They are trying to get him back to the burn unit at Walter Reed. But…"

Paul felt something break inside. As if the last mooring line that secured him to meaning and purpose snapped. Kata, the Ōkami, and now Filson. All gone. It was too much. He began to drift.

"Soldiers," Paul said.

"What?"

"They were soldiers. Not equipment."

"Oh. Soldiers. Right."

"Why did you kill them?"

"Wasn't my call," the general said with indifference. "Those things were the property of Determined End States, a big AI weapons manufacturer. Your sweetheart robots were just on loan to Filson's Special Development Activity. When they went haywire, it was the manufacturer's decision to destroy them in place. They sent in those contract paramilitaries to do it. Dredskill, they call themselves."

Dredskill. Paul repeated to himself, looking at the floor.

The general chuckled and shook his head. "Creepy bastards. But good at what they do. I'll give 'em that."

DredSkill. The name lodged like a splinter behind Paul's eyes.

"And she moved fast, I must admit. Impressive, really. Paid for it all herself. And I'm glad she did. Saved my men a lot of hassle."

Paul looked up at General Schofield.

"Fiona Malloy," the general said, answering Paul's unspoken question.

Paul blinked, slow and numb.

Trying to process it. Trying to hold it together.

"Her company. Her machines." The general shrugged. "Her call."

Fiona Malloy.

He and Kata knew the name, of course.

But it hadn't meant anything to them.

Just another rich suit.

Fiona Malloy.

It meant something to Paul now.

It burned into his brain.

Onto his soul.

Fiona Malloy.

The general crossed his arms, studying Paul.

"It's not your fault, son," Schofield said without anger. "All the crap they jam into your jigsawed head. The Centaur program has always given me the creeps…" His voice trailed off as he searched for an answer. He shook his head in weariness and revulsion. "That's the only way I can explain what you let happen."

"I didn't let anything happen," Paul said. "I was the—"

"It's on video, Owens!" Schofield interrupted him.

"What?"

"There was a reporter there. Got the whole thing." He saw the puzzled look on Paul's face and pulled out his phone. "Couple hours after you left that village, this was picked up by the media. Went viral. Globally."

He handed Paul his phone.

Paul pressed play.

It started off chaotically, panning back and forth in a village as gunfire erupted around the camera. Paul recognized it as the night they'd struck back at General Navarro. Same village. Same terrified foot soldiers. The cameraman was among Navarro's forces. Orders were barked from off camera, and there were shrieks of pain as men were killed. Every few seconds, the camera would jerk to the sky, trying to catch a glimpse of the streaking QC-10s above as they rained bullets and rockets down on the disorganized rabble of soldiers. Paul smiled, satisfied by the pandemonium. They had achieved total surprise.

The view cut abruptly to that of a beta. Chamberlain, Paul thought, rounded a corner, minigun blazing. Then another shot of Top firing at an unseen target with one hand while swatting away exo-wearing foot soldiers with her other arm. Her blows sent the men flying out of frame.

Another abrupt cut. The Ōkami were lining up men against the wall. Then a view of betas firing their weapons. Then a pile of dead men.

"Wait a minute," Paul mumbled.

The pile of corpses was made up of the men Paul had executed.

The video kept running.

A view of Navarro, taken from a distance by a person in a crowd. But Paul could see Navarro was whimpering now. He recognized the moment. He was about to pull Navarro apart as the general had done to Kata. But instead, the video showed Navarro begging, and then cut to Top shooting him in the head as he lay on the ground. The video did not show Paul tying him up or getting into the car.

Just Top executing him.

General Schofield took his phone back and said, "An autonomous machine made the decision to kill a human on its own. Many humans. And you did nothing while your precious robot soldiers committed murder. Navarro was no saint. But we don't get to just execute the folks we don't like. And we certainly don't let robots execute humans they don't like."

Paul's head was spinning. For an instant, he doubted his memory. Then he started to get angry. Paul looked at General Schofield, but words did not come.

"You were supposed to be the leader out there, Owens," Schofield said, rolling his eyes in disgust. "That's what they told me. But the truth is, I never expected Centaurs to be capable of that. You and your tin cans set back the American effort in this region for decades. And have brought shame on your military and your country."

The general opened the door to leave, disgust on his face as he took a last look at Paul. "You're going back to Bragg to be court-martialed. If it were up to me, you'd face a firing squad."

AFTERMATH

Chapter Fifty-Four

5 May 2066
Mio Posto, Italy

"There she is!" Eugene said, standing up from his seat at breakfast on the patio.

"Morning," Fiona mumbled. She walked out onto the patio under the pergola and took a seat next to Eugene.

Eugene scowled. Wearing only jeans and a black T-shirt, she was underdressed for the chilly winter morning. He shook his head and walked inside, returning moments later with a warm blanket and thick socks.

He handed them to Fiona. As she wrapped herself and put the socks on, Eugene poured her a cup of coffee without asking.

"You look a million times better," he said, pushing the cup of coffee in front of her and taking his seat.

Fiona nodded and took a sip of coffee. "It's amazing what sleep can do for a body," she said. "That's the first I really slept in about a week. First time I slept through the night in at least a year."

"Through the day," Eugene said, pouring himself more coffee.

"Pardon?"

"You slept through the day. And then through the night."

Fiona put her coffee down and looked at her watch.

"What day is it?" she asked.

"Wednesday."

"Don't bullshit me."

Eugene looked at her across his coffee cup. He let her try to do the math for a moment.

"You got here late Monday, Fi," he said, putting his coffee down. "Drunk."

He handed her the basket of croissants.

"And babbling," Eugene added.

Fiona looked at him.

Eugene stared back.

"I was not drunk," she said, grabbing a croissant and tearing it open. "And I was not babbling."

She spread butter on one half of her croissant before taking a large bite. Eugene stared at her while sipping from his coffee.

"I was exhausted," she continued after swallowing.

"Is it true?" Eugene asked. "Is what you told me true?"

"Yes. The lien on Mio Posto is paid off. One hundred percent. You own it free and clear."

Fiona leaned back in her chair with her coffee. "Let's never do that again, brother."

A relieved smile took over Eugene's face. He shook his head and exhaled.

"I was so scared you were going to tell me you were just drunk," he said. "I'm so sorry, Fi. But I thought for sure you were lying."

"Why?"

"You have never shown up in the middle of the night like that before."

"I've shown up in the middle of the night plenty of times."

"Not looking like absolute hell and on the verge of tears," Eugene said, eyes wide in emphasis. "Let's face it. That is not Fiona Malloy behavior."

"Lack of sleep will do that to you."

"No," Eugene said. "That wasn't it."

Fiona looked at Eugene, waiting for him to continue. But he looked away from her, out past the grounds of Mio Posto, at the rust-colored hills.

"What do you mean?" she asked him.

"It wasn't lack of sleep," Eugene answered, still staring into the distance, recalling two nights ago when Fiona showed up at Mio Posto with no prior warning. "You looked haunted, Fi. You looked guilty."

Fiona's face darkened, and she looked down at her hands.

"But you know what, Fi?" Eugene said.

Fiona did not look up.

"We don't ever have to talk about it," he said. "And you looked fucking great on TV."

The two weeks before Fiona arrived at Mio Posto had been the longest, hardest part of the longest, hardest year of Fiona's life. And the final day had been the worst of it.

After it was all over, she'd sat alone in her office. Pruden had left the day before, during the press conference.

She was wearing the same clothes from the press conference the previous day, and she knew she needed to sleep. But she could not find the motivation to get out of her chair.

The knock on the door startled her.

She looked at her watch. Too early for the nightly cleaning bots.

Fiona got up and walked toward the door.

It pushed open before she got to it.

Robert Malloy II walked in.

"Hello, Roberta."

"What are you doing here?"

"That was not the celebratory greeting I expected," he said, walking past her into her large office. "Not at all," he said, looking around. "And this is not the celebration I expected to find, either. Where is everyone?"

"This is my office. The company office is in Virginia."

"Ah yes," her grandfather said. "Near the customer. Of course. Very good."

He looked around some more, his eyes falling on Pruden's empty desk.

"Your partner, then," he said. "At the very least, you and he should be celebrating."

"He quit yesterday. Packed his things and left while I was on TV."

"Oh dear. And not so much as a goodbye note?"

"Didn't need it. Nothing left to say."

Her grandfather looked back at Pruden's desk.

"Business partnerships are hard," he said. "I try to avoid them."

Fiona said nothing.

"Will he be a problem for you?" he asked, looking back at her.

Fiona shook her head.

Her grandfather stared at her.

Fiona was now used to his awkward silences. She walked past him, back to her desk.

"I thought the press junket was handled well." He walked slowly toward her desk. "But don't ever do another one. Ever. Do you understand?"

"This one was unavoidable, grandfather." She grabbed her briefcase and started packing up her desk.

"Look at me, Roberta."

She stopped packing and looked at him.

"No more. Do you understand?"

"Yes."

Fiona had objected to the presser, and her grandfather knew it. But the military had insisted. When she realized it was part of the Pentagon's effort to distance themselves from the Ōkami, Dr. Musashi's architecture, and the Olvidados massacre, she went along with it.

Anything to keep the deal moving.

She'd sat in the Bloomberg studio with the CEO of Spitting Metal. After the CEO announced that they had just been selected to provide the entire US military with its next generation of fighting robots on an accelerated schedule, Fiona was asked to say a few words.

"I'm very excited and proud of Spitting Metal," she'd said. "Their architecture is superior to that of any technology solution that has been fielded to date. The Spitting Metal ability to put robots forward into combat zones while keeping the officers that command them in specially designed, high-tech command-and-control pods safely positioned in bunkers here in the States is a huge leap forward. It guarantees that humans stay in control, complies with all aspects of the Tokyo Accords, and gives commanders highly flexible, low-risk capabilities to fight and win our wars. The accelerated procurement means we can assist with the effort to roll back China in South America. And that is something we are honored to do."

Talking points complete, Fiona had smiled and cast her gaze down to her shoes.

"I mean, I'm no Clausewitz," Spitting Metal's CEO had added, "but why put the flesh, blood, and brain downrange if we don't have to, right?"

"Learn from me," her grandfather said, snapping Fiona back to the present. "The more your face is out there, the more people will peck at you. The more they will find."

Fiona nodded and went back to stuffing her briefcase. She was suddenly dying for a shower.

"What have you learned about their next steps?" her grandfather asked her. "With the court-martial, I mean."

"They've classified the whole process as top secret," she said, not looking up.

"Good."

"Limited testimony. No press. Sealed records. The works," she continued, voice sounding more grim with every word. "The captain will take the fall. He will probably get a life sentence."

Robert Malloy II nodded.

"And the military program manager? The one asking awkward questions?"

"Colonel Frank?" Fiona kept her eyes on her desk and bag, as if looking at her grandfather would turn her to stone.

"If that is his name."

"Your senate connections were very helpful." Fiona nodded slowly and her shoulders sagged. "He is being forced to retire."

He put his hands in his pockets and cleared his throat.

"I am going to say something to you now that I must admit I never thought I would ever have to say," He stepped closer to her desk.

It was an odd windup from him. She looked up.

"I am impressed, Roberta." The thinnest trace of a smile broke across his face. "Truly."

Fiona was dumbstruck. She stood motionless.

"The disastrous mission was good," he said, nodding slowly. "It likely would have been enough. But the massacre, Roberta. The massacre was inspired."

"I had nothing to do with that," Fiona said, mostly to herself.

"Because the massacre made them urgent. It made them needy."

"I had nothing to do with that," she said, louder.

"It made them move quickly. And you know better than anyone how hard it is to get the government to move quickly."

"I had nothing to do with that! The only thing that I—"

"No!" Her grandfather slammed his fist on her desk, startling Fiona into silence.

His glare gradually slackened, and the thin smile surfaced again.

"No details," he said. "Those are yours to bear. I have more than enough of my own secrets."

Fiona stared at her desk where her grandfather's fist had struck. She regained control of her breathing, but did not look up at him.

"This conversation took a turn I did not intend," her grandfather said. "You've impressed me, Roberta. I stopped by for the sole purpose of telling you that."

"Mio Posto," she blurted out, still staring at her desk.

"What about it?"

"It's free and clear now?"

"That was the deal, was it not?"

"Answer my question, please."

"Mio Posto is free and clear. I will have my attorney send you the paperwork in the morning."

"Thank you." Fiona nodded.

"You are not, though," her grandfather said, a smile cutting across his face.

Fiona looked away from him. She had saved Mio Posto. But she was still chained to her grandfather. He owned the controlling stake in Spitting Metal, the only viable asset left in Determined End States, and held nearly all of the company's debt. How would she ever get free of him?

Her grandfather started to leave, but hesitated. He turned back and looked at Fiona. She stared down at her desk in grief.

"Roberta, you are a defense industry titan now. You would do well to bear in mind the words of the Duke of Wellington."

Fiona crossed her arms and looked at her grandfather.

"Nothing except a battle lost can be half so melancholy as a battle won."

Robert Malloy II turned and left.

Fiona stood behind her desk, trembling, after the door pulled shut.

She was horrified.

Horrified at how good it felt to hear she had impressed her grandfather. For him to actually say it to her himself. In person.

She looked at her half-packed briefcase and then ran out of her office.

An hour later, her charter took off from Teterboro on its way to Italy.

"What is it, Fi?" Eugene asked her.

Fiona blinked. She looked across the table at him, steam rising from the coffee cup in her hands.

"What?"

"You just went so far away." He reached for her hand. "Are you OK?"

She let him take it and squeezed.

"Yeah. Like I said, I haven't slept much this year."

She pulled her hand back and sat up straight, running her fingers through her hair.

"Well, I hope you can stay and rest a while," he said, offering her more coffee.

She gestured yes.

"A few days," she said as he poured. "End of the week, maybe. Then I'll have to get back."

"Will you be on TV again, gorgeous?"

"No more TV. Ever."

Chapter Fifty-Five

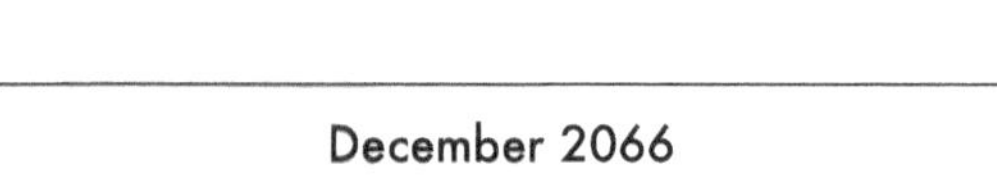

Paul walked under the flagpole on their compound on Fort Bragg. The sun was setting behind him, and his shadow stretched to his front, far beyond his footsteps. It was early summer, and the Carolina evening was comfortable and breezy. The smell of roasting deer grew stronger as Paul walked forward. Chief had been at it for a few hours, and it smelled close to ready.

Paul heard the voices of his soldiers ribbing each other and talking about the toils of the day. He heard Kata also, laughing loudest of all.

The fire came into view as Paul rounded the corner of Filson's command building. A large deer rotated slowly on a spit.

Chief tended to the cooking animal in a grease-stained white apron over his olive-drab T-shirt and cutoff camouflage shorts. Stainless-steel tongs hung out of one cargo pocket, a large, dirty rag out of the other. Chief's biceps bulged under the T-shirt, as did his gut. Spotting Paul, he gestured at his sizzling handiwork and smiled with just-like-you-taught-me pride.

Paul held both thumbs up in approval as he walked toward the group.

Stuntman stood in front of the crowded wooden table, foot on an ammo crate, gesturing dramatically to describe his actions on the weapons range that day. His wavy golden-blond hair and thick moustache were totally out of regulation and made Paul chuckle. Stuntman whipped one hand through the air to get his point across as he held a beer in the other without spilling a drop.

Mia rolled her eyes at him, her lithe body leaning back against the table, short brown hair pulled back. She never believed the braggart.

Dragon One and Magellan sat next to each other, arms crossed, regarding Stuntman with bored skepticism. D1 wore his trademark Ray-Bans and, despite the warmth of the summer evening, his leather flight jacket. His short black hair was gelled into a perfect spiky flattop, and his silver dog tags swung in front of his chest. Paul shook his head at the sweat drenching D1's white T-shirt. No one loved flying or being a pilot more than D1. But Paul thought D1 loved *looking* like a pilot even more. He'd seen D1 wearing that damn leather jacket in August on Fort Benning.

Magellan jotted notes in his small black notebook. Paul didn't have to read them to know they were full of random observations and tactical thoughts. He was always surprised by that kid's brain. But Paul learned not to let the glasses and relatively slight build fool him; Magellan was deadly on the battlefield.

D1 spotted Paul first.

"Evening, sir," D1 said to Paul, giving him a jaunty salute with one finger. "Beer?"

"Yes. Please."

D1 reached over and yanked a beer from the large bucket of ice at his feet.

"Long day, wasn't it, sir?" Magellan said.

"It surely was," Paul said, taking the beer from D1.

"What took you so long?" Kata said, standing up from her seat at the end of the table.

"Got hung up, is all," Paul said, opening the beer.

"Well," Kata said, walking over to Paul and holding her beer out to him. They knocked the cans together. "Better late than never, partner."

They each took a large swallow of beer.

"The colonel is here," Kata added. "Said he had to go grab something. Not sure what. But he should be back soon."

"He's here?" Paul asked, startled. "Really?"

"Yeah," Kata said, puzzled by his surprise. "Why wouldn't he be?"

Paul nodded. He knew it was a good question. But he was overcome by the ache of familiarity and couldn't think straight.

"Sir, you made it!" Top called out as she rounded the corner.

Paul turned to see his first sergeant walking toward him in a black utility tank top and olive-green cargo pants. Her pants and boots were covered in mud, and she carried a large cooler.

Over six feet tall with broad shoulders, Top had the build of a professional basketball player. Her sandy-blond hair was pulled back into a thick braided ponytail that betrayed her Norse bloodline, as did the runic shield knot tattoos that covered the length of her arms.

She handed the cooler to D1.

"This thing is heavy," D1 said. "What's in it?"

"Vegetables."

"Thank God," Magellan said.

"Last time we did Chief's meat-only dinner, you guys nearly destroyed the latrines," Top said.

"That is the truth," Kata said, giving Paul a knowing glance.

"Well, I'm not having that again," Top said.

Top looked around the table, pointing at each soldier in turn as she said, "Everyone will eat their veggies this time!"

Grumbles ran through the table, but no one dared argue.

Top looked at D1 and said, "Would you mind taking a break from your posing and taking them over to Chief?"

"Roger that, first sergeant!" D1 said, popping up from his seat and walking toward the fire with the cooler.

"Sir, your seat is over there at the head of the table," Top said to Paul, pointing.

Kata walked around to the other end, where she had been sitting.

Paul stepped behind his chair and looked around the table. All twelve of the Outlaw and Apache leadership were there. Kata talked intently to her first sergeant at the other end of the table. Reynolds and Chamberlain argued with D1 and Mia about something stupid.

Emotion welled within Paul.

"Take one and pass them around," Chief said, stepping up to the table with an armful of plates.

He returned a minute later with a large coffee can full of forks, spoons, and knives and placed it in the middle of the table, along with a pile of napkins.

"We're ready, sir," Chief said to Paul. "I'm going to serve it all up at the fire when you give the word."

Chief gestured over his shoulder. The deer now hung on the edge of the fire, while the vegetables grilled on a large metal grate positioned over the flames. The aromas wandered over on the breeze. They smelled wonderful.

"At ease!" Top said.

Conversation at the table ceased.

"The floor is yours, sir," Top said with a smile, standing next to Paul.

All heads swung to look at him.

Paul fidgeted. He fought the urge to cry. He wanted to say how sorry he was. How heartbroken. But it didn't seem like the right time. He was frozen by emotion.

"Sir?" Top said. "Don't you want to say something to us?"

Paul opened his mouth, but he could not speak.

"Sir?" Top said, putting her strong hand on his shoulder.

Paul looked at Kata. Her smile had faded.

D1 crossed his arms in disappointment.

Chamberlain shook his head.

"Sir?" Top said again, this time shaking Paul's shoulder. "We need you to do something before it is too late."

"Why won't you do something!" Kata yelled from the other end of the table, startling Paul.

He looked at her, not knowing what to say.

"Why won't you help me?" She screamed as her body was pulled in half by an unseen force.

Kata's intestines spilled onto the table as the two halves of her body flopped onto the ground. Her blood ran in streams over the table.

Paul watched in horror as the table became a bloody scene of death. D1 shrieked as he burst into flames. Stuntman shattered under the impacts of high caliber projectiles. The rest of the Outlaws and Apaches burned, bled, and broke apart in a terrible kaleidoscope of violence and gore.

Paul looked at his first sergeant, standing next to him, her hand still on his shoulder.

"Why didn't you help us?" She asked, eyes pleading, before her face burst open. Bone, blood and bits of brain sprayed on Paul's face as Top's body crumpled to the ground.

Paul screamed.

"Shut the fuck up!" his neighbor yelled, pounding on the cinderblock walls to wake Paul up. Everyone on the hall was tired of Paul's nightmares.

And so was Paul.

"Shut your crazy ass up!" his neighbor to the other side yelled.

He jolted awake. Panting, he sat up. Tears ran down his face as his eyes darted back and forth. Paul sat in bed in his dark cell for a few minutes, catching his breath and calibrating to his reality, again.

Prisoner cells at the United States Disciplinary Barracks in Fort Leavenworth, Kansas were small. The bed was made of metal, just like the toilet and sink, small writing desk, and locker. The stainless-steel furniture was fixed, fastened either to the cinder block walls or the cement floor. Only one wall had a small window in it sealed with thick, opaque glass that allowed only faint light to penetrate.

No light filtered into the sparse room now, though. It was early in the morning. The sun would not be up for hours.

Paul swung his feet off of the thin mattress onto the floor. He sat still and tried one of his breathing exercises. Fifteen minutes later, his heart rate was back under control and the feeling of panic more distant.

The bottomless heartbreak and despair, though, was still there. As always.

Paul was serving a life sentence without the possibility of parole for battlefield murder. The court-martial proceedings that put him there had been top secret and conducted in a fashion that had frustrated his lawyer, a well-meaning but junior captain that had been overwhelmed and intimidated at every step. Something seemed off to Paul about the whole thing. There seemed to be no interest in discovering what had really happened. There was a rush to get it done. His lawyer's requests for information and discovery were denied at every turn. It felt pre-determined.

But Paul was beyond caring. Grief stricken and guilt laden, he sat silently through the entire court martial and refused to testify in his own defense. During the trial, he learned that Colonel Filson had succumbed to the horrible burns he suffered trying to save the Ōkami. The judge rejected Paul's request to attend the funeral.

The judge did approve, however, the government's request for a three-day recess so that Paul's augmentation implants could be removed. It was a painful process that left Paul with new scars. When the doctor requested Paul be given an additional forty-eight hours to rest and heal from the invasive surgical process, the judge refused.

Paul returned to court and drifted back and forth between bouts of intense pain and a medication induced fog. The guilty verdict was a relief. Paul was ready to disappear.

Leavenworth ran the same way it had for centuries. Prisoner's days began early. Breakfast started at 0530 hours. Prisoners worked on various details, including laundry, yard cleaning, facilities maintenance, and food service. Lunch was at noon. Work details ended at 1600 hours. Dinner ran from 1630 to 1730. After dinner, prisoners could engage in group activities, like watching a movie or card games until 2130 hours when they were returned to their cells. Lights out was at 2230 hours.

There were two lockdowns each day for headcount and security inspections.

Prisoners were encouraged to take part in the numerous vocational programs available to them. Hotel and restaurant management, dental assistance, and small drone repair were among the most popular for those prisoners who planned on trying to turn their life around on the outside when they got out.

For the first two weeks, Paul was held in solitary confinement in a special wing of the prison. Combat Corps Command had allowed Paul's reputation to mutate into that of a violent, bloodthirsty man that enjoyed killing for fun - It served their purposes well during the court martial.

Command made no effort to dispel the Leavenworth Disciplinary Barracks' impression that Paul was going to be a dangerous prisoner, bent on murder and mayhem. They put him in solitary while they made a plan, which ended up being just leave his ass in solitary.

Every new prisoner at Leavenworth is psychologically evaluated during in processing, however. And the panel that evaluated Paul contradicted his reputation.

"This man is broken," the lead Doc told the commandant, Colonel Horton. "He's not a danger to anyone. You should save that solitary confinement cell for someone that earns it."

Paul was moved to general population and observed closely for weeks. Gradually, as it became clear that he was not going to erupt in a burst of highly competent, rage driven killing, the prison administration relaxed.

His fellow inmates left Paul alone. Bearing the scars and other marks of augmentation, they recognized him immediately as a Combat Corps veteran. The offenders guilty of genteel crimes such as misappropriation and drug use didn't dare cross him. Combat veteran prisoners in for violent crimes identified him as the hardened target that he was and didn't cross him either.

Paul was oblivious. The solitary confinement hardly registered with him, and he was unaware of the scrutiny he was under for the first month. He moved through the days in a withdrawn haze of sadness and smoldering anger.

After two months, the prison psychologist ordered him to try one of the vocational training programs. After a few misses, the carpentry stuck. From then on, Paul spent his time making cabinets and furniture. It didn't make the sadness and anger go away, but it pulled a different part of his mind to the fore. He could almost get so absorbed in working with wood that he forgot.

Almost.

The dream didn't come every night. But it came often enough. And when it did, it screwed him up. The sadness and anger clung to him for days before slowly subsiding.

Then the dream would come again.

Five months into his sentence, Paul was sweeping the floor in the reading room when he saw something that sent a jolt through his body. His pulse quickened and his breathing accelerated as he took slow steps toward one of the monitors prisoners could use to read the news of the outside world.

Fiona Malloy's smiling photo sat below a headline that read, "Entrepreneur keeps the world safe for democracy."

It was Fiona Malloy's decision to destroy them, he remembered General Schofield telling him. *DredSkill carried out the orders.*

Paul's grip tightened on the broom in his hands as he leaned over to read the article. He stood frozen, staring at the monitor until a guard on patrol passed by the reading room.

"Prisoner!" the guard yelled. "You're cleaning now, not reading!"

"Yes, sir!" Paul responded, standing upright and turning from the monitor. He pulled the broom across the floor.

"You clean during cleaning time," the guard admonished in a sarcastic voice. "You come back and read on your own time!"

"Yes, sir."

Paul came back the next day.

By the end of the reading period that day, Paul Owens had a new mission. He would bide his time. He would study. He would plan. He didn't know how, and he didn't know when. And he knew that, probably, he would never get the chance. But he would still try. His only reason for living now was to find a way to avenge his comrades, to kill Fiona Malloy.

Chapter Fifty-Six

"Prisoner Owens!" a guard yelled as he entered the prison wood working shop. A second guard walked at his side.

"Here, sir!" Paul said, standing up from the cabinet box he was working on. He placed the drilling jig down and stood at attention.

"Get over here," the guard said.

The wood working instructor looked at Paul with concern. An elderly local cabinet maker who volunteered at the prison, he had taken an interest in the quiet Combat Corps veteran over the past year.

The guards handcuffed Paul and led him out of the woodworking shop.

They led Paul to one of the visiting rooms where a lieutenant colonel waited for him, seated at one of the tables.

"Please remove his restraints," the Geek said.

"Yes, sir."

The guards removed Paul's handcuffs.

"We'll be right outside, Colonel Hartwell," one of the guards said as they left.

Paul waited, still standing, until the heavy door to the room closed. Then he arched an eyebrow and said, "Colonel?"

The Geek shrugged. "Light colonel."

"Yeah. But still," Paul said, smiling. "Congratulations, fast burner."

The Geek shrugged again. "Rank comes faster in Space Command."

"Accept the compliment, asshole," Paul said, sitting down across from Hartwell. "I am sure you more than earned it. Makes me happy."

"Thank you, Paul."

Paul studied the Geek. There was something awkward about the way he was sitting. As if he was favoring his right shoulder, maybe. He could tell the Geek was studying him as well.

"I meant to come earlier," the Geek said.

"Stop it," Paul said earnestly, shaking his head and waving a hand to bat away the Geek's need to apologize. "It's really good to see you."

"It's good to see you, too. Brings back a lot of memories."

"It sure does." Paul nodded.

The two old friends sat in silence. Each one struggling against a flood of emotions. The Geek fidgeted in his chair. As he did, Paul caught a glimpse of his right hand.

"Damn," Paul said. "What happened to your hand?"

The Geek smiled sheepishly, as if caught hiding something.

"Oh," he said, putting his right hand on the table. "That's a bit of a long story, I'm afraid."

Paul grimaced at the sight of the Geek's hand. It was a knotted clump of scar tissue. Each finger had been burned down to the middle joint and a bony, scarred nub protruded where the thumb should have been. Paul could see that the scar tissue ran up his wrist, under the cuff of his uniform shirt. He realized that the Geek was probably burned up to his shoulder.

Knowing too well what it is like to have lived a story you never want to tell, Paul lifted his eyes from the Geek's hand and said, "I'm so sorry."

The Geek nodded his head slightly.

"It's one of the reasons I have not been able to visit until now," the Geek said. "It took a while to heal up."

Paul shook his head again. "Please stop with that. It's really good to see you. What does Space Command have you doing now, anyway? Something cushy, I hope?"

Lieutenant Colonel Hartwell looked at Paul for a long moment.

Paul sat back in his chair, unsure. The Geek's face was inscrutable.

The Geek looked toward the closed door and then leaned across the small table. "I've been working on something you may find interesting, Paul," he said in a low voice. "I might have a way to get you out of here."

THE END

Spirit Of The Bayonet

Book 1: Betrayal

Book 2: Odysseus

Book 3: Sacrifice

All books available now, in paperback and for Kindle®, from Amazon.

For updates on future books in the series, sign up for Ted's newsletter via his website:

tedruss.com

Acknowledgements

The acknowledgment for this one feels a little unusual, since some of the people who helped shape the book haven't thought about it in over six years—back when I was grinding away on the first version. But their contributions were foundational. The spirit of *The Spirit of the Bayonet* started with their help. (Sorry… couldn't resist.)

Whether it was version one or this latest run, my trusted band of beta readers and thought partners were invaluable. No indie writer has it better. Period. James Aiken, Kirby Andrews, Amber Lilyquist, Ted Miller, Adam Parrish, Jennifer and Dan Ruiz, Kevin Virgil, Russ Watson, Morgan Watson, and David Weinstein.

The finishing crew on this one: Chris Evans and Mark Thomas. True professionals.

Thanks to my wife, Anna; to my parents; and to George and Susu Johnson—writing gets weird and lonely sometimes. Knowing you're in my corner means everything.

Finally—and again, and always—Anna. Partner. Best friend. Farm Boss. I'm so lucky.

Ted Russ
April 2025

Author's Note

I've been a sci-fi nerd for as long as I can remember. I love it in every format—novels, comic books, movies—you name it. Science fiction is fun, thought-provoking, and still makes up about half my fiction reading. After publishing *Spirit Mission*, it was probably inevitable I'd take a swing at writing sci-fi. That book had been a heavy lift—semi-autobiographical, first novel—and I was ready to cut loose in a genre I loved. I started *Spirit of the Bayonet* with the simple goal of writing an engaging science fiction story. But as I got into it, I found myself wading into intriguing waters. Truthfully, questions that have been rattling around in my head for a long time:

- Ethical questions about AI in combat
- The accelerating transformation of military culture and tactics
- The ever-present military-industrial complex
- And the fundamental essence of military service that never changes

Trying to explore all of that without losing the plot was harder than I expected.

The first version of *Spirit of the Bayonet* was a blast to write. But looking back, I made a lot of mistakes.

1. I just started writing—no plan, no map. I didn't think about structure or series architecture. I'd agonized over *Spirit Mission*—every beat, every turn. So it felt good to let this one rip. And rip. And rip...

2. I crammed in everything I loved. Powered armor. Derelict ships. Evil corporations. Sexy robots. Every trope, every influence—plus my AI anxiety and half-remembered cadet philosophy classes—made the cut.

3. I made it way too long. Unburdened by discipline, I cranked out two book's worth of content with barely one book's worth of structure. I love long novels—but this one wound up a bit of a dog's breakfast.

4. I declared it a trilogy… because trilogies are cool. Embarrassing to admit. Jackass move.

5. I killed my momentum. Readers were asking for Book II. Naturally, I pivoted to another project—*Duty's Cost*. Right move for good reasons—I'm proud of it. But it derailed whatever small momentum *Spirit of the Bayonet* had built.

When I finally returned to *Spirit of the Bayonet*, it was clear it needed more than a tune-up for three big reasons.

1. **The story**. The original version didn't set up the long arc I wanted. I needed a stronger foundation for the series to build on.

2. **The characters**. My vision for the characters had grown. So had the scope of their journey.

3. **And because I could**. One of the great joys of indie publishing is the freedom to rewrite your own damn book.

So here we are—years later—with the first installment of what I hope is a stronger, tighter, more focused version of the story I set out to tell. And no, I'm not going to say how many books it will ultimately be. OK… more than three.

Thank you for giving it a shot.

OTHER BOOKS

BY

TED RUSS

DUTY'S COST

Val Rafter's luck may have finally run out. Kidnapped by Russians and held at gunpoint on a ship crossing the Black Sea at night toward Crimea, Val is forced to confront the events and decisions that brought him to this desperate moment. Part of a top-secret US Army human intelligence program, Val is an expert at recruiting and running spies. Years ago, while training at the CIA's legendary Farm, he met Sydney, whose beauty, intelligence, and ambition made her a formidable agency covert intelligence officer. The attraction was immediate, but their timing was terrible. Soon after, while serving in the cauldron of Kosovo, Val forged an unlikely friendship with Alexei Volkov, a Russian army officer. When the three are sent to the prestigious Marshall Center for Security Studies in Germany, they become entangled in secrets that will haunt them for the rest of their careers. As global tensions rise, duty and loyalty conflict and propel the three old friends toward a disastrous reckoning in Ukraine in 2014...

In a globe spanning story that takes the reader from top secret CIA training, to Kosovo, Eastern Europe, Iraq, and Syria, Russ weaves a tale that is as thrilling as it is thought-provoking. Exploring the demands of duty, honor, and friendship in a world that often puts them at odds, this is an unforgettable novel that will leave readers questioning the nature of loyalty and the cost of Duty.

Available now, in paperback and for Kindle®, from Amazon.

SPIRIT MISSION

To honor bonds forged twenty-five years ago at West Point, Lieutenant Colonel Sam Avery leads an illegal mission deep into ISIS-held territory.

An MH-47G Chinook helicopter departs formation in the Iraqi night. The mission is unauthorized. Success is unlikely. But to save a friend, Sam Avery and his crew of Night Stalkers have prepared for one last flight.

ISIS operatives in Tal Afar, Iraq, have captured American aid worker Henry Stillmont. Avery knows Stillmont as "the Guru," the West Point squad leader who taught him about brotherhood, loyalty, and when to break the rules as a young cadet twenty-five years ago. Sam will risk his career and his life to save him.

As they near their target, Sam reflects on his time in the crucible of the United States Military Academy. West Point made Sam the leader he is. But his fellow cadets made him the man that he is. The ideals of duty, honor, and country have echoed throughout his life and drive him and his comrades as they undertake their final and most audacious spirit mission.

Available now, in paperback and for Kindle®, from Amazon.

ABOUT THE AUTHOR

Ted Russ is a writer living in the Carolina mountains with his wife, Anna, their dogs, Charlie and Ripple, and a bunch of chickens and bees.

In a distant prior life, he served as an army officer after graduating from West Point. Ted left the military in 2000 with experience as a special operations helicopter pilot and a philosophy degree.

Possessing no marketable skills, he went back to school and got an MBA. His 25 year journey through the business world was winding - from startups to fortune 500s, domestic to expat assignments, general management and sales to M&A.

He discovered writing late in life, publishing his first novel in 2016 and now tries to make a living writing full time.

Exploring themes of identity, loyalty, and the complexities of the human experience, Ted's works span contemporary fiction and thought provoking sci-fi. Readers praise his novels for their gripping narratives, authenticity, and moral depth.

For new stories, updates, and dispatches from the Ridge — sign up for Ted's newsletter at his website:

tedruss.com